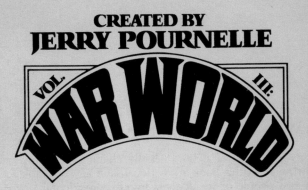

CREATED BY
JERRY POURNELLE

VOL. WAR WORLD III:

SAURON DOMINION

BAEN
BOOKS

WAR WORLD III: SAURON DOMINION

Copyright © 1991 by Jerry Pournelle

A Baen Books Original.

Baen Publishing Enterprises
P.O. Box 1403
Riverdale, N.Y. 10471

ISBN: 0-671-72072-4

Cover art by Stephen Hickman

First printing, August 1991

Distributed by
SIMON & SCHUSTER
1230 Avenue of the Americas
New York, N.Y. 10020

Printed in the United States of America

NIGHT OF THE LIVING DEAD ...

Stocky and broad, that was the Sauron's first impression. Her torso was covered in armor of overlapping plates of lacquered bullhide, with armguards of the same material. A sledgehammer drawn on the armor, over a six-pointed star. Her helmet had been torn away, and he saw a square, blade-nosed face, olive skinned, narrow blue eyes, a braid of black hair down her back. Blood from a graze on her cheek. A long red-wet saber in one hand, a shield in the other. White teeth showed as she bared her lips and twitched the blade back and forth *wheet, wheeet.*

Ah. She was favoring one knee.

"No further, Sauron." A heavy accent to her Americ, liquid and guttural.

"I can probably draw my pistol faster left-handed than you can attack me with that saber," Gorthaur pointed out. Meanwhile he made sure, looking with eyes that saw into the IR frequencies; yes, the bodies were all cooling fast. All dead.

Unexpectedly, she laughed; more of a sour chuckle, but still ... *What a woman to sire Soldier sons upon!* the Assault Group Leader thought in sincere admiration. *Only a dozen cattle to kill four Soldiers, and this one survived. Alone and confronted with an armed Sauron, she laughed. What genes!*

"Why do you laugh?"

"To hear two corpses threaten each other," she said.

"Corpses?"

"Your arm is broken. I have a wrenched knee. We are each a thousand klicks from home, no horses, scavengers coming, and the nomads around here scratch their heads to decide if they hate Saurons more than haBandari."

NIGHT OF THE LIVING DEAD . . .

Stocky and broad, that was the Sauron's first impression. Her torso was covered in armor of overlapping plates of lacquered bullhide, with armguards of the same material. A sledgehammer drawn on the armor, over a six-pointed star. Her helmet had been torn away, and he saw a square, blade-nosed face, olive skinned, narrow blue eyes, a braid of black hair down her back. Blood from a graze on her cheek. A long red-wet saber in one hand, a shield in the other. White teeth showed as she bared her lips and twitched the blade back and forth *wheet, wheeet.*

Ah. She was favoring one knee.

"No further, Sauron." A heavy accent to her Americ, liquid and guttural.

"I can probably draw my pistol faster left-handed than you can attack me with that saber," Gorthaur pointed out. Meanwhile he made sure, looking with eyes that saw into the IR frequencies; yes, the bodies were all cooling fast. All dead.

Unexpectedly, she laughed; more of a sour chuckle, but still . . . *What a woman to sire Soldier sons upon!* the Assault Group Leader thought in sincere admiration. *Only a dozen cattle to kill four Soldiers, and this one survived. Alone and confronted with an armed Sauron, she laughed. What genes!*

"Why do you laugh?"

"To hear two corpses threaten each other," she said.

"Corpses?"

"Your arm is broken. I have a wrenched knee. We are each a thousand klicks from home, no horses, scavengers coming, and the nomads around here scratch their heads decide if they hate Saurons more than haBandari."

CREATED BY JERRY POURNELLE

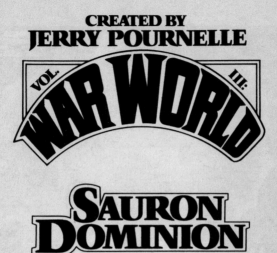

VOL. III:

WAR WORLD

SAURON DOMINION

With the editorial assistance
of John F. Carr.

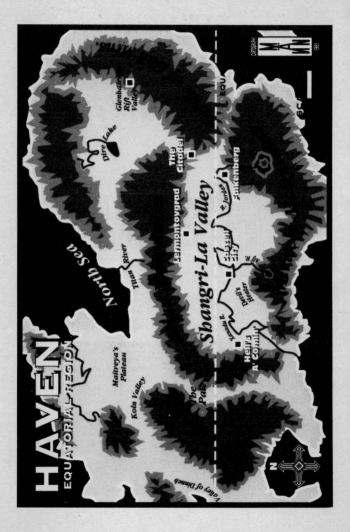

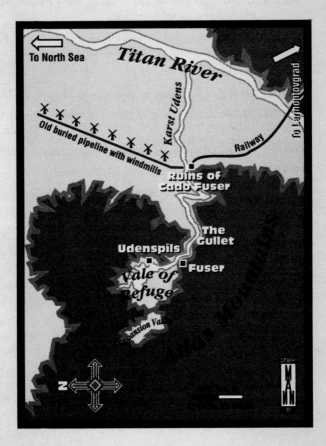

Chronology

2103 Great Patriotic Wars. End of the CoDominium rule. Exodus of the Fleet.

2110 Coronation of Lysander I of Sparta. Fleet swears loyalty to the Spartan throne.

2111 Formation Wars begin.

2250 Leonidas I of Sparta proclaims Empire of Man.

2250–2600 Empire of Man enforces interstellar peace.

2284 Haven is rediscovered by an Imperial warship.

2432 First cyborg is created on Sauron

2590 First brigade of Sauron cyborgs is formed.

2603 Secession Wars begin. St. Ekaterina nearly destroyed in surprise attack.

2618 The Third Imperial Fleet is destroyed off Tabletop.

2623 Seventy-seventh Imperial Marine Division ("Land Gators") is withdrawn from Haven along with all Imperial officials.

2637 Sauron-supported Secessionist armada and Claimant fleets fight to a draw at the Battle of Makassar.

2640 Sauron First and Second Fleets destroyed at the Battle of Tanith. The Home Fleet is destroyed off Sauron, the Supermen exterminated, and Sauron bombed back to the Stone Age.

Sauron Heavy Cruiser Fomoria disengages from Imperial fighter squadron and through a series of Random Jumps reaches Haven.

Table of Contents

PROLOGUE

From *A Student's Book* by Myner Klint bar Terborch fan Reenan, Eden Valley, Ilona'sstad, 2927:

... so good places to live are few and widely spaced out on Haven, apart from the Shangri-La Valley, which the Saurons dominate. People must live widely scattered where there is water or good land, or move in little bands across the steppe; even rarer are areas low enough for women to bear their children safely. Wide distances and little travel mean that customs and beliefs grow very differently. Greed or need often makes it necessary to fight, to take away what is needed for life from others. The Saurons take much from many peoples, leaving them to struggle over the scraps. We haBandari fight to hold what is ours, but experience has shown us it is often more profitable to talk and trade. ...

WAR WORLD ECONOMICS

"Ayo Gorkali!" A deep-chested shout from forty, fifty throats.

"Here they come again!" the guard-captain of the haBandari caravan shouted; his name was Johann bar Pinkas, and he had worked the steppe trade-routes of Haven most of his fifty T-years.

The wagons were laagered in around the bubbling water of the oasis hot spring, in a big shallow bowl covered in reddish screwgrass and eggtree bush. Oxen and camels, yak and muskylopes milled around; the cold Truenight air was pungent-steamy with their breath and the sulphur-mineral smell of the water. Torches on long poles blazed with the sputtering brightness of fat-soaked wool; outside the darting figures of the attackers were black shapes against the dark, except where the firelight gleamed on edged steel. Cat's Eye was an arc of ruddy light on the horizon, almost set.

"Wait for it, wait for it, pick your targets," Johann roared; a bull-bellow for volume, but calm.

His own target was the suggestion of a bush behind which a shadow *might* have moved; whoever this was had cursed good fieldcraft. He braced one knee against the boards of the wagon's outer wall; the tilt was drawn up overhead on the hoops. The arrow slid through the centerline cutout of his bow, the pulley wheels at each end of the *bare* levering against horn and wood and sinew.

"Now!"

Arrows and crossbow bolts and javelins slashed out into the night; *crack-crack* and stabbing spears of orange light, from the two flintlock rifles this caravan boasted. Screams, one from the bush he had been aiming at, and it thrashed. Then he dropped the bow, snatching up saber and shield from their racks to either hand.

"Ayo Gorkali!"

That shout, and a dark figure bouncing up to try for a foothold in the wagon. A blade chopped at him overarm; he caught it on the metal rim and stabbed low, feeling the ugly soft resistance, all too familiar. A choked grunt, and the man fell away; his blade stayed, driven through the steel and tough leather and drillbit gut lining. More of the raiders came up; spearheads flashed from beneath the wagons into their legs and guts, swords and axes hacked at them from above. Once there was a shout, and Johann leaped down to the trampled ice-crackling mud to lead the reserve around the circle of the livestock. They were ostlers and wranglers, not fighters, but everyone in a caravan had *some* training, and hitting an enemy with a line of spears was not exactly the most difficult thing in the world.

At last the noise died away, everything but the moaning of the wounded and the restless animals. Johann looked meditatively at the shield, suddenly noticing the extra weight. He pulled the strange weapon free of it, grunting with the effort and then grunting again in surprise at the depth of the cut. Three-ply muskylope leather boiled in vinegar was tough, and the woven drillbit-gut glued to the back tougher still; drillbits ate their way through medium-hard rock and had exactly the sort of insides you would expect. The . . . sword-knife, he supposed . . . was odd, a half-meter blade that curved inward, in two broad lobes.

Interesting. The p'rknz fly away with interest-

ing. Why don't I retire? It wasn't as if he needed
the income all that much; he had saved carefully.
A farm rented out to an Edenite back home, livestock out on shares with his clan-kin, a house in
Strang. *I should retire and let my granddaughters
fuss at me.*

"Now that was more than somewhat strenuous,"
a voice said. Johann looked up; it was his
employer.

Josepha bat Golda was a small, square-built,
deep-bosomed woman, handsome in the full-lipped,
hawk-nosed way of the People, with streaks of silver in her strong mane of black hair. She wore her
armor with an air of irritated competence, and
carried a two-handed war pick over one shoulder,
a curved spike ending in a serated hammerhead,
forged with its meter-long handle out of a single
billet of steel. It had seen recent use; Johann
reflected that he was glad she had never hit him
with it, though she had broken a jug over his head
once in a contract dispute. Her apprentice Filippa
bat Henriett was with her, looking younger than
sixteen, and scared; a cousin of some sort, in the
usual way.

"I hate a *gayam* who won't stay bought," she
went on. "Kuchuk Khan gets enough passage
money—"

"I don't think these were Kuchuk's men," he
said, turning and calling sharply for a light. One
of his guards ran up with an alcohol lantern, and
raised it above a dead enemy.

A short, stocky man, barrel-chested even by
Haven standards. Noticeably flat-faced and slant-
eyed, even on the high steppe where Mongoloid
was the predominant racial type. Gaunt with hun-
ger, and his sheepskin clothes were thin and worn.
Johann whistled soundlessly with surprise at the
gleam of raw hammered gold on his belt buckle.
Josepha stooped to examine it, ignoring the ragged

wound where a spearhead had been wrenched out of his chest.

"Electrum," she said, going down on one knee. "Platinum and gold, natural alloy. No, he's no Uighur."

"*Sekkle nu tvaz,*" Johann muttered in Bandarit: *it wasn't reasonable.* "Kuchuk had no reason to attack us."

Josepha nodded. "Nu, I think we should treat these *gayam* very well. Take their wounded to *mediko* after ours are cared for. And we should let a couple who can walk go."

"It's a *mitzvah* to be merciful," Johann said. Although usually cutting throats was safer; the haBandari did not sell prisoners and kept no slaves.

"Merciful *myn totchkis,* this could be useful."

"I am Haribahadur Gurung, Subadar of the Gurung villages." The little *gayam* was a proud man, from his looks, despite his ragged clothes. When he knelt, it was stiffly. "We thought you were Kuchuk Khan's men, and so attacked peaceful travellers. We are ashamed." He spoke the pidgin *turki* language of trade fluently, although with a thick accent. "You show great honor by returning our wounded. We bring blood-payment to show our sorrow." One of his men spilled a small sack on a cloak laid on the ground; nuggets of raw electrum, and a small shimmerstone.

Johann raised a brow, invisible beneath the brim of his bucket-shaped helmet, and whistled mentally. Josepha was in full merchant fig, to show her respectability; a long coat of fine scarlet wool embroidered with silk, a tall conical hat, baggy maroon pants and tooled boots with turned-up toes sporting silver bells, a cloak of supple-tanned tamerlane hide. She stayed mounted, to show who was the dominant party; there was a table set out with

mutton and pickled eggs, flatbread and baklava
and Finnegan's Fig brandy for potential hospitality;
and the wagons stayed laagered, with Johann and
a dozen mounted haBandari warriors nearby, for
practicality. They sat on their horses in grim
silence, armored in black leather and brass and
steel, armed with bow and lance, sabers and the
two precious rifles. Wind ruffled the horses'
manes, and the short stiff horsehair crests of the
helms; behind them stood the pikes and axes of
the caravan workers.

"Why are you at war with Kuchuk Khan and his
people?" Josepha asked.

Several of the ragged figures behind the *Subadar*
spat. When the chief spoke, it was with passion:

"Kuchuk Khan is a liar and a thief!" he cried.
"Always the Uighurs have charged too much,
when our young men went to fight and so earn
bread for us—" he waved backward, toward the
cold fangs of the Atlas mountains behind.

They live up there? Johann thought with respect.
Hardy. The high steppe hereabouts was bad
enough.

"—too much for passage for our women to the
Akaj valley." That was the local birthing ground;
too high to be really good, but at least the Saurons
had never bothered with it. This was a little too
far west to go to the Shangri-La and the Citadel.
"Cheated us on trade for our gold and fine musk-
ox wool! But now he goes too far, trying to take
the pick of our women as if he were a Sauron!"
Another chorus of spitting; some of the haBandari
joined in. "So we fight him, even though we starve
in the meantime."

Johann's eyes met his employer's; hers were
wide and liquid-black; there was almost a cooing
in her voice as she dismounted. Her fingers moved
in the sign-language version of Bandarit: *Make
camp. If there isn't a profit in this, I'm a* plaats-

man. The guard-captain nodded fractionally; if there was one thing Josepha bat Golda was not, it was a farmer.

"Stand, stand, my friend," she said gently, taking him by the elbow and urging him toward the laden table; many of the others in his party were looking at it with open longing. "Come, eat, tell me of your troubles. Perhaps we haBandari can help you—" Her voice rose questioningly.

"Gurkhas."

"—Gurkhas. Tell me about—"

From *A Student's Book* by Myner Klint bar Terborch fan Reenan, Eden Valley, Ilona'sstad, 2927:

. . . few people ever came to Haven of their own will. Even the first settlers, the Church of New Harmony, emigrated to escape persecution and came to Haven because it was all they could afford. During the CoDominium, the United States and Soviet Union used Haven as a place for those they were ashamed to kill openly, instead letting the planet do it for them. Even with advanced machines such as we know only through stories, this is a hard place for humans to live. When the CoDominium died there was hardship almost as terrible as that which followed the coming of the Saurons centuries later. The Empire of Man made life a little easier, and large populations grew up around its fusion plants and food factories; after a while, it also began sending its troublesome people to Haven. Our Founder, Piet van Reenan, was one such. When the Empire fell, it was those who had kept to the outback and had as little as they could to do with the Imperial machine-economy who were most likely to survive. . . .

* * *

From an address to the Military History and Analysis Board, Human Norm Combat Capacities Seminar by Vessel First Rank Galen Diettinger:

"No idea in human history has met with more widespread acceptance than that war is about the infliction of human suffering.

"And no idea could be further from the truth.

"Politically, war is about the imposition of one entity's goals irrespective and often at the expense of another's. It is usually in the political aspects that attach themselves to the conduct of warfare that the above statement has found whatever support may be rationalized for it.

"But militarily, war is about the destruction of the enemy's *ability*—not necessarily his *will*—to fight. The evolution of warfare has been an upward rise toward maneuver, with a concurrent de-emphasis on direct contact, and hence conflict, with the enemy. Ancient battles far outstripped modern ones in their casualty lists. Troops under the command of the Sauron Role Model, Hannibal, in one day at Cannae killed more men than in any other single battle in human history (the suicidal Patriotic Wars whose indiscriminate use of nuclear weapons ended all advanced life on Terra, and with it, the old CoDominium, were an aberration possible only to the excesses of civilian minds, and will not be discussed here).

"In Terra's Twentieth Century alone, warfare made a great leap forward in its method. From grinding wars of attrition, to fluid maneuver and breakthroughs made possible with man's conquest of the air and development of armored fighting vehicles, to the advancement of the individual's weapon systems, which not only increased firepower a hundredfold over his predecessors, but allowed complete accuracy in the delivery of that combat strength to the target; through these factors, warfare was changed forever. Soldiers could still, *would* still kill one another, but it was no longer *necessary* to do so, not when the command and control centers of the enemy could be destroyed and his logistics capabilities neutralized.

"Far from being about the infliction of human suffering, the age of the professional soldier, begun two thousand years before by the Sauron Role Model, Julius, now made the actual incidence of the wasteful murder of men in war drop to its lowest point in history.

"Ironically, it was that very pinnacle of operational theory which put the evolution of war, and thus the evolution of mankind, in danger. Like the *Condottieri* of the Post-Roman era, armies were developing into dancers with lethal capabilities, but nonlethal intent. This carried the danger that military thought would develop the dangerous complacency for which it was, until that time, justly famous.

"The solution was to increase the training of the individual soldier, not merely toward discipline, but toward initiative. The ability to do something in combat, anything, *even the wrong thing*, is the hallmark of the militarily dominant society, and it was the development of this trait which directed the training of all victorious soldiers throughout the Twentieth and early Twenty-First Century, until the reactionary military theories of the late Twenty-First Century brought on that century's Dark Age of military thought.

"It must be remembered, however, that the definition of this sort of individual initiative varied greatly from society to society; it was not standard, nor was it new. Primitive societies used it to great effect against more advanced ones, and there is no reason to assume that they will not continue to do so in the future, so long as civilized Man retains his dangerous capacity for personal aggrandizement, indulgence, and delusion."

THE GATES OF PARADISE

DON HAWTHORNE

"La illah illa Allah . . ."

Yurek was finishing his third rifled barrel of the month when the *muezzin*'s voice drifted through the thin mountain air into the cave where he worked, calling the faithful of Haven to mid-morning prayer. He stood, stretching the stiff muscles of his legs, and carefully replaced his tools in their felt-lined case. Yurek was a weaponsmith, a bearer of the Gift; it was largely through the efforts of himself and those like him that their people had survived for so long.

And not just on Haven, his father and uncles had taught him with justifiable pride. Since time immemorial, before the days of Alexander the Great, Yurek's Gift, and the Gift of those like him, had kept his people free.

He was regarded highly by the other men of the village for it, and his importance to their security exempted him from many obligations. *But no man may shirk his duty to God.*

For Yurek knew that the Gift, as all gifts, was the touch of Allah, and he never forgot the debt it imparted. So, gathering up his prayer cloth and skull cap, Yurek pushed aside the thick skins over the cave

11

entrance to join in devotion the rest of the men who lived in the south of his village.

Haven's frigid cold assaulted his face, scoured his eyes, made his gums retract from suddenly aching teeth and froze the hairs in his nostrils. Yurek gave a small grunt of pleasure; not even noon, and the mountains were warming up already.

Snow crunched under his boots as he crossed the open area between the stone huts and the cave entrances in this, the stronghold of his people. The *mullahs* had taken their bearings from the stars during the last Truenight; all were competent astronomers, a new requirement for the title since Islam took to the stars. Now they were organizing the faithful into rows, kneeling to face in the direction of that star around which spun the Earth, for there lay Mecca.

"Allah-u akbar . . ." The *muezzin*'s prayers enfolded him, bringing the peace that only the faithful knew, and the only peace the faithful seemed ever privileged to know. For on Haven, a man took what peace he could find in his heart and treasured it; there was none to be found in the world around him.

And on this day, even that inner peace was to be shattered. No sooner were the men in their prayers then explosions in the surrounding hills announced an attack, and the response by Yurek and the other men of the village was immediate.

Snatching their weapons from the prayer mats beside them, each moved quickly to their assigned positions. They passed the huts wherein the women and smallest children of the village worshiped, and who were now also leaving that worship to arm themselves for defense of their home. The mid-morning prayer would not be finished this day, but Allah would understand. No less pragmatic a God could ever have won the hearts and minds of such people as Yurek's, descendants of Old Earth's fierce Afghan *mujahadin*.

Yurek's station was the house of old Fahd the

Healer, in the southwest corner of the village. His fire team commander, *Aga* Yani, was already in position, scanning the perimeter with his binoculars.

"*Salaam*, Yurek," *Aga* Yani greeted Yurek without turning. "You are the first here."

Yurek nodded at the compliment as he dropped to his belly and crawled up to the firing slit. He flicked the safety off and watched his area very carefully; *Aga* Yani could not see everything at once, not even with the precious binoculars, and it was part of Yurek's job to warn him of any approaching attackers he might miss.

"It's the Chin, again," *Aga* Yani explained, the binoculars never leaving his face. "North wall outposts spotted several of their patrols just before dawn."

Yurek did not need to ask why they were thus guarding the southwest so carefully; Haven's Chin nomads had not earned their reputation for cunning with suicidal, frontal assaults; nor had her transplanted Afghan population survived so long by accepting the obvious.

Mulli, another member of the fire team, arrived with a machine gun. He unfolded the bipod and positioned the weapon in the firing slit, then pulled an ammunition case from the bag slung over his shoulder, all without a word.

"*Salaam*, Mulli," *Aga* Yani said, then lowered his binoculars and looked at him. Mulli's blank face was streaked with tears. "Where is your ammunition feeder? The new boy, what is his name?"

"Sadhar," Mulli answered. "Killed in his prayers by a Chin bullet." He added: "My sister's son," in a voice meant only for himself and God, but Yurek heard it, too.

"*Insh'allah*," *Aga* Yani said compassionately, and went back to his binoculars.

Was it, though? Yurek wondered. *And if it truly is God's will that the boy be taken in the act of prayer, is there a message to be seen in the fact? There must be, for God gives both life and death, and there is nothing He does that is without purpose.* Yurek sighed, putting the matter in perspective: *A youth, and devout; surely Sadhar was taken directly to Paradise.*

"There, a Chin squad, just to the left of the marker stone," *Aga* Yani said, carefully storing his binoculars and picking up a portable rocket launcher.

Yurek squinted at the serrated rock walls in the distance, their surface lit with the diffuse glow of both Byers' Star and the yellow-brown gas giant Cat's Eye that Haven orbited. The plateau that held his people's village dropped off sharply to the south, and the mountains rose up sheer on the other three sides, so that on the left side of his view their rippled expanse dropped at a sixty degree angle to the floor of the Shangri-La valley below. It was on just such a horribly difficult attack route that the *mujahadin* expected the Chin to come, and the infidels did not disappoint them.

Yurek suddenly picked out movement in the rocks, but he was well-trained; *Aga* Yani would tell them when to open fire. Part of the effectiveness of this position was its field of fire over an area which an attacker had every right to expect would be lightly defended, if at all.

"They're coming very slowly, *Aga* Yani," Yurek said after a moment. He was still young, and his eyesight was very good, despite his years of work with the intricate tools and precise tolerances of his trade.

"Yes," *Aga* Yani said. After a silent minute, he picked up the binoculars with one hand. Finding the Chin squad's position, he spoke: "Three men on the ridge, watching this area. Nine seem to be looking for something; if it's a full strength squad, that leaves three unaccounted for." *Aga* Yani abruptly hissed through his teeth. "Aah! The dogs have a mortar! The squad is looking for a flat area to emplace it!"

Yurek looked to Mulli, but the gunner's face was pressed into the stock of his machine gun like a bridegroom's face to his wife's thigh, his eyes never leaving the ridge. A mortar was very bad indeed. Yurek's village, tucked safely into the mountains, had endured many raids over the years, and while it had always survived, it had suffered greatest at the hands of raiders with mortars. Even the Walls of Allah, as Yurek's people called the Atlas Range, did not protect the faithful from death that could be dropped within those walls from above. And a mortar situated here, firing into the village from the southwest, would bring uncounted tears.

"Yurek, come with me. We'll try to get above them. Don't try to keep their heads down, Mulli," *Aga* Yani said, slinging the rocket launcher over one shoulder as he rose. "We'll soon be high enough on the slope for them to shoot at us without standing up. Wait until they expose themselves to fire at us, then kill as many as you can."

Yurek was grateful to get off the cold floor of Old Fahd's house; Haven's icy air and frozen stones leached the warmth from a man's body faster than Mulli's gun could draw Chin blood.

"*Allah-u akbar,*" Yurek heard Mulli say behind them as they left, then something like "*Sadhar,*" and they were off and away up the hill.

With the sound of the first shot from the cliffs above, Sauron Squad Leader Gav had dropped to one knee and signaled the nine men in his patrol to do the same. Looking up into the mountains above him, his normal vision saw clouds of smoke and debris rising and spreading into the air, while his infrared sensitivity defined the ripple of greater fires beyond, and his preternatural hearing discerned the cries of men in battle and the chatter of weapons.

Gav turned to his assistant squad leader, Goren.

"*Mak twa; cho dah kum vwa.*" It was a long series of commands in the Battle Tongue, but Goren had shown he was capable of remembering and carrying out the most complex orders.

Gav looked up the mountain once more. No other Sauron patrol had been assigned that area; it was regarded as too high for habitation by human norms. Haven's thin atmosphere dwindled gradually up to about eight thousand feet, then dropped off drastically to almost nothing. At fifteen thousand, it wasn't much more than vacuum. Yet now it seemed as though human norms were not only living up there, but fighting as well. To Gav, that could only mean there was something up there worth fighting over, and that had to be a settlement. Gav estimated the firefight to be occurring at eighty-five hundred feet, at or even above the ceiling of the breathable atmosphere. Gav swung his half of the patrol in the opposite direction from Goren, executing his part of the complicated encirclement to approach the fighting above.

Within ten minutes, they had captured a wounded norm, and spirited him away from his village without any of his comrades being aware of it.

If the human norms have a settlement up here, Gav thought, *living, working, and most importantly, birthing, First Citizen Diettinger will want to know about it.*

More explosions and the rattle of gunfire could be heard from the far side of the village; that would be the Chin's main assault, meant to draw off men while they set their mortar up here. Once emplaced, the device could bombard Yurek's people until they were all dead or the Chin ran out of ammunition, whichever came first. Even the Chin were not so foolish as to believe the *mujahadin* would surrender.

Yurek and *Aga* Yani raced up the glassy hill behind the house. The snow on the floor of the plateau was months old; the mountains of Haven were far too dry to get much snowfall at this altitude, and almost none was left now. Thus, their footing was sure and the gray-brown sheepskin coats they wore blended well with the rock slopes up which they ran.

Neither man spoke; breathable air was thin everywhere on Haven, and thinnest here. Their people had acclimated over the years in exile, but there was still only so much the human body could be expected to do. In any case, both knew where they were going: a spot in the rocks chosen for precisely this purpose, months ago. The Afghans had learned long ago the value of knowing the terrain, and it was no exaggeration to say that Yurek's people knew every inch of the territory surrounding their village.

They were almost there when a hollow *thump* was heard, the sound of the first mortar round being fired.

"Down!" *Aga* Yani pushed Yurek to one side as he fell, and both men curled up into the shelter of the rocks. They waited, straining to hear the whistle of the incoming mortar shell. In Haven's thin atmosphere, those sounds were so long in coming that a new round could be well on the way before the first was even heard.

Below and behind them, a fiery blossom of snow and stone leapt up from the plateau not twenty yards from Old Fahd's house. Yurek looked to *Aga* Yani; the fire team leader raised one hand, counting to himself. The next round came less than ten seconds later, closer to the stone hut by the same distance in yards.

"Mulli!" *Aga* Yani shouted through cupped hands, "Mulli, get out! Get out of there!"

Yurek watched, gripping the stock of his rifle with one hand and the lip of stone before him with the other. Mulli did not come out, there was no shooting from the house of Old Fahd the Healer, and the next Chin mortar shell was a direct hit that obliterated the building.

Aga Yani dragged Yurek to his feet, and they continued up the slope. The squad guarding the Chin mortar crew had seen them, and the rocks all around were shattering under the impact of their bullets, filling the air with stone splinters and fragmented steel-jacketed slugs. They had reached the position to fire down on the Chin when *Aga* Yani stopped and abruptly sat down, turning to reveal that the left side of his head was gone.

Instinctively, Yurek grabbed for the rocket launcher in *Aga* Yani's hand, but the weapon slipped from the dead man's fingers and went clattering down the slope, gaining speed, bouncing off the rocks to fly over the heads of the jubilant Chin and disappear into one of the great rifts of the mountain range below.

Yurek felt himself struck by two bullets in the thigh and another in the chest, but there was no pain. *Insh'allah.* Yurek acknowledged his destiny. *Only let me live long enough to kill but one Chin,* he prayed. Perhaps Allah heard him, for his pain was slow in coming.

Another bullet grazed his forehead as he pressed himself against the rocks and pulled another of the rockets from *Aga* Yani's pouch. Yurek had no launcher, but the rocket was fin stabilized, and he knew how to arm its warhead manually. Many said such a thing could not be done, but Yurek knew differently; it was but another part of his Gift, the *khan* used to say in admiration. The warhead was a shaped charge, not meant to be used against men in the open, but it would have to do.

The Chin had stopped firing as they made ready to move onto the plateau, where their observers could direct their mortar's fire into the village with deadly accuracy. Yurek looked down on them from the ambush point, and saw them gathered in the tiny bowl of cleared rock, some even pointing to him and laughing, or taking the occasional stray shot to keep his head down. No matter. Crouched behind the rocks, Yurek was completely hidden. Let them think him a coward. The Chin's opinions of his fighting prowess meant nothing to him, for they were but infidels and he was not a soldier, but an artisan.

Yurek plunged his knife into the rocket tube at the base of the warhead, cutting free the solid propellant engine. The black rod of hardened powder dropped into his lap, and he stored it in the lining of his coat for reuse later; Yurek's people wasted nothing.

Another thrust of the knife, this time into the tip of the warhead, and he had exposed the detonator. Below, the Chin had detached the mortar from its base and were preparing to carry it over the lip of stone that had concealed their approach. Yurek pulled the detonator from the base of the shaped charge explosive, pushed it hard into the nose, and spliced two wires. Jumping to his feet, Yurek took brief aim and threw the makeshift bomb high overhand into the air.

One of the raiders yelled something that might have been "grenade" in Chin, and Yurek had the satisfaction of seeing them all look frantically about the crater for cover that did not exist. Yurek watched as his throw, guided without doubt by the Hand of Allah, put the bomb directly into the center of the Chin. The blast scoured the crater, throwing the mortar tube over the side to follow the rocket launcher that *Aga* Yani had dropped earlier.

Moments later, Yurek had retrieved his rifle, and was methodically squeezing off single shots into the Chin that were still moving below. *Allah-u akbar*, he prayed, tears of gratitude streaking his face. *God is great, God is great; I testify that there is no other God but God, and Mohammed is his prophet.*

He was starting to put second shots into the dead raiders when a shadow fell on him from behind; he tried to turn, but his assailant was far too fast. His weapon was wrested from his grip. Yurek rolled over, but his assailant was silhouetted against the morning sun. He tried to draw his knife, but he had lost too much blood, and his shock was worsening in Haven's cold; the knife was batted from his hand with insulting ease, and Yurek lost consciousness without ever seeing his foe.

Heart pounding, his vision closing in at the edges, Mulli fought to draw air into his lungs; he was too high; the *mullahs* warned every child in the village not to climb above the rim when the wind was low. But he had disobeyed *Aga* Yani, leaving his post to get a better firing angle on the Chin, and a good thing as it had turned out, for their accursed mortar would have killed him, and his nephew Sadhar would have gone unavenged by a blood relative.

Mulli was racing up the back slope to a position even higher than that which Yurek and *Aga* Yani sought; the air was thin up here, dangerously thin, but he begged God that he be allowed to survive it for the few moments he would be above the rim. He was just crawling over a blade-thin ridge when he heard, far below, the sound of Yurek's makeshift grenade, amplified by the bowl the Chin had been hiding in; Mulli at first feared they had something larger than a mortar.

Standing too fast, Mulli blacked out, and losing his grip, saved his own life. The vengeful *mujahadin* slid a dozen meters down the slope, back down into the rim, pain threatening to split his skull from within— the first symptoms of anoxia. He opened his eyes and saw that he had not dropped his machine gun.

Allah-u akbar. He grinned fiercely. Below him, he could see Yurek firing into the dead and wounded Chin, and he was about to shout a cheer when he saw—something.

A black shape flowed over the rocks toward Yurek,

and before Mulli could recover his wits, the devil was upon the tribe's weaponsmith. In seconds, the strong, agile Yurek was beaten senseless, and with a gesture, the black shape called more of its fellows to the scene.

Whimpering with frustration, Mulli twisted the useless machine gun in his hands; what good were bullets against demons? Then, squinting against the late morning glare, Mulli saw one of them pull back a hood, to reveal a pale face and yellow hair. The figure raised a hand to its mouth and appeared to speak, then he and his comrades were gone again, moving across the rock faces like shadows on water.

Mulli stared after them for some time, trying to convince himself that firing the machine gun would have killed Yurek; the weaponsmith had been in the middle of those men—if they were men—and Mulli could not have avoided hitting him.

Mulli breathed deeply, slowly, gathering his thoughts.

They looked like men; they must have been men. Yet what sort of men could do the things he had seen them do? What tribe bred such warriors?

Revenge for Sadhar would have to wait. Mulli climbed carefully down the slope; it would not do to fall and die without bringing back the news that their best weaponsmith had been captured by warriors of an unknown tribe.

Mulli had to get this news to the *khan*.

While Gav was leading his men down the mountainside with their captive, First Citizen Galen Diettinger stood on a parapet of the Citadel and looked a little way to the northeast and a very long way down.

Four thousand feet below on the valley floor, the narrow pass into the Shangri-La from the Northern Steppes was a bustle of activity. Down there, Combat Engineer Denbannen's men were clearing the ground for the foundation of the most ambitious Sauron project on Haven since their invasion three years previous. Among the Saurons, only a handful understood Diettinger's reasons for believing the endeavor was necessary, and only Denbannen believed it could be done.

Diettinger turned and walked across the patio into his office in this, the highest meeting hall in the highest tower of the Citadel. On a table within stood a scale model of the project as Denbannen had proposed it: A featureless slab of gray concrete wedged between the southeastern point of the Atlas Range and the northwestern extents of the Miracle Mountains.

Five thousand feet high, far above the highest passes into the Shangri-La, a wall of stone and steel to forever seal off the valley from the Northern Steppes, and make the Saurons undisputed masters of the most crucial land mass on Haven. The wall would shut out the steppes nomads and raiders beyond the valley, ending their attempts at depredation of the Shangri-La. More importantly, it would prevent any escape of the valley dwellers who had survived Haven's first two winters since the Coming of the Eye, as the locals sometimes called the advent of the Sauron race on Haven.

But it was not a solid wall, of course. Denbannen's detailed model included the dozens of gates at the wall's base which would allow the flow of tribute from the steppes and the valley, tribute that would allow the steppes dwellers to enter the Shangri-La for their birthing women and allow the valley dwellers to trade with the more tractable nomads. It would be some time yet before Haven's economy would stabilize sufficiently to require all those gates, but already the human norms from within and without the Shangri-La had sent representatives to the Saurons asking permission to institute trade. Diettinger had agreed to accommodate them, eventually. And he would, for he was nothing if not a far-thinking man.

But the accommodations would be on the Saurons' terms, and that meant via the Wall.

Still, despite the power the Wall would provide, the project had its detractors. Nothing very vocal, of course. Saurons absolutely did not argue with the policies of their leaders, most in fact were incapable of doing so. But many of the Deathmasters had sent "recommendations" to the First Citizen that too many able-bodied Soldiers were being drawn off for work on this project, when the mountains surrounding the Citadel had yet to be fully explored and secured. The map on Diettinger's wall gained pins daily, each one showing yet another clash between Sauron patrols and bandits in the passes surrounding the Citadel.

But although Diettinger appreciated the situation of his commanders, there was nothing to be done about it. The *Formoria* had brought less than three thousand Saurons to Haven. In three years, two hundred Soldiers had died in the battles of pacification and consolidation resulting in the Sauron's mastery of the Shangri-La. The Breedmasters, under the capable guidance of Breedmaster Caius, had overseen the natural births of one-hundred fifty True Saurons, with Sauron parentage on both sides, and eighty-seven hundred Sauron/Havener progeny, only about five thousand of which were from fertilized Sauron ova carried to term by Haven women. It would be at least fourteen T-years before those Saurons reached adulthood, and it was that gap in the Saurons' population growth that made the Wall a necessity.

Dominance of the Valley would have to be maintained for those young Soldiers until they matured. By then, the next generation of Saurons would be only a year away, and life could proceed normally. But for now, the Saurons were vulnerable. Their combat losses could not be replaced until this new generation matured, and while casualties had dropped sharply since the initial invasion, they still lost an average of one Soldier a month in combat with Haven's diverse, warlike peoples. Diettinger thought it ironic that the Empire that had obliterated Sauron could have been so repulsed by her eugenics policies. Haven was a eugenics project the likes of which Sauron had only dreamt of: A harsh, merciless world forcefully colonized by some of the most violent and aggressive peoples of the old CoDominium and later of the Empire itself. A crucible, brewing a genetic steel that tested even the Sauron's mettle.

Diettinger looked up at the wall over the fireplace, where a tattered banner had been hung. A flag of the Haven Militia under Cummings, it was all that had been captured during a bloody, fruitless raid on a Havener stronghold that had cost the lives of three Soldiers. *They will never be defeated,* he thought, *not entirely.* And he smiled. *So much the better.*

The events that had brought them here after the destruction of Sauron, at the end of the Secession Wars, were beginning to take on near-mythic aspects in the minds of some of the Breedmasters. Haven was a world which might possibly improve upon even the Soldiers themselves.

All well and good, Diettinger thought. But mastery of Haven, with its thin air and concomitant poor birthing effects, meant mastery of the sheltered, fertile, oxygen-rich Shangri-La Valley. *And that mastery begins with the passes from the Valley to the Northern Steppes.* The original builders of the Citadel had known that; they had carved a splendid fortress from the stones of these mountains, a fortress which had stood secure until the Saurons came to annex it.

But even beyond a mastery over the Valley, which is by no means guaranteed even with *this Wall, something more is needed. Haven is practically secured, if not pacified. In the interim between the last battles of conquest and the primacy of the first New Generation, we will need a unifying purpose to prevent the faction-*

alism Haven could make us prone to. The Project,
building this Wall, will keep us busy, productive and
united; the inevitable Havener raids on its progress
will keep us alert.

And those raids had already begun. The worst were
a large faction of dispossessed Haveners known collectively as the Chin; little was known about them beyond
the fact that they had been driven out of the Shangri-
La some fifteen years previous, shortly after the
Empire had withdrawn its last legions from Haven for
the Secession Wars. They had been living as raiders
on the steppes ever since, and they had the ferocity
to prove it. They were constantly probing the perimeter of the Citadel's defenses, harassing the survey parties in the mountains and on the valley floor.

But they were only human norms, and what little
threat they posed would be eliminated if only the hundreds of problems with the Wall could be solved. Denbannen had given him a new list this morning, and
even Diettinger's enthusiasm flagged. He leaned over
the table, staring at the model as if prepared to *will*
it into existence.

"You will stare that wall down, Galen."

Diettinger started, turning to the voice of his wife
Althene as she entered the room. He favored her with
a rare smile, pointing to the patch that covered his
left eye. "Only half of it, Lady."

"Slow going?" Althene asked. The former Second
Rank of the *Formoria* was respected by the entire
Sauron population, and cherished by her husband. She
had been an expert Staff officer, continued to be an
excellent administrator, and had shown herself to be a
shrewd diplomat. But most importantly, she was fertile.
She was carrying their second child into the sixth month.

He nodded. "Acquisition parties have scoured the
Shangri-La for processed concrete, structural steel, all
manner of materials. Most of what is needed is available, just lying about for the taking, but getting it

here will take time, and a great many laborers. Several contacts with Haveners from the Valley have indicated willingness to work for food and shelter." He smiled at her. "Your recommendations for fair trading with them had precisely the effect you predicted; they will never love us, but they have grown to accept the fact that we are here, and already they see the wisdom in cooperation, however reluctant."

Althene smiled at her husband's compliment. "They are only human, after all, Galen."

A knock on the door was followed by the entry of one of his aides, Savin. Savin had been a Gunner on the *Fomoria,* and was currently retraining for ground artillery.

Not that we have much of that, these days, Diettinger thought. He acknowledged the young Soldier's salute. "Speak," the First Citizen said.

"Squad Leader Gav has brought back a prisoner from his patrol, First Citizen. A human norm, slightly wounded. Gav took him directly to the infirmary, but he believes you will want to see him."

Diettinger nodded. "Very well. Inform Fourth Rank Milsen and have him meet me there."

Savin left to comply, and Diettinger turned to his wife. "Would you care to accompany me?"

"I would. The Breedmasters treat me even more delicately than with our first son. I am prepared to suffer no such further indignities today."

Diettinger smiled. *True,* he thought, *Sauron is dead. Her children are scattered, and perhaps only this pitiful, tenuous remnant on Haven preserves the race.*

He held the door for his wife, and in his innermost heart, he acknowledged once more that secret he would take to his grave: *If such was the price for me to have found this woman, unnoticed all those days serving in my crew, then I am content with the bargain.*

*   *   *

Mulli held his chin against his chest so his tears could not be seen. He cried for the *khan,* but he knew his sympathy to be water poured into an ocean; the *khan* cried for them all.

Abdollah Khan vented his frustration and rage in the same way he ruled his tribe, killed a foe, or made love to his wives: with great vigor and utter commitment. Now was the time for grief, and he grieved, and his people grieved with him. When he had rent his clothes and stopped pacing, the *khan* took a deep breath, held it a moment, then let it out.

His eyes shone less with tears than with feral cunning, and Mulli thrilled at the sight as the *khan* turned to him.

The time for grief is past, Mulli thought. *Woe to the infidels that the time has come now for revenge.*

Abdollah Khan spoke aloud, and Mulli knew that meant he was planning a battle. "I have seen such men, and we have all heard the tales. They came in the starship that made the Great Wasting of three summers ago. Their ship was destroyed by the lowland infidels with one of their great missiles, but there has been much fighting in the valley ever since." The *khan* turned to face Mulli and the rest of the men gathered in his chambers; outside, the women wailed for the deaths of their neighbors and loved ones, and the loss of Yurek.

"Yes," Abdollah Khan decided. He paced slowly about the room as he spoke. "These are men from off world. Enemies of the Empire. They fight with the infidels of the valley and the steppes, and word comes to me that in them, the lowland peoples face a terrible foe these days. These men have a name that in Old Anglic sounds like the serpents of old—saurians, or something like that. Ah! I remember; they call themselves *Saurons.* They have taken over the old fortress which guards the northern passes between the outland steppes and the valley below." The *khan* shook his head, clearing his thoughts. "No matter."

Abdollah Khan crossed the room and gripped Mulli's shoulders in his hands. "Mulli, you would know such men if you saw them again?"

Mulli nodded. "*If* I saw them, *aga;* they moved very swiftly. And Yurek's ears are sharp; he should have heard them, but I think he did not."

Abdollah Khan nodded. "Hm. Did I not say they were like serpents?" He held out his hands to the assemblage of men, and all nodded at his wisdom. "Such men will leave little mark of their passing. But they *took* Yurek; they did not kill him out of hand, and they were not fighting beside the Chin." The *khan* grew quiet, and Mulli knew *that* meant he was plotting, trying to find the small advantage in any situation that could be turned to the advantage of his people.

"Mulli," Abdollah Khan said in a thoughtful voice, "take three of our best marksmen and three of our best trackers. Find out where these men took Yurek. Watch, and send me word." The *khan* raised a finger. "But do nothing without my command. If you should attempt a rescue and fail, Yurek might die because of it."

Mulli nodded firmly. "I understand perfectly, *aga khan.*"

"Good. Then do not fear. Go, Mulli, and try to find out what these infidels want with my son."

The first thing Diettinger noticed in the infirmary room was the rifle. Smeared with blood, it lay with its detached ammunition clip on a table beside the body of the captive. Frowning, he picked it up as Squad Leader Gav announced himself.

"First Citizen; it is the weapon of the captive."

"So I gathered. Why was it not taken to the armory?"

Gav looked to the surgeon, who answered the question as he was cutting the bloody ruin of a sheepskin coat from the body of the man on the table. "They couldn't get it out of his hands, First Citizen; Squad Leader Gav was afraid of injuring the man further, so they disarmed the weapon and left it in the captive's grip."

"And how did you get it, Surgeon Rank Vaughn?" Diettinger's tone indicated that it had better not have been by use of their precious stocks of sedatives.

He needn't have worried. Surgeon Rank Vaughn lifted one of his patient's hands to show the splinted digits. "Broke his fingers, of course. He never even woke up."

"Will he live?" Althene asked, moving closer to examine the man: dark skin, several days' growth of beard, curly brown hair, good teeth. Lifting an eyelid revealed the bottom sliver of a blue-gray pupil.

"Oh, I think so, Lady." Vaughn spoke as he continued working. "His wounds were not serious. Only his blood loss and resultant shock in such frigid cold put him in danger. He's quite a healthy specimen, actually."

Diettinger was still examining the rifle. The Saurons used linear accelerators, commonly known as "gauss" rifles, from the magnetic fields generated by twenty sequentially charged rings. A ferrous metal-jacketed slug of depleted uranium was push-pulled down the array of magnets, accelerating as it went to a velocity that made the weapon the ultimate development of the slug thrower. Not as effective as the high energy weapons used during the Secession Wars, but close to the limit of what the Sauron's light industrial capacity on Haven could produce and maintain.

And for how much longer? Diettinger thought. They were perhaps only five years from phasing out the high energy weapons completely; how soon before the gauss rifles went in favor of something simpler still?

Diettinger considered the weapon in his hands.

Something like this . . . He was an expert on antique weapon designs, and this one was excellent, a superb conventional firearm. A robust design that required only simple maintenance, an easily produced and replaceable stock and grip made of local woods, a large clip holding at least seventy rounds of ammunition. Diettinger sprung one of the bullets from the clip and examined it.

Long case, with a heavy charge; a copper jacketed slug with a disintegrating soft lead core. A civilian might misinterpret that as a needless cruelty, but Diettinger knew it to be simple expedience.

His interest piqued, he turned the weapon over in his hands several times. Try as he might, he could find no serial numbers, at least none where they belonged. In three places, however, he found what appeared to be some form of writing, graceful, fluid characters, strokes and curves and dots. They were inscrutable to him. He turned to Gav.

"Report."

"While patrolling Sector eight-zero, three-niner, we heard sounds of combat between locals. Deployed unit to investigate and found this man on the edge of a village currently engaging a band of local raiders, possibly Chin."

"This man's significance?"

"The village was situated at an altitude of eighty-five hundred feet, well beyond known human norm tolerances for Haven."

Diettinger, Althene, and Vaughn exchanged looks in silence. "You confirmed this altitude?"

"Yes, First Citizen." Gav pulled out his sealed barometer; the needle had locked in at eight thousand, five hundred and seven feet, but there was a long scratch in the calibrated wax altitude track.

"Has this been tampered with, Squad Leader?"

"No, First Citizen. There was some fluctuation as we reached the perimeter of the Havener village."

"Fluctuation?"

"The needle began dropping, First Citizen, but it is designed to lock at its highest mark, to confirm our readings."

"Are you saying that air pressure *increased* as you entered the village?"

"We carried no equipment to confirm such a statement, First Citizen, but some of the men did claim that breathing seemed easier nearer the village."

Diettinger considered this for a moment; he was not sure how such a thing could be possible, but it would bear looking into.

"Good work, Squad Leader Gav. Your initiative may have discovered a new birthing area for your fellow Soldiers. Remain on station here with your squad at the Citadel until this matter has been resolved. Dismissed."

Pleased at the First Citizen's praise, Gav acknowledged the order and left. He would order recreation time for his squad, and prepare his report with a mention of them all.

Fourth Rank Milsen arrived as Gav departed. Surgeon Rank Vaughn was probing the captive's chest wound, apparently satisfied that the bullet had exited as cleanly as it had entered; Haveners were known to use soft-slugs on each other as readily as they did on Saurons.

"First Citizen, Lady Althene." Milsen was one of the fastest rising young officers in Diettinger's command. A low ranking Engineering Tech during the invasion of Haven three years ago, he had gone directly to Warrant Officer when it was discovered that he had a gift for the varied languages used by the human norms here. He had made Fourth Rank last month, when the total number of languages he had learned reached twenty. Milsen had extensively studied the various cultures that produced those languages, and Diettinger had come to depend on him as an indispensable intelligence asset.

"Fourth Rank Milsen, can you identify this man?"

Milsen picked up the clothes from the floor where Surgeon Rank Vaughn's scissors had sent them. "Hill dwellers, I would say, First Citizen." He looked at the man's boots. "A much colder region than we've seen so far; his clothes are worn from use, not travel, so he was not dressed to cross the mountains but to live in them. The workmanship is by hand, of extremely high quality." Milsen studied some of the captive's other items. After a moment he frowned, obviously puzzled.

"Something?" Diettinger asked.

"The metalwork of his belt; the few buttons on his coat. The production quality is exquisite, but the material used is of very poor grade." Milsen looked into the eyes of the First Citizen. "These artifacts appear to be the result of a technological mass-production process, First Citizen. And they are new."

Diettinger's grip on the rifle tightened slightly. He went to the table, where Surgeon Rank Vaughn had turned his attentions to the wounds in the captive's leg. "Wake him."

True to his Sauron nature, Vaughn switched gears without pause, producing a syringe seemingly from thin air. The needle went into the human norm's forearm, and Vaughn said: "Within ten seconds, First Citizen."

It took eight. Yurek's eyes rolled slightly, then squinted against the light of the surgery. He tried to raise a hand to his eyes, but Vaughn restrained his arm.

Diettinger waited for the captive to speak; when he did, the language was somehow both fluid and stilted, lilting and guttural at the same time. He glanced to Fourth Rank Milsen, whose frown deepened as he concentrated on the alien words.

The captive's vision seemed to focus; he looked first

at Vaughn, then to Diettinger. His gaze rested for a moment on Althene, and he seemed abruptly embarrassed at his nakedness, trying to cover his manhood by drawing his wounded thigh over his groin, obscuring Vaughn's operation on the limb. He began chattering at them in a wounded tone.

Not all of us, Diettinger realized. *He's ignoring Althene completely, as though she were of no consequence.*

Milsen suddenly began speaking in a loud, authoritarian tone; the captive relaxed, but only a little. Diettinger understood nothing but what might have been "Sauron-dah" near the end, at which point the man on the table slumped in despair. He whispered something, then closed his eyes.

"What did he say?"

"He said: 'Mighty Satan,' First Citizen, or 'The Great Satan.' Something like that."

Bewildered, Diettinger looked to Althene.

The First Lady shrugged. "A religious reference, I believe. Old human norm, quite common; usually referring to the antithetical totem of most belief-oriented mythologies."

"Was he praying, then?" Diettinger wondered, curious.

"Perhaps, sir." Milsen said. "Or, he might have been referring to us."

Althene turned to the Fourth Rank interpreter. "If he is from a technological culture, such a primitive transference seems unlikely."

"I cannot tell, Lady," Milsen admitted. "But his tone did seem to indicate us. Also, he is evidently disturbed by his nakedness in the presence of a woman."

Althene nodded. "Hmm. That *is* typical of less-developed races." She raised an eyebrow. "Ah, perhaps he is a slave?"

Diettinger took the man's jaw between thumb and

forefinger and turned his gaze to meet his own. There was a cool resignation in the gray eyes, and absolutely no fear. *Not a slave, then. Even human norms are not so foolish as to keep slaves without fear. Interesting.* He had seen hate, bloodlust, and a hundred other reactions that human norms evinced on contact with Saurons. But never, not once, had he ever seen a look of such complete and utter peace.

Suddenly, he realized the man was whispering, and gestured Milsen closer.

" 'I testify that there is no other god but God,' " Milsen translated the captive's words as he spoke them, " 'And Mohammed is his prophet.' " He looked up at Diettinger. "He goes on to repeat that several times, First Citizen."

"What does it mean? Who is Mohammed?"

"A religious figure of Old Earth," Althene said. "He is most certainly praying, then." Althene had effortlessly identified what most Saurons could have only guessed at.

"Stop him," Diettinger said, the first faint stirrings of impatience creasing a line in his brow over his eye patch. "Confirm that his village is at the elevation stated by Squad Leader Gav." Diettinger did not doubt Gav, and anyway the details of how this particular band of Haveners could thrive at that altitude was more for the Breedmasters to sort out than himself. But he was curious about how much the man would try to conceal.

"He confirms it, First Citizen, but he offers no other information."

"Ask him about this weapon." Diettinger held the rifle before the man; whether it came from some hidden stockpile or was purchased with hides, wherever savages could acquire arms like this, a great danger lay for the Saurons. "Where did he get it?"

To their surprise, the captive answered immediately.

Milsen translated: "He says he made it, First Citizen."

After the morning's concerns, Diettinger's patience was nearing its end. "Fourth Rank Milsen, I have dealt with one Wall long enough today; kindly pierce the one in this savage's head and ask him where he got the parts to assemble it."

The captive looked puzzled at the question, and his simple answer made Milsen blink. The interpreter looked up at Diettinger.

"First Citizen, I—he says he made those, too."

The long silence that followed was broken by a keening wail of utter despair. The Saurons looked to the table, where the captive had freed one hand and brought it before his face, and was regarding the broken fingers with undiluted horror.

In his own village, Yurek would most likely have died within days. Blood loss in Haven's thin, cold mountain air induced rapid, deadly shock, and it was not likely he would have been found by his own people. But here in the Citadel, tended by Sauron doctors, well fed and warm, his body mended quickly.

His spirit did not.

Restrained in his bed by straps, he never tried to test them. He answered their questions, responded to their interrogator—a Sauron about his own age named M'ahl Hassan, or something like that—and prayed. He'd had trouble at first explaining why he needed someone to wash his face and head, then a small cloth to cover his scalp, but eventually M'ahl Hassan understood.

The Koran also dictated that he clean his hands before prayer, but Yurek still could not bear to think about them. Five times daily he prayed that the Devils had not taken his Gift when they had broken his fingers.

When he asked M'ahl Hassan, tentatively, about his

hands, the interpreter had spoken briefly to the
Sauron doctor, then told Yurek not to worry about it.
Keep them still, do everything the Surgeon Rank told
him to, and they would function perfectly once healed.

Yurek's heart fluttered at the prospect of regaining
the full use of his hands, but he crushed the hope
quickly. Hope was the prerogative of God, and He
would dispense reason for it as He saw fit. It was not
for Yurek to tempt His mercy by petitioning for it.

"Insh'allah," Yurek said quietly. M'ahl Hassan asked
him what it meant.

Yurek's temper flared for a moment at the ignorance of all infidels, then subsided. He knew very little
about Saurons, but he had heard they followed no
God of any name. He shook his head slightly. *To be
blind to His mercy, deaf to His word, ignorant of His
miracles; to never know Paradise.* They were more to
be pitied than hated.

"It means: 'As God wills,'" he explained. M'ahl
Hassan was a faithless man, but he seemed decent
enough for all that.

The Sauron's eyebrow lifted as he studied Yurek,
and the young Afghan realized that the infidel seemed
interested by what he had just heard. Could it be—
was it possible that this Devil was ready to hear the
words of the Prophet? Yurek could read, the *khan* had
insisted he learn the skill to further nurture his Gift,
but he was no *mullah;* he could not sing the Koran to
ears hungry for His truth, to hearts waiting to be filled.
Still, the Prophet admonished all men to spread God's
word in all ways, and never to fail to bring His truth
to those who asked.

Yurek was an artisan, true; a bearer of the Gift. But
he was, first and last, a good muslim. He would try,
despite his pain, despite his ignorance, and above all,
despite his hatred for these creatures who had brought
him to this crippled captivity, if they asked. To his

shame, he realized that he fervently hoped that they would not ask.

"Tell me about this 'god' concept," M'ahl Hassan said, activating a recording device.

Yurek sighed, took a deep breath, and began to speak.

"Fascinating," Althene said as Milsen finished his report. "A completely fatalistic belief system."

"But poetic," Diettinger said. "Quite beautiful, actually, in its way. And the ingrained belief in an afterlife is an inevitable part of a primitive warrior ethos. Particularly warriors of a culture surrounded by enemies, many of whom share the same faith."

Milsen nodded, speaking almost to himself. "An altogether brilliant social engineering tool; most religions are, of course, but they tend to erode with the advent of science. Notice how this one very cleverly embraces knowledge gained as an expression of the 'god's' favor. The more its adherents understand of the physical universe, the more that knowledge is taken to edify the 'miraculous' nature of that universe."

Althene was at her computer, consulting the historical database that had been her unofficial specialty even when she was Second Rank aboard the *Fomoria*. "It worked particularly well with these people, too. This Yurek and his people are evidently descendants of an Old Earth culture known as 'Afghans.'"

Diettinger frowned. "That name is familiar. They are mentioned in several texts on military history and adaptive warfare."

"The strain was wiped out during Earth's Patriotic Wars," the First Lady continued. "But what data I have indicates very large portions of their population had already been forcefully relocated, particularly the mountain tribes. Apparently they had made a strong enemy of one of the two planetary powers that comprised the old CoDominium."

Diettinger could not conceal his surprise. "They've been here on Haven that long?"

Althene nodded. "And virtually unchanged in their lifestyles and beliefs for all that time. The single dominant feature of their history appears to be an almost pathological devotion to self-determinism." She turned to her husband. "There is no record here that they have ever been conquered, Galen; *ever*. Not even the Ancient, Alexander, was able to subdue them."

"A romantic notion, Althene, but I remind you that during our history, Sauron Soldiers have put paid to that same reputation about a great many other peoples."

"Granted. But given that heritage, this religion of theirs takes on a whole new significance. They believe that death in battle against nonadherents to their faith is a *de facto* defense of that faith in the eyes of their 'god,' and so *guarantees* them admittance to their paradise. Thus, they have, potentially, no sense of self-preservation whatsoever."

"Then what you are telling me," Diettinger said, "is that these people will not submit to Sauron rule, making it necessary to destroy them; and that they will charge headlong into our soldiers' guns, making it convenient."

Althene shrugged. "Unfortunate to lose such a dynamic and promising gene pool, but that is probably the case."

"What about the weapon?" Diettinger asked. Engineering sat at the end of the table, examining the automatic rifle in silence, and evidently with great respect.

Milsen shook his head, frankly puzzled. "First Citizen, I know that it sounds incredible, but he maintains that he fashioned that weapon—a chemically fired slug thrower capable of full and semi-automatic fire—out of raw materials, *by hand*. He says that the shells are frequently stolen from other human norm tribes, but they are more often retrieved after battle and reused. He also claims that he personally produces several such weapons in the course of a year, and enjoys a special status among his people because of that."

Diettinger gave a short laugh. "I don't doubt that he would, Fourth Rank." He turned to Engineering. "Is this possible?"

Engineering thought for a moment. "In theory, certainly. First Citizen, every tool made by Man, even Sauron Man, is simply an extension of his own physical capabilities. Hands can kill, hands holding rocks can kill bigger opponents. Thrown rocks kill opponents at a distance, while a bow makes a better projectile weapon than an arm; a rifle better still. And a fabrication unit which produces a thousand rifles a day really does nothing more than the work of a thousand men in a fraction of the time they would require for the same task."

Engineering picked up the rifle. "Certain tolerance requirements grow in importance as the technological levels of the weapons increase, and it is arguable that a ceiling would be reached, beyond which human senses and manual dexterity could not go." He stopped and looked up at Diettinger. "But until one reaches the realms of microscopic circuitry in those arguments would be in error."

"Human capability is the founding principle of the entire Sauron race," the First Lady put in quietly.

Engineering nodded. "Exactly, Lady. Briefly then, First Citizen, only three things are required to do what this human norm claims he can do. First: tools, of at least a minimal level of quality, but doubtless his people even know how to fabricate and improve upon those. Second: time, the ability to work undisturbed, for weeks, perhaps months, in an area of security; that, of course, would be an end product of having such weapons. And third: expertise. Years, more likely generations of training and practice, to learn to do, implicitly, what a man at a higher technological level, dependent on better tools, would have to think about constantly. Eventually, even cutting and finishing metal to the finest tolerances would transcend mere technical expertise, and be elevated to an art form."

Engineering looked up to see the First Citizen smiling broadly. "I'm sorry, sir, did I say something?"

"Indeed you did, Engineering," Diettinger said. He turned to Milsen. "Can he walk?"

"Yes, First Citizen. He's quite improved over the past few weeks."

"Good. Exercise him regularly. Keep him healthy, and when Surgeon Rank Vaughn says he is ready, take him to the workshops and allow him the use of some simple tools. Tell him to indulge himself, but watch him carefully. More importantly, observe his procedures, and present me with a report on the feasibility of teaching them to our own people."

After Milsen had left, Diettinger stood and went to the map of the area surrounding the Citadel. "Beyond these walls, dozens of patrols are out every hour of every Trueday and Truenight, monitoring hundreds of passes and almost as many bands of raiders." He turned back to face Althene and Engineering. "And every Soldier of those patrols is armed with a weapon that is technologically superior to those of the locals." He picked up the rifle.

"For now."

Diettinger returned to the table and continued: "What you described, Engineering, are not just the requirements for a craftsman of this sort. They are also the ideal conditions for the training of a Soldier."

Yurek's convalescence was brief; if the Saurons' medical equipment was sparse, their knowledge was extensive. Yurek was walking on crutches within a week after his capture, on a cane within two. He waited for the Sauron Devils to begin torturing him for information about his people, but no such abuses ever occurred. Finally, he asked the interpreter, M'ahl Hassan: "What became of my people?"

"I am told that the patrol which captured you watched your village drive off the Chin raiders; evidently the mortar which you destroyed was the Chin's best hope for victory."

Yurek tried to see if the Sauron Devil was flattering him, but they showed little in their faces; he had come to think of them more as machines than men. M'ahl Hassan added: "You might be interested to know that our patrol destroyed the rest of the Chin raiders during their retreat."

Yurek blinked. "The Chin are your enemies as well?"

M'ahl Hassan shook his head. "Not specifically. But they are disruptive. We will tolerate villagers, townspeople, farmers, fishermen, even nomads. These people produce, and thus contribute to the social infrastructure. But simple raiders are counterproductive to our purposes."

Yurek was taken aback; the infidel had spoken from the Koran! Not the same words, of course, but the idea . . . was it possible that something of the Truth had touched this soulless one? *Ah, God, forgive me!* Yurek hissed a sharp intake of breath at his near-blasphemy. The Word of God was the Word of God, and nothing could stand before it, not man, not machine, and least of all the Devil and his servants!

"Is something wrong?" M'ahl Hassan had asked, seeing his distress.

"Ah, no, nothing. Some pain." Yurek's thoughts scrambled wildly; if he could convert this one, at least, then they might both escape to return to his people. But he was being tempted by his hopes again, and he pushed them down, below where they might reveal his purposes to these infidels and thus betray him. The fact was that he was a prisoner here; *remember that,* and only that, and trust that God will dispose of you as He sees fit, blessed be the name of God.

"Has your *khan* made contact with mine?" he asked, ordering his thoughts and watching the Sauron.

"Not yet."

He offers little, Yurek thought, *and asks much.* He knew he should not speak to these infidels more than necessary, but the inactivity of the past month did not sit well with the mind of a man like himself. *I am alone, and yes, may God forgive my faithlessness, I am frightened. And if I might not be allowed the use of my body, I would wish to use my mind. I want only to have someone to talk to.*

"What will you do to my village?"

"If the First Citizen wants to make contact with them, he will send a patrol to meet with your *khan*. Such patrols explain the terms of peace with the Citadel and the forms and quantities of tribute required of the contactees."

" 'Explain,' you said. Do you not mean 'offer'?"

M'ahl Hassan looked directly at him with an expression that might have been compassion. "No, Yurek. The terms are accepted, or the patrol destroys the village."

Yurek nodded. *"Insh'allah,"* he said. But the words brought little comfort.

He could not understand the Saurons. He knew them to be fierce warriors; the least among them was more than a match for any of the *mujahadin,* even big Amir, who had once killed a tamerlane with nothing but a short knife, and could still walk. But when it came to personal honor, these people were less than women. They accepted any order to any task, however menial, without hesitation. Old, scarred warriors could be commanded by fresh-faced youths, strong young men returned from patrol one day with head counts of twenty enemy dead, and the next they could be seen mopping floors, and not one grumbled. The Saurons did not even hold Meets around their tables at night. Soldiers talked, but it was about inconsequential things; no one boasted of his or his comrade's valor, no one wagered on the morrow's successes, and no one—and this was the most difficult for Yurek to understand—no one *ever* criticized the *khan* of the Saurons, Dihtahn Shah.

It was not fear, Yurek knew. He had seen men who lived under bad *khans,* where a word of dissent was the last thing their tongues did before leaving their mouths. These Saurons accepted the decisions of Dihtahn Shah without a council, and the orders of their other leaders as if each man was an *imam.*

And the women! Yurek could not help shuddering in dismay. The women were the worst. They conducted themselves absolutely without shame, taking their food with men, monitoring the activities of men, giving orders to men—to *men*—and worse, the men obeyed, and thought nothing of it!

Yurek could make no sense of the way these people lived, for they seemed to have no rational social structure, and they certainly had no God.

Of course, Yurek considered, *they have no enemies, either, at least none who are any real threat to them. So they must be doing something right.*

And they were courteous, if not friendly. Within certain limits, Yurek was allowed the run of the Citadel. He was always accompanied by at least two Sauron guards, one of which was invariably M'ahl Hassan. When the time came for the splints and bandages to be removed from his fingers, the Sauron doctor took great pains to instruct him in the exercises necessary for full recovery of the use of his hands. This seemed only slightly less important to the Saurons than it was to Yurek himself.

M'ahl Hassan waited until the second day after the bandages on Yurek's hands had been removed, then asked: "How is your leg today?"

"It is well; the stiffness is less. I think it wants exercise."

"And your hands?"

Yurek's eyes narrowed. "I do not know."

M'ahl Hassan turned to the young Sauron beside him and said something in a language Yurek had not yet heard; a clipped, toneless language with no inflections to gave him any clue as to its meaning. The youth nodded and left Yurek's room. M'ahl Hassan turned back to him.

"Surgeon Rank Vaughn has approved a new therapy for you, Yurek," M'ahl Hassan said. "If you feel well enough for a long walk, I think you will appreciate it."

Is this it? Yurek thought. *I am healthy now, healthy enough to be interrogated and survive. Have they nursed me to this health for that purpose?* It was what *his* people would have done, of course, but Yurek had heard that the Saurons were not much for subtlety.

The other Sauron returned with a larger version of the recording device M'ahl Hassan had used during Yurek's explanation of the Faith to him. This one had a glass lens set in one side, and Yurek assumed it was a video camera. He had seen such things once as a boy, during a rare trip to the lowland cities of the Shangri-La Valley, in the years before the Saurons came. If they were going to torture him, they were apparently eager to miss nothing.

Very well, then. He would show them that death holds no fear for the Faithful. *Inshallah*, he would sleep this night in Paradise.

"I will go with you," Yurek said.

They had walked for nearly an hour without once exiting the Citadel, or even passing a window. Up stairs, down stairs, past work crews refurbishing the interior, through halls where the Saurons met, or ate, or marched. Past row upon row of sealed doors clogged with dust, into brightly lit chambers so clean that Yurek would have believed even a muslim could eat food from the floor without sin.

Yurek was completely lost. Twice his leg had cramped, and the two Saurons had linked their arms behind his back and beneath his buttocks, lifting and carrying him in one motion without even breaking stride. Both times he had insisted they put him down the moment his leg had loosened sufficiently to bear his weight. Yurek found their effortless superiority humiliating.

Finally, when his leg was about to give out a third time, M'ahl Hassan said, "We are here."

Yurek took a moment to realize that the door they were facing was set into one of two much larger ones; light shone through the crack between the great panels, and for a moment he had the crazy thought that they had brought him to an outside door, that they were letting him go.

Then M'ahl Hassan opened the small door, and in the light of the brightly lit room beyond, Yurek saw that they had something far different in mind. He followed M'ahl Hassan into the chamber where dozens of the Sauron Devils were busily occupied in all manner of tasks, all of them involving equipment of one form or another.

M'ahl Hassan had brought him to the workshop.

"How did he react?" Diettinger was taking Fourth Rank Milsen's update on their curious captive while Combat Engineer Denbannen waited to brief him on the latest problems with the Wall Project.

"He is quite shrewd, First Citizen. At first, he openly refused to produce weapons for us which might be used against his people."

"Reasonable, if imprudent."

Milsen nodded. "Then I allowed him to watch a calibration test for a Mark VII manpack fusion gun;

after that he seemed satisfied that nothing he could produce would be of any interest to us."

Which could not be further from the truth, Diettinger thought. But there was a thread of unease running through his thoughts; should Milsen have shown this Yurek a weapon as advanced as the Mark VII? He didn't really think there was any danger of this— *mujahadin,* he called himself—copying such a device, still . . .

No matter. In ten years, the Mark VII will be a memory. And in another generation, it will be less than a memory. It will be . . . what is a good word? He turned to look at the model of the Wall, now covered with revision marks made by Denbannen.

A myth, Diettinger decided.

"And now?"

"He is fabricating a lathe, First Citizen." Milsen seemed bewildered. "He is making it from scrap metal with hand tools and a simple forge, and the work so far is indistinguishable from that of a low grade, but undeniably technological process."

"You have surveillance teams emplaced?"

"Yes, First Citizen," Milsen acknowledged. "Whenever I am speaking with him, I always have at least one Soldier along who is learning his language, but under strict orders not to reveal the fact. Seven recorders cover his workstation, and Engineering himself is watching him closely on a hidden monitor."

"Good. Tell him to fabricate a simple weapon; a sidearm, perhaps, modelled after one of the chemically fired hand weapons in captured stores. Tell him such a task is to be a condition of his release. See that your men observe the process scrupulously, and bring me both weapons when he has finished."

"At once, First Citizen."

Diettinger stood quietly for a moment. "Your Soldiers are having no difficulty learning this *mujahadin's* language?"

"No, First Citizen. It is a simple, logically structured tongue."

"Fortunate. It will be necessary to have an interpreter for the captive's tribe within two weeks. Accelerate training for the Soldier among your staff who has made the most progress with their language."

"At once, First Citizen."

"Dismissed."

"First Citizen." Denbannen called Diettinger's attention back to the Project as Milsen left.

The Combat Engineer pointed to a series of marks along the sides of the Wall, where the construct met the cliff faces on either side. "I have completed my analysis and located the stress points in the design."

"Serious?"

"My calculations show that the Wall cannot bear its own weight for more than twenty years without them. Each one will have a load-bearing reinforcement brace sunk into the mountain at a forty-five degree angle, running the length of the wall's interior, arching in the center, and extending one hundred feet into the mountains on either side."

"So much metal," Diettinger said. Denbannen's plans would use up the Sauron's strategic reserves of steel and then some. "You see no alternative to this problem?"

Denbannen frowned in concentration. "No, First Citizen. I reiterate, however, that my expertise rests primarily in temporary structures, battlefield enhancements, and the like. Even with the aid of the *Fomoria*'s database and computers, I am somewhat out of my depth. I may be missing something obvious."

"Very well. But if these struts are unavoidable, I would prefer they use the minimum material necessary. Is there a way to reduce their mass without seriously weakening them?"

Denbannen thought for a moment. "There are several computer models I could use to find out, First

Citizen. I will generate their specifications and ask Engineering's staff to fabricate scale versions as physical test pieces. May I take this model with me for the purpose?"

Diettinger nodded, dismissing him with a wave. Denbannen gathered up his datapads, and the First Citizen watched in silence as the Combat Engineer rolled the table with its model of the Project out the door.

The Sauron guard behind Yurek stiffened as the young Afghan braced himself with his cane and leaned out over the parapet. The view into the valley below was spectacular, the air crisp and biting, and the wan light of Byers' Star mixed with the waxy illumination of Cat's Eye gave the day an amber quality that reminded Yurek of the tallow candles in the hut of the *khan*.

Yurek considered that it was a beautiful day to die.

He had been in the workshop all morning, and had asked to go outside for the noon prayer. M'ahl Hassan and the other Sauron, a scarred Soldier named Tong, escorted him as always.

When he had finished, he'd bundled up the sheepskin that served as his prayer mat and gone to look down into the valley. Far below, he could discern movement, as the Saurons on the valley floor labored with machines and tools to build something. He leaned forward a bit more.

There was something down there in the rocks.

Less than fifty feet away, a flap of sheepskin blew out of a crevice in the stone and disappeared back in again. Yurek turned his head, and could just see the brim of a sheepskin hat above it. The brim moved slightly, and for a moment, a sharp profile was exposed, then the face turned and looked directly up at him.

Mulli! His blood went cold. *And there are at least*

two more. . . . If the Saurons found strangers this close to their Citadel, they were doomed. He had to try to warn them away.

He made a circle with forefinger and thumb, then waved it before him as he sang a few snatches of prayer about health and well-being. *Please, please understand it means that I am all right, and GO AWAY!*

He heard a small stone strike the rock face below the parapet, but he could not see if they had left the crevice for safety, and he must be sure they did not reveal themselves while M'ahl Hassan and Tong were nearby to see or even hear them.

Yurek had learned that the Saurons were eerily aware of changes in facial expression, posture, and other body language, but they did not always interpret it correctly. He tried to lean over for a better look without arousing their suspicion.

"You will not fall," M'ahl Hassan said matter-of-factly. The Sauron had been watching Yurek closely as he stared out over the pass, and had suddenly appeared at his side.

Yurek shrugged. "I am not afraid."

"You misunderstood me," M'ahl Hassan said. "It was a command, not a reassurance." M'ahl Hassan stepped back to afford Yurek his privacy.

Yurek looked back at the Sauron, fighting an urge to strike him; he would be knocked down, he knew, before he could clench his fist. And besides, M'ahl Hassan had meant no insult. Yurek knew that if M'ahl Hassan should allow him to die, the wrath of the Sauron *khan* would be great.

Then if my suicide thus causes an infidel death, Yurek wondered, *have I died in the service of the Faith?* He sighed. *Probably not.* He wished he could speak to a *mullah.* "I would like to go back inside, now."

M'ahl Hassan and Tong flanked Yurek as they returned to the door set in the stone of the mountain, which led to the workshops deep within.

When they reached the halfway point, Yurek spoke without looking at M'ahl Hassan. "Why do you not kill me?"

"You interest our *khan*. And you may be helpful in our negotiations with your people."

Yurek started. "Negotiations? Dihtahn Shah will send one of his patrols to my village?"

"Yes."

"And they will deliver his ultimatum."

"Yes."

Yurek's jaw clenched. "Then my people will die."

"You cannot know that. You are a young man; your *khan* is presumably older, therefore more pragmatic. Our conditions are severe, but reasonable, considering they are absolute."

Yurek watched M'ahl Hassan with sadness. These Saurons would never understand him, or his people. The Soldiers were so disciplined that Yurek had never seen one object to the most insulting of tasks, let alone refuse a direct order.

They have no concept of freedom, he thought. *To them, Paradise would be an anthill.* He finished the trip to his workbench in silence, and in silence he picked up his tools again and returned to his work. He had finished the lathe, adjusted its bearings, and was satisfied with its performance. Today he would turn a small bar of metal, forming a rod that he would later carve down into a drill. That drill would not be hard enough to bore metal, but Yurek would use it to make a mold for casting a drill that would.

He placed shields around the lathe to catch the metal filings; they would be used for something else later. Even the frugal Saurons were learning from Yurek's stinginess; many of their larger lathes sported such catch-shields now, too.

Yurek turned as the doors opened to see two Saurons pushing in a large table with wheels on its legs. Resting on the table was a pile of rocks with a slab of white stone wedged between them. Behind him, M'ahl Hassan and Tong began clucking quietly to one another in what Yurek had come to recognize as the Sauron's Combat Tongue.

"Is that something important?" he asked M'ahl Hassan.

"A model of the Project, Yurek. It is not your concern."

The two Saurons were turning the table, and Yurek could now see that he had been looking at the back of a scale model. They were going to pass his workstation, and he watched the model's approach curiously.

As they pushed it toward him, Yurek could see that it resembled nothing so much as one of the great dams that had been built in the foothills in his grandfather's time, dams which had channeled water from mountain rivers to generate hydroelectric power for the valley dwellers. Yurek could also see that the front of the model was a maze of red lines, numbers and notes written in Sauron.

"What's wrong with it?" Yurek asked one of the Saurons pushing the table.

The Soldier stopped abruptly and stared at him, then shared a look with M'ahl Hassan. They spoke quietly to one another for a moment, then M'ahl Hassan asked:

"How do you know something is wrong?"

Yurek shrugged. "It has many marks, many numbers, but it is a finished thing. It must have been built wrong. And those wire frames look to be holding it up until it can be repaired."

M'ahl Hassan spoke to the other Sauron again, and Yurek noticed the new Soldier watching him with increasing interest. The stranger spoke to M'ahl Hassan again, who then turned to Yurek.

"This is sub-sub-*khan* Din b'ahn Ahn. He is a war-builder, a maker of fortifications and redoubts. This is not a finished thing, but a model of one. He has built it this size to see what problems may arise when it is built larger."

Despite himself, Yurek grew excited. "Ah! I know this thing! A splendid idea! When I apprenticed as a boy, I made small weapons of wood, copying the motions of my master as he worked in metal. That way I did not waste steel with mistakes, but learned the rules of the craft that is part of my Gift." Yurek stood and walked around the model, studying it from several angles. "It is a beautiful toy."

And indeed it was. Though he could not fathom its purpose, the detail was nothing short of exquisite. On closer inspection, Yurek could see that the large rocks flanking the gray slab had been carved by hand with some fine tool, details added with extraordinary care. On the left-hand rock, facing the slab's front, he could see an indentation carved into the stone on which lay several small blocks of painted wood. Looking up and down the stone, Yurek saw several more such artificial plateaus, each with its own cluster of buildings; all were connected by paths carved into the face of the stone, but the highest was the largest and the most detailed, and Yurek could see that its buildings blended into crevices carved deep into the rock.

He caught his breath. One of those areas was a perfect re-creation of the tower roof where he had stood less than an hour ago.

Yurek took an involuntary step backward, taking in the whole of the model from his new perspective, and understood. He looked from the face of Din b'ahn Ahn to the marks and wires on the model, and when he looked back to the Sauron, he could not keep the triumph from his eyes.

"You will never make it work," the young Afghan said. "Not like this."

M'ahl Hassan did not translate, but Din b'ahn Ahn snapped a word at him, and he recounted Yurek's statement to the Combat Engineer. There followed a hurried exchange between the two, and Denbannen went to Yurek's workbench, examined his tools and the lathe, then turned and spoke again to M'ahl Hassan.

"Sub-sub-*khan* Din b'ahn Ahn instructs you to explain yourself. Why will the model not work?"

Yurek's knees were shaking, but he managed nevertheless to do the same with his head. "I will not tell you."

Denbannen heard the translation and shrugged, then signaled his assistant to continue moving the table.

"I will tell your *khan*, if he will grant me an audience."

M'ahl Hassan shook his head. "Dihtahn Shah has not expressed any desire to speak with you, and you may not dictate his audiences."

Yurek nodded. "I understand." He watched Din b'ahn Ahn moving away, and called after him in the smattering of Sauron he had absorbed during his time at the Citadel: "Remember the winds, *aga;* the Breath of Allah must flow."

Din b'ahn Ahn stopped, looking over his shoulder at Yurek for some time before he continued on to his own working area.

Yurek turned back to his workbench, singing softly under his breath as he began to work the foot treadle that powered his lathe.

"He lives, *aga khan.*"

Abdollah Khan did not react to the news. So many days had passed, so many weeks. "Is he guarded, Mulli?"

"Yes, *aga;* and apparently comes out only for pray-

ers. Had we not heard him praying, we might never
have known."

"You have lived in harsh circumstances for weeks
to learn this, Mulli," the *khan* said, "and you have put
aside your own well-deserved vengeance to see that
the news reached me. I proclaim myself in your debt."

Mulli bowed his head in gratitude.

"They allow him his prayers," the *khan* said
thoughtfully. "They are infidels, but they are civilized." He stroked his beard with one hand. "Even
courteous." The *khan* stood slowly and walked to the
window. The room full of *mujahadin* behind him was
silent. Their people had never submitted to an enemy
in their history, and while all of them had heard of
the might of the Saurons, none were afraid to die
fighting them.

After a long time, Abdollah Khan spoke: "I have
lost sons before. Likely I will do so again." He waved
a hand: *"Insh'allah.*

"But we cannot afford the loss of our weaponsmith.
Bring my guns. We go to parley with the Saurons."

Surgeon Rank Vaughn was summarizing his report
to Diettinger and his advisors. The windows in the
First Citizen's office were wide open to the frigid
morning air, and a fire roared in the open hearth,
creating a bracing comfort zone less than a meter wide
directly between the two. Vaughn stood just within it
on the fire's side; the First Citizen was just without,
closer to the window. His other advisors were placed
as they preferred, although Breedmaster Caius scowled
repeatedly at the Lady Althene's choice of a seat
almost beside the window.

"The captive is whole, First Citizen. And all my
tests indicate that he and his people have lived on that
plateau for almost a century. Evolving from mountain
dwellers, they have simply adapted still further."

Diettinger turned to Breedmaster Caius. "How can

this tribe exist? The birthing of their women in such an environment must be close to impossible."

Caius gathered his thoughts for a moment before speaking, and Diettinger and the others braced themselves for one of his diatribes. "In normal environments, the most dangerous period of a pregnancy is during the first trimester; ten percent of all human norm pregnancies terminate during this time for one reason or another. This number is higher for native Haveners, approximately eighteen percent, even higher than the fifteen percent normal for Saurons. But consider: the thinner Haven air would long since have killed off all the fetuses carried by mothers who could not adapt to the atmospheric conditions here. The normal vulnerability of the first three months of life still exists, but the mothers who could not compensate for the lack of oxygen have either"—he ticked off the results on his fingers—"A, aborted naturally; B, died in childbirth; or C, given birth to severely deformed and/or retarded offspring."

Caius noticed the look of discomfort crossing the Lady Althene's features and took some pleasure that he'd made her as uncomfortable as her proximity to the window was making him. "In each case, the genetic consequence was to end the strain of atmosphere-vulnerable genes. This Yurek's people were fortunate enough to have adapted so quickly, before the lowered birth rate could wipe them out."

"Could our people birth there, as well? Naturally?"

"Possibly, given a minimal period of adaptation. Say four to six generations."

The First Citizen closed his eyes. Why were even the most enlightened of Breedmasters nevertheless incapable of seeing things from any perspective but their own? Caius' "minimal period of adaptation" would see them all in the grave by at least a century. He looked up to see Fourth Rank Milsen frowning in concentration. "Milsen. Speak."

"Something Yurek has spoken of, First Citizen. The plateau where his village is situated is sheltered on three sides by sheer walls, one of which actually overhangs the village. More than a natural redoubt, it forms a pocket which could trap the normal winds crossing over the mountains between the steppes and the Shangri-La."

"Resulting in a higher air pressure than would normally be possible at that altitude," Diettinger concluded; suddenly he remembered Squad Leader Gav's barometer, and the Soldier's report that his men found it easier to breathe as they approached the town. "And making the air pressure on the plateau almost as comfortable as that on the floor of the valley."

"The Breath of Allah," someone said, and everyone who was familiar with the name of Yurek's god turned to see it was Combat Engineer Denbannen.

"What's that?" Diettinger asked.

"First Citizen, something the captive said. He saw the scale model of the Wall when I brought it into the workshops for the structural tests we spoke of. He claimed it wouldn't work the way we had designed it."

Deathmaster Quilland almost laughed. "Really? May we assume that when he is not fabricating chemically fired antique rifles, he is hand carving fifteen hundred-meter walls?"

Diettinger gestured for silence. "Why will it not work, Combat Engineer, and why do you think his statement has merit?"

Denbannen shook his head. "He would not elaborate, First Citizen, unless he was allowed to tell you directly. As to the veracity of his statement, I can only say that he referred to something called 'The Breath of Allah,' and reminded me that 'the winds must blow.'"

"Not 'blow', Combat Engineer," Milsen corrected him. "The word he used was 'flow.' His Sauron was poor, but I remember it precisely."

"In any case, he seems aware of the phenomenon,

and if he is educated enough to understand it, perhaps he saw some crucial flaw in your Wall at that," Diettinger concluded.

"Query, First Citizen," Quilland's consternation was evident in his tone.

"Speak."

"This meeting represents my first encounter with the data on this savage, but I have seen nothing so far to warrant such interest. He claims the ability to fabricate weapons, but the only evidence of that claim is no more than a primitive assault rifle."

"Your question, Deathmaster," Diettinger's tone made the window seat seem cozy.

"Of what importance is the opinion of one savage Havener craftsman?"

The First Citizen did not answer. Instead, he opened a box that sat before his place at the table. Removing two cloth bundles, he placed them beside one another on the table. He unwrapped them simultaneously, revealing two antique-style revolvers.

"One of these weapons was taken from a Havener bandit. It is a revolving-cylinder, gunpowder-fired hand weapon known as a double-action revolver. Those of you familiar with antiques will understand its action. Suffice it to say that it is a simple, robust design, with a minimum of moving parts, capable of delivering a three gram slug with killing energy at a range of one hundred meters." He picked up both weapons and placed them in the center of the table. "The other was made by the captive during his convalescence, and is identical in every way to the original."

Quilland picked up both weapons, scrutinizing them carefully. "Which is the original?"

Diettinger smiled thinly. "I don't know. I had expected a serviceable copy. But in telling the captive that the quality of his work would bear on the likelihood of his release, I apparently motivated him to new heights. He copied every production mark perfectly.

He even added the appearance of normal wear to the outside. Only firing the weapon gives away its identity. The copy has a smoother action and a freshly rifled barrel, and is noticeably more accurate."

Quilland nodded. "Your pardon, First Citizen. I appreciate his importance now."

"Your pardon, First Citizen," came a flat indictment from the end of the table. "I do not."

Cyborg Rank Koln watched the proceedings with the utter lack of emotion that characterized all members of his species. He looked, acted, smelled different than his less genetically enhanced fellow Saurons, was in fact almost an alien in their midst. He never confronted Diettinger directly on any issue, and that alone was enough to keep the First Citizen on guard wherever the Super Soldier was concerned.

"I will elaborate. We have one hundred eighty-seven Mark VII manpack fusion guns in stores, but they must be held in reserve for highest priority crises. Our troops are thus armed with substandard projectile weapons, linear accelerator gauss guns. Nothing like as effective as the Mark VIIs, but still far superior to the majority of Havener weaponry encountered." Diettinger picked up both revolvers and went to the window. "That is because we have destroyed the industrial infrastructure of Haven; and to ensure that they never send word off-planet which might bring the Empire down on our heads, we are committed to keeping that infrastructure destroyed. We can tolerate no level of technology above steam power, and even that must be strictly monitored.

"We have been successful at this; the Haveners are no longer capable of manufacturing gauss weaponry. But once our stocks of such weapons wear out, neither will we be."

"But, First Citizen," Engineering interrupted, "the only moving parts in gauss rifles are the ammunition feed mechanisms in the clips; there is no reason why they should not last for a century or more."

"What about the power packs, Engineering? What will happen when we can no longer recharge them efficiently? What about metal fatigue in the accelerator magnets, or the guidance rail on which they are mounted? What about weapons damaged in accidents, stolen by bandits, captured in battles? We have lost firefights to the Haveners before, we will lose them again. Indeed, such losses will be minimal, and granted, the weapons we retain *should* last for more than a century."

Diettinger held each of them with his gaze before he concluded: "*Is there still one of you who doubts we will be here on Haven for at least ten times that long?*"

He paused to let the reminder of their predicament sink in. "The only thing keeping us technologically superior to the Haveners is our military capacity to supress their technological growth. And that military capacity depends on an extremely fragile industrial base: the remains of the machine shops and production facilities salvaged from the *Fomoria*."

Diettinger went back to the head of the table. "Nothing lasts forever. Not gauss rifles. Not dark ages." He picked up the Afghan's duplicate pistol, aimed briefly with his good eye, and fired out the window; a flagpole on an outside wall shattered, the banner tumbling down out of sight.

"Not even Sauron dominance. All such things fade away, *because we forget that it is natural for them to do so.* 'Entropy is the nature of the universe, but only if it remains unopposed by the actions of Man.' We learn this from our first educations, but we must always remind ourselves of it. With these *mujahadin* producing weapons for us, we may just possibly stave off the decline of our military-industrial capacity until such time as our genetic dominance of Haven is completed."

"You propose an alliance with these cattle?" Cyborg Rank Koln asked quietly; his voice was toneless as ever, but his inflection bespoke disapproval.

Diettinger faced the Cyborg for the first time. "I *propose* nothing. I am informing this board of *advisors* that we will make use of these people in the manner best suited to the continued dominance of the Sauron genotype on Haven." He turned to Althene. "First Lady, you have examined the available historical data on the behavioral patterns of these Afghans, and correlated with Fourth Rank Milsen's observations of the captive?"

"I have."

"Assessment."

"Pathologically incapable of servitude."

Diettinger nodded once. "Briefly then, we can simply obliterate these people, since they will never submit to dominance, and gain for ourselves nothing more than another birthing area; albeit more convenient than those we must construct or otherwise seize. We may even capture some of their women as birthing personnel, but this is by no means assured."

"That has been standard procedure with all Haveners since the invasion," Quilland objected. "I wish to remind the First Citizen that modifying such a policy now may be taken as a sign of weakness on our part by the inhabitants."

"Only if they find out about it, Deathmaster," Diettinger answered. "This Afghan village is sufficiently isolated that the other Haveners need never know of our dealings with them."

"Query."

Diettinger paused a moment before acknowledging the speaker. "Speak, Cyborg Koln."

"If these tribesmen are permitted to manufacture

weapons for us, what guarantee have we that they will
not produce extras for themselves and other Haveners?"

"None." Diettinger said. "Which is why we must
make it important for them to know where their
greater interests lie."

"Your pardon, First Citizen," Koln said quietly.
"But I fail to see any advantage to be gained from any
liaisons with cattle."

"Then perhaps Breedmaster Caius can prepare an
introductory lecture on the subject for you," the First
Citizen ended the debate coolly.

Diettinger rose and addressed his staff as a group:
"The Coalition of Secession was an acceptable political
maneuver to the Sauron Council. They devised it in
order to provide us first with votes in the Imperial
Parliament, and later with buffer worlds in the war
against the Empire. Instead, we gained weak, petty
tyrannies which required constant rescue from Imperial forces, and to what gain? Most of the 'allies' in
the Coalition had less to offer Sauron than these people have to offer us." He held the pistol before him,
admiring the workmanship, the accuracy, the feel of
expertise with which it was imbued.

"And somehow," Diettinger finished, "I doubt that
these *mujahadin* will be running to us for help very
often."

He put the weapon down. "This meeting will
reconvene in two hours. In the meantime, Combat
Engineer Denbannen, return here with your model in
ten minutes. Fourth Rank Milsen, collect the captive
and bring him here, as well."

"Will you require my computer data on the Project
as well, First Citizen?" Denbannen asked.

Diettinger thought a moment and said: "I doubt this
Yurek would understand any of it, Combat Engineer.
We have been relying on a detail-planning method to
solve the problems with the Wall. Let us see what

can be accomplished by embracing a more intuitive approach."

Yurek had been praying steadily since M'ahl Hassan had come to collect him; he had vowed he would not be afraid, but his nerve left him as the double doors opened and he was ushered into the presence of the Sauron *khan* and his council.

Yurek had met other *khans* before, and even as an artisan, a bearer of the Gift, he knew what was expected of him. The cold stones of the floor grated against his knees as he knelt before the only one standing, who must, therefore, be Dihtahn Shah.

M'ahl Hassan spoke after a brief exchange with his *khan*. "Yurek, you have been granted an audience with the Khan-of-All-the-Saurons. You understand that this is an extreme honor?"

"Yes, M'ahl Hassan."

"The *khan* desires that you inspect once more the model you saw in the workshop."

Yurek nodded and rose to his feet. Though careful to avoid confronting the Sauron *khan*'s gaze directly, he stole glances at the man from the corner of his eye. Dihtahn Shah was tall and fair, his hair straight and almost white, with sharp, straight features. The man's face was utterly uncompromising, a study in planes. He reminded Yurek of a snowhawk his cousin had once trapped. Yurek saw too that Dihtahn Shah wore a patch over his left eye, and the Afghan youth's respect for him climbed a notch to know that the Khan-of-All-the-Saurons was obviously a warrior in his own right.

The model had been delivered only a few moments before Yurek arrived, and its surface was still cool from its sojourn along some outside parapet of the Citadel.

Uncomfortable with being the focus of the flat, un-blinking stares of the Saurons, he poked and prodded the model, trying to compose himself as he studied it carefully.

Yurek noticed the war builder, Din b'ahn Ahn, watching his every move, but there was no hostility in his eyes. Rather, he seemed to be intensely curious about—and baffled by—Yurek's methods of inspection. Yurek himself could not have described what he was doing, exactly. From childhood, Yurek had only to look at a thing to know intuitively what its strengths and weaknesses were. It was all part of his Gift, nothing more. *Insh'allah*.

Finally, when he thought he could speak without squeaking, Yurek faced Dihtahn Shah squarely and said; "It will fall apart in three winks of the eye."

Diettinger frowned at the translation, until Milsen explained. "It is a local term of measurement, First Citizen, a literal statement, not a euphemism . . . According to local legends, the oscillations in the 'storm-pupil' collapses and the blank 'iris' of the main body of the storm makes the Eye appear to have closed or gone blind. After a period of some weeks, the storm will reassert itself and the 'pupil' will reappear. There was a 'wink' shortly after we arrived in the *Fomoria*. . . . It happens approximately once every eleven standard years."

The other Saurons were upset by degrees over that, but Dihtahn Shah only smiled slightly. "Thirteen years," he said. "Close enough to your estimate, Combat Engineer Denbannen, to make me want to hear more. Fourth Rank Milsen, translate as we speak."

Diettinger stood next to Yurek, both of them looking down at the model. "What did you mean when you said that 'the Breath of Allah must flow'?"

Yurek shrugged. "The winds over the mountains carry the seasons to the valley. Without them, the lands will wither and die."

Diettinger turned to the young Afghan with a thin smile. "You are not a superstitious savage, young man, and I am not a fool. Do not insult my intelligence by pretending the one or assuming the other."

Yurek looked back for a moment, sizing up the Khan-of-All-the-Saurons, before answering. "Very well. The *mullahs,* the learned men of my village, say that the warm air rising from the valley floor and the outland steppes meets cold air moving down the mountains or in from the northern seas. The high-speed winds which result are trapped in the sheltered plateau where our village rests, forming a year-round pocket of overpressure. The air on our plateau is only a little thinner than that on the floor of the valley."

"We surmised that," Diettinger said, ignoring the surprised comments of the other Saurons in the room at Yurek's apparently sudden increase in sophistication.

"But what I said about the land withering is true in a way, as well," Yurek continued. "The pass which the Citadel guards is the main low-altitude access for winds between the steppes and the valley. Most wind from the seas never gets over the Atlas Range—what we call the Walls of Allah—since it cools so rapidly as it climbs the mountains that it drops back before cresting the peaks."

"Like rocking a bowl of water?"

"Precisely, Dihtahn Shah. But think of it as a bowl with a pinched middle, where one side has oil and the other water. The fluids cannot mix, but in order for them to mingle that crimp must remain unobstructed."

"Why should we care if they mingle or not?"

Yurek blinked. "Because there are so few birds and insects on Haven."

Diettinger was lost. "What has that to do with it?"

"Of course," Breedmaster Caius suddenly spoke. "Pollination on Haven is mostly wind-driven. That's why so many of the local tree species are primitive conifers. Wind patterns generated within the Shangri-La could never be strong enough to cross-fertilize all the plants growing within the valley, not with Haven's thin air, not without the help of the high pressure system of currents generated at the pass."

Yurek nodded. "And such birds and insects as we do have ride those wind currents back and forth, between valley and steppe, year 'round. The air above the mountains is too thin for them to survive flying through."

Caius continued: "There is a far greater consideration as well, First Citizen. The Shangri-La is the breadbasket of this hemisphere, true, but it is also the only environmentally secure birthing area we know of on the entire world. The valley with its sheltering mountain ranges is simply a larger version of Yurek's plateau. Enough of an obstruction in the structures which govern atmospheric conditions could result in equalizing the air pressure globally, which would mean dropping it significantly within the Shangri-La."

Diettinger kept his eyes on Yurek as he addressed the others: "Then the need for controlling the valley—and thus the need for the Wall—is clearer than ever."

"Wind vents," Denbannen said abruptly.

"Clarify," Diettinger said, still without taking his eyes off Yurek.

"I can modify the design to accommodate large openings in the upper two thirds of the Wall, First Citizen. That will allow for the natural maintenance of atmospheric pressure, and save a great deal of weight in the bargain. Perhaps enough to stabilize the Wall." Denbannen thought a moment and added: "I might even be able to rig wind turbines in the vents to generate extra electrical power."

Diettinger was still watching Yurek. "But that won't do it, will it?" he said.

Yurek did not answer.

"The Wall is still flawed, and you know how."

Yurek tried to hold the Sauron's gaze, but found he could not; the man was an infidel, but he was touched by Allah whether he knew it or not, and he was a *khan* the likes of which Yurek had never seen.

"Yes, *aga*," Yurek said quietly. He pointed to the model. "I cannot say it any other way, *aga;* it is *clumsy*. It tries hard where it need not, and ignores important places that must be considered. It is too complicated."

"It's almost a mile high and three miles wide," Denbannen protested. "Of course it's complicated."

Yurek shook his head. "No, no, that's wrong. Forgive me, *aga* Din b'ahn Ahn, but you are mistaken. At this scale, the more complex you make it, the more weaknesses *must* be part of it. And enough weaknesses will destroy anything."

"Can you suggest a better way, Yurek?" Diettinger asked quietly, and Yurek was sure that his life depended on the answer.

Taking a deep breath, he said: "You have planned support braces, which will be needed for the shape of the Wall you designed. But why use a shape that needs supports when you have *mountains* on either side to hold the wall up? Form the Wall in overlapping vertical wedges, which will strengthen each other as they settle into the pass. The mountains will press them together, with that stress adding to the strength instead of weakening the structure."

"'If you can't solve the problem,'" Diettinger quoted the Sauron tactical primers, "'change the problem.'" He gestured for Milsen to translate it to Yurek.

The *mujahadin* smiled a little. "Precisely, *aga*," he said.

Diettinger addressed Milsen: "Is your new interpreter ready?"

"Yes, First Citizen."

"Detail him to Squad Leader Gav's unit. Savin." Diettinger's aide materialized as if by magic. "Inform Squad Leader Gav his unit is to escort the interpreter to Yurek's village for a meeting with their chieftain. Have them standing by for departure on one hour's notice." He dismissed Savin and looked up to see tension evident on Yurek's face.

"What is the matter with him?" Diettinger asked Milsen.

After a brief exchange with the captive, Milsen said: "He apparently understood some of what you said, First Citizen. He says that his *khan* will never submit to our rule."

"We've heard that one before," Quilland's bored voice carried from the table.

Diettinger held the young Afghan's gaze for a long moment before saying: "Yes. I know."

"First Citizen." Diettinger's aide, Savin, picked that moment to enter without knocking.

"Speak."

"A band of twelve human norms has arrived at the main gate; they ask for an audience."

"The main gate?" Deathmaster Quilland, charged with security for the Citadel, and having waited patiently through all the engineering discussion to make his own reports, was instantly on his feet and headed for the door. "Up here? How did they get up from the valley without being spotted?"

"They came down, Deathmaster Quilland," Diettinger said, a quiet look of satisfaction in his eye. "Didn't they, Yurek?"

Yurek nodded, once.

"First Citizen, they will not surrender their weapons."

"Bring them in. Here."

Diettinger looked at Althene. The First Lady lowered her eyes and left the room. *I will hear of this, later*, he thought. Quilland, too, looked distinctly disapproving.

"The day we cannot subdue a dozen armed human

norms," Diettinger told his advisors, "we *deserve* to be removed from the gene pool."

He looked back at Yurek. "This parley may save your life, Yurek. Do you know that no human norm has set foot in this Citadel, or received an audience with me since—" Diettinger's hand went up to rub the patch over his left eye "—well, let's say since we arrived here on Haven?"

Yurek bowed his head. "I am honored, Dihtahn Shah."

Diettinger nodded. "Yes. I believe you are. I confess that if your people are all like you, they are unlike any human norms I have ever met. I find that a most refreshing change."

Diettinger was looking from Yurek to Caius and back again. "Who *are* your people, Yurek? And how can you make high-quality firearms by hand, have a scientific understanding of weather patterns and biology, and yet wear animal skins and live in caves?"

Yurek shrugged again, apparently his stock answer to whatever bewilderment he caused infidels.

"*Insh'allah,*" he said.

"I have come to parley for the life of my son."

Milsen was translating from the fluid Afghani tongue into Sauron even as the *khan* spoke, allowing Diettinger the opportunity to study the man. The Havener called Abdollah Khan was square-jawed under a bushy beard, with a large, powerful frame. Diettinger saw that he was missing the last two fingers of his left hand. *I like him already,* the First Citizen thought.

"No parley is necessary," Diettinger said evenly. "Your arrival has made your son a guest, no longer our prisoner."

The *khan* sat quietly, scrutinizing the Sauron.

"He may leave?"

"At once. Now that he is healed."

The *khan's* eyes glinted. "Ah. You have cared for him. How may I repay your kindness?"

"You cannot."

Diettinger watched the man stiffen. "You wish to have me in your debt?"

"No. It is simply that the care provided to your son was freely given for our own purposes. You owe us nothing, so there is nothing for you to repay."

The *khan* leaned slightly toward one of his own men, the trusted Mulli, and whispered: *"Have these Saurons no social grace at all? We have opened negotiations, I have spoken the correct formalities, and still there is no mention of the ransom they must surely demand!"*

The *khan's* bodyguard shrugged, his grip on the armed grenade beneath his coat never slackening. *"Perhaps they plan some treachery, khan; shall I throw the grenade now?"*

Abdollah Khan considered a moment, then shook his head. *"No, Mulli. But keep it ready."* He turned back to Diettinger and Milsen. "Does my son still live?"

"He lives." Diettinger turned to another of his Soldiers and said something in the Sauron's indecipherable clucking. "He will be brought to you. Then we will eat, and you may leave."

Abdollah Khan's men bristled, and he said, "I will leave whenever I wish."

"No, Abdollah Khan," Diettinger said simply. "That you will not do."

Beside Abdollah Khan, Mulli tensed, but the *khan* put out a hand. "I am here under a truce."

"You are here as my guest," Diettinger corrected him. "And an uninvited one at that. There is no truce, for we are not at war with your people. And if we were at war, no truce would be necessary or possible, for your people would all be dead."

"My khan!" Mulli gasped in horror. *"How can you*

bear this infidel's arrogance? Let me feed him this grenade, aga, *I beg of you!*"

Abdollah Khan sat back, making himself comfortable. If he was to die, he would enter Paradise with dignity. "What do you gain by making me prisoner? My people made me *khan* by their own free will; they can make another just as easily."

Diettinger shook his head. "You stubbornly refuse to accept the absolute meaning of my words; this is frustrating, and dangerous. I ask that you put aside all your conventions of negotiation for the next few minutes, and *listen*."

Abdollah Khan watched the one-eyed Khan-of-All-the-Saurons carefully for a long time before he spoke to his bodyguard. "Disarm the grenade, Mulli," he said, loudly enough for Milsen to hear. There was no response, and he turned to berate his nephew for disobeying him.

Mulli was pinned in the viselike grip of another Sauron, who had clamped one hand over the Afghan's lips and used the other to calmly remove the grenade from his grasp; and Abdollah Khan had never heard.

"We do not view this as treachery," Diettinger said as the Soldier released the bodyguard and carefully handed him the grenade. "No Sauron ever goes to a meeting with strangers unarmed. But a misunderstanding could have disastrous consequences for both our people, and I suspect we have both seen disasters enough to last."

Warrant Savin arrived with Yurek in tow. The young *mujahadin* went to sit at the feet of Diettinger, the traditional place for hostages, but Savin re-directed him to a place between his father and cousin.

"We have been on Haven for three years," Diettinger said. "We have never met your people before, and yet you are only a few kilometers away from our stronghold here. Why is this?"

"You have nothing we want."

"Yet you have something the Chin want. Your plateau allows for safe birthing in the thin upper atmosphere of Haven. This is a great prize, more so since we have taken control of access to the Shangri-La Valley."

"They have tried many times to take it," Abdollah Khan acknowledged with a smile. "They have failed."

"How many men have you lost to the Chin?"

The *khan's* eyes narrowed. "Some. What does it matter? The Chin are infidels. Those who die killing infidels sleep the same night in Paradise. *Insh'allah.*"

"And is it God's will that *all* your people sleep in Paradise?"

"Paradise is the reward of the Faithful," the *khan* said, making an expansive gesture.

"Just as the betterment of the world is their responsibility," Diettinger returned. "In the words of your Koran, 'Accursed is he who leaves this world no better than how he found it.' Is that correct?"

Abdollah Khan nodded. "It is." This Dihtahn Shah was now speaking of the Holy Word, and the conversation required seriousness.

"Then we may come to the purpose of our discussion, Abdollah Khan. Our goal on Haven is survival. We employ all means we deem necessary to ensure that result. Peripherally, our goals sometimes benefit the peoples of Haven, but that is never a consideration except as such effects may be likewise beneficial to us."

"You are a selfish people."

"Rationally selfish; yes, of course. And you are an unique people. Alone among Haveners, you have something of value to offer us besides your women, your food, or your land. You have *expertise.*"

Abdollah Khan looked at his son. "You are speaking of the Gift my son possesses?"

Diettinger nodded. "Your son, and the others like him in your tribe. This expertise will prove of great value to us in the years to come, as the machines which we rely on inevitably break down."

"We work for no one but ourselves!"

"That must change," said Diettinger. "You have a long history of resistance to authority; I am willing to accommodate this, up to a point. Here are my conditions: Your son will instruct our engineering and fabrication Ranks in these 'arts.' He will likewise serve as liaison between your tribe and the Citadel. His expertise, or that of another of your weaponsmiths, is to be made available to us on demand. Your tribe will secure and guard the passes up to and through your plateau, allowing free passage and providing all aid only to Sauron patrols or Haveners cleared and accompanied by such patrols. Your plateau is to be made available on a need-only basis to those of our women who require safe-birthing areas. Your women, presumably competent midwives, will receive additional training by our Breedmasters to bring them up to our standards."

Abdollah Khan listened without a flicker of reaction crossing his features. "I have heard the 'absolute meaning' of your words, Dihtahn Shah. You *tell*, but you do not *ask*. You have no respect for others."

"On the contrary, Abdollah Khan, I have the greatest respect for you and your people, *as they relate to my designs*." Diettinger leaned forward. "Understand my position; in the last three years, I have ordered the destruction of twelve tribes which have rejected our terms. I will not tolerate resistance. I cannot afford to." Diettinger told Savin to bring in food and drink. "Now, as to what your people may expect from us—"

"We want nothing but to be left alone!"

"The Chin do not leave you alone."

"And we kill them as they come!"

Diettinger's remaining eye fixed on the *khan* from under a white brow. "You will not have that option with us. You and your people have possibly the most fearsome reputation as guerrilla fighters in human history. I will not waste any Soldiers for your destruction. Your plateau can be sterilized by a single radiation-enhanced bomb. Our reconnaissance indicates that your tribe consists of less than six hundred people; in an enclosed area the size of your plateau, such a weapon can kill twice that number immediately. Four times as many would die from radiation poisoning within a week, ten times as many within a month." Diettinger sat back. "Note that I assume a great many of your people are hidden away; you are clever enough to keep your true numbers secret from prying eyes, and I am clever enough to take no chances with such dangerous foes."

Abdollah Khan was aghast. "You would kill all who live there, women and children, the old and sick?"

"I would. If I must, I shall. But I hope that it will not be necessary. I said your plateau *can* be sterilized by such a weapon. I do not threaten you, I merely point out your vulnerability."

"If we must serve you to avoid such a fate, then we are all hostage to you."

"You have not heard the rest of my terms."

"I do not *wish* to hear more! You give us no choice but servitude or destruction. We have faced that choice before, and our answer has always been the same."

"I require that you change."

"You *require* that we surrender our destiny to you! That is the province of God; no believer may willingly do such a thing."

"Untrue," Diettinger countered. "Your teachings specifically allow false conversion to infidel faiths to preserve the life of one of your own."

Abdollah Khan took a deep breath. "You demand that we become slaves."

"I demand order."

"Cemeteries are very orderly."

"Indeed they are. Doubtless because they have so few debates."

"Do you expect us to just kneel before you and surrender?"

"I do not *expect* anything of you. I am informing you of the situation which now exists. Whether it is resolved by negotiation, or genocide is immaterial to me."

"You enjoy *telling*, Dihtahn Shah. Then tell me this; have my people *anything* to gain by staying alive in a world dominated by you?"

"First, I do not 'enjoy' this, Abdollah Khan. I look on my people's presence on Haven as another battle, of great duration and uncertain outcome. I perceive you as a potential ally in that battle, but you must understand that I am in command. I am a Sauron Man, and thus incapable of involving my ego in this matter whatsoever. The irrationalities such an involvement would necessarily create would be counterproductive. As to what your people have to gain," Diettinger gestured to Savin, who went to a set of large double doors, and opening them, ushered in several Soldiers pushing wheeled palettes. "Let me show you."

Diettinger stood and went to the palettes; the display and its timing had been orchestrated by Althene to appeal to the primitive sensibilities of the *khan*, and it worked perfectly.

"Metals, high quality, suitable for conversion to tools, weapons, or any other purpose you choose. Medicine, and access to the medical facilities here at the Citadel, with women doctors to see to your own women; I understand you have societal taboos that interfere with male doctors examining, and thus effectively caring for your women. Food in the winter months, and fuel for your fires. Structures if you wish them." Diettinger threw a tarpaulin over a rack of metal stock and returned to his seat.

"You may have as much or as little of these things as you wish. Your faith will not be interfered with in any way. Your tribe will be exempt from the provision of tribute maidens; a singular concession, I might add. Your only obligation of arms will be to function as you always have, keeping your plateau—and the passes into the Shangri-La which it straddles—secure from steppes raiders and valley refugees."

"You do not fear that we will manufacture weapons to use against your own soldiers?"

"I have the bombs, Abdollah Khan. The first such verified instance will be the last."

Abdollah Khan had grown quiet as he considered the offer.

"We could simply leave our plateau; go down into the valley, or the steppes."

"In point of fact, *khan*, you could not." Diettinger's voice held real regret. "There is no food to spare in the valley, and the Chins of the Steppes would hunt you down; they are the masters of the flatlands, even as your people are of the mountains. Worse, should either the valley dwellers or the steppes nomads realize your true value as weaponsmiths, they would wipe you out, for they know they could never truly enslave you."

The *khan* was frowning hard. "Our lands remain our own?"

"Only make our people welcome in need."

"You will dictate none of your laws to us?"

"Your laws serve well enough to govern your people. We do not attempt to fix things that already work."

Abdollah Khan went to look out the window. "Yurek," he called to his son without turning. "Attend me."

Yurek rose and joined his father, looking out at the forbidding peaks of the Wall of Allah.

"Are you troubled at teaching them the Art, my son?" Abdollah Khan asked in a low voice.

Yurek thought a moment before answering. "Some will be better at the Art than I am, father."

Abdollah Khan shrugged. "Then perhaps it is good that we get along with them."

"But what if they break faith with us?"

Abdollah Khan laughed under his breath. "You have forgotten your lessons, my son. Has anyone ever *not* broken their faith with us? What difference has it ever made? That is what our people rely on we *mujahadin* for; to make it too *expensive* for people to break faith with us. We have *never* broken faith, not in all our history. But we must always be prepared for those who are less honorable than us."

Yurek smiled. "When I was a little boy, you used to tell me to 'Trust in Allah, but tie your camel.' I *still* don't know what a camel is."

"Neither do I, Yurek." Abdollah Khan laughed. The Khan-of-the-Faithful-on-Haven turned back to the Khan-of-All-the-Saurons.

"I look for cruelty in your face, Dihtahn Shah; I see none. I look for cunning in your words, and find only cold truth."

"I have no gift, nor use, nor time for lies, Abdollah Khan."

"I will abide by your terms."

Diettinger nodded. "Good." He gestured to the table of food. "Then let us eat."

Abdollah Khan noticed several flasks and shook his head. "Muslims do not drink alcohol."

Diettinger pulled a cork and poured water into a goblet.

"Neither do Saurons," he said.

Two months and half a dozen visits after first coming to the Citadel, Abdollah Khan was marching with his men back toward the main gate feeling very pleased. The Khan-of-All-the-Saurons was a man he could deal with, had even come to respect. The Abdollah Khan had finished one of his visits with Dihtahn Shah; they were always by invitation, never summonses, and Abdollah Khan enjoyed them.

He liked the Khan-of-All-the-Saurons, he had told his men after that first meeting. He liked his eye.

For his part, Diettinger appreciated the *khan's* company. The Afghan was the first human norm Diettinger had met in decades who did not consider Saurons *de facto* monsters.

He escorted the leader of the *mujahadin* to the door, watched as his aide led him outside.

So our Wall will be built, and built to last, Diettinger thought. *And we will all be kept very busy while doing it. Too busy, one may hope, to get into mischief.*

He crossed the room to the table holding the new model of the Wall, the one without a single mark; Denbannen's computers had tested Yurek's design thoroughly, and found very little room for improvement.

He thought about his meetings with Yurek and the *khan*, and what he was learning about both men.

I wonder what the youth is passing to his father today? His men at the gate always reported it to him; one day a phasing trigger, the next a power cell mount.

Not that it mattered. Even if Yurek returned to his village and fashioned a Mark VII manpack fusion gun, there were still many more Saurons than *mujahadin,* and there were still plenty of the nuclear weapons Diettinger had warned Abdollah Khan about. For the first time in their history, the Afghans were contained. The plateau that was their refuge was also their prison, and periodic reconnaissance flights had already mapped the area in detail.

In a way, Diettinger hoped Yurek would do just such a thing; better weapons for Abdollah Khan's people would provide a grim surprise for the first Chin raiders in the Spring, and the message would go out that at least one tribe had profited by dealing with the Citadel. As for the Saurons, they now had a guaranteed supply of spare parts for a variety of weapons Diettinger had not thought would last out the decade.

Diettinger was, if not content, satisfied with the way things had turned out. *And more than weapons: by allowing a single "primitive" enclave of human norms to indulge themselves, the Saurons will control the door to the Shangri-La, and with it, the destiny of all the peoples within and without that valley.*

Within and without, Diettinger reflected, thinking about the Afghans in their aerie.

But not, perhaps, above.

In the courtyard below, Abdollah Khan waved to Yurek, hurrying down a flight of stone stairs to greet his father.

"My *khan*," Yurek said, smiling broadly, "you are well."

"I am well, son. How goes your work with the Saurons?"

Yurek nodded, pleased. "Very well. The Wall progresses ahead of schedule; of course, at this stage that may not seem like much, but there are still so many problems to overcome before we can begin serious construction—" He stopped short. The Khan's look of pleased interest was severely strained.

"Forgive me, father; I grow too full of myself." Yurek realized that he was sounding more like a Sauron every day.

But the *khan* dismissed the thought with a shrug. "Youth," he declared simply.

They walked on together, chatting.

"Do they learn?" the *khan* asked.

"Slowly, father. But they are grown men; no other people can learn the Art at all once grown." His voice dropped. "And their children are growing. Soon they will be old enough for some to begin training. The children will learn very quickly."

As they reached the main gate, Yurek embraced his father, and slipping a hand into the Khan's pocket, deposited a finely crafted metal ring. A Sauron guard noted the exchange, and began casually eavesdropping.

"It's the fourteenth accelerator, father," Yurek said in a low voice; "Mark it 'm.066' and store it with the others. I'll need it for the master molds before I start copying."

"Do you have the spacing rail, yet?" Abdollah Khan asked conversationally as he gathered up his cloak at the gate.

"Another week. Look for it in a cart of rifled barrels. It will be marked with white at one end."

Abdollah Khan mounted his horse and rode out to the trail, turning once to wave at his son by the gate. Looming in the mountains behind the Citadel were the first faint markings of the frame of the great Gate that his son would help the Saurons build.

A way down the trail, the *khan* pulled the metal ring from his pocket, idly sticking it to his buttons and a knife blade.

What was it Yurek had called it? A part of a key, he'd said. *A key to the Gates of Paradise, that they may never be closed against his people.* He was proud of his son; he would make a good *khan,* one day, if the people would have him.

Abdollah Khan shook his head. *Magnets,* he reflected with wonder.

What would people think of next?

From *A Brief Atlas of the Planet Haven* by Colin Lyon Jones and Lilya Ivanovich Egorov. Oxford Press, AD 2427, folio:

The Shangri-La "Valley" on Haven is more than a valley. It is a great equatorial (but by no means tropical) basin of some 12 million square kilometers, large enough to hold the old United States of America. Ringing it are volcanic mountains which almost define the term "forbidding". . .

North of the Shangri-La Valley and high above it—beyond the brutal mountains that rim it—lies the high steppe, a vast, continent-spanning expanse of grassland, using the term "grassland" in the Haven sense. The term *moor* would be almost as appropriate, because low shrubs are very much a part of it; also *tundra,* because much of it is underlain with permafrost. But during the long summers it thaws deeply, despite occasional long Truenights that in summer can send the temperature to −15° C and even colder, covering the shallower pools with centimeters of ice. Also, although the atmospheric pressure on the steppe is typically about 700 millibars, the partial pressure of oxygen is only about 120 millibars, less than 60 percent of Terran sea-level normal. The Haven biota, of course, have long since adapted, and in summer the high steppe

produces abundant forage for livestock and
wildlife.

The steppe is by no means uniform. Rugged
ranges of hills and low mountains interrupt it.
Lakes and ponds are more or less numerous in
some locales, though many dry up by late summer.
Most are more or less drinkable. Elsewhere it is
necessary to dig for water, rock permitting, or drill
for it. Here and there are raw lava flows, sometimes extending for scores of kilometers, virtually
barren of forage or wildlife, their sharp rough sur-
faces capable of ruining boots and the hooves of
horses or muskylope in an hour's passage. In other
areas are badlands—tangles of gullies, many of
them blind—almost impossible to pass without
guides, and as unpeopled as the lava flows.

*   *   *

From *A Student's Book* by Myner Klint bar Terborch fan Reenan, Eden Valley, Ilona'sstad, 2927:

. . . Within a few years of arriving on our world,
Sauron soldiers had subdued the tribes on areas
of the steppe nearest to the main eastern entrance
to the Shangri-La Valley. Bit by bit, in the generations since coming here, the Saurons have expanded
their hegemony—the area whose people are under
their control and required to pay them tribute. This
process continues, but it has been difficult and
bloody. They could not have done so well, except
for their control of access to important birthing
valleys. . . .

MAITREYA AND THE CYBORG

John Dalmas

Assault Group Leader Borkum lay on thin, dry snow atop a rock pinnacle. Cat's Eye was a dull and ruddy orb, rimmed on one edge with a sickle of brightness like some enormous new moon, and Borkum peered through its russet light. It was a dimmer phase of dimday, but to his Sauron eyes, the sun might almost as well have been up. Before many hours, Cat's Eye would set in the east, and Borkum wasn't sure whether the sun would come up first or not. Judging by the elevation and phase of Cat's Eye, it would be close.

In the stone fort he spied on, it seemed the troops were less alert than most cattle fighting men. Looking down at it from his vantage on the pinnacle, he could see no one at all on the battlement. Probably they didn't expect anyone up the trail in winter; the last time he'd checked, the temperature had been −72°F, and he was glad for electrically heated winter gloves. This had to be the highest, coldest inhabited place on the planet, and he didn't look forward to the fifteen or so hours of Truenight that would follow the next Trueday.

Ahead, the trail they'd come up passed through a gate in the fort's wall, a closed gate. Inside the wall he could see the slanted roofs of buildings built against it, no doubt barracks, armory, stable, and what not. Thin smoke rose from chimneys to settle over the fort—dung smoke by the smell. In a place like this, dung would be hoarded for fuel; there couldn't be a tree for 400 klicks—nothing this side of Koln Valley, and nothing there but low scrub. His infrared perception told him that some of the smoke came from the gate tower. Whoever was on watch would be holed up there, perhaps asleep.

If, as seemed likely, these cattle knew nothing of Soldiers, they were in for a surprise. Blow the gate, and the place would be his. There might even be women there. Without turning, he gave instructions to Under Assault Leader Gerrit beside him. Then, still on his belly, Borkum backed away, and deftly, skillfully, climbed down the off-side of the basalt column he'd observed from.

A cone charge bent and separated the narrow, steel-faced gates, and left them hanging on a single hinge each. Borkum sent most of his men through at once—all but the weapons section. It stayed outside and fired rockets at the gate tower. Almost at once, one went through a firing slot and exploded inside, followed quickly by two more. It was excellent marksmanship, given their single-shot, shoulder-fired weapons and simple optical sights.

Then Borkum went in himself, making his command post just inside, beside the gate house. His squads had spread throughout the small fort, each to an entrance in some building. Resistance seemed meager. Enemy gunfire, audibly from black-powder weapons, was sparse; apparently most of the garrison had been caught asleep.

From where he knelt, he could peer around a corner and see the entire bailey. Except for what appeared to be sheds, the fort's buildings were of stone, mostly with two low stories, and built with their backs to the wall. Nothing seemed designed for defense against an enemy who'd gotten inside—the type of oversight that few cattle on this world would be guilty of.

Standard orders were to take prisoners when feasible, and he'd given no counterorder, yet prisoners were not immediately forthcoming. For two or three minutes longer, shooting continued, most of it from the Soldiers' nitrocellulose-charged cartridges, but some from primitive gunpowder. There were occasional shouts and screams—not by his men. Then he began to get reports on his belt radio: The enemy had resisted with whatever came ready to hand, mostly with swords, and most had fought till dead, disabled, or unconscious. His men had also had a few casualties.

He moved into what had been the enemy command room then, a room pungent with dung-smoke and less identifiable smells, and heated by a ceramic stove. Almost nothing was clean. There was a bathhouse, he was told, with a large tub for bathing, but without water. It seemed that the fort lacked a system for melting large volumes of snow.

The tally of his own dead was two, both killed by gunfire. Four others had been significantly wounded.

The enemy garrison had numbered sixty. Thirty-one were dead and twenty wounded; only nine had surrendered unscathed. There hadn't been a woman among them. Now that the fighting was over, the captives seemed entirely docile, showing no sign of defiance or even sullenness.

Borkum had the wounded of both sides taken to the messroom. Judging from his ornate if grimy uniform, one of the conscious enemy wounded had been an officer, and Borkum tried to question him. The man understood nothing, and made no intelligible reply—merely gabbled. He seemed to know no Anglic at all, or understand anything that Borkum's Mongol guide said.

Besides his human prisoners, his men had captured twenty-three muskylopes kept corraled as riding stock, and he ordered two of them butchered. The metabolism of Sauron Soldiers required a lot of food. His force would spend the rest of dimday here, he'd decided, eating and resting, and leave at once when the sun came up.

There was also a small herd of yaks in the vicinity, and several milk cows in a shed, but the Soldiers didn't trouble with them.

He had the able-bodied prisoners stripped of their baggy, padded clothing so he could judge their fitness, and selected the three who looked most able-bodied, to take with him. They'd be useless as interpreters, but they could tell anyone they came to how powerful and dangerous the invaders were, and how quickly they crushed resistance. And no doubt he could get some sort of useful directions from them, even without language.

He assigned a squad to stay at the fort and take care of his several wounded. The six unwounded prisoners to be left behind would be their servants. Meanwhile he had the wounded enemy taken outside the fort and shot. His remaining prisoners were forced to witness this, letting them know what it meant to resist Sauron Soldiers.

The prisoners, both those who knelt to die and those who watched, showed remarkably little fear, nor any sign of hatred, open or suppressed. Borkum had experienced a variety of cattle in his years of duty: Mongols, Americans, and Chinese; Uzbeks, Russians, and Armenians . . . but none as peculiar as these. He assigned this no significance, however. They were all cattle.

The scout fighter settled in a cloud of dirty snow. When it was down, its engines off and the cloud of snow settled, First Cyborg Hammer could see Base

First Rank Krell striding toward the pad. The gullwing door lifted smoothly, and Hammer swung down the extruded ladder to meet him. The outside air, thin and frigid, was like a kind of energy sump that sucked warmth from him. Consciously, Hammer ignored it; unconsciously, his body made subtle adjustments. From beneath their epicanthic folds, his black eyes took in the unfinished base around him: the completed command building and fire towers; uncompleted barracks; and the temporary hutments for Soldiers, construction specialists, and impressed laborers. All surrounded by minimal and temporary defensive works. Construction was substantially behind schedule.

Base First Rank Krell arrived and saluted. He didn't intend that his resentment show. His threefold resentment. This was not a routine inspection visit, and he was sure he knew why Hammer had been sent: First Soldier Diettinger was not only unhappy with progress here, he was also unwilling to accept the responsibility as his own. Also, this inspection had been unannounced; he'd been told by radio, ten minutes earlier, to meet the First Cyborg at the pad.

His third resentment was more intimate: First Cyborg was *old*, even for a cyborg, the only person still alive who'd arrived on the *Dol Guldur*, sixty-eight T-years earlier. He had to be ninety T-years, or damned close to it. Probably older. Krell himself, on the other hand, was unlikely to reach fifty; some critical organ of his supercharged body would probably break down before he was forty-five. Many died by age forty. And he was forty now, still with the superhumanly strong athletic body of a Sauron Soldier, but without many years left to him.

Yet despite his ninety years, First Cyborg in a fight could destroy any Soldier.

"Welcome to Koln Base," Krell said.

Hammer's black eyes had caught the slight—very slight—signs of resentment, and let it be. Resentment was irrational but endemic. If the planet was culled for it, there'd be few Soldiers left, and no cattle at all for them to rule. He acknowledged Krell's greeting with a curt nod. "I'm here to get the construction of Koln Base back on schedule," he said.

Krell took the cyborg to his office, picking up his construction chief on the way, and together they reviewed progress and problems. Krell had a manpower shortage that couldn't be corrected by simply rounding up more forced labor: He'd need to feed, train, supervise, and police them. Skilled Sauron construction personnel for training and supervision were in short supply, assignment priorities being given to construction requirements at the Citadel. Further, Soldiers were always in short supply, being needed to fight the cattle. And a Sauron Soldier required twice the food that a Sauron construction specialist did— four times that of a forced laborer. The Soldier's peculiar metabolism and his need to stay fit required abundant exertion more or less regularly, and his genetically supercharged system burned calories and used up vitamins and essential minerals at remarkable rates, even on garrison duty.

Any added food for additional personnel would have to come from local tribes, and existing agreements didn't provide for further levies, except for forces in the field. While to enforce increases would require even more Soldiers, perhaps bringing about a major outbreak of fighting that could even threaten Koln Base, unfinished as it was.

Beyond that there was the matter of construction in winter, this far north. Construction slush could only be poured during Trueday, unless heated forms were made and used, and resources for producing forms were short. Furthermore, although the shortest day was well past, the weather was still getting colder. Cat's Eye, with Haven in tow, was just approaching the longest radius of its slightly elliptical orbit, and the total solar energy received per day would continue to decrease for another T-month.

None of these considerations were new to Hammer, or to the First Soldier's staff, back at the Citadel. The Citadel itself was incomplete, partly for similar reasons, and work had been in progress on it for more than sixty years. But the Citadel was an enormous project, considering the resources available. Also it was the administrative, military, industrial, and strategic center of the entire Sauron hegemony on Haven, and its completion was of highest priority.

By contrast, Koln Base was a small outpost, like a shed compared to a vast mansion. Its sole, though important, purpose was to control access to a small birthing valley, called Koln Valley by the Saurons. Its construction was simple, straightforward, and involved no unusual technical problems; it was appropriate for the First Soldier to demand more rapid progress. And the acceptance of excuses was foreign to Sauron philosophy; to accept excuses could lead to the collapse of Sauron dominance, Sauron goals, and eventually Sauron survival.

Finally, with records examined and difficulties described, Hammer got to his feet. His deep rich voice was calm but implacable: "I've seen enough. When I am ready to leave, in one hundred hours, you will have a plan ready for delivery to First Soldier Diettinger, describing how you will reverse the situation here and complete the base by the scheduled date. It must be a feasible plan, complete with programs, projects, and targets. I will courier it. Meanwhile, I will inspect your troops, construction work, completed installations, and current military operations if any."

Base First Rank Krell had stiffened. "As you order, First Cyborg," he said.

*　　*　　*

The Soldier, at present arms, stood stiff as his rifle barrel. First Cyborg Hammer stopped in front of him and looked him up and down. Like the others in his rifle company, the Soldier's face was olive tan, not the glare-darkened near black of a Sauron who spent a great deal of time on the steppe in winter. Obviously the training schedule was slack. With a slap that might almost have broken it, the First Cyborg snatched the rifle from the Soldier's hands. He spun it so it nearly blurred, examined it, then slid back the bolt, held the muzzle to his eye, and peered up the spiral-grooved barrel.

Finally he slapped it back into the man's hands. "Dirt in the butt plate grooves; dirt in a screw slot," he said to the platoon officer beside him. The officer wrote it on his clipboard.

Grim-faced, Hammer strode down the line to another Soldier. Something had been unacceptable with almost every man, a sure sign of general laxness in discipline. There was nothing intrinsically wrong with dirt in a screw slot, but if discipline was slack in little things, it was likely to be slack in others. While a tough training schedule did more than maintain combat fitness; it maintained morale, and reduced behavioral problems.

He wondered what he'd find at Operations Center.

The swarthy officer in charge of Operations Center gestured at the double-plated thermal window and the frozen landscape outside. After a dozen hours of sunshine, it had warmed considerably, but it still was bitter cold. "We do not routinely pursue military activities in winter here," the man said.

Hammer had noticed the temperature read-out: –17°F. On the steppe above the valley it would be colder; windier at least. At sunrise, after forty-seven hours of dimday, it might have been –58°F; by two hours before sundown it would probably have warmed to 14°F on the steppe, and be ready to start getting colder again. And occasionally there would be forty or more hours of Truenight, with the temperature dropping to as low as –94°F.

"Do not belabor the obvious to me, Second Rank Morens," Hammer replied. "I am interested in what operations you may have, routine or not."

Ops Center in-charge Morens nodded, feeling the beginning of gooseflesh at the implied criticism. "Yes, First Cyborg." It was natural to feel ill at ease when being inspected by any cyborg, and First Cyborg was even uncannier than others. He'd been appointed First Cyborg when First Cyborg Koln had died, though several others had been senior to him then. Even his voice was not quite like the other cyborgs'. His resonant bass almost sounded electronically altered. The rumor was, he'd been part of an experimental batch, back on Homeworld, and the only one of it who'd survived gestation.

"We have one military operation in progress," Morens answered. "Recently we learned of an inhabited plateau rising fourteen hundred meters above the steppe. About four hundred klicks northeast."

Hammer nodded. He'd heard a report of the place; the Mongols had spoken of it.

"They must have a birthing valley somewhere," Morens continued. "One we don't know of. Base First Rank sent out a reconnaissance in force, about a hundred and seventy men, to feel out the cattle there, and if feasible, to establish dominion and interrogate their leadership."

A long-range reconnaissance in force, with troops in short supply here! In winter on the steppe, four hundred klicks was at least four T-days' march for Sauron Soldiers, perhaps as much as eight, depending on snow depths and on the detours necessary to commandeer rations from the winter stations of steppe herdsmen. More equipment and supplies had to be carried, and more time was needed to set up and break down camp. Say six T-days out and six back, with an indeterminate time spent on the plateau. This action of Krell's might produce interesting results, he told himself, but it should have been postponed till Koln Base was finished.

Perhaps Krell was beginning to fail mentally; occasionally that was where deterioration first showed.

Morens had continued talking. "A few hours before daybreak, they reached the head of the trail to the plateau top, and took the fort there. They had six casualties, two of them dead, and killed most of the garrison. No one alive there spoke Anglic or any other known language. Assault Group Leader Borkum left a squad to hold the fort and care for the wounded, with a few cattle to serve them, and left with several other cattle to find whoever rules there."

"Hmh! Inform me when you learn anything further," Hammer said. For Krell, who'd complained of a lack of troops, to send a sixth of what he had on a lengthy, low-priority mission was irrational and irresponsible. He'd initiate a fitness and replacement action when he got back to the Citadel.

Following his inspection, Hammer slept for four hours. He'd just eaten when an orderly from Morens found him: there was further information from the reconnaissance force on the plateau. Hammer took a final swig of mittenwort tea, then strode to Ops Center.

The new reports were on tape, and at Krell's orders, they had descriptive as well as situational information. Like the steppe at its foot, the plateau was covered with from two to five decimeters of wind-slabbed snow. But their Mongol guide had been useless to them up there; the local language was something quite different. The Sauron force's three captives had been useless, too, even after one had been killed as an

incentive. The only indications of roads or trails had
been stacks of rock—cairns—and Assault Group Leader
Borkum had selected the route himself. Where cairn
routes crossed or forked, the junction cairn was somewhat larger, its rocks painted with what seemed to be
words in some non-Roman, non-Cyrillic alphabet. A
thin staff, two splinted-together thighbones of yak or
muskylope, stuck out the top, sometimes with the
wind-tattered remnant of a flag. There was no way of
telling what route might be more important; even digging away the snow and examining the ground itself
had failed to help.

The troops had come to an inhabited place—winter
quarters for a herding operation. They'd stopped to
butcher some yaks, eat, sleep for three hours and eat
again. No one there appeared to speak any known
language, but Borkum had stood before the frightened
ranchhands and had one shoved up to him. He'd then
ordered the man to guide them to their capital,
demanding loudly, with gestures. The man stood
frightened and mute till Borkum struck and killed him
with his fist. Then he'd repeated his command to a
second and third, killing each when they'd failed to
respond. When he'd begun to order a fourth, one of
the others had seemed to comprehend. He'd come
forward and indicated that he would go with them.
Whether the man actually knew what was wanted was
uncertain. Borkum's radioed report had been made
just prior to leaving.

When he'd heard it all, Hammer got to his feet. "I
am going to overfly the plateau," he said. "Get me a
map and mark the location."

Koln Base First Rank Krell watched the scout
fighter lift vertically from the cloud of snow and dust
it raised. He himself had requested an exploratory
overflight of the plateau a T-month past, and had been
refused. *Only three aircraft were left,* high command

had replied, *and only two of those were operational. Neither could be spared for such a mission.* Also, though it wasn't pointed out, aircraft fuel was a problem. Groundmaster Fosse had signed the rejection, and was no doubt responsible for its tone of disdain. It was in response to this disdain, Krell recognized now, that he'd sent Borkum out with 170 men to explore. By hindsight it had been an unwise, irrational decision, and with First Cyborg's inspection report, he expected to pay for it.

And now First Cyborg, without anyone's approval, without even consulting with anyone, had departed to do what Groundmaster Fosse had disapproved.

Krell supposed he should feel vindicated, but what he actually felt was resentment. He wasn't sure why, and was disinclined to the kind of introverted analysis that he might have turned to to sort it out. All he knew was that First Cyborg disdained the chain of command of which he, Under Regiment Leader Krell, Koln Base First Rank, was a part. And no one would do anything about it.

Though Groundmaster Fosse would be unhappy with it, might even take it out on his, Krell's, hide, Krell suspected.

Hammer was piloting himself, the assigned pilot idle but alert beside him. The mid-afternoon sun glittered on a snowscape broken only by patches of black rock, precipitous and windswept, on a range of broken hills. Like some bird of prey's, his vision had shifted into magnification mode, to examine briefly Borkum's reconnaissance force, five klicks below him, 154 Soldiers trotting through shin-deep snow, the wind-slab broken for them by their mounted guides and several pack muskylopes, hard-pressed to keep ahead.

The column of Sauron Soldiers had passed other livestock stations since the first, without stopping; apparently its commander was satisfied with his new guide. Ahead, visible on Hammer's horizon but far beyond their own, was what might have been a fortress on a ridge. Unaware, the Sauron force was headed directly toward it. A moment later he could see a town at its foot. The ridge was not high. Hammer switched on his microphone.

"Reconnaissance force, this is First Cyborg in the scout that just passed above you. You are headed directly toward a town. Continue on your present heading. Over."

"First Cyborg, this is Assault Group Leader Borkum. Your message and order received. Borkum out."

Hammer banked off then toward the unseen south rim of the plateau. He'd investigate the fortress and town later. It would be hours before the reconnaissance force arrived there. He had time to explore, perhaps find the birthing valley the locals used—the valley and the route to it.

When he crossed the south rim, he banked eastward, following it. It was even more precipitous there than it had been near the canyon route the reconnaissance force had climbed. And that had been passable only by pack animals and by men mounted or on foot. Here and there, as he flew, he found rough canyons cutting back into the plateau wall. Men active and strong enough might have climbed them—Sauron Soldiers could have easily enough—but not animals with riders, and downward they led nowhere except to the high steppe. There was nothing remotely like a birthing valley.

At near-sonic speed he continued. The east edge was more precipitious than the south. Here the lava caprock was more recent and higher, and as yet no canyons had developed. On the north, the plateau reared into volcanic hills, almost mountains, that northward broke off steeply into badlands. Beyond the badlands lay more desolation, less high than the plateau but higher than most of the known steppe.

Hammer broke off his exploration; his fuel was limited. There was more north rim to see, and the west rim, and still some of the south. He could examine them later; somewhere there had to be a birthing valley. But for now he'd fly to the town he'd seen, land nearby and wait for the reconnaissance force. It should be in sight of the fortress by now.

He landed on the ridgetop less than a hundred meters from the "fortress," which seen close-up was no fortress at all. It had no artillery, no battlements, no enclosing defensive walls. Its several outer doors seemed neither strong nor guarded. It was simply a large, four-story stone building partly carved into the ridge, with a squared tower at an upper corner tapering upward another three stories.

In the town below, a few of the larger buildings were also square and of stone. Most, however, were domes, or domes atop cylinders, made of large, crude bricks. Probably, he surmised, to minimize the need for construction timber. Presumably these people had carried on a modest commerce during the First Empire, with timber from the Shangri-La Valley brought in, perhaps by airship. Expensive, even then. The round buildings may have been built since that time, some of them at least. Walls would be thick, for insulation. The smoke that rose from their chimneys were mere wisps.

He'd been down only minutes when the locals arrived, eighteen of them, on foot and without apparent weapons. Some were dressed in bulky sheepskins loosely open in the afternoon sun, the side flaps of their caps turned up. Others wore loose, orange-yellow robes, and orange-yellow skullcaps on shaven heads, as if it were actually warm out there. Two carried banners on short poles. Several others played flutes of bone or horn, making what Hammer supposed was music. Except for the slitted eyes, their faces reminded

Hammer of some of the Dinneh—brown-near-black, with high cheekbones. Their noses varied from aquiline to almost flat, their faces from broad and round to long and angular.

Though it was late afternoon now, his control screen told him the temperature was –11°F, but the wind was only one to two meters per second, its direction variable.

He sensed no intended threat from this entourage of—greeters?—stopped some twenty meters away. When, after several minutes, Hammer had not responded, one of the men in yellow approached. By that time, Hammer knew from his radio that the reconnaissance force had the town in sight from a distance of about three klicks—under the conditions, about a fifteen-minute loping "march" for the nearly tireless Sauron Soldiers.

He touched a key, activating the loud hailer, and another, activating the external sound pickup and recorder. "Who is in charge here?" he demanded into his microphone.

For several long seconds, the only visible response was concern or consternation by a few, uncertainty by others, and calm by the rest. The music had stopped. Then the nearest of the yellow robes spoke, loudly and slowly, in a language which to Hammer sounded rather like Mongolian. Local or Mongolian, he understood none of it.

He interrupted. "I will speak with someone who speaks Anglic!"

Again uncertainty. The one who'd spoken before spoke with companions now, in some decidedly different language. Then he turned back to Hammer again, speaking again in Mongolian, or whatever it was. This time the man's speech—entreaty?—was backed by pointing with one hand toward the large stone building.

Hammer switched his microphone to the band being used by the reconnaissance force. "Assault

Group Leader Borkum, this is First Cyborg. You have a Mongol guide with you, is that not so?"

"That is correct, First Cyborg."

"I am being spoken to here in a language that may be Mongolian. Bring your Mongol to your radio. I'll play it back for him."

Hammer heard Borkum call a halt. By that time the yellow-robed speaker had finished what he'd been saying, and stood quietly as if waiting. A long minute later, Borkum spoke again. "First Cyborg, our Mongol guide is here listening."

Hammer played back the yellow robe's speech for the guide. When it was done, the guide spoke in understandable Anglic. His voice reflected what might have been awe; perhaps fear. "Your lordship, what was spoken to you is very poor Mongolian, maybe some old dialect. He say that—" the man paused. "He say that *Maidari* waits to talk you. He say Maidari will speak you language."

Hammer's tone was impatient. "Who is Maidari?"

"Maidari—is the Buddha Yet to Come."

Ah! Buddha! Hammer thought. *The religion of the Mongols!* This could provide opportunities; also problems if poorly handled.

His cyborg senses had been tuned to maximum sensitivity, his mind with them, and there wasn't the slightest hint of danger out there. He made a decision, one that the First Soldier would not like when he heard about it. Inwardly, Hammer smiled sardonically. "Assault Group Leader, there is a set of buildings, apparently a livestock station, just short of town. Billet your force there, and do not enter the town itself until I tell you to. I am going to investigate this person who supposedly speaks Anglic."

When he had Borkum's acknowledgment, Hammer turned to the pilot. "Fighter Rank Stuart," he said, "take the controls and activate engines. I will then disembark."

He drew a sidearm from its holster and examined it. Stuart recognized the weapon, an energy pistol. He'd been trained on one himself, had dry-fired but never used it. The Saurons' supply of energy weapons and irreplaceable power slugs had long since been in storage, waiting for some emergency that might never come. Meanwhile, Soldiers fought with projectile weapons—bolt-action rifles, double-action projectile sidearms, Gatling guns, crude rockets, and mountain artillery. *Leave it to a cyborg to get privileges*, Stuart told himself. *It's not as if he needs an energy pistol. He could waste this place with his bare hands.*

"I will accompany those people to the building you see here on the ridge," Hammer continued, and reholstered his sidearm. "You will keep a channel open to me, prepared to take any action I order. Meanwhile, activate your engines for their psychological effect, then shut them down when I have entered the building."

Stuart acknowledged, and from the copilot's seat activated the engines, which hummed to life. The locals backed away nervously. A systems status rundown showed green on the control screen. Hammer's gullwing door lifted; he swung his legs out, ignored the ladder which extruded automatically, and hopped down the meter and a half to the frozen, snow-covered ground. The door lowered silently shut behind him. His vision took in most of the crowd; his central focus was on its speaker.

"Take me to Maidari," Hammer said.

The yellow-robe speaker understood, though presumably only the name Maidari had meaning for him. He bowed slightly, turned, and spoke to another yellow robe. That one led off toward the stone building. Smiling then, the speaker gestured to Hammer, who responded with no particular expression, and they followed side by side, the rest trailing behind.

* * *

Assault Group Leader Borkum had been paying close attention since they'd come in sight of the livestock station, just outside town. Given the fact of Sauron superiority, both of vision and speed, he didn't doubt he'd seen it before they'd seen him. He was equally sure that no one had carried or sent a message ahead of him. And there was no sign of alarm or discovery, even now, halted in full daylight with 154 white-clad men, some 400 meters from the town's nearest building, and more than 200 from the station's nearest.

Borkum had more than just infantry with him; there were two mountain gun teams from Battery A. He had them assemble their howitzers. Fire from even such light artillery often had a strong morale effect on cattle, especially if they hadn't experienced shellfire before. Then he sent a Gatling gun team around to the right, to cover the rear, and two rifle squads to protect the Gatling gun, which would be within bow shot of town. With them he sent two rifle squads to provide flanking fire on the livestock station, if needed. With those in position, he sent two rifle squads forward toward what clearly seemed the main building— he thought of it as the headquarters—the one with thin smoke drifting from a pair of brick chimneys. He didn't expect trouble, but he was prepared for it.

His eyes in magnification mode, Borkum watched the two squads stop before the headquarters, in a single spread line, the men two to three meters apart. Pistol in hand, Assault Leader Hanko and two others went to the door. Roughly, Hanko shoved it open, and the three pushed inside. A moment later, Hanko stepped back out and called to the rest of his two squads, which moved on the building and went in. Borkum barked more orders. Squads trotted toward others of the station buildings as assigned.

* * *

They must have, or have had, some trade with the outside, Hammer thought as he entered the monastery. *The door is wooden.* Wooden but not massive, and neither bound nor bossed with metal—nothing to repel force. There was a wooden drop-bar to hold it shut against wind or animals, but it could be raised from either side and the door opened. *A trusting people,* he added to himself; *perhaps even an honorable people. Or perhaps only their religious structures are safe from criminals.*

He was aware of the attitudes toward religion in some societies. Saurons, on the other hand, were devoutly rational materialists, and rarely stole from one another. It was foreign to their culture, and fatal if discovered. What they took from cattle was not considered theft, of course, but even that was constrained by policy, and by the politics of the situation.

He entered with the speaker, and was followed by most of the others. It was cold inside, too, but far less than outside. Hammer felt no unease at being enclosed here. He was engineered and trained to notice the smallest clues of human moods and reactions, even when they were suppressed: movement and tension of muscles, including facial muscles; dilation and contraction of the pupils; coloring of the episclera; moisture on the face, especially the forehead; changes in loudness, pitch, and modulation of the voice; and certain smells. And while interpretation of some of these varied with the culture, a cyborg and most Soldiers could pretty well read the attitudes and mood, and to a degree the immediate intentions, of cattle. The First Cyborg perceived no threat, and walked in arrogance.

From a large vestibule, corridors left in three directions, lit by lamps burning yak butter. The ceilings and upper walls were black with their soot. Most of the cattle dispersed into two of the corridors; the speaker led him down another. At a staircase, the speaker turned and gestured, then led Hammer upward, the three who had followed them continuing down the corridor. The stairs were basalt, with concavities worn by centuries of footsteps, and climbed steeply without turning till the fourth landing. There they entered the base of the tower, the stairs following the exterior walls around. Here the lamps were cold, and daylight filtered through windows covered with stretched yak gut.

At the topmost landing was an open door, and a room with rich soft light. His guide stepped aside and gestured Hammer in. There was nothing of evasion, of nerves or deception in the man. Thus Hammer walked in with only his normal vigilance, which was abundant.

The room was surprisingly clean. A man stood waiting, looking old by Havener standards but not ancient—perhaps 50 T-years. He was markedly less dark than the others Hammer had seen, his hair pale reddish-brown, a sort of tarnished copper lightened by threads and streaks of silver. To one side stood a boy, an adolescent, dark like the others. "Welcome," the old man said, in archaically proper Anglic, and gestured at a cushion on the floor. "Please be seated." Then, without waiting, he sat down himself on another, folding his legs under him strangely. "Would you like tea? I'm afraid our ingredients here are not those you might be accustomed to."

For a moment Hammer stood scanning, his mind recording, classifying. This old man was apparently his only suitable information source here. "Have him bring me food," he ordered, then sat down himself.

The old man spoke in his own language then, a tonal language which sounded quite unlike Mongol. He could have been saying anything, but there was no sign of treachery or ill intent in face or voice or smell. The boy left the room quickly but smoothly, closing the door behind him.

Hammer, meanwhile, was murmuring into his wrist

radio, first to his pilot, then to Assault Group Leader Borkum, using the Sauron battle tongue for privacy and brevity. Their voices answered, small and tinny. The old man seemed neither alarmed nor awed by it. His gaze was as absorptive as the cyborg's, but not hard at all.

When Hammer was finished, the old man spoke. "You are one of the soldier people we heard of, many years ago. I've been expecting you to come here someday."

"Your guards killed two of our soldiers," Hammer said.

"Yes. And your soldiers killed the garrison there, in reprisal."

Hammer's eyebrows rose slightly, for him a strong facial reaction. "How were you informed?"

"I wasn't informed. It is in the nature of such encounters, between such as you and such as we."

The old eyes, too, were unusual. Their epicanthic folds were notably less pronounced than on the men who'd met the cyborg, and the eyes were gray-blue. "You say 'we,'" Hammer replied, "but you are of a different race than the people you rule here."

"Rule?" The old man chuckled. "I am not the ruler here. Tenzin Gampo, the man who brought you to my door, is the ruler. I am only Byams-pa—he whom the Mongols call Maidari. In English, Anglic, my name is Maitreya."

"What is your function, if you do not rule?"

"I am the one to whom Tenzin Gampo turns for guidance."

"The 'Buddha Yet to Come.' So I've been told. How does that differ from ruler, if you control the throne? Even from behind it."

The old man's face and voice laughed together. "The Buddha Yet to Come? That was a prophecy fulfilled long ago on Terra, in Tibet."

Hammer interrupted. "Old man," he said coldly, "I

warn you this once: I have no tolerance for riddles, and I do not hesitate to kill. Now, clarify."

The old man's face, his eyes and voice, showed no sign of shock or fear at the hard rebuke, and the threat. A fact which Hammer noticed and registered. "Tenzin Gampo rules as he wishes," the old man continued gently. "If he asks my opinion or advice, which he sometimes does, and if I then give it to him, as I sometimes do, he invariably follows it. But usually he does not ask, and if he does not ask, I say nothing. Maitreya is a teacher, not a ruler, not a counselor.

"Maitreya was born at Gyatsho, in the state of Tibet, on Terra, in the year 2005 by European reckoning. He was a *tulku,* specifically a reincarnation of the lord Gautama, the Buddha." He paused. "Does this have meaning to you?"

Hammer nodded curtly. The Saurons had planned to—had expected to—conquer the First Empire, and he had been intended as a would-be trouble-shooter who would travel from world to world. Thus his education, though not completed, had been far broader than the purely military, and he had at least a passing familiarity with many cultures, philosophies, and governments outside Sauron. Thus he knew that on Terra, Tibet had been a state conquered and ruled by China; 2005 was shortly after the founding of the CoDominium; Buddha had been a holy man in some early millenium of history.

The old man continued. "The boy, while still a small child, was recognized as Maitreya by certain lamas, holy monks, and they proclaimed him so. And because the civil authorities were undertaking to further liberalize their rule, this was allowed. At age fifteen he began to preach, reforming and purifying religious practices and teachings, which gained him a devout following. In this he offended both the civil authorities and certain leading members of the orders of monks.

Monks approved by the civil authorities, who themselves were either Chinese or obedient to the Chinese."

Hammer interrupted, suspecting what the answer would be. "That was seven hundred T-years ago. What has that to do with you?"

"I am Maitreya."

The old man's gaze, as he spoke, was utterly unperturbed, without fear or any sign of artifice. *So, he is insane*, the cyborg told himself. *Deluded at least.* Insanity usually included fixations. Sometimes those fixations could serve as axioms from which whole systems of consistent logic might be derived, to form a rational, if erroneous gestalt. The same was true of more ordinary delusions, though the results were less compulsive. Know this man's fixations or basic delusions, and something of his logic, and he might prove useful.

"You are old, but you do not appear to be seven hundred years old."

The old man laughed with delight. "You know the answer to that one, too, Hammer. I have died more than a dozen times, over those centuries, and each time ensouled another newborn among these people, each time to be recognized by the color of my hair— coloring foretold of Maitreya."

And after conditioning you, they taught you what your predecessors had said and done, Hammer thought. *Very tidy. And you believed them—still believe them.*

He heard softshod feet on the stairs, the lower flight, although the door was closed. Interestingly, the old man heard them, too; his ears would do credit to a Soldier. "I believe your supper is coming," said the man who called himself Maitreya. "We shall see if Lobsang truly comprehended the strength of your appetite."

Assault Group Leader Borkum looked at the middle-aged man and woman before him in the room, seemingly a mated couple. The other human cattle here, at what was obviously a livestock holding yard and slaughtering place, had clearly looked to this pair as their superiors; presumably they were the manager and his woman. They stood meek and humble before his gaze. *Damn all cattle that don't understand Anglic! Well . . .* He gestured forcefully at himself, thumb rapping his chest, then put his hands together beside his head, rested his cheek on them, and snored.

The man brightened, gestured enthusiastically, and turning, began to walk, his woman still beside him. Borkum followed, his orderly a step behind. They went down a dim hall to a doorway with a well-tanned cowhide hanging over it to the floor. The man pushed it open. Borkum shoved past him and stepped into a room which was equally dim, lit by a small butter lamp and a gut-paned window, its deadlight of stiff hide laid back against the brick wall. The man slid past him and hurried to light two more butter lamps.

He had no notion that to Sauron eyes, dim light was more than light enough.

Borkum looked the room over. The bed was the top of what seemed to be a brick stove—an intelligent arrangement—and topped with a crude mattress that by the smell was stuffed with raw wool. He walked over, and opening the firebox door, looked inside. No fire. He straightened, peering around. The couple stood side by side, watching, smiling nervously. Dried yak dung, like large disks of gray bread, were piled close at hand, and next to it a pile of coarse grass, twisted and tied into knots, to help the dung burn well. Hanging from the wall was a thin sheaf of paper, or parchment more likely. Borkum stepped to it and pulled it down, crumpling the sheets, then turned at the gasp he heard. The man looked horrified; the woman's knuckles had gone to her mouth.

Borkum scowled, knelt, and laid a fire of parchment, grass, and dung. The woman began to wail as

he lit a twist of grass at an oil lamp. He snapped an
order, then knelt again and lit the parchment while
his orderly slapped the couple around, knocking the
woman sprawling. The wailing shrilled for just a
moment, then cut off. *Damn all cattle!* Borkum
grumped inwardly. *They're hard enough to understand
when they speak Anglic.*

The First Cyborg, even more than the Soldiers, was
relatively indiscriminate with regard to taste. Food was
food. Which was not to say he found no pleasure in
it: He enjoyed stoking his metabolic fires, and when
he ate, preferred to give it his full attention. When he
was done, he looked at Maitreya again.

"Where do your women go to give birth?" Hammer
asked.

Maitreya's eyebrows lifted. "It is usual to go to one's
home, to one's bed. Whether it be one's winter home,
or one's tent in summer, when most of our people
travel with their herds."

Hammer detected no trace of irony, sarcasm, or
banter in the man; he seemed to have answered hon-
estly. "Other people," the cyborg said, "feel it necessary to take their women to low valleys for birthing.
Otherwise the newborn usually dies at birth, or lives
brain-damaged. Not infrequently the woman dies,
too."

"Ah, of course. We heard of that, in the days when
we traded with the Mongols. But these, my people
. . . Many of us who came together from Terra were
born at forty-five hundred to five thousand meters
above the sea, as were our forefathers. Most were
herdsmen, nomads. Sometimes newborn died there,
too, more than at Lhasa, at only thirty-seven hundred
meters. This place is hardly more severe. Even here
most newborns live—enough to provide bodies for
those souls wishing to live among us, to heal in our
quiet. And our women do not often die giving birth."

Desirable genes, Hammer thought. *These people can provide valuable tribute maidens. Breedmaster Dekker will be pleased.* The genetic engineering equipment landed from the *Fomoria,* the "Dol Guldur," had mostly become inoperable, its functional components salvaged to help keep the jerry-built cyborg production facility operating a little longer. To maintain the Sauron genome at something close to its current superiority would take careful selection, attribute matching, and culling.

"When were you brought to this world?"

"In 2052 by the European calendar. There were nearly three thousand of us."

Hammer accepted the answer. *If they were brought here as a penal shipment in that decade,* he told himself, *they'd have been landed as convict labor at some mining development. And forced relocations of other than criminals hadn't begun yet. So presumably these people had been brought here at their own request, perhaps even at their own expense. Was there some resource of particular value on this plateau?*

"Why were you settled in such a remote and inhospitable location?"

"Precisely because it was remote and inhospitable. Already, colonies on the more desirable sites were being encroached on and disrupted. There were conflicts, and they would become worse. And we were a peaceful people, then as now, avoiding violence. Our purpose requires that we do not harm anyone, and we benefit from separation. Before ever petitioning the Chinese government for relocation, I learned what I could about possible locations, on this and other worlds. This plateau had been explored for minerals. It was considered to have little of value—there are minor deposits of iron and copper ores—and to be unsuited for human occupation because of its latitude and elevation.

"Thus I requested it."

Rational, given the basic purpose. "You have wood here. Lumber. What did you trade for it?"

The old man didn't hesitate. "In the early years, in digging iron and copper ores, three shimmerstones were found. And at times we've sold copper to the Mongols, though apparently they turn to others now."

To others, yes. To the troublesome people who'd begun to call themselves the haBandari. As for shimmerstones—Hammer had heard of them, though he'd never seen one. They were the sort of thing a degenerate society put great store by, and they were rare. In the days of the Empire, three sizeable shimmerstones could have purchased a great deal of lumber, even on forest-poor Haven.

"You say you do not believe in violence," Hammer said.

"One may use violence, but one is caused thereby to continue longer the cycle of rebirth in the material universe, postponing one's reunification with God."

Remarkable! Controlling these people should be relatively simple. "God? I have seen no evidence of any God. Can you show him to me?"

"In the material universe, one does not *see* God with one's eyes. One 'sees' God only with an Inner Eye, so to speak, rather as a blind child may come to know his father or his nurse. For nearly all it requires long discipline; in some societies it is nearly impossible. Here we have created a society where more than a few see God, and by that seeing, take a great stride toward oneness with God. On Terra, holy men undertook to create such a society in different lands, in different ways, but progress was slow, very slow. Even where they followed the Buddha.

"That is why, long ago, I promised to some day return to a body: to create a place, a society, where each person could most easily refine his or her Karma toward oneness with God. . . ."

Hammer interrupted. "Karma? I do not know the word."

"Karma is that milieu of psychic energy one creates in life by one's actions, words, beliefs, and thoughts. One creates karma and one is influenced by karma. When one's karma is sufficiently harmonious with that of God, one sees God, so to speak. And when that harmony is more nearly perfect, one unites with God, though retaining one's awareness. Each person creates his own karma, but each person's creation of karma is influenced by the karmas of those around him. Or around her. And influences theirs in return."

An interesting superstition! A system of more or less consistent logic rooted in delusion. "So you had promised to return to a body," Hammer prompted.

"Yes. I chose Tibet because the people there, and the circumstances, were most ready. There the work of reforming and purifying was not so difficult as it would have been in some other land. There I prepared a brotherhood and sisterhood to come here, to this quiet place."

"If you do not believe in violence, why did your guardsmen kill two of my Soldiers and wound four others? Why did you even have a guardpost at the access trail?"

"Not all of my people have seen God, though almost every one of them wishes to. But almost none wish to kill, even among the guardsmen. It was simply that some wish fervently to protect their land, to keep it a safe and quiet place in which to seek God. Even Phabong, who first ruled here and who was close to God, felt it was necessary to fortify the access."

"But you do not."

"Never. Not under Phabong, not under Gampo."

"You let them do it though."

The old man was not perturbed by the pointed questioning. "I am not the ruler," he said mildly, "and they did not seek my counsel on it. They knew what it would be."

Hammer seldom needed time to think about a matter. He didn't now. "Maitreya," he said, "the Soldiers of Sauron are your new masters. But we will not enforce a way of life on you: As long as you commit no further violence against us, and meet certain tribute requirements and other conditions, you will be free to live and worship as you please. The Soldiers of Sauron will also guarantee your safety from possible intrusions of other peoples. But if you are violent or treacherous or disobedient toward us, you will be punished, the severity of the punishment being in proportion to the crime.

"Someone will come to you later to formalize the agreement, but I will describe the usual terms to you now. . . ."

The original Sauron stock had been almost entirely Caucasians, largely from northern Europe and North America, and having rationalist traditions and affinities. But the Breedmasters had produced from them a people quite different—flat-faced, flat-nosed, with mouths unusually wide and eyes slitted by epicanthic folds. In those respects, their faces were designed for endurance, of both exertion and severe climates. And in those respects they resembled many of the plateau people, the Haven Tibetans.

Thus, to Assault Group Leader Borkum, the husky, round-faced girl before him was quite attractive. With unconscious vanity he brushed his hand over his thick, resilient cap of auburn hair, a throwback to a Norwegian great-grandfather. He especially liked the way she'd lowered her eyes when he'd motioned her to wait while he ate. Now he put aside his empty bowl and spoke sharply, though not, he thought, harshly to her. When she looked up, he beckoned her to him. He'd show her what a real man was, an officer. She should like it, sometimes they did, but cattle were hard to predict.

"And your people will need to learn Anglic," Hammer said. "Each of them must be able to answer questions, should a Soldier ask one. In each group, there must be someone who speaks it well."

A question occurred to the First Cyborg then, one it seemed he should have thought of before. "Who taught you Anglic?"

"I once grew up with it. My father, on that occasion, was a British embassy official in Thailand, a beautiful country. It is in the nature of the material universe that there are things most effectively learned within it, and I spent a short lifetime gathering useful experiences, before being born as Maitreya. At age fourteen I was killed by terrorists, in order to be born at the appropriate time in Tibet."

Hammer's gaze was intent. Almost certainly, the old man believed what he'd just said. It even fit with his archaically proper Anglic.

"And as my recall is quite complete from life to life . . ."

Maitreya stopped there. From below, somewhere below the tower, they both heard a loud voice, an angry voice. A Sauron voice. Seconds later there came the sound of booted feet on the stairs, not a single set, but numerous.

A squad, Hammer thought. And one pair of soft-shod feet. He stood. The men who burst in were an officer, two lesser Soldiers, and the Mongol guide. One of the Soldiers gripped Tenzin Gampo; the left side of the yellow robe's face was swelling. The rest of the squad waited outside the door, on the landing and upper stairs.

"What is this about, Senior Assault Leader?" Again Hammer spoke in battle tongue.

"Assault Group Leader Borkum has been murdered, First Cyborg!"

"Under what circumstances?"

"He was—in bed with a girl. I believe it was her parents' bed. She had called out—it sounded as if she was unwilling—but none of us went to investigate. The Assault Group Leader would have been angry with us. Unfortunately, one of the cattle entered and split his skull with a meat cleaver." The young officer sounded embarrassed for his late commander. "Apparently the Assault Group Leader was in the midst of an orgasm. Otherwise the man could never have gotten him."

The First Cyborg's face and voice were ice. "What else?"

"Then the murderer, the man apparently in charge of the place, came into the main room with his cleaver bloody, and started for one of the men—Soldier Gilmak. Gilmak took the cleaver away from him and killed him with it."

Hammer turned to Maitreya. "So, old man! Your people reject violence? One of them has murdered the commander of these Soldiers."

The old man met his eyes calmly. "As I said, not all of us have seen God. And sufficiently provoked . . ."

"Umm." The First Cyborg's irritation had died at the old man's words; he paused for brief seconds— three or four. "I've described to you in general the crimes and punishments."

"Indeed you have."

"The murdered man was second in rank among us here." He turned to look at Tenzin Gampo. "And he is second in rank among you. Therefore he shall be executed."

"No. He is first in rank. I am second."

That wasn't true, Hammer thought. Perhaps formally it was, but not in fact. And the old man who called himself Maitreya was needed alive. He was the only one of them who . . .

"Lobsang speaks Anglic, too," Maitreya added. "Not fluently; I realized only recently that I should teach him. But he is remarkably adept in all things; more than anyone else here. You will find his ability adequate, and perhaps one of your men can remain here to teach him further."

"Very well then. It will be you whom I execute." He looked at the Under Assault Group Leader. "Because of the circumstances, the rape, the family of the murderer will not be executed."

"Yes, First Cyborg!"

"They are all right now?"

"To the best of my knowledge, First Cyborg!" The officer was nervous; uncertain.

"I'll look into it when I get there."

"Yes, First Cyborg!"

"Return there. I'll follow shortly, bringing this person with me." He indicated Maitreya. "And leave that one here," he added, gesturing at Tenzin Gampo. "I will have him instructed on the need for an audience at the execution. Which will take place at sundown."

When the Soldiers were gone, Hammer spoke to the old man. "Send for the one who speaks Anglic— Lobsang. He must serve with that one—Tenzin—as his communicator and deputy, at least in matters to do with the Soldiers. There are things which Tenzin must know and do, after your execution. Particularly, he must ensure that there is no violence or demonstration following the executions. It is undesirable that we butcher large numbers."

"Of course." Maitreya turned and spoke to Tenzin Gampo, who bowed and left the room. Hammer followed the sound of his feet all the way down the stairs.

Before a compulsory audience of all the local monks, both trapas and lamas, First Cyborg Hammer executed Maitreya himself by compression of the carotid artery, followed by breaking his neck. But not before the old man had spoken to that audience in Tibetan for several long minutes.

Policy required that the execution be publicly witnessed, to demonstrate the laws and power of Sauron, and so that the execution would be widely known by first-hand accounts. And it seemed to Hammer that monks were less likely to riot and require bloody suppression. As expected, there had been no trouble, though many had wept, and a few had wailed loudly.

After they'd gone back to the monastery, taking the body with them, the First Cyborg had lectured the Soldiers on discipline, and they'd been suitably subdued. A First Cyborg was like God to them. Or the Devil.

It was nearly two hours after the executions before the scout fighter left for Koln Base. Hammer allowed Fighter Rank Stuart to pilot. Outside was Truenight, and as dark as it ever got on Haven, except for nights when clouds blotted out the stars. The snow surface had cooled to below air temperature, and his optical sensitivity to infrared added little to Hammer's view, except for the glow of a smokehole in a faraway herdsman's hut, and the warm spots of a yak herd resting in the snow. But starlight on the snow gave abundant visibility, even for normal human eyes.

How cold would it be when Cat's Eye rose, a dozen hours hence? And how cold when Byers' Sun finally showed its disk again? The people up here were hardy stock, even by Haven standards. Birthing their children here! The partial pressure of oxygen could hardly be much more than fifty percent, by T-standards, possibly fifty-five. And when the intricate movements of Haven, Cat's Eye, and Byers' Sun gave them their occasional fifty-hour winter night, by sunup the frost that formed might well include frozen carbon dioxide.

Beneath him the rim dropped away to the steppe, itself an arctic wilderness in this season. But its tough tribesmen took their women to a deep valley to give birth. He still needed to survey the rest of the rim and document that there was no birthing valley for the people of Maitreya, but he had no doubt that there wasn't.

He looked back at the plateau then, receding behind him. And wondered if, sometime soon, a red-headed child would be born to some woman there.

From *A Student's Book* by Myner Klint bar Terborch fan Reenan, Eden Valley, Ilona'sstad, 2927:

. . . some of the peoples we know today on Haven bear the same names and have many of the same customs and language as their very ancient ancestors. Our world is a place where it is very easy for small groups of people to live apart from their neighbors. The coming of the Saurons was a period of great change; in the generations that followed, many settlements were broken up, many people forced to wander in search of new homes. Most of these died, but some—our own ancestors among them—settled and formed new, mixed peoples in refuges they found or made. . . .

BUILDING A PILLAR

John LaValley

For any true civilization to exist three things are essential: unhindered communication, unrestricted travel, and the free exchange of goods and values. If these pillars, if you will, are maintained, a civilization can last almost indefinitely. Remove any one and total collapse is inevitable.
— from the introduction to
Civilization and Empire, Vol. I
(Hans Kattinger's personal library)

"This tastes like muskylope urine, Johann." At nineteen years of age Daerick Kattinger had few discretions against expressing an opinion on his younger brother's latest experiment. The brown, steaming fluid in the mug was simply horrible.

"I didn't know you were that familiar with animal fluids, brother," Johann retorted easily. "Besides, you gave me this stuff, remember?"

Daerick did remember, and not without a twinge of sadness. He had given Johann the colony's last few pounds of coffee beans to try to find some way to make them grow. Before Grandmother Heidi died, she had implored Daerick to try one last time to grow coffee. Daerick then gave the beans to Johann as Johann was by far the better farmer.

But what was supposed to be just another chore became a passion. Johann answered the challenge of growing the beans with a vengeance, partly because he hoped to become a hero, but mostly because he was one of the few colonists who actually liked the taste.

Daerick remembered how Johann had come running from the special greenhouse he'd built for the coffee. In the thin air of Haven even a descendant of Frystaat became exhausted easily. "I found it!" he said, catching his wind. "I know why the Fathers couldn't grow it! It's so damned simple no one thought to look for it. Come on."

In the small greenhouse, Johann had set up a table with several bowls, each with a different soil sample. On the table was a small microscope that had been brought down from the *Fledermaus* by the first settlers of Acropolis.

Johann placed a glass slide on the viewing plate. Of the two hundred-odd slides brought with the microscope, nearly a third were cracked or broken. The colonists had set up a small glassworks but its product was nowhere near optical quality and would not be for some time. Johann handled the slide with excruciating care. "Look," he said.

Daerick looked. Among the fibers and dust on the slide he could see what appeared to be a tiny, twelve-legged spider, bloated and fat and partially squished onto the slide. Its size was just outside the range of human visibility but the microscope showed it nicely.

"All this time," said Johann, "everyone thought it was the soil, something chemical. No one thought to look through a microscope. Or maybe they did but not in time to catch the things in the act."

"So what's this?"

"I don't know, some bug that's not in the book, but

you put a coffee bean in the ground and these things go after it. Probably attracted to the smell."

"How common are they?" asked Daerick looking through the microscope again.

"How should I know? I just found them. A bean I planted just yesterday was covered by them this morning."

"Well, the Fathers tried growing it all over the southern region and failed, so the little bastards are probably everywhere," Daerick concluded.

As it would turn out, he was almost right.

Johann had spent the next several of Haven's long days working in the greenhouse and making many trips to Frau Gartner's baking ovens. At last she chased him out, railing about cleaning the ovens so many times after his visits. But Johann ran away smiling. He had what he needed.

Baked soil hung in ten half-barrel pots from a reinforced ceiling in the greenhouse. In each, freshly transferred from its germination pot, was a little plant sprouting its first leaves. After nearly eighty Terran years, coffee was growing on Haven.

It was with sadness that Daerick remembered Johann's early triumph, for Grandmother Heidi had told him what might have to be done with the coffee if it grew.

Johann had answered back with carefree indifference to his brother's remark, but Daerick regretted it anyway. The blow, when it comes, should not be augmented by memories of callous words.

"It's not that bad actually," Daerick lied. "At least it wakes me up. So, do you have a name for this brew?"

"Yes, as a matter of fact. Considering the original stock of the beans and their new home, I would say 'Acropolis Blue Mountain.' What do you think?"

"Sure, sounds good."

Johann smiled. "You don't have to pretend to like it for my sake. Some of the others have been itching to try it. See you later." Johann left to share Haven's first pot of native coffee with neighbors and enjoy his moment in the sun. . . .

. . . Twenty years later and Daerick still remembered. By a combination of lineage and a good track record, he had become leader of the colony.

His brother was the undisputed expert on agriculture, having studied the books and practiced their knowledge. He had produced increased yields and a number of grain and tuber hybrids.

But the Blue Mountain coffee was always his favorite work. Through sweat and patience, Johann had produced no fewer than seventy-five bushes. Coffee, in small amounts, had become a staple drink, rather than something consumed only on special occasions.

The time had come, according to Dr. Gettman's original genetics plan, to find some new blood. Some new genetic material had to be brought in to the Acropolitan gene pool. The genetic diversity of the original settlers had been played out to the fullest. Further generations would only increase the risk of recessives breaking out.

After five generations of isolation on Acropolis, someone would have to go out and meet the natives.

Martin Krusenstein, descendant of one of the Imperial ship *Fledermaus*'s enlisted technicians, was the closest thing Acropolis had to an ordained Methodist minister. But like so many ministers and priests in frontier settlements throughout the galaxy, the Reverend Krusenstein had another, more secular occupation. He was the colony's blacksmith.

After leading the congregation of his small chapel in prayer for the ten-man expedition to be sent out, Krusenstein met with the expedition members themselves. He had forged each a sword, a large knife, and a number of arrowheads for hunting.

"We've asked the Lord to watch over you," he said, "but you'll have to take care of your equipment yourselves. Everything I've given you is high carbon steel. If you get blood on it, your own or . . . or something else's, like an animal, clean it off as soon as you can or the surface will pit. Too much pitting will ruin the blade and that will really irritate me.

"This stuff represents just about the last of the ship's bar stock, and as you know, we haven't found any workable iron ore, so try to bring everything back if you can.

"And, gentlemen," he looked at each man in turn, "bring yourselves back, too. God bless you."

The men left to make their final preparations as Krusenstein closed the church doors, then returned to his foundry, making what implements he could with the lighter metals mined on the eastern face of Acropolis.

The next morning, the citizens of Acropolis who could spare the time turned out to see the men off. With muskylopes carrying their supplies of food and water, the men left. Armed with their swords, two of the remaining rifles and a haltingly practiced old Finnish language, they descended the mountain and headed north toward a vague outline on a map called Novy Finlandia.

Oleg Klobregnii felt his heart pounding at the news his wife brought into the tent. The advance party had found a group of men and surprised them. The strangers were armed with steel swords and rifles! Their countenance was described as one of angular features and sharply defined muscles. This could have only one meaning.

Saurons!

One of the scouts entered the tent just then. "Sir, we encountered—"

"I know. Tell me what happened, quickly."

"Sir, they entered a clearing before we did, so we saw them first. They were pretty small for Saurons, but they looked the same so we took aim and shot. We dropped two of them before they even knew what was happening. They had rifle weapons and kept us away."

"Away from what?"

The young scout seemed nervous. "Sir, Ragnar was injured. We couldn't get to him. They had us pinned down—"

"Where is Ragnar?"

"They . . . they captured him. We tried, sir, we—"

Klobregnii placed a hand on the scout's shoulder. The young man flinched slightly.

"It's all right, lad," Klobregnii said. "Is that the first time you've faced gunfire?"

"Yes, sir."

"I remember I was older than you when I hid from a rifle that spat many rounds at once. Only fools and madmen are brave in the face of that. Is there anything more?"

"Yes, sir. There is." The man ran out of the tent, then returned a moment later, carrying a long bundle. "When they took Ragnar and the two we shot, they left this."

Klobregnii sat on a chair and unwrapped the layers of cloth to reveal one of the Acropolitan's steel swords. The blade had a number of day-old fingerprints on it which Klobregnii couldn't quite rub away with the cloth. It was otherwise polished smooth.

Something about it didn't make sense. A Sauron group should have wiped out his scouting party, especially after losing two of their own, instead of apparently fleeing.

Klobregnii dismissed the young scout and called softly to his wife. "Lissa, please come here."

After first entering the tent, Lissa had gone to the back to put their two young daughters to bed. At the sound of her husband's voice she stepped back into the light.

It had been many days since their five hundred-plus member band had fled Novy Finlandia, burning their fields and homes and heading south rather than submit to the growing Sauron dominion to the north.

Not since that first night had she seen the look on her husband's face that she saw now.

"There are Saurons several days to the south." He stood up to hold her. "They have our son."

"A prisoner? What?" Daerick Kattinger got up and followed the messenger out of the stone and wood house to the commotion outside. The crowd parted to let him through.

Lookouts on the north side of the mountain had reported a return of the ten much sooner than expected, but they could not see that the one riding a muskylope had his hands bound at the wrist.

"All right," said Daerick, shouldering through the onlookers to the nervous-looking stranger on the muskylope. "Let's see him."

The man under Daerick's scrutiny was young, early twenties. He stared back with apprehension and loathing. And something else, an edge of curiosity.

"What happened?" Daerick asked of Otto Hermann, the expedition leader.

"They attacked us in a meadow two days march north, sir. We lost Heinrich, and Willem was hit in the shoulder."

Heinrich was Frau Gartner's second oldest son. Daerick was glad she wasn't here to get the news firsthand.

"All right," he said. "Take this young fellow and Willem to the Gettman's."

Like so many colonists, Marcus and Olga Gettman followed their forbears in a family trade. Along with their medicinal duties, the Gettmans were the current ministers of the colony's breeding program originally set in motion by Dr. Liza Gettman of the *Fledermaus*.

The wound in the Novy Finlandian's leg had been given a field dressing but it would need better care and soon. Daerick sniffed the air slightly. "He'll need a bath and some clothes. Then you and the others should get some rest."

A few minutes later, Daerick knocked on his brother's door. "Why don't you have supper with us, Johann? I'll need your linguistic services, for our special guest tonight."

An old, worn book on Haven's more common languages had been the colony's only tool for communication with the locals. The Fathers' plan had been for the fourth generation to begin studying the language of the nearer tribes to the north.

Johann had done as well as one could at learning the Finnish-Russian of the north, without having natives to practice with. It had only been his responsibilities in the fields and greenhouses that kept him from the first expedition. It was something for which Johann was secretly glad.

Oleg Klobregnii did not like the sounds coming from the large tent in the center of the camp. Voices laden with fear and anger argued with increasing volume.

It went silent when Klobregnii entered. The eyes of the men told which of the opposing sides each was on.

Varushin Byorin had been Klobregnii's friend for many years. He was the first to break the silence. "Oleg, we must return to Novy Finlandia."

"Why?" But Klobregnii already knew the answer.

"I think you know why. Some of us believe it is better to be a live dog than a dead lion."

"Those were not your words when we left, Varushin."

"We were not surrounded by Saurons then!" Byorin shouted.

"I do not know that we are surrounded by them."

"Then you are a fool, Oleg Pyotrovich," Byorin said sitting back down.

Klobregnii clenched fists, then relaxed them instantly. "Tell me, then," he said, "why did they flee after our scouts hit two of them? Why did they not fight when they had superior numbers and guns? And why did they leave a precious steel sword behind?"

"A precious sword that you have been hoarding, Oleg."

"Yes!" Klobregnii's voice rose slightly. "And I will continue to hoard it until I have buried it in the chest of whoever is holding my son."

"Your son, Oleg Klobregnii," said Byorin. "What about our sons? They are here, with us, and we don't want them to die."

Klobregnii realized that Byorin and some of the others had already made their choice. His next words he must aim at those who still had doubts. "And what about your daughters, hmm? With the fields burned, what will be your medium of exchange to trade for your lives and a few scraps to eat?"

None of the others, not even Byorin, could meet Klobregnii's stare. His words, like arrows, had struck home too solidly.

"I don't want to hear your answer tonight," he said. "At first Eyelight we will strike southeast, around the flat mountain instead of toward it. I'll know if you are with me then."

With the first faint light from the not-quite-brown-dwarf star known as Cat's Eye, some three hundred Novy Finlandians with their animals and goods began to move southeast, toward the sea. The rest turned and headed back the way they had come. By the end of the day some eighty more had broken off from Klobregnii's group.

For a full day, after the last of those who broke off and ran did so, the caravan headed seaward. Then, at a signal from Klobregnii, they turned ninety degrees to the right.

Hilde Munsen swore as she accidentally cut her thumb with the whittling knife the Rev. Krusenstein had given her. She had been carving a small model of the *Fledermaus* from a sapling when a motion at the corner of her eye distracted her enough to break concentration. She sucked the drop of blood from the tiny cut and began to forget it instantly. Her thumb already had several such cuts and would acquire more as her hobby developed.

Standing lookout watch at the mountain's edge was not the busiest of Acropolis's chores. It gave Munsen time for carving and the view was—

Something moved! Carving and small cuts were forgotten in favor of the carefully padded binoculars on a tether.

There, at the base of the foothills to the north, was a dotted black line that hadn't been there before. A look through the glasses revealed that while some of the dots in the line had four legs, others had two.

Munsen quickly mounted what would have been a bicycle, except that it didn't move. Instead, it turned a flywheel which in turn spun a small generator. Munsen didn't understand much about electricity, but she did know that she had to keep pedaling or the message she tapped on the wire key would not go through.

"No, it's not a war party. It's my people," Johann translated Ragnar's comment. He'd become rather good at the language, now that he had someone to practice with. It had not been easy, at first, but Johann

had at last convinced Ragnar that there were no Saurons on Acropolis. Barriers fell more swiftly when
Johann saw Ragnar react with delight at having
another cup of his Blue Mountain coffee.

I hope, Daerick thought to himself, it will be that
easy with their leader.

At the foot of the mountain, Daerick stood with a
party of one hundred men. Across the glen he could
see the new arrivals milling. At last a group of perhaps
twenty separated itself and advanced across the clearing.

Daerick motioned to the five men with rifles to join
himself, Johann, and Ragnar, who stood with the aid
of a crutch.

At two hundred and fifty meters distance the
riflemen stopped. "We have them in range, sir," one
said to Daerick.

"Keep walking," he answered.

Klobregnii watched with interest as the men with
guns tried to stop outside the range of his bowmen.
He shook his head with wonder as he saw their leader
motion them forward again, well into arrow range.
What kind of Sauron would do that?

The two groups stood about thirty meters apart
when Klobregnii shifted his attention from the rifles
to the three men in the lead. One of them was—

"Ragnar!"

Ragnar Klobregnii hobbled over to his father. Their
embrace lasted nearly a minute. "Are you all right,
Ragnar?"

"Yes, father. Look, they made this crutch and salves
for my leg—"

Klobregnii was momentarily shocked. No Sauron
had ever, as long as Klobregnii could remember,
spared precious medicine for people they called "cattle." "All right, son," he said. "Go to your mother."

A lone woman had left the caravan and was racing across the glen.

Ragnar turned back to his father. "These people, father, they say their ancestors came from one of the other worlds. They have a wonderful drink. They have rich food, they—"

"I understand, son."

"Father, they never once called me 'cattle.' "

For a moment Klobregnii was still. "Good, son. Now go."

He turned and walked slowly toward the men staring across the short distance at him.

Daerick began to walk as well. "Stay here," he said, "You too, Johann."

At a distance of five feet, the two leaders stopped.

Daerick could not believe the size of the individual before him. The man was a full head taller than Daerick, who was not short by any standard. The shoulders were broad, the hands huge and calloused from years of hard work. But under the large, blond brows were bright green eyes that fairly glittered with intelligence.

Klobregnii scrutinized the man before him. He could easily see the muscle tone of the arms and estimated similar tone and strength throughout. This was the man whose warriors had wounded and captured his son.

Slowly, Klobregnii began to reach into his cloak. Blue eyes held his gaze as the man spoke in a low voice, using a language Klobregnii couldn't understand.

"Men, keep the guns down."

Daerick's heart raced as the man in front of him drew his hand from the cloak. There was a quick flash of sunlight on metal— And Oleg Klobregnii handed the steel sword to Daerick Kattinger.

After the caravan reached the top of the mountain, a feat more easily accomplished by the burdened muskylopes than the Novy Finlandians, a formal meeting was held between the leaders, to be followed by a feast.

Daerick had never felt more alone than he did when drawing up a proposal for a treaty with the Novy Finlandian exiles.

At last he finished and was about to call his brother to tell him and try to apologize. He knew Johann would hate him for what he was about to do. If only there was a way to keep—

But there was! Yes, thought Daerick, it could work. And Johann would probably agree.

"What we ask, with greatest respect," Daerick said across the table, using the formalized speech the Fathers had said to be used for negotiating, "is for our sons and daughters to marry with your sons and daughters." He paused, partly for effect, partly to catch his breath. "If they'll have each other."

After Johann translated, the Novy Finlandians talked among themselves for a moment.

Klobregnii's translated reply was short, "Why?"

Daerick could see that the big Finn knew why, just by the amused smile on his face. But again, the Fathers had warned of this sort of thing in formal talks. There was nothing for it but to answer the question. "As a farmer and herdsman, you know of the need for large numbers to keep the animals healthy. So it is with men. Neither of us have those numbers separately, but together we do."

Klobregnii understood Daerick's reasoning before it was spoken. He only wanted to see if the man was honest, which he was.

Klobregnii looked around at the faces on his side of the table. "It is done. Provided, of course,"—this time it was his turn to pause—"that they'll have each other."

A number of other items were discussed. Daerick's greatest fear was that the Novy Finlandians would continue migrating and possibly come into contact with others and thereby allow word to reach the Saurons about Acropolis.

But they agreed to stay. The thus far untilled foothills of the northwestern side of the mountain would be theirs. And the mountain itself was more than large enough for everyone.

They would trade knowledge and skills in farming, breeding, and harvesting. In mining, metallurgy, and foundry as well as medicine and dental care, such as anyone had.

Two items remained for discussion.

First, the new arrivals would be shown how to increase the range of their bows by stringing them through a series of compound pulleys. This, in addition to being given two of the remaining five rifles and forty percent of the ammunition, perhaps some three hundred rounds.

This last removed any remaining doubt as to the Acropolitans's integrity. No Sauron, no matter how kind-hearted, *ever* gave a weapon to a native Havener. It simply did not happen.

Last, so that the Novy Finlandians would have at least one exclusive property for trade, all seventy-five coffee bushes would be given to them.

Johann just sat at the table, stunned.

Daerick spoke softly, "I'm sorry, my brother."

Johann cast his brother a withering stare. His response was not quite what Daerick expected. "They'll die! I've spent years babying those bushes! You can't just give them away to these people. They have no idea how to tend them—"

"That's why I'm going to miss you, Johann," said Daerick, relieved that his brother was more concerned for the coffee bushes' well being than the idea of personally losing them. "You speak their language better than any of us, so I'm appointing you as ambassador. You will live with them on the west end of the mountaintop. You can personally supervise and teach them to tend the coffee."

After a moment Johann looked back at his brother, his anger gone. "You will visit, won't you?"

"Only if you promise me that you'll get married and have children. I've seen some of these young ladies of theirs looking at you, Johann."

Klobregnii had watched with interest as what looked like a heated exchange cooled rapidly. Johann's translation confirmed what he suspected. He nodded his approval, feeling his respect for Daerick Kattinger deepen that much more.

Feast! Resources being what they were, feasting was not common on Acropolis, but it was sometimes necessary to relieve boredom or celebrate living through another year. This year, both parties had much to celebrate.

Just before the feast began, Klobregnii disappeared into one of the tents. He reappeared with a huge basket under his arm.

"You have given us an exclusive item for trade. If there is to be stability in the future you must have one, too."

"Yes," answered Daerick, "but we have—"

Klobregnii held up a hand, politely interrupting Johann's translation. "No, your spices are wonderful but they are not equal to the coffee. This is." He put the basket on the table and opened the lid. "There are seven more baskets in the tent. They are yours."

Klobregnii paused, enjoying Daerick and Johann's curiosity. "This requires careful growing, like the coffee, but that's no problem. We'll send our ambassador."

"What is it?" asked Johann, dipping his hand into the unfamiliar grains.

A wide grin spread across Klobregnii's face. "Hops."

*   *   *

Hops began and coffee continued to grow. Other things grew on the mountain as well.

Of his many ministerial duties, none were so pleasant to the Reverend Krusenstein as the one he had now.

He stood in the chapel before a packed congregation. Standing in front, were Johann Kattinger and Klobregnii's niece, Solvieg.

The reverend smiled slightly, placed his hand on an ancient bible, and began to speak. "Dearly beloved . . ."

From *A Brief Atlas of the Planet Haven* by Colin Lyon Jones and Lilya Ivanovich Egorov. Oxford Press, AD 2427, folio:

Haven may be divided into roughly three main areas, each with its characteristic settlement history. The great equatorial lowland of the Shangri-La Valley was first claimed by the Church of New Harmony, religious sectaries of Americ descent; subsequent settlers were mainly also Americ and Russki, adopting an economy of farming, sedentary ranching, mining and, under the Empire of Man, some urban development. The massive spread of continental steppes surrounding the Shangri-La and its ring of mountains received a much more varied immigration, most of whom adopted ranching or even nomadic pastorialism as their means of livelihood; small peripheral valleys suitable for marginal agriculture were claimed by a wild assortment of smaller groups.

The southern and equatorial oceans and their islands—some of which are as large as Earth's Ireland—are a relatively favorable zone, by Haven standards if no other. Their potential attracted a variety of voluntary emigrants during the last years of the CoDominium, mostly NeoLibertarian and Royalist groups from Northern Europe, who built on native traditions to establish a pelagic culture. . . .

*   *   *

From *Report on Sector Twelve*, Citadel Intelligence, Archives, Threat Analysis Division, Ethic Substudies, by Analyst Fifth Rank Grishnak, 2915; ammend:

. . . further operations in the eastern-hemisphere islands are contra-indicated until substantial forces can be spared from the Citadel-Shangri-La sectors. While disorganized, the cattle communities are very numerous, due to the high productivity of their aquaculture; and the continuous inter-state warfare maintains a very high degree of military preparedness. Recent probing actions indicate that the cattle kingdom known as *Scandia* (for related groups see *Norskuna, Dannarik*) will serve as a satisfactory buffer against the more active elements, with an occasional punitive expedition to prevent excessive concentration of forces. . . .

AEGIR'S CHILDREN

Phillip Pournelle

The sea rocked *T.M.S. Duty* and sang to Midshipman Scott Brindle as he swayed in his hammock, accompanied by the gentle creak of timbers and a splash of breaking water at *Duty*'s bow. The slippered feet of sailors slapped across the ship's deck as they moved to the deck officer's commands, trimming sails and hauling on lines. The cat padded her way through the stores hunting for rats. The canvas sails boomed and cracked from the final remnant of one of Haven's all too common storms.

Scott heard Petty Officer Goodmark walk up to his post: he had the gait of an old enlisted seaman, as natural and unaffected as Cat's Eye's eternal stare. Goodmark rang the bell as he always did, one double ring followed by another.

AEgir, Sea King, protect me! Scott thought. No one had called him, and he was an hour late for his watch! He washed and then struggled to dress, hopping on one leg as the ship came about and the deck sloped. He put on his coat, pausing to inspect the two bronze anchors on his collar—they would need shining tonight if he was going to eat in the wardroom—and rushed up the ladder to his post. The sextant was in his hands by the time Lieutenant Tryker spotted him and walked over.

"Have a good night's sleep, Midshipman Brindle?" Scott blushed. "Sir, forgive me."

"You wore yourself out last watch during the storm. I allowed you an extra hour of sleep—I'll need you wide awake today. Here, eat this and don't bother the cook."

Lieutenant Tryker had been Scott's guide and teacher since he arrived aboard the *Duty* almost three months ago. The transition from the Academy's theories to the dangerous reality of Haven seas was tough, but Scott had survived—in part because of Lieutenant Tryker's tutelage. Scott wondered if he would ever become the officer Tryker saw in him. He hoped so.

While handing the youth the batter-covered sandwich, Tryker gazed over the foggy sea. "There are strange corsairs we're after today, Midshipman. The attack at Stanjord was too professional a job for our local brigands. Get a fix on our position, then report to me."

Using a sextant wasn't hard to do on Haven, once one learned how Cat's Eye behaved and how to use her other moons to help find the ship's location. The trick was to do it quickly, and Scott felt sweat break out on his brow as he struggled with the instrument.

"Sail off the starboard bow!" the lookout cried from the crow's nest. "Looks like the ship's launch."

The catamaran had been launched late last watch to search for corsairs. As she sailed into closer view Scott recognized Coxswain Jorwin's muscular frame. Manipulating his sail and rudder like an accomplished juggler, Jorwin cut speed and came alongside *Duty* as cleanly as a 'dactyl might land on the ship's rail.

The captain, Lieutenant Commander Lloyd, was on the quarterdeck receiving reports from his lieutenants. Scott joined the coxswain and handed Lieutenant Tryker his notes.

"I spotted a schooner ten nautical miles east of here making way north east," the coxswain said. "She took damage from the storm last night and was only traveling at two or three knots. Her rigging was poor but I recognized her as the pirate *Shining Pearl*."

"Are you sure she's the corsair?" the captain asked the leather-faced coxswain.

"Aye, sir. She sails with the same crew but she flies new colors, a red eye."

"Did she spot you?"

"I saw no sign of such, sir, and I took great care to avoid silhouetting my sail."

"Thank you, Coxswain. Go below and get something to eat. Then make sure to report your findings to the watch officer for the log."

"Aye, aye, sir."

The skipper was already writing in his log as he called out orders to the first officer. "Load the catamaran and alert the crew. Have Lieutenant Harper prepare his Marines, and set course of northeast under full sail. Mr. Tryker?"

"Aye, sir?"

"You and Mr. Brindle will prepare the ship's rifles for combat."

"Aye, aye, sir."

"Mr. Barnswith, please prepare your gunners. See that they do their usual best."

The captain's orders were still ringing out when Scott reached his battle station. With a small division of sailors, he inspected the ship's rifles, making sure they were not fouled and otherwise ready for combat. The rifles were twenty millimeter-rifled cannons mounted on the rails of the frigate and used mainly to assist boarding operations.

Opening the breach of one rifle, Scott inspected the chamber and the barrel and then turned to the gun captain.

"This barrel is wet from the storm. Clean it and report when you are ready."

"Aye, aye," the sailor answered, his face an unreadable mask.

The midshipman moved on to the next rifle and prepared his crew for combat. Lieutenant Tryker would doubtless check his work prior to action, but that was no reason to be less careful; quite the opposite.

All hands were at general quarters as the frigate approached the schooner; a tense silence filled the ship, broken only as the boatswain relayed orders to the men in the rigging. *Shining Pearl* was running slowly, as if searching for other ships. When the *Duty* came close enough to be seen through the early morning fog, Scott heard horns from the schooner. When the *Duty* failed to answer, the schooner sounded her bells, and a bustle on deck revealed that she was clearing for action.

Soon both ships were at full sail, their deck crews laboring to keep sails perfectly trained in the cat and mouse duel that was playing itself out in Haven's wild winds. The storm from the night before had not blown itself out and another would likely be along soon. Haven's slow rotation rate created severe weather patterns that kept all but the bravest (or most desperate) from going down to the sea in ships.

Duty was the faster ship. *Shining Pearl* moved sluggishly, as though battle damaged or badly fouled, but she was hard to approach as she dipped into the deep swells and came up again.

At the moment, Scott noted, the captain had the *Duty* on a broad beam tack. The executive officer was working with the boatswain on the relative motion board, using precious paper to compute the most efficient path to close the gap with the other ship. The captain shouted leather-lunged orders to trim the sail.

"Heave, heave, heave!" Sailmaster Saulin called to the deck crew. "You men aloft, retrain the mainsail. Make ready to come about!"

The sailing master had spotted the other ship doing likewise and wanted to keep pace with them. He could do no more without orders, of course.

"Prepare to come about!" the executive officer called.

The rest of the deck crew hurried to clear the rigging as the sails were readied for a new wind angle.

"Hoist the trap sail!" Chief Saulin ordered.

Men and rigging groaned as the large triangular sail was brought up to where another crew of men aloft could train it into place. At the same time, yet another crew rolled up the mail sail and tied it in its overhead rolls. The near perfection with which this evolution was accomplished allowed *Duty* to quickly gain several more meters on her prey.

The frigate was now quickly approaching the smaller and slower schooner. The corsairs never cared for their ships as well the Navy did; now—and not for the first time—they would pay the price.

When *Duty* was within twenty minutes of overhauling the smaller craft, the captain luffed the mainsail slightly; he did not want to give the schooner's gunners the opportunity for a broadside.

As *Duty* daintily closed the remaining gap, Scott borrowed Lieutenant Tryker's glass to study the target. The colors stood out over her stern as the wind whipped it around. The burning eye was now brightly visible against the gunmetal sky. The design was disturbingly familiar. Where in his studies had he run across it before?

Before he had time to remember, the captain interrupted his train of thought: "I need the ship intact. Her colors are new to our waters, so make every effort to capture her skipper alive." He then spoke directly to the Marine officers who would lead the boarding party.

Assault Group Leader Protonus studied the enemy's colors. With his enhanced vision Protonus could easily make out the iron cross with its companion crowns of silver and gold underlined by a harpoon. Another Nordic tribe, he decided, plying the waters with delusions of grandeur.

The Sauron turned and ran an experienced eye over the Soldiers assembled on the top deck, frowning slightly at the sickly green tinge to many complexions. Any one of them on land was worth twenty of the cattle that crewed the ship, but his men were ill at ease with *Shining Pearl*'s motion. Last night's storm had convinced him that Saurons really had no business on the sea. The corsairs claimed his people did not have the blessings of AEgir, for they had not paid him his due respects.

Protonus spat as he thought about the disgusting customs of these cattle. *If only we knew how to conquer the sea, we wouldn't have to be carted around by these parasites.* Then he reviewed the magnitude of the diversion of resources necessary to accomplish that task and dismissed the matter from his thoughts as he had so many times before. Besides, as long as they were kept unaware of the reality of Sauron power, the seagoing cattle who pursued them provided—all unknowingly—a great service to the Race. Not that that mattered just now. . . .

"Wait till they're in range. On my command shoot their officers and Marines. They do not have enough men to take this ship against us."

Protonus gave out individual instructions to his sharpshooters, including the placement of the Gatling gun. Two squads of Saurons was more than enough to handle whatever Marines and sailors were on the pursuing ship. Patting the mastiff that had been so useful to him in controlling the female cattle, he snapped the cylinder of his revolver open to check the rounds.

He was ready, his Soldiers were ready. These wild cattle would soon get their first taste of Sauron steel.

The frigate quickly closed to cannon range and fired—only a couple of rounds—aiming for the schooner's rigging: the captain wanted to create confusion, not destroy the ship. The corsair answered the shots, but its fire went wide—a hazard of sailing with unrifled cannon.

As her rigging fell, the *Shining Pearl* coasted to a dead stop in the water. The skipper took the frigate in, being careful not to place her within good firing range of the schooner.

Scott ordered a full powder charge loaded into each gun's chamber, setting up the ship's rifles for maximum range. He aimed one gun at the *Pearl*'s quarterdeck and stood by for Lieutenant Tryker's command.

Suddenly small-arms fire from the deck of the *Pearl* struck out with deadly accuracy from a range Scott would have thought impossible. In a matter of moments an officer and six sailors went down, as Marines scrambled for cover before the next volley could strike. Through the crackle of another volley he heard Tryker's voice cry "fire."

Mustering his men as best he could, Scott returned fire with the ship's rifles. He was helping reload when a sailor beside him fell from a shot to the throat, blood spraying in a wide fan. The enemy might not have rifled cannon, but their small arms were surely impressive—and the men wielding them were as good as their weapons. Better. *Much* better.

Scott sprinted across the cluttered deck for the ship's magazine. A shot cracked past his head and set his ears ringing. He dove into the mess deck, down the companion way. Wood hammered at him, and his head rang as it bounced off a railing.

Momentarily stunned, he was helped up by the Master-at-Arms. Tomorrow, if he lived to see it, all the flesh on his left side would be one big bruise.

Snarling past the Master-at-Arms' remarks about who was abandoning his post, Scott ducked into the passageway that led into the magazine. There was no way the frigate could take the enemy ship without eliminating her Marines first. He had to admit it: their own men were no match for the enemy's sharpshooters. Attempting to board the schooner without first silencing its small arms would be nothing but suicide. *We need to overcome their advantage with one of our own,* he decided.

Scott quickly located the brightly colored box he was searching for and carried it up to the main deck. He turned and passed several of the burnweed rockets to the Master-at-Arms who had followed him out of the hold. "Take these to Lieutenant Tryker."

Meanwhile, he slid the box across the deck to a gunner's mate and dove after it. The crew instinctively loaded the rockets into their guns, and fired when Lieutenant Tryker gave the order.

The rockets burst out of their barrels with a bang and a cloud of smoke, arching for the schooner. Three hit the smaller ship's deck and exploded, releasing an orange gas. The results were immediate as the *Pearl* was swept by an orange fog of death. Small-arms fire sputtered within seconds. Scott could hear the crew coughing and hacking, mixed with the occasional thud of sailors falling from the riggings and smashing into the deck. Only the gunfire from the topsails continued.

The captain's voice rang out. "Gunners. Load cannons five and three with grape and rocksalt. Clear the rigging!"

As the gunners loaded and *Duty* closed in, Scott

saw a very large corsair heading for what appeared to be a bomb.

He couldn't make it out through the thinning orange fog and stood frozen for a moment wondering what or how the man was moving in gas strong enough to bring down a charging bull.

Then he shook his head, realizing it didn't matter. All that mattered was stopping that man. He turned to the swivel gun, saw that it was primed, gazed down its sights and fired. The twenty millimeter round smacked into the giant and sent him flying off his feet. Then for a second it looked as though he was going to use the mast to pull himself upright, but the giant shuddered and stopped moving.

Scott released a deep breath he hadn't even known he was holding. *They're not human*, he thought. *Nobody should be able to even move a muscle after a twenty millimeter hit*. It was at that moment Scott realized they were fighting the ancient invaders, the sons of giants.

His people had long known the story of the Saurons, the warriors from the stars; they still sang the old ballads and when sufficiently drunk searched the night sky for their ships in the University towers late at night. Fortunately, they had never met—the Citadel, the legendary capital of the Saurons, was half a continent away—until *now*. Now, when *Duty* was fighting a Sauron pirate ship.

"Captain, we are fighting Saurons!" Scott shouted without thinking.

A noticeable chill swept the crew like a wave rippling after Scott's voice; Saurons, the bogeymen of parents' warnings and children's late-night yarns. The captain's voice, as steady as the *Duty's* course, rang out, "Very well."

Mindful of the ship's morale and how important it could be in the fight ahead, Scott regretted blurting out his thoughts. But there was no time to think about that now; another lesson learned.

The *Duty* came in awkwardly, and it took grappling lines to bring the two ships together. The Marines went across first, wearing lacquered filter masks, although the burnweed gas was now mostly blown away by the strong breeze. Sporadic fights occurred whenever the Marines discovered a Sauron, who even in near-death spasms fought like five men.

Lieutenant Tryker and Scott went aboard with their sailors to back up the Marines. Armed with swords and revolvers, they dispatched the surviving corsairs who'd survived the gas long enough to cough up their lungs on the deck.

"Be careful," said Lieutenant Tryker. "The lower decks should be mostly intact. Be on the lookout for more Saurons."

Some of the older men cursed, others drew back from the hatch.

Leading the six survivors of his gunny crew, Scott approached the hatch under the cover of Marine rifles. A harsh growl brought his attention to the rear. He spun around, drawing his sword, to find a giant mastiff charging down upon him. While several rifles fired without stopping the charging mastiff, a Sauron burst out of the hatch and gutted a sailor with a boathook.

Lieutenant Harper's constant drilling and training took over, as Scott went into an automatic crouch and brought his sword to bear. Wishing he had a trident instead, Scott leveled his sword at where he expected the mastiff's jaws to strike.

The giant dog leaped and Scott felt bone splinter as his sword pierced the mastiff's mouth. The beast died, but not before its momentum wrenched the sword out of his hand and its body slammed into Scott, knocking his head against the mast.

All Scott remembered of the next several minutes was the vague impression of shots fired and mortal cries. When at last he tried to rise a petty officer leaned over and hauled him upright while anxiously informing him that the captain was about to board. Scott could hardly stand upright in the roll of the ship; his mind thick with concussion and the soles of his shoes slick with the blood that washed out over the deck.

While Lieutenant Harper informed the captain that the *Shining Pearl* was secured for Their Majesties, Scott caught his breath and tried to locate the missing members of his gunny crew.

With the last of the Saurons dispatched, they searched the rest of the schooner and opened the holds to inventory. Her cargo: grain (and plenty of it), cooking wood, a store of wine, and about thirty women. Their expressions ran the gamut from fear and rage to apathy. None seemed hopeful.

The captain turned to Scott, who, having somewhat recovered, had thrown himself into the work. "Well done, Midshipman Brindle, especially for the burn-weed." The captain paused for a moment, looking bleakly over the aft rail.

"Lieutenant Tryker is dead."

Scott shook his head in dismay. "I didn't know . . ."

"He distinguished himself and his family with honor. As did all my officers in this engagement; alas, I am short of officers due to this unprecedented resistance. As of now you are promoted to the rank of ensign. You will act as executive officer of the prize *Shining Pearl*.

"Mr. Campbell will skipper the prize. Your first task, Ensign, is to interview the prisoners. Report to me at the evening meal of your progress.

"Mr. Brindle, will you take these responsibilities?"

"Aye, aye, sir."

Breedmaster Brehman had always disliked the sea, but after last night's storm he hated it. His small fleet of hired ships was scattered and his prize ships lost. The only ships remaining were the two he needed most, the brig *Hunting's Tomb* and his flagship, the newly named *Proteus*. The brig held the captured professors, and in the flagship's hold was the prize he had sailed almost halfway around the planet for.

It was hard to believe now that Saurons had once conquered a wet realm like this on the Home World. Unfortunately, the records of those days were long lost.

Brehman was known for traveling far for what he sought. Each time a Sauron center reported a new civilization or the legends of a university or library, the Breedmaster marched off to find it, categorize it, and take its knowledge, books, scholars, and women back to the Citadel.

Few of the Soldiers other than the upper Ranks and other Breedmasters, understood why. Those few realized just how far Sauron technology had fallen since the arrival of the *Fomoria* and the Invasion. The constant warfare among Sauron and Haveners had resulted in many Soldiers and far too few engineers and teachers. The few remaining computers were scattered throughout Sauron bases or cannibalized to keep the others working. All computer time, except for that needed by the Breedmasters and the First Soldier, was dedicated to defense and battle-threat estimations.

The Saurons needed those few Haven scientists who had survived the dark ages and what few tools remained. Almost as important was the need for intelligent female breeding stock. The stress of everyday life on Haven was such that Haveners were bred for military and survival skills rather than intellectual abilities.

During every generation since the Invasion the Saurons had lost a sliver of their technical edge. Brehman's dream was to resurrect the weapon makers of the Home World.

Now he had found a nucleus for that dream: the steam turbines in his hold and the men who had built them. All that was left was to collect his ships and get out of these waters. He would have liked to disembark and return by land, but the mass of the steam turbines precluded this. Ahead his party faced a long journey, including the rounding of Firga's Point, then across the Harph, the southern ocean, and across the Main Continent to the southernmost Sauron base, Champlon.

He wrapped his cloak tight against the icy winds as he watched an orca surface and blow steam into the frigid air. Brehman recalled how the killer whales worked together like wolves in a pack. Despite the orcas' intelligence, strength, and killer instinct, they were vulnerable as individuals. As a pack there was nothing that could stand up to them, not even here in Haven's deadly seas. He saluted them as he would any Sauron brother and turned back to his rankers. . . .

The *Pearl* was badly damaged from the battle. Not only were sails in tatters from the storm, but the burnweed destroyed them wherever it had come in contact with the sails' fabric. Nor had the *Duty*'s grapeshot done them any good. He already had his small crew repairing both sails and rigging, as well as some of the damage done to the hull. Any Royal Navy man could sew sailcloth or reeve a rope; most had learned it from their fishermen fathers before enlisting. The few boards that *Duty* could spare were already being put to good purpose by the ship's carpenter and his assistant.

The sounds of sawing and hammering and the creaking of rigging as it was repaired was like music to his ears. Despite the sense of loss he felt toward his former friends and crewmates, the *Pearl* was his to command. And he couldn't deny the exhilaration that brought to him.

A squeal from one of the female prisoners brought

him back to more mundane concerns. It was already clear that most of them saw the Scandians as little better than their former Sauron captors.

"Miss Lockman," he said in his most commanding tone, "please cooperate with the surgeon. You will not be molested."

"Why are we being examined like this? With no privacy, nor any concern for modesty. Are we cattle to be sold at the next harbor? Or do you plan to use us for breeding as the Saurons had planned?"

"The *Shining Pearl* is now Their Majesties' ship and she is to be conducted as a man-of-war. The decks still contain patches of burnweed and are not safe until completely cleared. The physical examinations are to make certain that none of you have any diseases that could be passed on to our crewmen.

"Of course, you won't be sold as slaves! You are now provisional subjects of Their Majesties' Triumvirate and will be introduced by the Huguenotic Order. They will assist you in acclimating into our civilization—now that your own island has been burned of human habitation."

Less afraid but far from mollified, she continued to press: "What kind of life will that be for a woman?"

"I'm sure most of you will find husbands," Scott answered in a matter-of-fact tone, to hide his own growing interest in the beautiful and brave young lady.

She looked as if she'd just bit into something sour. "What if I told you I was educated as an engineer?"

"Most surprising, Miss Lockman. Those few women scholars in the Triumvirate are in the monastic orders and content themselves with the classics." Scott saw a flush of anger creep across her cheeks. It did not make her less attractive.

"What if I told you I helped build the steam turbines?"

Scott felt his jaw drop, and closed it with a click. His limited experience in engineering classes had taught him the importance of the turbine and even the basic principles behind it. Its military and economic value were obvious, but the Triumvirate's engineers had never been able to manufacture one; the precision machining was beyond the Kingdom's reach. The steam piston was extensively used on shore and aboard larger ships, but such devices could not be made small enough for use aboard frigates.

Collecting his wits, Scott asked, "Where is it now?"

"On the Sauron flagship."

"Where are the other engineers?"

"Does this mean you believe me?" she asked.

"Yes. Your people at Stanjord were extremely capable gadgeteers. Where are the male engineers?"

"You people are overbearing sexist bigots!"

Scott felt his own face flush. He realized that once again he'd asked the wrong question; yet it was difficult to accept that this young girl could achieve success where the Triumvirate's best men had failed. Why he himself had failed the mathematical section of the engineering school's entrance examination! *Time for another approach.*

"Miss Lockman, you've lost your home, family, and friends to the Saurons. We all sympathize with your plight. We want to help you: Wouldn't your people rather be under our guidance than the Sauron heel?"

Scott could see her intransigence begin to soften, but he was too inexperienced to know how to exploit it. Nor did he know what to present as evidence of the Kingdom's good intentions aside from hospitality.

But shouldn't that be enough? *Damn her beautiful eyes!*

When it became obvious that she wasn't going to answer he decided on a tactical withdrawal. Turning to the orderly, he said, "Tell the coxswain to prepare a boat to ferry Miss Lockman and me to the *Duty.*" Turning back to his lovely passenger who *persisted* in thinking of herself as a prisoner, he muttered, "Excuse me," and fled.

While waiting for the ship's boat, Scott reviewed the crew's progress in refitting the *Pearl*. The job was going well, but much work remained. Some of the sails were being replaced and the decks were covered with canvas and spare materials. The women who had inhaled trace amounts of the burnweed were resting on the quarterdeck.

Scott shook off a feeling that he was personally responsible for their fate. True, had they known the nature of the *Pearl*'s cargo they would never have used the gas—but they had *not* known, and his men had been dying all around him.

Unfortunately, some of them would not survive the voyage back to New Wales. There was no known cure for blister pneumonia.

After relaying to Lieutenant Campbell what he had learned, Scott sent for Miss Lockman and they were rowed to the frigate.

Several things had convinced Scott that these people were capable of building a turbine. Their teeth were surprisingly well maintained and their clothes were not hand spun. All of them wore manufactured clothes, and not just the upperclass ladies either. Lieutenant Tryker had shown him an account gathered from far traders sailing these waters that reported Stanjordian machined items were generally *at least* as good as those from New Wales.

He also noted that a few of the women, including Miss Lockman, had the hands of skilled laborers, hardened from tool use, not chapped from household chores or gnarled from fieldwork.

It was also obvious that Miss Lockman was not used to the sea. She had apparently adapted to life aboard the *Pearl*, but the *swoop* of the small boat undid her, and she was soon bent over the side paying tribute to the sea gods. Well, the ride *was* rough; the storm from the first watch was threatening to return. Fortunately, the coxswain and his men did their usual quick job of the crossing, and within minutes he was hoisted up into the *Duty*'s quarterdeck and speaking to the captain.

As soon as Lloyd understood what Scott was saying, he invited him to his cabin, leaving Miss Lockman to the delighted care of the quarterdeck officers.

"So the Stanjordians made a steam turbine, which the Saurons captured along with the engineers who designed and built it," said Captain Lloyd. "Saurons in our waters—who would have believed it? No one's seen a Sauron in the Triumvirate since the Invasion. And now you say the Saurons are headed back to their base."

"Aye, sir," Scott replied. "Miss Lockman told me the Saurons put the turbine on their flagship and the engineers and professors on a ship I suspect to be a brig by her description."

"How certain are you that this machine is truly a turbine?" the captain asked with a penetrating stare.

"I questioned Miss Lockman on the turbine based on my knowledge of the steam cycle. It quickly became a lecture in which I was the student."

"Then you believe this engine to be valuable enough for me to chase a small fleet into enemy waters?"

"Yes, sir."

"Well, you're quite correct. And where do you think these ships are headed?"

"There's really only one place, given their heading."

"Right again, Ensign."

The captain sent Coxswain Jorwin to inform the Commodore of his plans and to ask for ships to meet *Duty* at Shark's Teeth Bay. The pirates traditionally used the island's fortress and shallow bay to slip away from deeper draft ships.

The captain quickly had them under full sail. Scott noted that even with the schooner's sails repaired, with which she should easily have been able to show a frigate her heels, the *Shining Pearl* was no faster than the *Duty*.

Foul bottom, he thought, looking over the rail. Sure enough, a skirt of weed below the waterline. How could the crew of a fighting vessel bear to have their ship so crippled? It made Scott queasy to look at it.

The prize crew of the *Pearl* soon relaxed back into cruising watches, each man on duty for six hours, on collateral duties for the next six-hours and then sleeping through the third watch. It was a schedule they had followed most of their adult lives. It let every man obtain eight hours' sleep per Terran day and allowed the ship to have two thirds of her crew ready at any given time. Not only did the watch system mesh well with the variable Haven days and nights, but ships were able to keep their men fit by feeding them at the beginning or end of every watch.

"The pirates never kept the *Pearl* so clean," Patricia Lockman said to Scott, who had joined her for the midday meal. She looked down at the bowl an able seaman handed her. "Nor did they serve as much variety in their meals, either."

Scott laughed. "A busy crew is a happy crew. We feed them with all the variety we can—not for their enjoyment, though never underestimate morale—but to avoid scurvy and other diseases that would keep them from serving Their Majesties' needs."

"I might have known it wasn't for their enjoyment," Patricia said. "Do you shoot them if they break a leg?" she added dryly.

"Of course not—" he began, then flushed. "Excuse me. It's my watch in ten minutes. Thank you for sharing your meal with me."

Scott's watch went quietly and he was able to spot the dorsal fins of a pair of orcas riding the ship's bow wake. He was always surprised at how the whales welcomed human companionship. He wondered if it was because they recognized that both species were far from home on a world where survival was more an opportunity than a certainty.

The Scandian legends said that the nine daughters of AEgir had spawned orcas to be man's brothers in the sea. The *Imperial Encyclopedia* had a reference about their having been brought, along with thousands of other sea creatures, from Terra by a biologist. The orcas, along with squids and eels, were among the minority of those who survived the battle against Haven's indigenous sea life and frigid waters.

Religious taboos among the Scandia prevented them from killing the orcas for oil. Instead they turned to the south and traded with the Yakuts for blubber from the snow lions.

It was during moments like this, while watching AEgir's children dance in the sea, that Scott truly felt AEgir's presence. Sailors held that AEgir ruled this wet realm in God's stead, protecting the good while his wife used her nets to catch the unwary or the unlucky or the careless. All the while his nine daughters would bear and keep watch over all his ferocious grandchildren.

Many of the officers were devout Christian Huguenots, but no sailor could spend his life on these treacherous waters without believing in AEgir and his evil wife. Sailors on Haven needed a *personal* god they could speak with; one who would provide solace against the awesome powers of the sea.

The Huguenotic Council would like to pronounce the sailors pagans, he thought. They had never pressed the point as long as the admiralty was willing to make them pray to God at mass. Wisely the Council treated the sailor's devotion to AEgir as if it were some childish superstition that one truly believed. While officers were indoctrinated into being devout Huguenots in low school by the monastic order, many found a new faith in AEgir after their first real storm.

Scott was explaining all this to a skeptical Miss Lockman in the *Pearl*'s wardroom when he was interrupted by a messenger. He felt a flash of irritation: it had been pleasant to have her attention. . . .

"Gentlemen," the rating said with barely repressed excitement, "the lookout has spotted several masts on the horizon."

Mr. Campbell nodded. "Keep sail for Shark's Teeth. We should be about twenty nautical miles away. Order the signal men to inform *Duty*. Mr. Harper, prepare your Marines below and see that the men we selected are on the main deck with the lights lowered. Distribute the Sauron weapons to those men. Mr. Brindle, make sure that the correct signal is sent to the enemy ship and have Miss Lockman tell you which ships hold what items. Then pass on a silent call to general quarters."

In the fading light of the Haven sunset the crew busily prepared for the rendezvous with the Sauron cargo ship; the beautiful sunset was wasted on them. Patricia Lockman had time to enjoy the brief respite before the coming storm of battle.

As she gazed out at the horizon and saw the silhouetted enemy ships, Patricia realized it was the same image her people had seen just before the Sauron attack. The ferocity and deliberate violence of the attack had taken her island by surprise. The resistance of the Voortrekker mercenaries was smashed within minutes. Also surprising was the restraint the Saurons had shown after their victory and the ease with which they had turned brilliant men mindless with fear.

Now these new actors in the same deadly play were preparing to bring those men back and save their work. Would the end result be much different for her people? She thought not. The Scandians might use

different semantics and act more politely, but in the
end her people were finished. Only a few fishermen
and farmers would roam the hallways of the University
now.

Yet, these fair-haired Scandians were not all bad.
Patricia felt something akin to remorse as she listened
to the sailors sing their Scandian battle songs. She
worried, too, for the young man next to her, who tried
to fill a new role as officer and to hide the fear all
sane men felt in the face of battle. Like a clumsy
puppy, he had wormed his way into her affections;
not that she could let him know that—not now, when
he would make more out of it than she could afford
to allow.

Her new life had started with her capture by the
Saurons. The University had been sacked, the town
burned, her family dead or in hiding, her people
enslaved or scattered. These Scandians offered a new
home, but she wasn't sure there was a place for her—
a woman who knew her own mind. It had been hard
enough for her to attain her position even in liberal
Stanjord. Certainly, this was no time to let herself
become involved with a man who accepted his society's view that women were mere chattel.

No, she would hold her emotions in check as she
had done most of her life. Maybe her knowledge and
mind would purchase the freedom and respect she
deserved.

The largest of the Scandian sailors, wearing Sauron
uniforms, strode about the *Pearl*'s main deck posing
as the enemy; only their sea legs gave them away, but
hopefully the enemy would not notice. Not even a
direct order could make a Triumvirate sailor walk like
a lubber. Meanwhile, the *Pearl* signaled to *Duty* with
bull's-eye lanterns in the stern.

As they entered Shark's Tooth Bay, Patricia Lockman pointed to a brig with green dragons emblazoned

on its sails. "That's the ship that took our scholars and engineers! I remember those sails."

Scott thanked her for her help and ordered the seamen to escort her below deck. Meanwhile, *T.M.S. Duty* lurked at the horizon's edge awaiting a signal rocket from the *Pearl* to bring her hurtling down.

It was well into the third watch by the time they drew abreast of the brig. Many of the sailors were now dressed as raggedly as the corsairs had been.

Scott used the horn to signal the *Pearl*'s "need" to come alongside the brig, whose name—the *Green Dragon*—could clearly be seen. It appeared that the small Sauron fleet had not fared much better than the *Pearl* during the recent storm. All five ships, two of which were being towed, were just entering the bay. Mr. Campbell positioned his prize ship to come in off the port side of the *Green Dragon,* placing it to the far side of the other entering ships, which included a small frigate.

As far as Breedmaster Brehman was concerned, the schooner *Shining Pearl* justified her name the moment she hove into view. He had thought her lost, and with her the best of the breeders, and—almost as importantly—a major part of the grain and gunpowder that were vital to the return voyage. Brehman had not relished the prospect of lingering in these waters after his business was done merely to replenish supplies; some of the local cattle were entirely too adept at warfare.

Now perhaps this expedition would be able to return to the Citadel some of the fruits he had promised the First Soldier and the members of the War Council. With the *Pearl* he now had six of his original ten ships, and while two needed repairs, including masts, none were serious enough that they couldn't be completed by the end of the next Truenight.

Soon his fleet would be safe behind the bay's appro-
priately named reefs and the island fortress' guns.

*Those merchants who had so gladly taken our gold
had better be there as well,* he thought grimly. While
all had been warned of the penalties of double-
crossing a Sauron officer, they also knew they were
half a world away from the heart of Sauron power, the
Citadel. Unfortunately, here Sauron might was more
legend than reality. Brehman fully intended to turn
that around.

The Breedmaster lifted a spyglass to his eye and
examined the schooner; she appeared to be in relatively good shape. His Soldiers were on deck and the
cattle were in the riggings. He watched as the *Pearl*
approached, sailing to the opposite side of the *Green
Dragon*. Something about the schooner made him
uneasy; he began to search the ship for anything out
of place.

Lines were being readied for casting and there was
nothing obviously out of place or character. The cattle
appeared to be the brigand's usual disheveled crew.
Yet, something still struck him as wrong.

Why are they sailing for the brig? he asked himself.

Suddenly it dawned on him. The schooner's crew
was too disciplined. The sails, while still showing signs
of recent damage, were placed with too much care,
and the men worked them with Sauron diligence
rather than the desultory manner typical of most brig-
and crews. As the schooner's path drew it closer,
another definitive fact pressed itself upon his consciousness. Those were not his Saurons!

The *Green Dragon*'s watch made only a cursory
check of the *Pearl* when she signaled to come alongside. Lines had already been cast and were being set
when an alarm rang out from the flagship. Marines
and Saurons came storming out of the holds of both
ships. The Scandia Marines were out because they

were no longer lying in wait, the Saurons because of their native speed; they seemed to have only one pace—a run.

The fight was fast and vicious. The Marines worked their bolt-action rifles as quickly as possible; those in hiding had already killed one and wounded two of the half-squad of Saurons that had bolted out of the hold. A Sauron Gatling gun rattled and several sailors dropped from the rigging.

Scott quickly lit the fuse on the green-colored rocket, firing it straight into the air. Its signal charge blew with a bright green flash that the captain could easily spot.

Meanwhile, the orders Scott had given the gunner's mates were being carried out. Two openings cut in the aft castle were uncovered, and two of the guns brought over from the *Duty*'s blew apart the Sauron Gatling gun, killing one Sauron and knocking another to the deck.

Although a third were dead and half the rest were wounded, the Sauron's rapid fire was decimating the *Pearl*'s crew. Half a dozen sailors, two Marines, and a gunner's mate dropped before the gun crews could reload with grapeshot. He watched in horror as a well-aimed Sauron shot took out the back of Lieutenant Harper's head.

I'm in charge! What do I do now? Calm down, breathe slowly. He quickly regained his equilibrium. He nodded when the remaining gunner's mate told him the guns were primed and loaded.

"Fire!" Scott shouted.

A living wave of metal cleared the *Green Dragon*'s main deck of Saurons and corsairs. The Marine sharpshooter in the crow's nest quickly dispatched the only Sauron who made it as far as the hatch with a shot to the head.

There was still return fire from the *Dragon*'s rigging, but her blood-stained deck was littered with the dead and the dying. The Marines fired at anything moving on the deck and in the rigging. Scott noted that almost half of his original command was either dead or severely wounded. He wished he could have used the burnweed like last time, but the captain had forbidden it for fear of injuring the professors and engineers in the *Dragon's* hold.

Now having seen Saurons in close action Scott doubted they would have won the first round without the element of surprise. He looked up at a sailor's shout to see the Sauron flagship steering directly for the *Pearl*. He felt as if a black cloud had just dropped over him, and struggled to lift it. He remembered one of Lieutenant Tryker's maxims: "Action, any action, is preferable to inaction."

Scott took out his spyglass and scanned the horizon for *Duty*. The frigate was closing with the Sauron flagship, but it was too soon to tell whether it would be in time to save the *Pearl* from a devastating broadside. Regardless, it was his duty to secure the *Green Dragon* and arrange the transfer of prisoners onto his ship.

As Scott put his spyglass down he noted with satisfaction that the other Sauron ships were quickly fleeing the bay; one had even gone so far as to cut a derelict adrift.

Scott put himself and the surviving Marine lieutenant in charge of the boarding parties. There were still shots ringing out despite the carnage on the *Dragon's* deck, so Scott ordered the guns, now mounted on the *Pearl's* rails, and grenades from the Marines to silence all enemy fire.

The deck of the *Dragon* was quickly turned into an inferno of smoke, flying splinters and shrapnel. When all enemy fire had ceased, Scott—under covering fire from the captured enemy Gatling guns—ordered his crew to board the *Green Dragon*. Using boarding planks that had been concealed in the fallen rigging, the Scandians spanned the water between them and the brig.

One of the Marines slipped and fell into the frothing sea, only to disappear in a red vortex as river jacks attracted by the battle's blood fed.

The remaining Marines rushed the main deck, while Scott led the crew's riflemen to take the quarterdeck. The wreckage and carnage was belied when a Sauron rose out of a pile of dead bodies and hacked two men instantly to death with a cutlass. Scott, with his pistol, and two riflemen, shot the Sauron a dozen times before he fell back to the deck unmoving. One of the sailors quickly bent over and sliced his throat with a flaying knife, and was quickly joined by the others who did the same to any Sauron body they encountered.

The Marines found a sniper in the rigging and poured rifle fire into his position. The enemy fought with chilling ferocity, holding their positions until blown to ribbons. Scott wondered how long they would survive against the Sauron flagship if the *Duty* did not arrive on time. Well, they *wouldn't*. Best hope the *Duty* made a timely appearance.

Though Scott was unaware, *Duty* had already saved them.

Breedmaster Brehman was furious. The Saurons were at great risk in this new medium of warfare. They needed sailors of their own. Brehman decided he would take the best of the pirate captains and mates for teachers back at Rajamann Base.

Now as his flagship approached the battling ships, a mate called out, "Sail ahoy!" Brehman looked up to see a large frigate flying the colors of iron, silver, and gold heading straight for the flagship. Though it was still a distance off, Brehman quickly ordered a change of course. "Head into the bay," he told the captain. "They will attempt to board us. We must protect the turbine at all costs. Soldiers to arms!"

*   *   *

Gaining entrance to the brig's hold was slow and difficult. It appeared that while half the Sauron squad had fought on deck, the other half remained below. The Saurons waited in the lower compartments where only two or three men could enter at a time. The Scandians didn't dare use grenades for fear of killing the scholars in the hold, or damaging the hull. Fortunately, the Saurons—for reasons of their own—held to the same course.

Scott would have liked to have locked down the lower decks until the *Duty* came to assist, but the captain's orders had been clear. They were to free the prisoners lest the Saurons in desperation or revenge killed them before the Scandians could release them from the hold.

Sword in his right hand and revolver in his left, Scott led a detachment of sailors into the lower decks. Below the decks the sailors were reduced to pistols, cutlasses, and hand axes. The small party entered the crew's mess deck ready for anything, or so they thought. Suddenly the room exploded, Saurons coming in from everywhere. Before he had time to think, Scott was parrying an axe blow with his sword while being backed into a bulkhead. He would have died there had a sailor not sliced the Sauron's forearm to the bone with his cutlass. This diversion gave Scott time enough to aim his revolver and fire into the Sauron's face.

Even at point-blank range, it took three rounds to kill the giant Sauron and three sailors to pull him off the young officer. While dying, the Sauron killed the sailor who had saved Scott, smashing the man's ribs with a blow from his slashed arm. Wounded men screamed; the Saurons died as they fought, in eerie silence.

Scott picked himself up to find out that a third of his men were dead or wounded; yet only two Saurons,

both slashed almost beyond recognition, were accounted
for. Before he had time to digest the implications of
this, a loud explosion and a crash of timbers sounded
from the brig's galley where the Marines had gone.
Immediately, another wave of Saurons barreled into
the cabin. The survivors of Scott's boarding party
threw up tables and chairs as a makeshift barricade,
while two Marines entered from another corridor firing shotguns at the wave of steel-and-iron-hard flesh
charging them.

A Sauron lost a hand, stared at the stump for a
moment; as Scott watched, the bleeding stopped, and
the Soldier returned to the fight without changing
expression. The heavy iron-copper smell of blood filled
the room below the powder reek.

The three Saurons, including the one-armed Soldier, were up and over the small barricade before
Scott heard the second blast of shotgun fire. One
Sauron head disappeared in an explosion of red, but
the other two slammed into the Scandian defenders.

His sword broken and his revolver long empty and
forgotten, Scott fumbled for a boat hook one dead
sailor had used as an improvised spear. He brought
the boat hook to bear on the one-armed Sauron; the
Sauron used a broken axe handle to knock the boat
hook away, almost wrenching Scott's arms out of their
sockets in the process.

Unharmed, the Sauron rose up—shaking off a sail-
or's pistol shot—to crush Scott. Scott set the base of
the boat hook in the joint of the deck and bulkhead
and waited for the crushing charge. The Sauron, who
up close appeared to have lost one side of his face as
well as an arm, impaled himself on the boat hook.
Only by AEgir's grace did the shaft hold his great
weight. Scott tried to roll to the left, but the hook was
torn out of his hands as the Sauron smashed Scott into
the deck.

Trapped as he was, Scott could not avoid the Sauron's iron hands as they clasped his neck. As the world began to blacken, Scott hazily saw a Marine strike the Sauron with a hand axe. . . .

Scott woke up groggily to learn they had taken the brig, although there were several Saurons still loose under battened hatches in the lower decks. According to the captain they would stay there until the ship reached port; Scott saw no reason to disagree. Not when he had barely enough able seamen to sail the *Pearl*. Of the original thirty-two man prize crew, only seven—including Scott—were fit for active duty.

Of the Sauron dead they could account for only four bodies; although Scott himself could swear to having seen three times that number killed or mortally wounded. He was now convinced they would have never taken the ship had there been a full squad; it was only the Saurons' unfamiliarity with sea warfare that had given them their own limited successes. It appeared there was more truth than fiction to the old legends.

When Scott reached the quarterdeck, he could see the Sauron flagship playing a game of cat and mouse with *Duty* in and out and behind the volcanic rocks that gave the bay its name. He watched as the flagship tried to lure the *Duty* within range of the island's batteries, mindful of the fact they were both of the same draft.

A number of ships had foundered or wrecked themselves upon the uncharted rocks and shallows of Shark's Tooth Bay during its infamous history. The river jacks and sea dragons who dwelled in its waters made certain that few survivors of the many shipwrecks ever made it to shore. It was a safe haven only to the foolhardy and the criminal.

Scott watched through the ship's most powerful spyglass as the two frigates closed. Captain Lloyd had forced the Sauron flagship close enough to the shallows that the pirate ship had almost no room to maneuver. Shots were fired from the pirate fortress at the top of the cliffs, but their range was well short of the *Duty*, and at this point fell dangerously close to the Sauron ship. The firing stopped when a ball punctured one of the flagship's sails.

The last thing Breedmaster Brehman had expected was the enemy to fire on *his* ship, with its valuable cargo. But being a Sauron his adaptation to a new situation was virtually instantaneous. As soon as the first round hit he ordered his own Soldiers to supervise preparation of the launch.

While the deck rocked and lurched under the first enemy broadside, Brehman gathered his drawings and the ship's captain's charts. Before the flagship had time to turn and return its own salvo, the ship was slammed with another broadside. The air was filled with sailors' screams and the burp of the Sauron Gatling guns.

Brehman was knocked off his feet for a moment when the ship foundered on a reef. He was halfway to the launch when another broadside shook the dying ship. Brehman had to dodge falling spars and rigging as the mainmast slowly began to topple.

As his men lowered the boat into the water, Brehman could see the water bubble as sea dragons and river jacks feasted on those who fell or were knocked overboard. Just as the launch reached the water, a final broadside of pyrotechnic rounds crashed into the doomed ship.

The charges exploded, spewing burning oil saturated with iron rust everywhere. The primitive thermite burned everything on the wooden ship it touched. Within moments the riggings began to fall to the deck like ghosts burning in the wind.

Brehman heard screams and shouts as the sailors fled the flames only to discover there was no place to go. Fire was the nemesis of all ships; on Haven the sea offered no escape. Fire lit the ship like a torch.

As the launch began to pull away from the doomed ship, sailors tried to jump aboard. "Fire at will!" ordered Brehman. If they could make it to shore, there would be fresh crews to be hired. He couldn't take a chance of capsizing the launch or attracting the sea dragons.

The sea dragons were six-limbed spiral sea creatures superficially not unlike the starfish of old Terra. However, the sea dragon had an armored exoskeleton, and at the end of each retractable limb it had claws that injected poisons to paralyze its victims. Full grown, it weighed about a ton, and was hideously dangerous when it weighed a tenth of that.

Even the orcas left the shallow bays of the sea dragon alone.

One sailor actually managed a leap into the boat only to have a Soldier toss him casually into the sea. The pirate captain pleaded with Brehman to spare his loyal servant. Brehman's answer was a gunshot through the man's forehead; his next shot took the captain's life. A loyal servant deserved a painless death if he was not worth saving.

Brehman considered his options as the launch began to work its way ashore. He had the drawings of the turbine, but not the engine itself or the men who designed it. He had the charts to get home, but not the ships to sail there. The task ahead was great, but if they survived, the Burning Eye would soon have a new weapon and a worthy adversary to use it against.

"Our work! You destroyed everything we spent our lives to create!" Scott turned from the burning and floundering Sauron flagship to confront a distraught Patricia Lockman.

"We could never have recovered the turbine from the Saurons." Scott pointed to better than a dozen canvass-shrouded bodies on the *Pearl*'s deck. The screams of the wounded below decks still rent the air. "This was the cost to save the *Sea Dragon*'s prisoners. Would you rather have the Saurons sail off with it?"

"No . . . but it took a generation to plan and build those turbines. It's our legacy—"

"No. It's the minds that matter. We have the scholars who designed it and the engineers who built it here. The turbines can be built again."

"Are we to be slaves, then?"

"No. Allies in the war against the Saurons. You will have places among us. Not as slaves, but as Citizens of the Triumvirate."

From "The Frontal Assault and Other Tactical Pathologies," in *The Way of the Soldier* (traditionally attributed to First Lady/Second Citizen Althene Diettinger):

The ancient Sauron role model Nietzsche said: "Beware if you fight dragons, lest you become one. And if you stare into the Abyss, the Abyss may open its eyes and stare back into *you*."

We have anticipated that as we struggle to subdue Haven, its peoples will learn as they fight, taking on as far as they are capable our methods, our philosophies of combat, even as many of our genes as they can garner. This is an integral part of our Plan, the Plan which will eventually bring forth the Haven Saurons and a reborn Homeworld.

However, a long-term problem is that this process is potentially capable of functioning *either way* . . .

CEREMONIES AT THE LAST BAR IN THE VILLAGE

John Hartnett

Byers' Sun was a distant dry teardrop sinking into the grassy brown hills at the western end of the Pale. A grove of Finnegan's fig trees was silhouetted against the sinking orb. The older officer sat on the terrace on a gray birch chair, drinking warm coffee from a small cup. Chief Assault Leader Saval swallowed his drink slowly and let the cool rays of the setting sun wash the days from his face.

The younger officer stepped through the dark archway and out onto the terrace. He stood against the wall with one boot on the empty chair. He wore field gray covered with a sheepskin cape.

"I was told that I'd find you here," said the young man.

"And so I am. I am here often in the evenings. As you will be," said Chief Assault Leader Saval.

"Is this really the last bar in the village?"

"Yes. The others are gone."

The waiter, a tribesman, probably a Turk, came. Chief Assault Leader Dagor ordered *kimiz*.

"That's a native drink, isn't it?" asked Saval.

"Yes. It's quite strong, rich."

168

"I prefer coffee. It's not as good as Angband Base, but they try. You're here only one day, but already you drink like a native," said the older man.

Angband Base seemed a long way south of the cold steppe grasses.

"You cannot conquer what you don't understand."

"Do you think that was my downfall?"

"No. There were other problems."

"You think I do not understand them."

"You don't drink *kimiz*," said the young man.

"I think I understand."

"I think you don't."

"My successes on this expedition have been noted."

"You can't fight from reflex here. It needs cunning. You cannot win the steppes from a Citadel textbook."

"I am not a barbarian."

"Too civilized to win their respect, then?"

"Yes. I am civilized."

The waiter came with cold *kimiz*. Chief Assault Leader Dagor stood, stepped to the edge of the old terrace, and cradled the fermented milk between his strong hands. He looked out at the village street. The low buildings were boarded. A Turkish laundry was still open at the end of the row. Soldiers' uniforms filled the racks inside the laundry. The sun nearly set behind the trees.

Twelve kilometers to the west, Dagor's men filled the bush. Crouching. Hiding. Waiting for the word.

"You don't fight like a Soldier," said Saval.

Dagor brought his drink to his lips, then inhaled the rich fumes. He took a drink.

"I've had my own successes."

"Ah, yes. Your *special training*."

"I fight. The enemy fights. I win."

"Is it winning to fight like a savage, yelping from the back of a muskylope?"

"I adapt. As you should have."

"Will you fight like them? Like the clans?"

"I will do whatever I have to." Dagor blinked. "It is as honorable to win as to fight well."

"Do you think you can? Do you think you can keep order out here, or even turn the clans against the Bandari?"

"I will do what's necessary. It'll be tough. Your men will have to be retrained. They won't like me at first."

"I thought you would say that."

Chief Assault Leader Dagor sat in the empty chair. He fixed his bright eyes into the sad blue eyes of the older man. Even without Sauron enhancement, he thought he could read what was there.

"Do you want a ceremony before you leave?" he asked Saval.

"No."

The young man sat back in his chair, his jaw clenched. The scar under his left eye twitched, then calmed.

"I thought you would want a ceremony," said Dagor.

"No."

"You needn't be embarrassed. You had some successes."

Saval looked away, over the plains.

"Half the expedition is gone, buried."

"Your concern is noted. You accomplished part of your mission. The ground was taken."

"Yes, taken. And filled with our bodies."

"Still, you can have a ceremony if you wish."

"No. It's too much."

"I know how important it is to you. You may pass a sword to me if you wish. Sometimes it helps . . . it helps the men. Formalizes things."

"No. They will understand."

"I'm surprised. I was told you'd want a ceremony."

"Perhaps we should have a ceremony. For the men."

Chief Assault Leader Saval finished his coffee. He

thought of his camp out to the west. He thought of
the neat rows of tents, the perfectly placed sentries.
Why was it so much easier to lose good Troopers than
to win respect from these tribes? Soon his men would
batter their old commander around the campfires.
They would play double-Jack and talk of how it was.
Later they would see Dagor's replacements approach.
Dagor's new men, some with Citadel water still wet
behind their ears, would march in column into their
new camp. March in to fill the gaps in the expedition-
ary force. Gaps caused by an unimaginative commander who refused to think like the cattle, to be like
the cattle.

Or perhaps not. Dagor was different. Like the clans
who had to be taught to surrender. He accepted nothing as given. Did Dagor always expect difficulties?

"You cannot leave without a ceremony," the young
man interrupted.

"I know."

"Without your sword, the nomads will never respect
me. They would fight me to the death."

"I was told."

"You need a ceremony. You have to pass me your
sword. The word must reach the *kabiles*."

"It is foolishness."

"Without your sword, I'll lose half the unit again.
We must have a ceremony."

"I do not want a ceremony. I cannot return to
Angband."

"Give it up, man! It's no disgrace. You gave up your
old post to lead this expedition. It's the same thing.
Pass the damn sword and forget about it."

"It's not the same."

"No one's going to rub your nose in it. If you don't
do it, if you sulk off back to Angband, or worse all
the way to the Citadel, everyone will know what the
cattle did to you. They'll draw their own conclusions.

You'll never get another posting. If you leave with a ceremony, it's just another change of command."

"I do not want a ceremony."

"You're quite sure?"

"Yes."

Dagor rose and paced back to the far end of the terrace. His sturdy boots echoed through the quiet evening's glow. Truenight would arrive in several hours. With the night came the noises, the danger, the uncertainty. Soon Dagor's men would teach their new comrades to hunt the plains at twilight when the cattle's eyes failed them. They would teach the other men how to hug the cool night earth of Haven like a whore. They would show them how to glide along the floor of their world, drop death on the enemy, then leave Bandari tracks behind.

"It could have been worse," the young man said. "The men were well equipped. That always helps."

"Don't, don't patronize me."

"I wasn't . . ."

"There's something else," the old man offered. Dagor turned. He stepped toward Saval.

"What is it?"

The older man hesitated. "A girl. Badri."

"Ah. I heard about her."

"She was given in tribute, this season. She's . . . exceptional. She has no one."

"No. I'm not like that."

"Someone told me the clans expect it."

"Yes, they do. But, no. I'm a Soldier."

"She won't understand. Neither will they."

"I have a countryside to subdue."

"She cannot go back, or have I misunderstood?"

"No. That's right, but, no."

"She knows the land, knows the peoples and their ways."

"I have my own scouts, and the new ones I'll train."

"When I go, she can't come with me. I have other . . . commitments."

"She can't stay here."

"She . . . she saved me."

"That's different. What did she do?"

"She is exceptional. She gives . . . confidence."

"I am already confident."

"She also gives compassion, understanding. Besides, you have no choice. I insist," said Saval.

"Insist." Dagor shrugged.

Chief Assault Leader Saval stood. He tugged at the corner of his Soldier's uniform. He brought his hand to his belt. "I want her at the ceremony."

"Ceremony?" The young officer cocked his head.

Slowly and deliberately, "Not regulation. Tribesman. Pass the sword, pass the prize. They understand that, I think. Will you accept the pair?"

Chief Assault Leader Dagor called out in Turkish. The waiter returned. Several of the clansmen around the laundry heard and took note of the young stranger on the terrace with the Sauron *kummandan* who was supposed to leave soon. They bowed just a little, keeping their eyes on the four men with weapons crouching around the last bar in the village. The men with weapons were dressed in capes like the stranger. They stood, slung their weapons on their shoulders, and came out into the open to join the two officers as they stepped off the terrace and headed to the west.

One of the men with weapons brought a box to his mouth, touched a button, and spoke a single syllable. Elsewhere, Dagor's men in the bush rose, slung their weapons, and organized a column to march into their new camp.

From *The Book of Ruth bat Boaz*, traditional. (Preserved in oral form from approximately 2630. Translated into Bandarit and printed, c. 2800, Strang, Eden Valley. Anthologized in *Sayings of the Judges*, 2910, Ilona'sstaad, Eden Valley.):

. . . Piet van Reenan was the wisest man I ever knew, and the saddest. In his last illness, he told me that the final irony of his life was that he, a historian—for that was how he thought of himself, not as a soldier or ruler—had outlived history. I asked him if our story would not be preserved for the generations yet to come; surely our wars and our wanderings, griefs and loves, the peace we made and the people we brought to being, all this would live? Yes, he said; but not as history, because history was the product of civilization. When the Saurons came, Haven stepped out of history, into the time of legends. It was as myths, archetypes, legends that we would be remembered, not as human beings. Our children and children's children would live once more through the endless turnings of the great cycle of myths. . . .

Traditionally recited at the Spring Festival
before the Great Sacrifice to the
Anima of the Founders

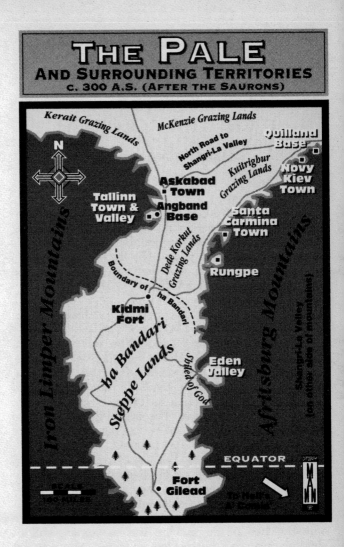

JUCHI THE ACCURSED

Harry Turtledove

Something moved, out on the steppe. The Sauron Soldier sentry came to watchful alertness, discarding like an unwanted cloak the boredom that is a sentry's normal lot in time of peace. His fingers caressed the trigger of the Gatling gun that covered part of the approach to Shangri-La Valley.

Even with his enhanced vision, the moving speck was only that, a speck. He used his left hand to raise binoculars to his eyes. The speck resolved itself into a pair of human figures, afoot. The sentry frowned, actively suspicious now. Haven's nomads were universally mounted, on horses or camels if they had them, on native muskylopes if they did not. *Dismounted nomad* was a contradiction in terms.

The two people slowly approached the entrance to the valley. One appeared to be leading the other. The sentry forgot them for the moment. By themselves, they had to be harmless. But if they were intended to distract him so raiders could attack the mouth of the cleft that led into the valley, they would fail. The Soldiers laughed at sneakier ploys than that.

At last, reluctantly, the sentry decided there were only the two of them. One was a woman, still of childbearing years but no longer young. She was not visibly pregnant, either, so there went the most obvious reason for her coming to the valley. The other, the man she was leading, had gray hair and a white, wispy beard that blew in the cold breeze. He walked awkwardly; the sentry needed a moment more to realize he was blind. Not only did his eyes stay closed, the lids seemed sunken into their sockets, as if no eyeballs lay beneath them.

For all his genetic modification, the sentry felt ice walk up his spine. The tale was from half a continent away, but it was not the sort that shrank in the telling; over a generation's time it had come to Shangri-La Valley. Unlike most folk on Haven, Sauron Soldiers were not supposed to be superstitious. All the same, the sentry jerked his hand away from the Gatling as if it had suddenly become red-hot. That blind man had known worse than bullets. Shivering and doing his best to blame it on the weather, the sentry let the woman lead the man into the pass.

Dirt and clumpy grass underfoot, by their irregular pressure against the soles of his boots and by the sound they made as he scuffed through them. More sounds came from either side: echoes from the nearby canyon walls. "Careful here," his daughter said; her hand on his arm was his sole link to a world wider than what he could feel and hear. "The slope gets ever steeper. Don't stumble."

"I shan't, Aisha, unless I trip," Juchi said. He heard the futile pride in his voice. He carried Sauron blood. His senses, those he still had, were swift and keen.

Automatically, he cocked his head for a better look at the terrain over which he'd pass. Futile again; his ruined eyes gave back only blackness, as they had since the day he took his own sight with his dead wife's brooch. "Where are we now?" he asked.

"Halfway through the cleft," Aisha answered. "The

Citadel sits above us on the rocks, armed and armored like a tamerlane."

Juchi sighed, long and slow. "I never dreamed I would see it." He laughed harshly, at himself. Like the head-cocking gesture, the word remained, half a lifetime after his eyes were gone. He sighed again. "I've wandered farther than ever I dreamed I would back in the days when I rode with Dede Korkut's clan. And what did it gain me in the end?"

"Great glory," his daughter answered stoutly. "Who but you ever drove the Saurons from one of their lairs, made a whole valley free of them?"

"A greater curse," Juchi said. "Who but I lay afterwards with the woman who proved my mother as well as Sauron chieftain's lady; who but I bred children—bred you, dearest daughter—who were also my sibs? How can I atone for such sin, make myself free of it? Blinding did no good; my mind sees still. For all the long years since, I have sought relief. If I do not find it here, I fear it may never come. Allah will spit on my soul and the spirits blow it round Haven forevermore."

Aisha said, "You have borne it, where a lesser man would have fled into death."

Juchi's laugh held nothing of humor. "That is your fault more than mine. Had you not come after me out to the steppe, come as I forbade you to do, death would have found me soon enough. Many time, oh, how many times, I've wished it had."

"No." Aisha had been a stubborn child; that had changed not at all since she grew to womanhood. She went on, "Allah and the spirits must have had reason for twisting your life as they did. Before its end, they will grant that you know that reason."

"Then they'd best hurry," Juchi said. "I cannot see my beard, but I know it is the color of snow. I need not see to know how my bones ache, how my heart pounds, how my lungs burn with every step I take.

Soon I will die whether you let me or no, daughter of mine."

"That is why we have come at last to Shangri-La Valley. Here sit the Saurons in their power, the Saurons but for whom your curse would never had arisen. By the god, by the spirits, I will see that you have justice from them before the end. If they do not give it to you, I will take it from them myself." Aisha spit on the trail to show her contempt for the overlords of Haven.

"What do they know of justice?" Juchi said. "They know only force. And why not? It has served them well over the years. And their blood is ours as well, to me through the father I slew; to you, poor child, through me."

"I am no child," Aisha said wearily; how many times had they argued this round and round? "And I do not willingly claim their blood, while you, father, you struck a great blow against it."

"You may not claim the blood, but the blood will claim you," Juchi said. Aisha did not answer, not in words. The pressure of her hand on his arm changed; she was moving forward again. Juchi followed. From the breeze that blew into his face, he tried to scent out what lay ahead in the valley.

With every step he took, the air seemed to grow thicker. That, he knew, was his imagination, but the Shangri-La Valley was far and away the greatest lowland Haven boasted. Women came from hundreds of kilometers around to bear their babies here; the steppe tribes paid the Saurons a steep price for the privilege, in goods and in women.

The breeze brought the fresh, green scents of growing crops. By Haven's standards, the climate of the Shangri-La Valley was tropical; a man from the Terra now long lost in legend would have judged it no worse than austere. It was mild enough to let wheat survive. In the Tallinn Valley that Juchi had once ruled, oats and rye were the staple crops. Of course, the Tallinn Valley could have been dropped anywhere here without being noticed as it fell.

The breeze also carried the odors characteristic of man, and man in large numbers: smoke and sweat (the amount of labor required to wrest a living from even the most salubrious parts of Haven was plenty to raise sweat even in the moon's icy climate) and ordure. Falkenberg and Catell City and Hell's A-Comin' had been cities once, before the Saurons smote them from the sky. Towns still stood not far from where the bombs had landed.

Another, newer town lay close to the inner mouth of the valley. Nûrnen had grown up to serve the Citadel, the Saurons' greatest center on Haven. After more than three hundred T-years as masters of the moon, the Saurons were not averse to such luxuries as it could provide them. Further, the more work the humans they contemptuously called cattle did for them, the less they had to do for themselves and the more they could remain fighting machines. That suited them. Thus Nûrnen throve.

"Take me into Nûrnen," Juchi said suddenly.

Aisha stopped. "Why do you want to go there? Of all the towns on Haven, Nûrnen loves the Saurons best."

"Just so," Juchi said. "Through all the long years since they came, simply hating them has not availed. They are too strong, and their strength repels hatred as armor will turn a sword stroke. Those who love them may know where they are truly weak."

The noise Aisha made, deep down in her throat, did not betoken agreement. But she led Juchi into Nûrnen all the same. She had guided him for more than twenty T-years now. When he gave her a destination, she got him there. Whatever she thought of the life she led, she never complained.

"I've given you a long, empty time, my daughter," Juchi said.

"You did not give it to me; I chose it for myself," Aisha answered. "And how could I have found a better one? Who would have taken me into house or yurt, bearing the burden of ill-luck I carry?"

"Through me, all through me. You could have left me behind, left your name and birth behind, gone off and lived among folk who knew nothing of your misfortune."

"You tried that, father, growing up as you did among the steppe tribes after you were rescued from Angband Base's exposure grounds. Yet your name and birth returned to work your fate. Why do you think it would have been different for me?"

To that, Juchi had no good answer. Allah and the spirits accomplished a man's fate as they would, not so as to delight him. The best he could hope to do was bear up under it with courage.

Soon after the narrow canyon opened out into Shangri-La Valley, Aisha stopped to pick a couple of clownfruit from a tree. She gave one to Juchi. As he bit into it, the mixture of sweet and tart brought to mind a perfect mental picture of the red-and-white fruit. Even after so long without eyes, he knew what things looked like.

Before long, they entered Nûrnen. The clamor of busy streets surrounded Juchi: men and women afoot and on horseback, wagons with squealing wheels, the rhythmic footfalls of litter-bearers. "Turn here," Aisha said. "This is a tavern."

The blast of heat from the door, the noise inside, and the smell of beer and tennis-fruit brandy had already told Juchi as much. The noise faded a little while the drinkers sized up Aisha and him when they stepped inside. A moment later, it picked up again: they were judged harmless, at least at first glance.

Juchi almost smiled at that. He'd worked more harm than any tavern tough could aspire to.

"Here is a stool," Aisha said. Juchi felt for it with his hand, sat down. Someone approached the table— a barmaid, by the rustle of skirts. "What'll it be, sir, lady?" she asked, her voice losing some of its professional good cheer as she got a look at Juchi's face.

"Kavass," Juchi said. He'd learned to like fermented mare's milk among the nomads who raised him.

"Beer for me." Aisha had grown up in Tallinn Valley, and had the taste of a farmer. "And a roast chicken for the two of us to share."

"I'll bring your drinks right away. The chicken will take just a little while—we're cooking three of them now, and they should be done soon." The barmaid hesitated, then said, "Maybe you'd better show me your money first, since by the look of you, you're new in town."

Aisha fumbled in the pouch she wore at her belt. A moment later, silver rang sweetly on the tabletop. "Will that do?" she asked.

"Oh, yes, ma'am." The barmaid retreated in a hurry. She came back very quickly, set a mug of beer in front of Aisha and a skin of kavass before Juchi. He tasted it, made a sour face. Town taverns had a habit of serving a thin, weak brew, and this one was no exception.

Someone new came up to the table: a man, and no lightweight, either, not from his stride. "The taverner," Aisha whispered to Juchi. She raised her voice to speak to the man: "How may we help you, good sir?"

"I'd talk to your companion, if I could," the fellow said. Hearing Aisha use Russki, he answered in the same language, though his voice had a shrill Americ accent: the Saurons spoke Americ among themselves, and Juchi had heard it more than any other tongue on the streets of Nûrnen. Americ made him nervous.

It was the language Badri had known best, Badri his mother, Badri his wife—

He pulled his mind back to the blackness of here and now, away from the image of Badri's face that burned always behind his eyes. "I will speak with you, good sir. Ask what you would."

That openness made the taverner hem and haw, and Juchi had never heard of a bashful taverner. He knew what was coming: "Forgive me if I offend, graybeard, but there are tales that stick to an old blind man who travels with a woman younger than he is."

"I am the man of whom those tales tell," Juchi answered calmly, as he had many times before. The tavern went deathly still. Juchi's shoulders moved up and down in a silent sigh. That had happened many times, too.

The taverner gulped, loud enough for Juchi to have heard even without his genetically augmented ears. Legends, by their very nature, dealt with the long ago and far away. To have one sitting at a table had to disconcert the taverner. He needed close to half a minute to gather himself after that gulp. At last he said, "I don't want your trade here. I ask you politely to leave in quiet and peace."

"Our silver is as good as anyone else's," Aisha said hotly. She took slights harder than Juchi, who felt he deserved them. The legs of her stool bumped on the rough planks of the floor as she started to get up so she could argue with the taverner face to face.

Juchi set a hand on her arm to stop her. "Wait, daughter." He turned his ruined face toward the taverner. The man gulped again. Juchi kept his voice mild: "Tell me, sir, if you would, why you want me— want us—to leave."

"Because— Because—" The taverner stopped, took a deep breath, tried once more: "Because you are who you are, curse it, and because you did what you did. And because Nûrnen is a town that depends on the

Soldiers and their goodwill. They'd not think kindly of me if I let you stay."

"Those are fair reasons," Juchi said. "We will go." Aisha started to protest further. He shook his head at her. "Come, lead me away. I would not stay where I am not welcome. Is it any wonder, then, that I have wandered all through these many years?"

"Everywhere you travel, folk treat you unjustly," Aisha said.

"No, only with horror, and horror I have earned. Now let us go."

As Aisha led Juchi toward the door, a man at a table he passed said, "And good riddance to you, too, mother-fucker." He laughed at his own wit.

Juchi reached out, effortlessly lifted the man with one hand. The fellow squawked and kicked at him. Juchi felt the muscle shift, heard the whisper of cloth against moving flesh. His body twisted to one side before the booted foot arrived.

"Mother-fucker!" the man yelled again. His hand slapped against the hilt of his knife. At effectively the same instant, Juchi's hand closed on his wrist. Juchi squeezed and twisted. Bones crunched. The man screamed. Juchi threw him away. He smashed against something hard. Juchi stood in a warrior's crouch, waiting to hear if he got up. He did not.

"Horror I have earned. I grant this," Juchi said. "The contempt of such a dog I have not earned. Come, Aisha; lead me away from this place where I am not welcome."

He reached out his hand for hers. She took it, guided him toward the doorway. Behind him, someone said softly, "More Soldier blood in him than in most Soldiers, by the saints. Check on Strong Sven, somebody—see if he'll ever get up again."

"Let him lie there," someone else answered. "He picked on a blind man; he deserves what he got. Maybe he'll keep his stupid mouth shut next time."

Slightly warmed at that, Juchi followed Aisha down
the street. He listened, tried to learn. Nûrnen was
indeed a town on good terms with the Saurons. The
best indicator of that was how seldom he heard the
term. Like the taverner and the other man in his
establishment, most people called them Soldiers, their
own name for themselves. Juchi did not care one way
or the other. Just as he was what he was, they were
what they were, and names did not matter.

"Most names," he amended out loud. Aisha made
a questioning noise. "Never mind," he told her. He
could still feel the quick, precise motions his muscles
had made as he chastised the foul-mouthed fool. The
memory would stay with him. That was his trouble,
he thought. He was blind, but the memories stayed
with him.

Soldiers lined up for a meal at the Citadel refectory.
It was first come, first served, regardless of rank. If a
simple Section Leader took his place in line before a
Chief Assault Group Leader, he was served before
him, too. The Soldiers did not make distinctions
among themselves where distinctions were unnecessary.

Glorund was no simple Section Leader. Nor was he
merely a Chief Assault Group Leader. Nevertheless,
the Battlemaster took his tray and waited for his turn
with everyone else. Once a young officer, an Assault
Group Leader with, everyone said, a promising future
ahead, had stood aside for him. The fellow was a
blank-collar-tab Soldier within half a cycle, and bound
for duty on the most barren part of the steppe Glor-
und could find. After that, no one curried favor with
him in the refectory line.

The refectory workers who slapped food onto the
tray were from Nûrnen. Soldiers did not need to cook;
therefore, they did not cook. The food was unexcit-
ing—stewed heartfruit, a meatloaf made from ground
mutton and muskylope, a chunk of rye bread, a mug

of beer. It was nourishing, though. And Glorund, like lower-ranking Soldiers, was no gourmet. No geneticist had ever found a good enough reason to bother amplifying the sense of taste.

Glorund's ears, however, were not only genetically modified but also had the bioengineered implants that accompanied the cyborg death's-heads on his collar tabs. He heard, and listened to, every conversation in the refectory. Differential signal processing let him pay attention to each of them in turn at not quite the same time. That was useful; even people who knew intellectually what he could do sometimes made interesting slips if the refectory was crowded.

"The blind man's come into the valley," he heard a Soldier who'd been on sentry-go say. His modifications did not literally let his ears prick up, but he willed into being the mental analog of that primitive physical process. If he heard the word *blind* again, he would key on it, correlate it with this first mention.

To Glorund, to all the high-ranking Soldiers of the Citadel, there was only one blind man, the one responsible for the loss of Angband Base and Tallinn Valley. Not for the first time, he thought the Citadel should have mounted a punitive expedition, no matter that Angband Base lay far, far to the west. Cattle should never be allowed to get the notion that they could beat Soldiers. So often in combat, what men believed counted for as much as what was true.

But more cautious heads had prevailed back then: Soldiers who had argued that an attack on Tallinn Valley would draw in the Bandari of Eden Valley. And in the end Juchi had destroyed himself more thoroughly than any mere outsiders could have destroyed him. The lesson Soldiers found most difficult to learn was that abrupt, straightforward aggression was not always the best solution to a problem.

"—blind man smashed him against a table, broke three of his ribs."

Glorund hadn't been consciously following that conversational track; the gossip of other ranks seldom held much of value. Now he replayed it, and learned of the bar fight in Nûrnen. Haven was a tough, unforgiving place; few handicapped folk could survive here. Fewer still could hope to win a fight against a sighted foe. Even for Juchi, that did not seem likely, not so many years after his fall. For anyone else, though, it seemed impossible.

Glorund kept eating. His metabolism was augmented, too, to power his implants. He needed twice the calories of an ordinary Soldier, or three times those of an unmodified man. No matter what he decided to do, he had to fuel up first, as if he were a river pirate's steamboat taking on wood before it sailed.

When he was done, he rose from his bench, stacked his tray, and left the refectory. He did not even pause to draw weapons: what need for them, against the old blind man he sought? He did stop a moment at the Citadel's outer gate, to record a message that he was going into Nûrnen for a while. He needed no one's authorization to proceed; Soldiers, and especially cyborgs, were supposed to use their initiative. "Each man his own army" had always been their motto.

Nûrnen was a dozen kilometers from the Citadel, down the pass and out its throat: a couple of hours' walk for an unmodified man, half an hour's run for the finest unmodified athlete. Glorund got there in less than twenty minutes, and was not breathing hard when he arrived. He paused to button his greatcoat just outside of town, to hide his collar tabs. That a cyborg was in Nûrnen would have raced through the place as quickly as word of Juchi's presence had got back to the Citadel. Sooner or later it would get around anyhow, but better later than sooner.

He needed to ask fewer questions than an ordinary man would have. He simply strolled through the

streets as if window shopping and let his enhanced
ears do his work for him. He kept keying on *blind*.
By the time he'd heard it three times, he knew in
which tavern Juchi had had his fight. He paused on
the way to buy a couple of barbecued lamb ribs. When
he was done with them, he tossed the gnawed bones
into the street. There they lay; he hadn't left enough
meat on them to interest scavengers.

The taverner bowed low as he came in; any Soldier
automatically expected that much deference in Nûrnen, and was likely to turn a place inside out if he
didn't get it. "Clownfruit brandy," Glorund said.

A barmaid fetched it for him. She was pretty. He
watched her appreciatively. He had a wife back in the
Citadel, but any Soldier who earned cyborg status was
supposed to disseminate his genes as widely as he
could. *Maybe another time,* Glorund thought with
mild regret. He'd come into Nûrnen for a purpose
more important if less enjoyable than spreading a barmaid's legs.

He had another shot of brandy, ordered bread and
cheese to go with it. "You eat like a land gator," the
barmaid said as she watched him methodically demol-
ish the meal. She meant it as a compliment; on Haven,
being able to put away large amounts of food in a
hurry was a survival characteristic.

Glorund smiled back at her, thinking that perhaps
he would bed her after all. That, too, was a genetic
imperative. But no. First things first. He stretched and
yawned, a good impression of a man who felt lazy and
loose. "Hear you had a strange sort of brawl in here
not so long ago," he remarked casually.

That was all the prompting she needed; if she was
as eager to screw as she was to talk, he thought, she
might well wear him out, cyborg Soldier though he
was. "We sure did," she said. "Blind man—Ivan over
there"—she pointed to the taverner—"says he's Juchi
the Accursed—whaled the stuffing out of Strong Sven.

Everybody in town knows Strong Sven, and nobody wants to quarrel with him. He has a good bit of Soldier blood in him, or so they say."

"Half the people of Nûrnen have some Soldier blood in them," Glorund said. All the same, word of who Juchi's opponent had been startled him. A T-year before, Strong Sven had fought a Soldier to a standstill. The Soldier was no prize, genetically speaking, but he hadn't been left out for stobor, either. So Strong Sven unquestionably was of mixed blood. And what did that say about Juchi?

Ivan the taverner spoke up: "I wouldn't let Juchi stay here, not after he admitted who he was. I like the Soldiers, I do, and I want naught to do with anyone who fought and hurt your folk." He puffed out his chest in righteous—and possibly even sincere—indignation. As he deflated, his right hand moved in a sign the people of Shangri-La Valley had learned from the steppe nomads. He went on, "Besides, I didn't want his ill-luck rubbing off on my place."

"Where would he have gone, then?" Glorund asked. As long as the cattle were so forthcoming, he would pump them for all they were worth (just for an instant, his thoughts went back to the barmaid).

She was the one who answered: "When they went out the door, they turned left, going south through town. Maybe they were trying to get a place to rest, but who would give them one, knowing what they were?"

It was a good question. Glorund knew not all the town of Nûrnen was as pleased with the Soldiers and their constant presence as Ivan professed to be. Still, though, Nûrnen depended on the Citadel for its livelihood. Few townsfolk would risk their overlords' wrath for the sake of a couple of wanderers.

The Battlemaster threw down a silver coin with the shark shape of the *Dol Guldur*—the ship that had brought the Soldiers to Haven—stamped on one side

and the old Americ motto KILL 'EM ALL AND LET GOD
SORT 'EM OUT on the other. Coppers jingled as Ivan
started to make change. "Keep it," Glorund said.
"You've helped me."

He went out into the street, glanced up at the sky.
Byers' Sun stood almost at the zenith; Cat's Eye was
low in the east: second cycle, third day noon, more or
less. Another thirty-five hours of daylight, at any rate.
Sleeping patterns on Haven tended to the peculiar.
Some people catnapped when they felt like it, regardless of where—or whether—Byers' Sun and Cat's Eye
were in the sky. Some tried to keep a rhythm of long
stretches of awareness and long sleeps.

Soldiers, for their part, usually went without sleep
as long at they could, then slept hard for ten hours or
so. Glorund had to think of Juchi as a Soldier. Likely
he and the woman would not have settled down to
rest, not here in a town where so many people had
reason to despise them, but would have pushed on
into the valley. If they did stop to sleep, it would be
away from people.

Working through the logic took but a moment. As
soon as he saw the end of the chain, Glorund went
into a Soldier's trot. Like a broken-field runner, he
dodged round the people and carts crowding Nûrnen
streets. Some Soldiers got into trouble when they tried
moving quickly in town—they forgot that people
would seek to dodge out of their way, and sometimes
zigged into them when they should have zagged away.

Glorund was a cyborg. He made no such stupid
mistakes. He saw a kilometer and a half of street as a
single unit, plotted his course through it with accuracy
and finesse. His processing equipment and reaction
time let him treat the journey as a series of freeze-
frames, with the men, women, horses, and muskylopes
essentially motionless as he moved past them.

Soon he was past the southern limits of the town.
He slowed, examined the dirt surface of the road with

care. He knew the shoes a man from Nûrnen or another valley town was likely to wear, knew also the boot styles of the local nomads and, of course, of his fellow Soldiers. All those, save to some degree the nomads', he mentally eliminated; his eyes literally took no notice of them. That disposed of more than eighty percent of his possibles; the rest he studied more closely. He did not need long to settle on two pairs of prints as most likely to belong to Juchi and his guide.

One of those sets of prints was a good deal smaller than the other. Since Juchi's guide was known to be a woman, that alone made those two pairs a decent bet to be the ones he sought. Legend said she was his daughter, his sister, or both at once, but Glorund, with resolute cyborg rationality, discounted legend. Data counted for more, and data he had: the smaller set of feet—the ones he'd tentatively identified as belonging to Juchi's companion—took firm if short strides. The other set of prints, the ones from the larger feet, was scuffed and dragged along through the dirt, very much as if the person who made those tracks could not see where he was going.

Glorund grinned a carnivore grin. He resumed his effortless Soldier's trot. Now to see to revenge for Angband Base. It would be late revenge, and minimal, but not to be discarded on account of that. Word of how Juchi met his end would also become legend, legend that would grow and make fear of Soldiers grow with it. Glorund's grin stretched wider.

Unlike an unaugumented tracker, the Battlemaster did not have to slow to keep track of his quarry's trail. Now he simply screened from his vision centers all footprints in the road save the two pairs he sought. Sometimes cyborgs made mistakes by programming themselves to ignore data that later proved important. Glorund did not think he was making a mistake, not here.

As he ran on, the trail grew fresher. He was not taken by surprise when Juchi and the woman with him left the road to head for the shelter of an apple orchard not far away. He mentally checked his weaponry. He had a knife—and he had himself. That was plenty. Juchi, after all, was unlikely to be toting an assault rifle. As for the woman with him, well, she was a woman, and largely (altogether, if the legend was a lie, as legends mostly were) of cattle stock. He screened her from his consideration as thoroughly as he had the irrelevant footprints.

He added two things to his inventory of weapons. He had privacy here, and he had plenty of time. Grinning still, he trotted toward the apple orchard.

Aisha looked up from the small fire she was building. "A man is coming."

"Yes, I hear him." Juchi turned his head toward the sound. Even after so long, he sometimes expected to see what he was hearing. Whoever the approaching stranger was, he had a gait like a muskylope's, tireless and easy. Juchi heard his quick footfalls but only calm, steady breathing, as if the fellow were just ambling along.

Suddenly Juchi did see, in his mind's eye that no brooch could pierce. He saw himself as a young man out on the steppe, saw another man approaching him at a trot. It had been just such a trot as this. The man had been Dagor, his father—a Sauron. He only learned that years later. At the time, he'd thought him just another outlaw. He'd fought him. He'd killed him.

The fellow now was in among the trees, weaving between them faster than a man had any business doing. Aisha said, "He has a gray greatcoat."

"He is a Sauron," Juchi said. "Well, if he wants me, he has me. I shall not run from him, nor would it do me any good to try." Less than a minute later, the Sauron came into the clearing. "Greetings, guest,"

Juchi told him. "Will you share salt and bread with us?"

"Yes," the Sauron answered, "but afterwards I will kill you all the same."

Aisha drew in a sharp breath. Juchi set a hand on her arm, shook his head. He turned back to the Sauron. "You are honest, at any rate. Shall we talk a while first, that I may learn who so baldly seeks my death?"

"As you wish. I just now thought to myself that I have all the time I need to do as I will with you," the Sauron said. "Think not to escape, either, for I am no mere Soldier. I am Glorund, Battlemaster of the Citadel. I know you cannot see them, but I wear the death's-heads on my collar tabs."

Cloth rustled. He was loosening his greatcoat, then. "He speaks the truth," Aisha said, her voice quavering. "He is a cyborg."

"I did not think he came here to boast and lie," Juchi said. He sounded calm. He'd passed beyond fear for his life in the red moment he'd plunged his wife's—his mother's—brooch into his eyes. He nodded to Glorund. "Well, Battlemaster, so you will take your revenge for Angband Base, will you?"

"Exactly so," Glorund answered. "Our reach is shorter than it was in the long-ago days; we have not maintained as much travel technology as we might wish. But we still know what examples are worth. Now that I have you, the cattle will quiver in fright and horror whenever they speak of your death. That serves the Citadel."

"Men quiver in fright and horror when they speak of me now," Juchi said, shrugging. "Allah and the spirits know I have deserved both. But no one yet has dared call me coward. I shall not flee you. Indeed, I warn you that I will strike back if I may. I began fighting Saurons long ago; the habit is hard to break."

"Strike if you wish," Glorund said. "It will not avail

you." Juchi had not dealt with Saurons for many years, but he remembered the arrogance they could put in their voices, the certainty that things would be as they said and only as they said. Glorund had it in full measure.

"You condemn me for taking Angband Base," Juchi said. "Why should I not condemn you and all your kind for what you have done to Haven?"

"Because you have not the power," Glorund answered at once. "Haven is ours because we are strong enough to hold it, to shape it as we will." Yes, he was arrogant, arrogant as a cliff lion stretching in front of a herd of muskylopes.

Juchi had thought that way once, till his own downfall led him to a different view. He said, "Your kind, Sauron, did not have the power to hold Angband Base. Thus by your own argument you ought to leave me in such little peace as may be mine."

"Had you stayed in that faraway valley, you would be right. But you are here now, in the Shangri-La Valley, the stronghold of the Soldiers, and here, I gather, by your own free choice. That makes you a fool, and for fools the death penalty is certain. I am but the instrument the universe chooses to carry out its will."

"Why not say you are a god and have done?" Aisha said.

"There are no gods," Glorund answered. "I am a Soldier and a cyborg. Here and now, that is all I need to be. I am a lord among the Soldiers, and the Soldiers are lords among the human cattle of this world."

"Do you take pride in that?" Juchi asked.

"Why should I not?" Unmistakably, Glorund was preening. "Year by year, we breed more Soldiers, shape this world in our image."

"And year by year, your grip grows shorter. You said as much yourself. When your kind came to Haven, you came in a starship. Where is your starship now,

Sauron? You had fliers, they say. Where are your fliers
now? You call your folk great conquerors? Were you
not then fleeing defeat, like a beaten nomad tribe
driven from good pasture country to badlands where
grass hardly grows? Boast of your might, and hear your
boasts ring hollow in your ears."

Aisha clapped her hands in delight at her father's
defiance. Juchi hoped to hear some sign of anger from
Glorund, the sharpness of an indrawn breath or the
small mineral noise of teeth grinding together. From
an ordinary man, even from an ordinary Sauron, he
knew he would have won them. Yet Glorund still sat
as relaxed as if they were talking about the best way
to trim muskylope hooves. The biomechanical implants
that made him a cyborg gave him inhuman calm.

A good word for it, Juchi thought. Many doubted
whether cyborgs truly were human beings any more,
or only war machines fueled on bread and meat
instead of coal. Juchi knew he was glad no cyborg had
led at Angband Base. That fight had been hard enough
as it was. But had he died in it, he would not have
gone on to sin as he had. Maybe better, then, if a
cyborg had been there.

He'd chased round such thoughts countless times
in his years of wandering, never to any profit. That
did not keep him from getting caught up in them,
from wishing his life somehow could have been different. He realized he'd missed something Glorund said.
He said, "I'm sorry; I was woolgathering."

"A fit trade for a nomad," the Sauron said, the first
trace of wit Juchi had heard from him. "Let me try
again: aye, we were defeated. The herds of cattle
gored down our forefathers by weight of numbers. Is
that warfare? Half a dozen drillbits may gnaw flesh
from a man's bones. Does that make them mightier
than men?"

"The fellow they gnawed will never worry about the

question again," Aisha put in. "He lost, and so did you."

"And what have you Saurons done with Haven since you came here?" Juchi added. "Have you made it better? Stronger? Or have you simply gone about the planet destroying anything that might get in the way of your quest for power?"

"Those who rule brook no rivals," Glorund answered. "So has it always been, on every world; so shall it always be. Accept a rival to your power and one day you will find you have a master."

"But your power is not based just on the fighting magic you Saurons have within your own bodies," Juchi said.

"By the Lidless Eye, what else is there, you bad-genes wretch?" The Battlemaster's words still came out in that perfectly controlled tone, but now they betrayed anger all the same.

Juchi nodded to himself. Flick a Sauron on his fighting ability and he bled. Juchi did not intend to let him clot. He went on, "You won Haven with machine magic, and slew everyone else's machines when you came. You had to—machines can kill from farther away than any Sauron's arm can reach. But now that that magic is gone for everyone else, it is dying for you as well. And fight as boldly as you will, how can you ever hope to leave Haven again without the machine magic you've spent all these years killing?"

"When we have fully mastered the world, we will restore technology—under our control," Glorund answered. "It can be done; cyborgs can outthink men of the cattle as well as outfight them."

Juchi snorted impolitely. "I've wandered widely across Haven this last half of my life. Though I do not see, I hear and I know. Aye, you hold Shangri-La Valley tight, here with your Citadel. Here you still retain some of your magic, enough to breed or make cyborgs—for now. But for how much longer, even here? In the other and lesser valleys where Sauron fortresses still dominate, they have lost the art. And, Battlemaster Glorund, think on this—is a Citadel a place from which to fare forth to conquer all the world, or is it a place to huddle, warded there against a world that hates you?"

Now Glorund sat some time silent. In that silence, Juchi was reminded of the electronic ruminations of the Threat Analysis Computer at Angband Base. He wondered how Glorund was analyzing the data he had presented, how the cyborg went about weighing those data against the ones he already possessed. No matter how Juchi had scoffed at it, the Threat Analysis Computer had proven abominably right. Could Glorund's augmented flesh and blood match the machine?

Juchi never learned the answer to that question, for Glorund said, "I can tell you what the Citadel and its valley are, Juchi. They are the fitting place for you to die."

"Aye, that is so, Sauron, but not for the reason you think." Juchi unobtrusively shifted his weight, readying himself for the attack that, he knew, would come at any moment. While Glorund hesitated still, he took the chance to get in the last word: "What better spot for me to lie than in the center of Sauron wickedness? Perhaps your land will gain some atonement from me, as I have already rid one part of Haven of your foul breed."

What would have been killing rage in an unmodified man ripped through Glorund. The cyborg Battlemaster felt it only as an augmented urge to be rid of Juchi once for all. He had no need for the rush of adrenaline that sped the hearts and reflexes of cattle, even of Soldiers. All his bodily systems functioned at peak efficiency at all times. Without gathering himself, without changing expression, he leapt at the mocking blind man whose very existence affronted the Soldiers, who would not be silent, and who somehow kept piercing, deflecting, the cool, perfect stream of Glorund's own logic.

A man of the cattle would have died before he ever realized Glorund had moved. The Battlemaster learned in that instant that part of Juchi's legend, at least, was true. He reacted to Glorund's attack with speed many of the Soldiers at the Citadel might have envied, knocked aside the first blow intended to snap his spine, struck out with the dagger that had appeared in his right hand as if by magic.

Glorund chopped at his wrist. That should have sent the knife spinning away. Juchi held on. He grappled with Glorund. His every kick, every handblow was cleverly aimed, Soldier-fast and Soldier-strong. The knife scored a fiery line across Glorund's ribs before the Battlemaster finally managed to knock it out of Juchi's hand.

"The Breedmaster who left you out for stobor was an idiot," Glorund said.

Juchi's only answer was to butt him under the chin. Even Glorund saw stars for a moment. Juchi's blindness mattered little in the hand-to-hand struggle in which they were engaged. Both men fought more by ear and by feel than by eye—and Juchi, however he had learned them, knew all the tricks in the warrior's bag.

But however skilled, however swift, however strong he was, he was no cyborg. He hurt Glorund a couple of times. Even so much surprised the Battlemaster. Glorund, though, made him first groan and then scream. "There," he snarled, snapping Juchi's right arm against his own shin. "And there—" He rammed his knee into his enemy's midsection. "And there—" A final savage twist broke Juchi's neck. It was not the slow, lingering kill Glorund had looked for, but it would serve.

Juchi's will to live on was stubborn as any Soldier's. His lips shaped one last word: "Badri," he whispered with all the breath left in him. Then at last he died. Glorund started to scramble free of him.

With a wordless scream, Aisha leaped on the Battlemaster's back. Glorund had looked for that, looked for it with anticipation. He would, he thought, have her two or three times and then either kill her or take her back to the Citadel for breaking. He swept out an arm to roll her off him. It was a casual sweep, not one he would have made against an opponent he took seriously. But he still thought of Juchi's legend as legend and no more; he did not believe Aisha was truly Juchi's daughter and sister both, did not believe she too could hold Soldier genes. When a cyborg did not believe something, he utterly banished it from his thoughts: for him, that possibility no longer existed.

The way Aisha smashed down his arm warned him he had made a mistake. He twisted desperately now, in full earnest. He was fast as a leaping cliff lion. He was not fast enough to keep her from drawing her knife across his throat.

Blood spouted, hideously crimson. Soldiers clotted far faster than ordinary mortals; cyborgs held their circulatory systems under conscious control. Glorund could will away bleeding in an arm, in a leg, in his belly. But in his neck—! Whether his brain lost oxygen from bleeding or from his own willfully imposed internal tourniquet, the result would be the same, and as bad.

Pieces of the world went gray in front of him. The color even of his own gushing blood faded. He kicked out at Aisha. If he was to die, he wanted to take her down with him, lest her genes be passed on to those who hated Soldiers.

He thought he felt his booted foot strike home, thought he heard her cry out in pain. But all his senses were fading now, not just his vision. When he fell to the ground, he hardly knew he lay against it.

Was his bleeding slowing? He forced a hand to claw its way up his side to the wound that opened his neck. Yes, the fountain had dwindled to a trickle. If he stayed very still, he might yet live.

Something dark appeared over him. He concentrated. It was Aisha. She still had that dagger. He tried to raise a hand to protect himself. Too slow. He knew he was too slow.

The point, sharp and cold, pierced his left eye and drove deep. All he felt at the end was enormous embarrassment.

Slowly, ever so slowly, Aisha got to her feet. She bit her lips against a shriek as the broken ends of ribs grated against each other. Even dying, Glorund had been faster and stronger and deadlier than anything she had imagined. Now she understood how and why the Saurons ruled so much of Haven. How they had ever been stopped, why they did not rule the human part of the galaxy, was something else again.

She wanted desperately to pant, to suck in great gulps of air to fight her exhaustion. Her ribs would not permit it. She sipped instead, and trembled all over. "Father, I have given you justice," she whispered.

A noise, not far away— Her head whipped around. Her fist clenched on the hilt of her dagger. The blade was still red with Glorund's blood. Even as she made the gesture, she felt its futility. If that was a Sauron coming through the apple trees, she was dead. She knew it. Only wildest luck and surprise had let her slay the Battlemaster. She would not enjoy surprise here, not standing over Glorund's butchered corpse. And as for luck, surely she had used it all in killing him. Her shoulders sagged in resignation as she waited for her end.

But she still did have some luck left, as she found when the newcomer walked into the clearing. He was no Sauron, only a peasant dressed in sheepskin jacket and baggy trousers of undyed wool. He carried nothing more lethal than a mattock.

His eyes widened as they went from her face to the dagger to the two bodies sprawled close by, back to her face, back to the bodies. They almost popped from his head when he noticed one of those bodies wore a greatcoat of Sauron field-gray. He shifted the mattock to his left hand so he could move the other over his heart in a violent crisscross gesture that Aisha had seen before in some of the valleys she'd visited. It belonged to a faith many farmers still followed.

"You killed them both?" the peasant whispered in Russki. Now he gripped the mattock in both hands and fell back into a clumsy posture of defense.

Aisha shook her head. The motion hurt. Every motion hurt. "No," she answered wearily. "The Sauron killed my father. I killed the Sauron."

"You are a woman," the peasant said, as if it were accusation rather than simple statement of fact. "How could you slay a Sauron Soldier?"

"I am called Aisha. My father is Juchi." She pointed to the corpse that was not Glorund's. Juchi's death had not hit her yet, save to make her numb—she noticed she'd still spoken of him in the present tense.

The peasant knew the name. This time he dropped the mattock so he could crisscross himself. "The accursed one," he whispered.

"So people have named him," Aisha agreed, more wearily still. "He taught me to fight—before misfortune cast him down, he was a great warrior. And I—I share his blood." The third repetition of the peasant's ritual crisscrossing began to bore her. She said, "If you're going to run screaming to your Sauron masters, go do it. I won't flee. I'm sick to death of wandering."

"Don't talk like a fool," the peasant said, crisscrossing himself yet again. "We bury these bodies, we maybe have time to run away, Bog willing." He picked up the mattock and set to work. Dirt flew.

"Why do *you* need to run away?" Aisha asked.

"This happens on the land I work for the Saurons, so they will blame me." He paused to wipe sweat from his forehead. "Drag the bodies over here while I work."

Aisha obeyed. She did not relish the idea of her father's sharing a grave with a Sauron but, as Juchi himself had said, perhaps that was only just. Glorund's greatcoat came open as she hauled him by his boots to the edge of the growing hole.

The peasant kept digging for another couple of minutes. Then he happened to look over at Glorund's collar tabs and saw the death's-heads embroidered there. As if drawn by a lodestone, his gaze swung back to Aisha. "You slew—a cyborg?"

Now, at last, he did not bother crisscrossing himself. He did not bother digging any more, either. He whirled and threw his mattock as far as he could. It clattered off a treetrunk. Then he dashed away, back toward the road.

"Where are you going?" Aisha called after him.

"What does it matter?" he yelled over his shoulder. "Wherever I run, it will not be far enough. But I must try."

The thump of his heavy strides faded as he dodged between apple trees. Aisha felt a sudden, almost overwhelming surge of pity for him—she was grimly certain that he was right, that he would be hunted down and killed. His crisscross Bog would not save him.

And what of herself? Only minutes before, when she'd thought the peasant a Sauron, she'd been ready to give up and die. Now she found that was no longer so. She looked down at her father. Yielding tamely to the Saurons would spit in the face of everything for

which he'd lived. She could not fight them all, not
here in Shangri-La Valley. That she'd killed Glorund
the Battlemaster was a greater victory than she'd had
any right to expect.

Which left—getting away. The foolish peasant had
fled at random, and probably would not go more than
a few kilometers from this land he'd been working all
his life. He could no more conceive of taking refuge
on the steppe than of building a booster and escaping
into space.

But the plains and their clans were Aisha's second
home. Aye, the Saurons might seek her there, but
seeking and finding were not the same. Before she
consciously came to a decision, she was jogging toward
the steppe. It was a slow jog, with knives in it, but
she kept on.

She skirted the town of Nûrnen, staying off the
main road in favor of the farmers' tracks that snaked
their way through the fields. Only at the inner mouth
of the pass did she perforce return to the highway.

She jogged on, ignoring her hurt, ignoring how tired
she was. All her life she'd been able to do that at
need. She seldom thought about why it was so. Now
she did, acknowledging the Sauron blood that ran in
her veins through Juchi. She felt she was putting it to
its proper use, as he had before her—using it against
those who had brought it, all unwanted, to Haven.

Had the Saurons in the Citadel or in their sentry
posts at the outer mouth of the cleft wanted her, they
could have taken her. She knew that. They had assault
rifles and Gatlings and no doubt deadlier weapons as
well, leftovers from the starship that had carried them
here. But now, without Juchi at her side, no one took
any special notice of her. She seemed just another
woman who had finished her business in Shangri-La
Valley and was on her way back to her clan.

She kept jogging for several kilometers after she left
the pass. Only when the tall grass behind her had

swallowed up the way back to the lowlands did she stop to wonder what to do, where to go next.

For long minutes, her mind remained perilously blank. All her adult life she had led her father-brother about, served as his eyes and as a staff in his hand. She'd wanted nothing more. Now he was gone. She still knew no grief, only vast emptiness. Without Juchi, what point to her own life? What could she do? What could she be?

"I am Aisha," she said. The wind blew the words away. She said them again. The wind still blew. What did her name mean? Her voice firmer, she declared, "It will mean what I make it mean."

She still had no idea what that would be. She turned west, toward distant Tallinn Valley where she had been born, and began to find out.

From *The Book of Ruth bat Boaz*, traditional. (Preserved in oral form from approximately 2630. Translated into Bandarit and printed, c. 2800, Strang, Eden Valley. Anthologized in *Sayings of the Judges*, 2910, Ilona'sstaad, Eden Valley.):

I have lived a long life, very long for this world and this age; I have known bitterness and great joy, and now I am only weary. My father began as a godly man of peace, and he hung me from a cross of iron to die; my husband and lover was a man of war, but took me down from the cross and made our peoples free and one. Ilona, dearer than a sister to me, don't weep! Even here, Piet and you and I will never die; because our children live, and what we taught them.

Come closer, all of you. Let your grief be light; it's only when a parent buries a child that grief is heavy; this is the way of nature. But remember me, remember all of us. Remember that you can see farther if you stand on our shoulders. . . . From my sister Ilona's heritage, remember that we are nothing without the Law that binds us one to another. From mine, remember that the Law was made for us, not we for the Law; love is the final commandment. From Piet; be strong,

205

for without strength and courage there can be no
Law, nor love, nor peace. Together we are the
People.

Goodbye. . . .

> *Traditionally recited at the truedark service
> Ruth's Day, throughout the Pale.*

SEVEN AGAINST NÛRNEN

Susan Shwartz

Bloody light from Cat's Eye glared over the steppe.
The wind lashed the high, coarse grasses into waves
like the seas of lost Earth. Aisha had heard stories of
them, but the only tides she could sense pulsed in her
temples. The only salt she tasted came to her lips after
she coughed, and she had been coughing too often as
she ran, slowed to a trot, then to a walk, one hand
pressed cautiously against her aching side.

She ran her tongue over dry lips. The last thing she
had drunk was the thin, sour beer they had served in
that Soldier-loving tavern in Nûrnen, that slut of a
town. And she, even she, with her doubly Sauron
blood, was cold now and sleepy enough to scare her.
She and her father Juchi had come far during this day
and now it was getting toward Haven's long night. All
her life, she had rested in the dark when she could. . . .

And now her father would rest forever. Tears filmed
her eyes briefly, then dried. He had died hard, but at
the end, he had had her mother's—and his—name on
his lips. And she had avenged him. Aisha's own lips
snarled.

Twenty years of wandering, of guiding a blind man
who called himself accursed; and now what? The burden was off her back now, disloyal as it was to think

207

of her father's care as a burden—or was it? At the last, though Aisha had avenged him, she had failed. She could not even offer him a proper funeral. That the best a man like Juchi could have would be a ditch shared with a cyborg wasn't just a reproach to her; it was a shame that cried all the way to Allah. It was almost as much a pain as the ache in her heart, or the burning of her broken ribs. The burning shifted for a second to a sharp stab, and she coughed. Not a good sign.

She knew—and mourned—what became of her father. But what would become of her? Hours ago, when she had left a cyborg dead behind her in the fields of Nûrnen, she had set herself on course for Tallinn Town and the range of the tribe her father had ruled. He had been cast out, accursed; and she had been proud to take his exile as her own.

Aisha coughed again and spat, a dark glob. Control, she warned herself. Enough blood in her lungs and even she could drown.

Would the tribe take her back? She feared not. Once, the tribe had been "we." Now, it was "they"; and, touched by her father and mother's curse, she was an outsider. She would be lucky if she were not killed on sight.

She did not believe in curses from the gods. Twenty years of exile with Juchi had proved to her satisfaction that men's curses were damnation enough. The long grass hissed against her heavy boots as the wind laid it flat. *Haven,* she remembered, once had meant harbor. There was no haven, no harbor, for her anywhere, unless she made one for herself.

Tallinn . . . she had counted it home long, long ago: a vanished haven of intricate red rugs and supple leather walls and care. She shut her eyes until red lights went off beneath her lids. So much red—blood from her father's ruined eyes, the way blood gouted from his mouth as he died, then from the cyborg's eye, the glare of Cat's Eye, the pain, like a coal held to her lungs, of ribs grinding against each other. Even the sullen luster of what she had worn into exile: the great ruby that the Judge of the haBandari had sent her by her son's hand.

A thousand times in the past twenty years, she had thought of selling it. Juchi needed medicines; she needed a sharp knife; they both needed better boots and winterwear. Once, she had even approached a Bandari trade caravan and held out the ring. The ruby—for what she and her father must have. Even the greedy, sly Bandari recoiled from it, excusing themselves to whispering among themselves, with the occasional glance flicked back at her. (They had forgotten her hearing, augmented by her mother's crime.)

"Judge Chaya's ring?"

"*Gevalt!* Is *she* here?"

"We can't take that ring in trade. Chaya would skin us."

"Any chance we could bring them both in . . . the *kapetein* . . ."

"Quiet! Haven't we got enough trouble without the tribes knowing we've got them? Give them what they need. It's a *mitzvah* anyhow."

And so the trader had offered them leathers—finer than anything Aisha had seen since leaving Tallinn— food, even a dagger with a blade shimmering with the intricacy of much-folded and hammered steel. She had wanted to hurl his charity in his big-beaked face. For her father's sake, she had not. So she had accepted the gifts. She had even managed to thank the man. And she had never told her father that she had traded pride for warmth. His shoulders had shuddered that night when he thought she slept; he had no tears, but she knew he mourned what he feared she'd traded. As she might have done, she realized. She just might.

They had never spoken of it.

Aisha shivered at the memory. Odd: she was no

longer cold. Heat spread out from that burning coal at her side. Like the heat of a fire within a yurt after a long day's ride, it was heat that sapped her strength and made her yearn only for sleep.

Her father slept forever. Surely, no one would begrudge her just one little hour of rest in Cat's Eye's light. Even the coarse waving grass of the steppe looked inviting as new-washed fleece. Her knees were loosening, her pace slowing. . . .

If she slept now, she would never rise. She met Cat's Eye with a feral snarl and forced herself into a jog. The impact of her feet on the hard earth and the stabbing in her chest made her gasp. The cold air, rushing into her open mouth, nearly stopped her breath altogether with its impact.

She coughed, and it felt as if she had swallowed clownfruit brandy that some fool had set on fire. She spat it out, and blood—more blood than she had will to stop—followed.

Father, I avenged you! She took that comfort, at least, down with her into red-tinged darkness.

"We've got guards out, so what do you want?" Barak snapped at the master of the trading caravan.

"The *kapetein* hears we went this close to Nûrnen, he'll have both ears and a tail."

Anyone else in the caravan might have been hooted at for gutlessness, but it was the physician who spoke; and physicians—badmouthing them was like damaging a book or sounding off at old *Oom* Barak. ("Old, am I, *yongk*?" Barak could hear the bellow of the man for whom he was named. "I'm still *Kommandant h'gana,* and I'll thank you to remember it. Until you settle down and take it over—let an old man rest his bones in whatever sun we get on this God-cursed rock.")

Barak grinned at the physician: lean, weathered, cynical. The winds of this journey had scoured him of the last of the grief for his wife, died of a too-late pregnancy last winter while he was riding circuit among the flocks. The scars of that sorrow remained in the deep wrinkles that webbed his blue eyes; but he was healed.

A Haller, not-so-old *Oom* Karl, for all his complaints; but for all the clan loyalties that set the old Edenites against the first Bandari, a good friend. Twisting the tail of the Saurons, however and wherever you could, was a fine thing. After all, hadn't they cast his mother out to die? But she hadn't; instead, his grandmother Dvora had rescued her, like Moses from the bulrushes (he thought of them as a sort of steppe grass), and raised her until today she was as strong a defender as the Pale of the Bandari boasted. Or almost. If it weren't for her Sauron blood, she'd have been a shoo-in to be elected *kapetein* when the old man stepped down.

If not her, maybe her son, if Barak could ever bring himself to settle down. His mother had simply shrugged off his wanderlust and ignored out of existence the whispers that the Judge went easy on her youngest child, the only one to follow full time the craft of arms. It was undeniable: every time someone mentioned that maybe young Barak would make a fine next *kapetein* she frowned. Well, she wouldn't be the last woman to spoil her youngest child, born after his father's death in the sack of the Sauron base outside Tallinn town.

There would be many such whispers during Ruth's Day, regardless of the spirit of reconciliation the summer holiday was supposed to bring. Barak had heard them so often that they weren't even marginally interesting.

The *kapetein* was old, and the Pale crisscrossed with factions, any one of which held three different opinions at once.

"Heir apparent." Sure, he knew he was a candidate.

So was the caravan master, Sheva bat Barak, and a damned sight more solid than he. To his way of thinking of it, he was a very dark muskylope indeed. After all, Heber, his father, might have been descended from Piet fan Reenan, but his family had moved from the Pale to Tallinn three generations ago. If the job came to him, he'd take it. But personally, he was grateful to his mother for trying to quash it.

That damnable rumor was a bigger burden than the arms all Bandari adults bore. It was no big deal to be a warrior; all Bandari could fight at need, and need usually struck. But to be *kapetein* meant you bore the burden of every life in the Pale.

He was almost sure he didn't want it. He was very sure that some of the clans—the stubborn Hallers, the tricksy Gimbutas—would rather have almost anyone but the son of Chaya the Judge. It would go as it would go, not, perhaps, as he wished it.

But Barak would have a long, long time to settle, to raise strong sons and daughters for the clans and guard the Pale; surely he was allowed one last, carefree ride or so as the leader of caravan guards? And it had been a prosperous trip, too. Now he had enough to pay off his bow, maybe start saving toward marriage.

"Not my tail, *Oom* Karl. I was told to guard this caravan and get it home in time for Ruth's Day, and I'm damned well going to do it. Whose idea was it to separate Nûrnen from its money at that trade fair, anyway?"

Sheva bat Barak the caravan master, an older woman, grinned and shook her head at him. The feathers on her braid danced. "It isn't as if we actually rode into Nûrnen's gates. We were a day's ride away, at any time."

"That's hairsplitting, and you know it."

The caravan master shrugged. "It's a fine point. What do you want? Sauron silver spends just as well

as any other. And I like separating those bastards from
their money."

"Then it's your tail he's going to get," Barak
grinned. "You interested?" He dodged the capable fist
she swung at him.

"After this trip, I can buy anything I want," Sheva
said. "Including bratty nephews, or almost nephews.
Next time, remind me to pack along more spices. They
take up less space and they're more cost-effective than
jewelry. Easier to transport than glass."

*And this close to Nûrnen, better trading goods than
drugs or arms.* The Saurons would probably pay in
gold, looted from the blood of their "cattle," for the
fine Bandari *wootz,* crude or worked into weapons;
and they'd pay in platinum for herbs and other phar-
maceuticals as their own stores failed: but not even
the greediest of the Bandari would sell those things
to their ancient enemies. Even the physician had ridden, as now, with his own bodyguard, and his supplies
were among the best-hidden of the caravan's goods.

"You don't need reminding," the physician snorted.
He started to ride away, but Barak held up a hand,
forestalling him. He whistled once, calling up *meid*
Sannie, who rode up, hand to knife, to escort him.

The patterns of the grass, bending before Haven's
fierce wind, were all wrong.

Actually, Barak ben Heber didn't so much think
that as observe a break in the stand of grass over to
his left, *so.* Even as he observed, he reached for his
bow. His vision, keen even though it was a full Haven
night and Cat's Eye was half-lidded, flickered, then
focused on the anomaly. He sniffed once. Blood
tinged the air.

"I'd better check, *chaverim,*" he called over a shoulder and pressed heels against his muskylope's flanks.
"Cover me. Use the rifle."

Sheva, oldest and richest of the small *kamandim,*

reached behind her for her rifle with its richly carved stock and priceless fittings.

No one called Barak back. There were some advantages, at least, to being a Judge's son. And even more advantages, in some things, of being the son of a Judge whose Sauron blood was well known.

As Barak rode and neared the oddness in the grass, he slung his bow again and reached for his lance. He urged his horse closer. Nostrils wide, it nickered and sidled, but he pressed his legs against its barrel and reassured it with one hand against its neck. He sniffed the coppery tang of blood—that must have been what spooked the horse.

For a moment, he was tempted to continue on foot, but dismissed that: that heroics had no survival value on Haven had been hammered into him since he had first sparred with other boys and girls in clan Allon till back and backside ached with the knowledge. His nostrils flared again. Human blood. Human scent: not the soaps and scents of town—which wasn't surprising—but sweat, sickness and, under them, the leather and wildness of the steppes.

But no grass had been trodden down, and—he focused attention on hearing and smell and extended his senses as far as he might—he could not detect the droppings or other spoor of a frightened horse or beast. Whatever lay before him had come here on foot and alone. It was not a tribesman.

Barak's lips skinned back from his teeth. Alone on Haven . . . only one type of man ventured the steppes of Haven alone or on foot. Saurons.

He heard a coughing, then a bubbling sound. If the Sauron hadn't been sick, he wouldn't be lying in the grass, bubbling out blood through his nose and mouth. Easy enough to finish off, Barak thought. He'd do that for any wounded enemy. But finishing off Saurons was positively a *mitzvah* even if you had to go a thousand klicks to do it. He rode forward.

Before him, the trampled grass rustled. The rustling turned frenzied as if the Sauron sensed his danger and tried to defend himself.

Poising his lance, Barak waited for his best opportunity. Even a dying Sauron could have one last, deadly spurt of energy in him. Anyone with any brains at all would count on just that.

Overhead the wind keened. Barak ignored it. The clouds blew free of Cat's Eye, just as the Sauron levered into a fighting crouch. An instant away from urging his horse forward into a deadly charge, Barak jerked its head to one side.

The "Sauron" wore, not the uniform of the hated enemy, but battered leathers that once, surely, had borne Bandari marks. And the face of his enemy, horrible with clotted blood around the nose and mouth, contorted with frustration at the weakness of limbs and lungs, was one he had seen long, long before.

("Give this ring to . . . your cousin," his mother had ordered him in her Judge voice. She had stripped the great ruby she always wore from her finger. Barak had been the one to take it to Aisha, daughter of Juchi, as their former ally, his eyes oozing blood and matter through bandages, stumbled out into the exile that was the best he could expect. Behind him, he could hear the Bandari whisper and the tribesfolk mutter oaths and prayers against ill-luck. Aisha had thanked him with the grace of the princess she had been until her father—and her brother, both—had found their mother Badri hanging by her own garments, unable to face the fact that her husband had also been her son. The elders had kept Barak from seeing Badri, but he had seen her daughter: hawk nose, dark hair, flashing eyes.)

Silver winged the dark hair now, and the eyes were dull with fever; but there was no mistaking, even now, the face of a kinswoman whose very existence had scandalized the Pale and all but called his mother's judgeship into question.)

"Cousin Aisha," Barak called. (Or was it *Tante* Aisha? No matter.) "And what are you doing here alone?"

Surprise made his voice harsher than usual.

The woman tried to hurl herself forward, then coughed rackingly. She glared at him for seeing her weakness. Blood and froth trickled from her mouth, and she fell.

Easy enough, when she lay defenseless in garments so shabby that the poorest Bandari woman would have disdained them, to pity her. Easy enough. And easy enough to die of it. Barak restrained himself until she stopped moving, even when his cautious lance turned her over.

Then he swung down from his horse. Opening her jacket, he saw that she still breathed, and saw something else beside: his mother's huge ruby, like a gout of blood, dangling from a thong against sweat-slick olive skin. With the leather strips he carried at his belt, Barak bound her hands and feet just in case. Hoisting her up onto his saddle, he rode back through the grass toward the caravan.

"Hoy, there! *Oom* Karl!" he called. "Got a patient for you!"

It was not Juchi who was accursed, Aisha moaned, but herself. She lay on soft blankets, but confined in a tiny yurt that reeked of herbs and sickness. Worse yet, it never ceased to sway and jolt as if some giant's hand shook it. And worst of all, Shaitan had sent a thousand djinni to torment her. She shivered, then sweated in the next instant; and always a raspy-voiced djinni hovered over her with an arsenal of stinks, steams, needles, and foul tastes. . . . "damn fool runs with a shattered rib . . . a wonder she didn't die of a punctured lung . . . or freeze . . ." The muttering trailed away into long words that Aisha was certain were incantations.

It was a ritual the djinni did, and it would call for blood. She knew it, she just knew that in a moment the djinni would stick her with yet another knife, and she had to get away.

"Barak! Come hold this madwoman!" shouted the djinni, and the armed man who had seen her in her shameful illness and watched as she fell thrust into the dark, tiny space and held her down while, sure enough, the djinni stuck her with yet another knife, needle, thorn . . . it didn't matter . . . she was slipping out into a warm tide of sleep.

Hard to believe, as she fought out of the riptide, only to sink again, that a djinni tended her with a father's care.

Something remained to be said, though, before she could drift happily away. "Not . . . not right . . ." she muttered, ". . . shouldn't be here . . ."

"What's that about?" muttered the man who, shamefully, watched her once again.

"She was born in the tribes," the djinni explained. Odd that his voice no longer rasped so harshly on her ears. The tide was warm, so pleasant. In a little while, she would forget. . . . "And she's delirious, or close to it. So she's returned to the customs she knew as a child. She's unmarried and by all the customs she ever followed, it's highly improper for either of us to be here."

She muttered and tried to nod. "Easy there . . . easy . . ." muttered the djinni. "I'm Karl. I'm a doctor. *Hakim*." He used a word she hadn't heard for more than half her lifetime. He patted her hand as if she were still an innocent who had not forfeited the protection of her tribe. She wanted to cling to that hand, and her weakness shamed her.

"Barak! Company coming!" A low, urgent voice called, and a series of whistled notes followed.

"Saurons," muttered the doctor. "Steady there, lady. Easy . . . we won't let them get you."

She was too weak to move. They would find her, and they would take her. Take her like that thrice-accursed Glorund, who had thought to have her on the ground beside her father's body, and whose body now mouldered in the pit that was too good for it.

"Scheiss!" Barak whirled toward the opening of the tiny yurt. *"Oom* Karl, get your supplies together. If they get to you . . ."

"I know the drill," the doctor nodded. "But you won't let them reach me. Give the Saurons hell, will you?"

Barak's teeth flashed in the lamplight. "My pleasure. And, by the way, tell her it's all family, will you? God, can you just imagine the talk when we get her home? When we get back to the Pale, I'm going to wish that all I had to fight was Saurons!"

Aisha tossed her head, her too-sensitive hearing bringing her the few low-voiced words she needed to know that Barak and his guards were readying what might need only be a show of force—but what might have to be an all-out war. Muffled hammerings and the click of metal told her the caravan would be well defended with everything from stakes to grenades. It was odd to sense incoming battle, know herself as one of its causes, yet be protected. It was a luxury she did not think she should indulge in. She tried to lever herself up, but fell back, dizzy.

Another click sounded beside her. Her eyes fluttered open; the healer held an iron ball. Near him, but not too near his weapon, was the lamp.

"You . . ." she moaned.

"I won't let them take us. Or my medicines. Now, *sha,* be still. Or I put you out again."

Now Aisha could hear the regular trot . . . trot . . . trot of Saurons patrolling the steppe.

A whistle came from outside.

"Stop right there." Barak's voice, not the caravan master's. Knowing the Saurons' hearing—how not? It was no keener than his own—he didn't even bother raising his voice.

The Saurons stopped. They were not even breathing hard.

Oom Karl shrugged. "They've got guts even for Saurons, taking on a fully equipped caravan."

Aisha snarled. She would have liked to wind their guts around a Finnegan's fig tree.

"We're looking for a woman."

"When aren't you?" Barak retorted. The caravan master, standing fully armed beside him, chuckled. "Sorry. We don't trade our kinswomen."

"This one's no kin of . . ." The Sauron broke off, clearly adding pieces of the old, damned puzzle together. "A woman, not too young, though not as old . . ." He gestured dismissively at the caravan master.

Sheva glared and did not stir. Though it was no laughing matter, having Saurons in their camp, Barak fought to suppress a grin.

"Probably injured."

"What makes you think *cattle* could survive alone and injured on the steppes?" he asked.

The Sauron glared. Barak let the silence draw itself out.

"This one's got Soldier blood."

The healer drew a careful breath. His eyes glittered warning at Aisha.

"What's she to you, Sauron? Aside from the obvious."

Aisha bared her teeth. Not fearing them as he probably should, *Oom* Karl laid his hand over her mouth. She would have wagered her hope of Paradise that the Saurons wouldn't admit that a woman had killed their precious cyborg Battlemaster.

She could almost see the Sauron shrugging. "No

matter. We came out here to remind you: stay away from Nûrnen. You won't be let in, and you could see something that might offend your delicate eyes—cattle, a failure and a motherfucker, tacked up outside our gates to stand watch against the likes of you. All they're good for. Take those poor sods as a warning, and keep away from Nûrnen." The Sauron's Americ was flat, almost nasal; Aisha instantly hated him.

All that poor man's mutters of Bog and his criss-crossing hadn't spared him a death as painful as her father's, then; and not even her father's honor and her own spared him this last exposure and her family such shame. Tears ran out of the corners of her eyes, then dried. Allah Himself would mourn; she had failed in a child's obligation to provide her father with a worthy burial.

Well, he could have more Saurons for company, she thought, all but growling. Starting with these. Drawing a deep breath, she tried to tap the reserves of wild strength she had always had.

"Lie *back*! I may be no match for your strength, but if I have to, I'll knock you a good one on the back of the head; and let's see you fight me with a concussion." Delirious Aisha might be; she wasn't stupid. She lay back, waiting and listening for the Sauron's next question. The physician's lips thinned, and he checked his weapon.

"Who do you have in there?" demanded the Sauron.

"My aunt," Barak answered with the ease of the practiced liar who, for once, gets to make a lie out of the truth. "She just had a miscarriage. Again. So you wouldn't be interested."

Aisha had had no miscarriage, no child; and never would. That, too, struck her as unutterably sad.

"Old for us," sniffed the Sauron. "Besides, she'd probably ambush us in our beds like Badri . . ." He spat out the name of Aisha's mother and grandma.

Barak let the pause draw out long enough that even

the lower-rank Saurons could realize that this was a
bad idea.

Aisha's hearing picked up a mutter, Sauron to
Sauron, that even an infertile Bandari woman might
be fun . . . *don't even think it, Soldier!* She flicked a
glance at the healer and quickly turned her attention
within. The fire of broken ribs had subsided to a discomfort she could override for long enough, she
thought, to dodge past the man and hurl herself at
the Saurons. If worse came to worst, she would do it,
too.

Barak would have heard that, too. Aisha could imagine him, his hands away from his weapons, but quick
enough to reach them, fast enough and strong enough
to stand against a Sauron. As she herself had done.
Though she had faced a cyborg, still there had been
but one. Barak faced several. He should not do so
alone, she resolved.

"Don't even think it," the healer's lips moved
soundlessly. She chuckled, puzzling him.

She wondered if her first impression—that he was
djinni, not man—had been right after all. In the darkness, his eyes seemed to glow. So did her own,
reflected in the tiny lamp: lambent and feral, like
those of a creature wounded unto death, but with one
last battle in her.

"He is of my blood," she hissed back. "But not
accursed. I cannot—"

"You cannot interfere. By God, woman, letting the
Saurons know we've got you would be the worst thing
you could do."

"The Battlemaster will pin our hides to the walls
next to the motherfucker's," a Sauron hissed behind
his leader, "if we don't bring her or her body back to
tack up there instead."

Aisha felt a surge of fierce pride. She had *killed* the
Battlemaster; this must be a new one.

"We're going to have to search that wagon."

"You and what *h'gana*? Smart Soldier like you, you should think of better ideas," Barak suggested.

"Such as . . ." Even *Oom* Karl could hear the suppressed eagerness in the Sauron's voice. It was well known that a Bandari would crawl halfway across Haven to do a Sauron a mischief—if the Sauron didn't meet him halfway.

Hoofbeats sounded from outside: other Bandari who had circled around and behind the Saurons, and who now rode up. Aisha could hear the *snick* of safeties being removed from firearms and the faint whine of strung bows.

"Such as turning around and going back to the women you *do* have," Barak said flatly. "As for us, we're headed back to the Pale for Ruth's Day. And expecting to join up with another caravan pretty soon. I'd really suggest you start on your way."

Oom Karl's mouth quivered and his eyes lit with appreciation at Barak's bluff.

The Sauron remained silent.

"Was there anything else you wanted?" Barak prompted, his voice quivering on the edge of arrogance. *Oom* Karl hissed. *Don't get cocky*.

"Yes, we had a message for you. Stay out of Nûrnen. We don't want your trade or your trash."

"Well enough," Barak agreed. "Slim pickings there anyhow; the trip to harvest them isn't worth our while. I promise, I won't be back unless I plan to move in."

"That arrogance could be permanent, Bandari."

"Not when I've got you circled. We have to get moving now if we want to get back to the Pale. Open it up, *chaverim*. Sauron, you've got till the count of ten . . . nine . . . eight . . ."

The thud of retreating footsteps vibrated in the wood of the wagon. Aisha let out a breath she had forgotten she was holding. Fire licked against her ribs, and she flinched.

Oom Karl sighed gustily, too. "Got off easy, for

now," he said. "Now, I'm going to make sure you sleep . . ."

"My father," she muttered. "He was dead, and they defile his body. I must turn back to Nûrnen and avenge him." She began to climb from her blankets.

He had a sharp-pointed glass knife in his hand. Before Aisha could catch his wrist, he had scratched her arm.

She raised a hand to punish him for the scratch, but her head swam, and the shadows in the tiny wagon closed in and engulfed her.

Since the day Aisha had found the courage to turn her back on her tribe and guide her blind father out of Tallinn, she had never doubted it. As the caravan wound its slow and eminently well-guarded way back toward the Pale, descending into Eden Valley, she found that courage sorely tested.

Her ribs had healed with a speed and cleanliness that drew grunts of admiration from *Oom* Karl. Her lungs had drained and her fever vanished almost overnight. But physical recovery was the least of the ordeals she faced.

The first day she was permitted to walk unsupported, *meid* Sannie appeared in the wagon that had been her sickroom. "Wrap up," she announced brusquely and shoved the blanket at Aisha.

She blinked and looked about for her clothes. "*Schmutzig,*" Sannie told her. "So filthy we had to bury them. The caravan master has others for you."

Aisha glanced around, as if expecting the clothes to appear. But, "How much?" she asked. She had had some silver when she left Nûrnen: not enough, probably, to cover the costs of the fine leathers and wools that haBandari merchant princes usually rode out in.

"Don't worry about it," said Sannie.

Aisha wrapped up in the blanket and glared at her. "Then I cannot accept them." Damn Bandari and their slap-in-the-face charity. She drew the blanket around her shoulders. Let her kinsman Barak come and command her, as the only living male of her line. She might even listen to him; for certain, she had no desire to enter the Pale wrapped only in rough wool. But to accept charity was to strip her soul as naked as her body.

Sannie's face went flat. She disappeared from the wagon. A moment later, *Oom* Karl put his head in.

"I sent Sannie in because I thought you'd do better if you had another woman around. There's not much water left, but we've got plenty of sand for a dustbath. Come on."

A dustbath. Then it was true what all Haven said of the Bandari: men and women not wed to each other went naked in one another's presence. Those of the tribes were more shamefast.

Yet had she a right to shame? Whether she did or not, she felt a blush starting from somewhere around the level of her belly.

"Yes, it's all true," the healer laughed at her and showed his uncanny ability to sense her thoughts. "We bathe, whether we need to or not. And you could use the sun on that skin of yours. Doctor's orders."

"She won't take the clothes . . ."

"I cannot . . ."

"If it's money, count them as a bounty. Didn't you kill the last Battlemaster of Nûrnen? We're in *your* debt. I promise, no one's going to look at you. Anything you've got, we've already seen. And right now, we've seen it in better shape." He must have seen her bare while she was sick, but he turned his back ostentatiously. She flushed like a fool for the relief— and the aggravation—she felt.

Before her world changed, she had been brought up among the tribes, where maidens were modest. And she was still—despite her age—a maiden. That too was a matter for shame. But in all her life, the

only man she had ever met before was her father/
brother.

"I'd like to stuff you back into your bottle, djinni,"
Aisha muttered. "And I would, too, if the cork
weren't . . ."

"Say what?" he showed surprisingly even teeth at
her in a grin that shocked an answering grin from her.

Moving unsteadily, she rose, the blanket clasped
about her, and clambered down from the wagon. After
so long riding, the earth felt nubbly, strangely solid
under her bare feet.

The day was surprisingly warm for Haven. She
glanced about, then away from the shocking spectacle
of naked Bandari (all but those on guard) lounging,
their weapons near to hand. Given Aisha's more efficient metabolism, she felt herself sweating, then felt
the sweat evaporate. She sniffed experimentally. She
did need a bath. Just as well her companions' senses
weren't as keen as hers.

"Like this," Sannie volunteered, skinning out of her
clothes. She was stocky, compact, with more body fat
than Aisha carried. She palmed a handful of dust and
rubbed it down a well-muscled flank and flicked an
inquiring glance around.

Did these people think she was a *total* barbarian?

"I know how to bathe," Aisha said. She turned her
back on the shocking, not-to-be-glanced at sight of so
many naked males, knelt stiffly to gather dust for herself, and scrubbed. Soon she glowed from the friction
of her bath—and from embarrassment.

Far to her back she heard the physician's voice. She
was glad he did not approach. She was glad that none
of the men did. She listened with half an ear to Sannie's chatter of this family and that. She mentioned
Barak often, and Aisha raised an eyebrow.

Even as she basked in the pale sun, Sannie scanned
the horizon for Barak and her fellow guards. Aisha
scanned it for Saurons.

Then she stiffened, her hand reaching for a knife, then curling into a claw of frustration at her nakedness.

"What's that?"

Used to Barak, Sannie didn't doubt the evidence of Aisha's hearing.

"Somebody coming!" she called. All about her, Bandari uncoiled, bare arms reaching for rifles, knives, spears, and bows. Two men ran past, dressed only in shields and their weapons. They no longer looked naked.

"How many?" she demanded.

Aisha flung herself ear down on the ground.

"Hoofbeats," she muttered, straining to make out the numbers. "Not many. Maybe five."

Not the nomads from which she was so long sundered. And not Saurons who had met reinforcements.

Someone dropped sun-warmed leathers on her. Aisha tugged them on, thankful that a knife hung from the sturdy belt. They trusted her then, to that extent. The sunlight gleamed off the ruby on her hand until it looked like a glob of blood squeezed from a puncture wound.

Sannie gestured her back beside the physician, then ran to take her place in what looked like a very thorough defense.

"Can you see anyone?" he asked.

So quickly she wasn't aware, Aisha's eyes locked on target, filtered away the scanty trees, the possible prowling beast, or even a puff of dust. "Riders," she murmured. "In leathers . . . they look like Bandari . . ."

"Could be a trick. . . ."

She heard a thin voice, half snatched away by the wind, calling out something in *Ivrit*, only to be answered by a sharp bark of a command. An instant later, the incoming riders had dropped their weapons and their mounts' reins. Hands held high, they waited for Bandari from the caravan to surround them.

"They're talking," Aisha reported back to the physician. "They're clasping arms."

"Where, girl? Point me in the right direction." From a leather case at his belt, *Oom* Karl took out binoculars. A rich djinni, indeed.

"Oxhorns, a leaping antelope ... the fan der Merwe, the fan Reenan ... even my own clan's crossed daggers ... why so many? Looks like they had trouble. Those jackets are torn ... oh God no!"

Aisha narrowed her eyes. Barak rode up to the newcomers. His eyes too went to the rips in their garments, the black bands ringing the arm of each rider. They spoke, fast and urgently. Barak reeled back, as if he had taken a blow from a lance.

A moment later, he dismounted. Drawing his knife, he slashed his own tunic. Then he bent and, taking up a pinch of dust, smeared it across his face.

The other Bandari dismounted. Slowly, they made their way into the camp. No one moved yet. Aisha could see skin pale and pucker as the wind licked across bare, motionless bodies. Hands tightened on weapons; faces bore the look, not of men and women facing combat or even people proved to be friends, but of people expecting bad news.

Barak led the newcomers in. Careful not to stand in each other's line of fire, the Bandari drew in and formed a semicircle.

Oom Karl raised a tentative hand in greeting to the man who bore the crossed daggers of his clan, then let it fall.

"It had to happen," he sighed. "Say what you came here to say, Hans."

Only a lifetime's self-denial prevented Aisha from demanding an explanation. In the next moment, the new Haller gave it.

"The commandant *h'gana* sent us out. It's the *kapetein*. He's gone. The Lord giveth and the Lord taketh ..."

"Blessed be the name of the Lord . . ." intoned *Oom* Karl, but his voice cracked and lacked conviction. He stared at his kinsman as if he were a cliff lion that might spring at any moment.

All around them, Bandari emerged from cover. They laid aside their weapons and pulled on their clothes. Then, almost as one, they drew their garments and slashed them in token of mourning.

"*Yisgadal v'yiskadash . . .*" Barak intoned. Bandari prayers? It was the will of Allah, Aisha thought.

With her new knife, Aisha politely tore the leathers she had only just put on. This Bandari king had died full of years and honors. He would be buried. Guilt caught her by the throat. But for her father there was no honor and never would be, unless she provided it. And she was honor-bound now to mourn another's death.

Haller and Haller drew apart and talked, low-voiced. She could see their eyes glint as Cat's Eye rose in the sky. They had no Soldier blood in them. Until the wind blew, their tears for the old *kapetein* did not dry.

Pillars of cloud by day; pillars of fire by night. Light and smoke flanked them as they hastened toward the caravan. Their muskies were tired, and their wagons slowed them. From time to time they were passed by other riders, heading in toward home, toward a funeral, and the selection of a new leader.

At the head of the train, Barak rode, wrapped in his own thoughts. Already it seemed as if the loneliness of a ruler had fallen upon him. The others did not trouble him, and Aisha did not dare.

She had hoped, but not expected, to ride alone. She had assumed they would watch her, and so they did. To her surprise, the physician left his place beside his kinsman and rode toward her. "Now what?" she asked.

"Now, we go home," he said. "And choose a new

leader." He looked over at the other man whose slashed tunic bore the symbol etched upon his own.

"There's a saying we have. 'May you live in interesting times.' It's a curse."

"I know," Aisha told him. "You stole it from the tribes."

The physician hissed under his breath. "This isn't the time I'd ... You couldn't be coming here at a worse time.... The old story about Judge Chaya being part Sauron," He shook his head. "No question about Barak's father, though. Even if Heber did choose to work in Tallinn."

"He's still of *Oom* Piet's line," Sannie blurted out.

Aisha shrugged. For one who was accursed, all times were bad. She was outcast. What was it to her if the Bandari fought about their laws? And what bloodline was as corrupt as hers?

"Look," said *Oom* Karl. "I'm a healer. If I say it's normal to worry, to be concerned, you shouldn't blame yourself ..."

"Fine words for *coward*!" Aisha flared at him. "All right, then. I *am* afraid. Now you can despise me for that as well as for the curse of my family. Watch the barbarian. Make sure she bathes. Show her how decent folk do it, just in case. And then you can watch how she walks. Watch how she talks. Watch to see if she eats differently and comment on her manners. And watch out, for the time will come when she breaks out in some god-cursed act that will bring everyone she ..." Her voice wobbled, and furious, she went on ... "cares about to ruin. I've spent a lifetime doing that."

"Too long," murmured the physician. To Aisha's astonishment, he patted her hand where it rested on her muskylope's reins. She jerked it away as if she had touched a coal. "I meant what I said. You come to us in sad times. But, Judge Chaya will do her best for you.... And she is the closest kin you have."

Aisha's eyes smarted as they rode down the last lap toward the valley. She thought she could sense the richer, warmer air. Green smells floated in the breeze, mingled with sweat and horses as, from time to time, Bandari rode up fast to exchange urgent messages with the caravan and with Barak in particular.

"Do you have any idea *why* my mother said that?" Barak demanded.

No one answered; then four people spoke at once. *Bandari manners,* she thought. They stared at her but ventured no comment. Not yet. The Haller who had brought the news of the *kapetein*'s death to the caravan rode up and spoke urgently to the newcomers, shaking his head.

"Too much, too fast . . ." was the mutter. Aisha shut her eyes. Her hearing, part of her Sauron legacy, brought her the words that were hissed or whispered, accompanied by vehement pointings and shaking of fists. Just so, Aisha had heard whispers, had heard her mother's soft felt shoes pad as she fled toward seclusion and the final, decent privacy of death . . . not even her Sauron speed had been enough to divert Badri from the path she had chosen.

Something about admitting women to the clan's council. They were not one folk, these Bandari, but several. They had a woman as judge over them; in fact, their first judge had been a woman; yet not all their women had a public voice. At that, more of them did than in the tribes. She had to allow that that had its attractions. She would have to learn.

"We need a moderate. *Any* of the ben Zvi, the Allons . . ."

"Tarred with the same brush as the Judge, is it?"

"It's not her Sauron blood we mind . . ."

"Bet me. Wager me your bow . . . or the rifle with the carved stock. . . ."

"It's her politics. How can we be sure she hasn't passed it on. . . ."

"Tell me Barak isn't fit. *Tell* me. You've served with him. Remember the time he went back and got your brother, the time he was cut off by bandits? Rode half the night, too. You thanked God for his Sauron blood then. . . ."

"Damn!" spat Hans Haller. "It's not his courage at question. You *Ivrit* are taking over, and my people— it's more than an issue of votes. Our young ones are running from our farms, trying to marry into *Ivrit* clans. Our girls stamp their feet and say, they won't. What kind of words are these for modest girls? Even Karl here . . . ever since he finished his medical train- ing he's been more *Ivrit* than Eden. And it was *our* Eden first till you came in. . . ."

"You can dare say that? When it was *your* people hung Judge Ruth on a cross. . . ."

"Dammit, shut *up*! Save it for when we get home." What could have been a highly informative fight dissipated in a flurry of mumbles, like far-off thunder.

Aisha shook her head. Dimly she remembered a time when her father ruled the tribe. What her father said was law. And no one dared question his judg- ments . . . except Badri, their mother. And she had never had to raise her voice.

Soon a new round of judgments would start. And she would be their target. With more than half a life- time of practice, Aisha put that thought from her. For now, though, she would pretend that she was no dif- ferent from any woman in the caravan. Like them, she sat clothed in leather so supple it clung to her body like fine cloth. Like them, she wore jewelry: only one ring, in her case, but a rich one.

Aisha arranged her cold fingers on the reins and waited to be discovered. They rode past wall and steading, past field and farmer and rider, hastening to call the clans together to vote upon a new *kapetein*. The richness of the air pressed down upon her: it was too much. It was for other women, fruitful women, who could retreat here and have healthy babies. It was not for her to savor as she anticipated children of her own. She would be punished.

The next time *Oom* Karl looked at her she flinched. They had come to their journey's end. She had come to the end of her courage, and she was disgracing herself. Though the air was warm and moist for Haven, she shuddered. As she had learned in the years of tears and curses, she drew into herself. After awhile, the tears ceased to prickle at the corners of her eyes, and she began to hope she might be ignored.

The caravan stopped beneath a ruin. To Aisha's surprise, Barak rode at her side.

"The bunker," he pointed out the ruin. "My mother used to like to go there when she was a girl. That's the place from which Ruth was taken out and hung on the cross; and which we took when we took Eden."

"When *you* took Eden from us," muttered *Oom* Karl's kinsman.

"We are one people now," the physician muttered. "We are one. We are."

Honored the place was, but it bore all the hallmarks of disuse.

Ruth's Day, Aisha recalled, was supposed to be a day of reconciliation. It would take more than one day, she thought.

A woman whose height marked her out among the stocky Bandari ran from a nearby building and headed toward the caravan. Her hair was silvered and her face lined. Despite that, she moved with astonishing speed. Three people came out after her, one of them a stocky man wearing the furs and felts of the tribes. The marks burned into his shield, emblazoned on his garments were marks Aisha knew well: long ago, she had borne them, too, when her father ruled the tribes near Tallinn town.

She thought she recognized the man. Kemal. In another life, he had bowed to her father and stam-

mered out how far along he was toward saving up a
suitable bride gift. By now, he could even be a grand-
sire, Aisha thought. He looked well-fed and secure in
his place. Emissary from his father Tarik? She thought
she could recall that Tarik took over the tribe when
her own father . . . left it. Her eyes flicked over the
knots of people. Sure enough: many men of the tribes,
come, no doubt, to join the celebration for Ruth's
Day, reaffirm the old alliances—and keep eyes out for
any sign that the Pale was splintering now that the old
kapetein was dead.

What would they make of her presence here? And
who was it betraying?

For the first time in her life, Aisha backed away
from an ordeal. Immediately, the doctor was at her
side.

"Steady there," he murmured.

She glared at him. Just let her sink into the background was all she asked. She would not run away;
where could she go in this Pale that she would not be
found and stared at and returned in disgrace?

At least no one had seen her nerve falter except
Oom Karl, and he had seen worse than that.

"Barak!" cried the Judge. Praise Allah, she hadn't
noticed. "Son!"

"Hey there, it's the new *kapetein*!" came a shout
from across the way.

The first woman out flinched. For an instant, her
face went pale.

"Not yet, he's not," muttered Hans Haller.

Barak shook his head at the people who had greeted
him. "Anyone who wants that job deserves to get
it!" he called. Despite their torn clothing and dust-
smeared faces, the crowd laughed, and he grinned
back.

"You haven't got it yet, *boychik*," growled a man
whose red-scrubbed hands showed he had left his
farm just recently to ride in for the funeral.

"Watch how you talk to him," snapped a woman wearing Gimbutas clan signs. "Can't control yourself, can't control your people. So let people who can . . ."

The Edenite farmer purpled under his weathering and started toward her, to be stopped by *Oom* Karl's companion. "That's not the way. You know that's not the way."

Aisha was certain that three of the tribesmen at least turned around and studied the quarreling Bandari as if they were traders calculating discounts at market.

"To honor Judge Ruth? It certainly isn't," Barak said. "And she was one of yours before she became one of ours, too. Remember this, *chaver*. I wasn't the one who started this disrespect."

Kemal of Tallinn's eyes narrowed, allowing it to be seen that he too assessed the disagreement and what it might gain him.

Standing near him, the older woman closed her eyes in aggravation. Or concentration. She would be sorting out voices and tones, Aisha suspected. Her hearing must be as keen as Aisha's own. And her wits, if she balanced factions, tribes, and ambitions, must be as sharp as the blades that her long-dead husband had once forged of the finest *wootz*.

Though a generation separated them—and did not—they were of a height. And in looking at the taller woman who ran to her son with the speed of a much younger woman, Aisha saw herself as she would be if she lived so long.

Judge Chaya withstood her son's hug. "How's it been, mother?" Aisha heard him ask and watched his mother's shoulders shrug minutely.

"How should it be?" she said. "The Edenites—Hallers and Tellermans—are raising Cain again. Just when I thought they'd give their women clan vote, Kosti Gimbutas's third son had to run off with one of the girls. *That* one . . . don't know how he manages to

walk. And then, old *kapetein* Mordecai, rest his soul
. . . he sure picked his moment." She shook her head.
"I'm glad to see you, son."

Barak turned, one arm still about the older woman.
She smiled kindly at Sannie and the others, then nod-
ded graciously at *Oom* Karl and the man he rode with.
"A good trip, Karl, *Oom* Hans?" she asked carefully.
The man nodded shortly.

"I thank you for notifying my son," the Judge
added, her tone consciously gracious.

Another short nod.

From the corner of her eye, Aisha saw *Oom* Karl
grin crookedly. When he saw her watching, he winked
at her and gestured with the flat of his hand: *keep
your chin up.*

For a moment longer, Judge Chaya's polite questions were met with nods; questions and answers had
the air of ritual, performed by actors well-versed in
their roles. The *kapetein* was dead now; all the roles
might change. The old rituals seemed to quiver with
tension because of that.

The nomads' dark eyes flashed as they listened to
the Judge: they *listened,* Aisha wondered, they actually
listened to a woman who raised her voice and spoke
with authority in public.

Karl Haller nodded, his eyes shrewdly narrowing.
She's going to pull it off.

The Judge did not look at Aisha. Would she even
speak to her? For a long time the careful politenesses
went on. Finally, with a gracious, "but you must be
anxious to get home," Judge Chaya ended the audience.

"You go on ahead," *Oom* Karl told him. "I've got
medical reports to file. And then you know the other
clan elders want to see me. Surprise." He grimaced,
and he patted his shoulder. Clearly, he had been dismissed, but he lingered.

"And now . . ." she turned toward her son. "Your
last message . . ."

"I bring you," Barak gestured at Aisha, "a kinswoman. She has been quite ill."

Aisha put up her hand as if it were a shield or a
veil for her weathered face. The sunlight winked off
the great red stone that she and the woman facing her
had both worn. Her hand trembled, and she brought
it to her lips to still their quivering.

*(She had been such a pretty girl when the screaming
started. One moment, she had been a princess, the
favored child of the tribe's chieftain, whose mother
delighted in combing her hair and adorning it with
the coins of her dowry. In the next, women's wails had
told her; her mother was dead, hanging, her tongue
all black and puffed out—though they would not let
her see. And her father . . . they wouldn't let her in to
see him, and they'd said it was by his orders!*

*She couldn't understand it. Always, always, even
when he sent everyone away, she could coax him into
smiles. So she had broken through the guards and
found him, his hands pressed to the bleeding wounds
that had been his eyes. And then she had learned the
truth: that he had been father and brother both.*

*Aisha's world had reeled. To go from favored
daughter to . . . what could she hope for in the tribe?
Nothing but a lifetime of sidelong glances while her
father brother wandered and died fast, if he were
lucky—and he was not a lucky man. Better to die with
him, she resolved. And then the tall woman, who
looked just like her mother, had sent a boy to her,
running, carrying a great red stone. It had been more
talk; more rumors; but all had known that the Bandari
woman judge had great strength than was a woman's
lot.*

*They had been kin, but Aisha's pride had made her
choose exile with her father instead of the alms of a
stranger who was also sister and aunt.)*

That stranger now faced her. And, after all these

years, Aisha faced the need to accept her charity at last. At least for now.

Abruptly, the weakness of Aisha's first days with the caravan struck her, and she flung up a hand. Sunlight caught the ruby and sparked fire from it off Chaya bat Lapidoth's face. The woman blinked fast, then returned to watchfulness. Sauron watchfulness.

"Khatun . . ." Her throat closed. The man from the tribe that had cast her father out affected not to watch, a pretense she did not believe. She sensed the stiffening in his shoulders, saw the minuscule widening of pupils: his very body betrayed him.

Once he had sought her as a bride.

Aisha wanted to toss her head, but she was afraid she might fall. She would not use the titles of the tribes that had cast her out and dishonored her.

Warmth at her side: *Oom* Karl, her own personal djinni. She stepped away. This was family; no one could help her. And yet she was not Bandari. Frantic, she recalled an Americ title she had heard once in her wanderings.

"Your Honor . . ."

The older woman shook her head, rejecting title, rejecting Aisha's hand outflung to ward her off.

"*Tante,* child, or Chaya. Whichever you prefer." She seized her in a grasp that Aisha knew was strong as her own, despite the Judge's age.

"Welcome."

The woman's eyes locked into Aisha's. Black eyes, keen, proud, and profoundly experienced . . . as her mother's eyes had been before they bulged and glazed in her purpled face, as her father's had been before he gouged them out. In the early days of exile, Aisha had changed the bandages and fought against her horror not to gag or shake.

She shook now, shuddering with half a lifetime's anguish. All the weeks of illness, all the years of exile came up on her like spoiled food.

To her horror, she was shaking. She felt Judge Chaya's shoulders shake, too, then steady; and she embraced the older woman, her aunt and sister.

"Let's get her out of here," she heard Chaya mutter. "If she breaks she'll hate herself." The Judge paused as if considering. "Worse than she already does."

Aisha felt herself steered into a building, thrust into a leather framed chair, and held, always held, by those strong hands. Other footsteps followed; for once Aisha couldn't count them.

"No, Karl, I don't think she needs a sedative. Did she cry once while you were nursing her back to health? Not even once? Then she has got to cry it all out. *Tell* me about it, little one, little sister."

Little one? The last person who called her that had been her father—when he still had his sight. It was the compassion that broke her where exile and even the caravan's care of her had not. Aisha tried to break free of Judge Chaya. When she could not escape, she turned her face into the chair's high back and wept, sinking down until she was curled up on its broad seat like an injured child.

Her tears poured down without drying this time. That too was a survival reflex, here, in this moist place, her body could afford the release of tears.

"They didn't even bury him," she sobbed. "The cyborg . . . he broke my father's arm—I heard him scream. He told my father 'the Breedmaster was an idiot who threw you out.' He *looked* at me, and I had to fight him or he would have . . ." She shuddered, fighting for control, and she drew deep breaths of the valley air. "I killed him, but they have slain my father's honor."

Chaya rocked her as if she had been an innocent. What a luxury; to be weak, to be little. She didn't think she ought to allow it. She didn't think she could stop it.

"I didn't hear this," she remarked over Aisha's tumbled braids. "What have the *mamzrim* . . . the Sauron bastards . . . done this time?"

"Ran into a Sauron patrol on our way back from Nûrnen or thereabouts. Apparently"—Barak lowered his voice—"they dug old Juchi up, quartered him, and put him on the wall for everyone to see. She overheard, of course."

Mother and son sat beside her and held her with a strength equal to her own.

"Karl, you had reports . . . ?"

"I haven't released my patient," Karl Haller announced.

Aisha looked up in time to see the Judge transfix the physician with one significant glance. Trouble? Her tears dried immediately.

"Reports, Karl. Before cousin Hans thinks we're trying to bribe you. Besides, young Kemal is probably prowling back and forth, dying to interrogate someone. I don't like it when any of the warriors from the tribes get that impatient. People have a way of dying."

"Of conspicuous knife-wounds," the Judge agreed. "Bad for your patients."

"Apart from the damage to my patients, they cause feuds. And this near Ruth's Day or with the election . . ."

"Definitely counterproductive." *Ivrit* and Edenite grinned at each other, allies for the moment.

Karl Haller nodded, his face thoughtful. "Allies, they call us. Honored brothers. Right. Like Cain and Abel. I can drive that, at least, through my cousins' thick heads."

Edenite and *Ivrit* nodded, in perfect amity.

His hand went out, almost irresolute, and Chaya's grasp on Aisha's shoulder tightened.

"Aisha is *my* kin, remember? I'll take care of her for you."

He was out the door before Aisha could thank him.

"I think . . ." Chaya began deliberately, "he likes

you. And he's a fine man. I think we might help you build a very acceptable future. His wife has been dead long enough . . ."

Aisha jerked away. "I have to go back. I have to avenge my father."

"He . . . my brother is dead," Chaya said flatly. "I left my husband Heber for others to bury and came back here where I was needed. . . . And that was my life, and that was my honor."

"With a young son . . ."

"Barak wasn't born yet," Chaya said.

"They didn't bury my father. They dug him up! It stinks to heaven, and Allah weeps . . ."

"God," Barak muttered, "don't let Hans Haller hear you say that."

"Quiet, son!" Chaya snapped. "Aisha, you are our blood kin. We'll do what we can. Judge's honor. *My* honor."

All over the Pale, books were being balanced before Ruth's Day. People who had not spoken for a year, clans that had snapped at neighbors or snapped up their land or livestock were talking again, hesitantly. It was not easy—whether you were Bandari or Edenite—to admit error, and no easier to accept forgiveness than to offer it. And there were a few people who would be skimping all year after paying back their debts.

Aisha, dressed in yet another fine new suit of leathers, followed Judge Chaya and Barak toward the Pale's meeting place.

"We have some of Judge Ruth's belongings. Would you care to see them?" Chaya asked.

"Watch it," muttered Barak.

"Oh?" Chaya raised a surprisingly elegant brow. "Kemal. He's coming our way."

Aisha braced herself as Judge Chaya greeted him in the language of the tribes and smiled as he flicked fingers at heart, brow, and lips. "Khatun ... Judge, I must speak with you," he began, though he faced Barak.

"We are on our way to show our kinsman Judge Ruth's belongings. Come with us?" asked Chaya. She turned to lead the way.

That left Kemal and Aisha standing, staring like fools, at each other. Like a girl more than twenty years her junior, Aisha lowered her head, waiting for the warrior to speak first, longing for the protective status of the *yashmak* she had renounced when she chose her father's exile. She felt her hand coming up to veil the lower half of her face and forced it back down.

"It is a long time, Aisha," he muttered.

She nodded. She did not understand why he feared the meeting. Tarik's son; possibly the next chief; probably married at least once to sleek women with no hint of a family curse about them. It was she who stood defeated, a beggar at her sister/aunt's ample table.

"You must have many sons," she observed.

"Three. And"—he turned to the Judge—"all dishonored. We are kin, all of us, in the tribe. And it shames us for one of our own to lie rotting under Cat's Eye."

You cast him out! Anger and a kind of astonished gratitude warred and kept Aisha silent just as surely as did Judge Chaya's hand upon her arm.

The Judge's hands worked deftly, unfastening a lock. "I say," she began deliberately, "that this is Ruth's Day when debts are acknowledged, quarrels are resolved, and all books are balanced. I honor you as a good guest."

She switched into the language of the tribes, in which the word "juchi" meant "guest."

"The man you speak of was cast out by his tribe, but acknowledged by his blood kin, who stand here. We shall not let him suffer dishonor, nor share in it.

But you must decide, guest of the Pale. Is it to your honor to join in avenging a man all believe to be accursed?"

Blood rose to Kemal's face. "The Saurons shame us," he muttered.

"Only if we let them. My kinswoman killed a cyborg; do you think she will let her father's disgrace live?"

The nomad's eyes widened. He nodded to the Judge, then bowed to Aisha as if she were still a princess in the yurts and strode off.

Smiling thinly, the Judge led the way into the meeting hall. Aisha stared about her, fascinated, for the hall had windows—not just skins stretched across openings cut into the walls, but windows wrought of precious, colored glass. All her life, she had heard stories of the wealth of the Bandari; she had eaten their food, worn their clothes, and profited from their medicines. But the luxury of those windows, with their stars and stags, their hammers, their swords, and all the other sigils of the Pale, startled her.

A table had been set up and covered with an embroidered cloth. On it rested treasure that none of the Bandari would covet, fond as they were of treasure. Its value lay only in the fact that once it had belonged to Ruth bat Boaz: the innocent vanity of frayed ribbons in pale colors, perhaps given her by Piet fan Reenan; a book, encased in some shiny stuff, with letters that Aisha could not read and a picture of a frail, blonde girl in a blue robe on its cover; some simple first aid supplies; the gleaming, well-kept menace of a handgun.

Beside the relics of the first judge lay a heavy chain from which hung a large enameled medallion—a springbok superimposed on a six-pointed white star and framed by flaming swords on a field of blue. It would go to the next *kapetein*, Aisha thought. Barak avoided even looking at it.

"Ruth's own father hung her on a cross for defying him when she was the age you were, Aisha, when you led your father into exile. Do you understand what I am saying? If she could recover from her own father's attempt to kill her and rise to be Judge over the Pale and the mother of healthy children, you, too . . ."

I saw you nod, tante, sister, when the djinni you call Karl Haller came to my side. What future do you plan for me? Sufferance in a clan that does not want me? "There goes our kinsman and his barbarian woman?" Watched, corrected, and not reminded of everyone's generosity and patience not more than thrice a day? Sooner would I flee to the steppe and make my way alone back to Nûrnen.

She turned to Chaya, and the reproaches died on her trembling lips. The Judge wore Badri's face, and Badri had always wanted the best for her daughter. That evil, not good, had come of Badri's care was not her fault. Light glinted off the book in which another woman cursed by her blood had found delight. Ruth's father was not her fault. Her care, perhaps, and a sorrow that would abide unto death: but she bore no blame.

"On Ruth's Day, we forgive," Chaya murmured. "It is no bad thing to start by forgiving yourself."

Tears welled. Again, Aisha did not begrudge them. Nor was she the only one, in the crowd of clansfolk who pressed into that room and sat on the narrow benches, to weep that day. She pressed her hands over her eyes as old Barak, who still wielded the armies of the Pale, spoke of the *kapetein*, who had been friend and brother to him. When young Barak laid an arm over her shoulder, she did not jerk away from its comfort.

She blinked away sorrow and glanced around. Quick reassurance twinkled at her from Karl Haller's eyes. How different he was from his stolid kin! Sitting well behind him in the seats reserved for the women of the Eden clans was *meid* Sannie, who glared at Aisha as if resenting her place.

The Bandari kept good order during the Memorial, if good order included the whispers of children, the footsteps of elders whose bladders would not let them sit still for the long speeches, the hasty, apologetic pad ... pad ... pad of mothers removing children who whimpered at the breast. The adults were quiet during the speeches; Aisha, schooled to the watchfulness of an untold number of camps in which she was the only guard, shivered with the tension in the air.

A General Council had been called. Members of *kamandim* and Church Elders not already present were traveling from outlying areas. The election of a new *kapetein* was too important to be left to proxies; and this vote, Aisha knew, was trouble.

Who will wear the chain of office? the tension seemed to demand. One by one, it focused on the leaders who sat near Aisha, at the front of the hall. *You are too frail,* it told some, like the dead *kapetein's* brother. *You? Unlikely:* to another. *It won't be you:* to the sour-faced Haller elder who sat, master of his kin, and glared at clans he could not master. *It might be you.* As if aware of the scrutiny, Barak shivered.

Sannie watched him intently, as if trying to make out which part of him was Sauron and which, Bandari. She would be a difficult kinswoman, Aisha thought.

It was past noon when the service ended. A cold wind drove the clouds from the pale sky. Then the sun seemed to brighten; warmth even seemed to come from the baleful Cat's Eye, visible even now: Ruth's Day came at the time of year when there was no darkness.

Barak groaned and stretched. "I can't sit for that long," he complained. "And with all those eyes on me."

"They'll be watching you at the feast, too," Chaya warned.

"I'll be too hungry to mind. Let's go!" He laughed and flung one arm about his mother, the other about Aisha, making a great show of hurrying his womenfolk along.

For all Barak's rushing, they were not the first to the feast. What seemed like hundreds of hungry Bandari and Edenites clustered about the trestle tables where roast lambs lay, surrounded by kebabs, stews, roasts, and more usual fare, such as cheeses, flat breads, and salads. On another table, guarded by women and under heavy assault by the children of every clan, rested sweets: baklava and other pastries, dried fruits, and decorated eggs.

Already, a few red-faced men—Edenite farmers from the look of them—leaned against yet another table on which rested a veritable army of bottles— *vadaka*, whisky, mead, ice-wine, and the treacherous liqueurs Aisha had never seen, much less sipped. Behind it stood barrels of ale.

Kemal and his followers drank and ate and belched politely, but their eyes never ceased the watchful flick ... flick ... flick of a beast wondering whether to challenge the pack leader. One of the nomads began to sway back and forth where he sat. Kemal snapped out an order, and one of his fellows led him away.

"Nipping at the whisky, I bet," muttered Barak. "I hope he's a quiet drunk. What about you, Aisha?"

I don't drink much. I don't eat much. Usually haven't had the chance. The feast would be ordeal, not celebration, for her. *Watch the barbarian eat. See her do it all wrong.*

"You'd drink kumiss, wouldn't you?" Barak asked her. "We must have some of it around. Mother, your usual?" He disappeared into the crowd.

"I take it you don't eat pork," Chaya led Aisha toward the tables. Without seeming to guide or observe her, she helped her fill a plate with more food than she had seen at once since she was a child. Barak returned with the mare's milk, and no one raised an eyebrow at her choice of drink. The talk and the food relaxed Aisha, and she found herself laughing, even when *Oom* Karl wandered by and offered, with a grin, to pay his admission to their table with a round of drinks. Not bothering to pull up a chair, he leaned an arm over hers as if he had a perfect right.

Chaya caught her eye and winked. Kemal, passing by with Sheva bat Barak and some other merchants, nodded gravely at the way her new clan seemed to accept her. Her relief at his approval didn't even annoy her as she thought it should. And when *meid* Sannie glared, she was able to smile and beckon her over. If Barak were to become *kapetein*, he would need a wife, and Sannie was smart and strong.

Sannie scowled (*Ya Allah! Does she think my cousin would even* look *at me? There's been enough of that in this family!*) and turned her back.

Barak chuckled. "She gets like that. She'll be back."

Two men wearing the sigil of Gimbutas came up, one holding an extra beer, which he handed Sannie.

"She's probably trying to make Barak jealous. Hasn't worked yet," Karl Haller said. "It's all a matter of time, time to heal. You'll see."

Two of Sannie's cousins came up beside her and wrapped arms about her, shouting that another caravan had just come in, and Sannie must come see. Two caravan guards, a very young man and woman, strode toward them, arms linked. The man had a long rope of blond hair, conspicuous against his dark skin and green eyes. The woman's blue eyes flashed, and her personality, though she was little more than a girl, blazed more fiercely than anyone's but Judge Chaya's. Following her, almost trotting to keep up, was a younger girl enough like her to be her sister.

Even Aisha knew enough of the Bandari clans by

now to know that the newcomers were of clans not
especially friendly to Sannie's. Still, she greeted them
with a grin. When they left, she and the Gimbutas
men hoisted their drinks in salute. Shortly thereafter,
they followed.

Karl Haller groaned. "They're back! I don't know
what's worst. Having another Karl about who gets into
fights, having him fight with Shulamit there, or having
them on good terms with each other."

"Thing is, you just don't like being called Little
Karl," someone threw at the healer, and he groaned
theatrically. "Not when Big Karl is young enough to
be your son."

Aisha felt the healer twitch under her hand.

"You want Shulamit and Big Karl to stay on good
terms with each other," Barak said. "When they fight,
they tend to throw things. But you can't break a bedroll when you pound it."

Aisha surprised herself by flushing like a tribute
maiden, then laughing. She felt engulfed by clan, by
friends.

Let it be real. Praise Allah, let it be real.

One or two tribesmen wove by—Kemal couldn't
keep a watch on all of them, apparently. They eyed
her owlishly. She started to look down, then met their
eyes with what was not boldness for a woman of the
Bandari. *This* was her clan now.

The long, long day went on. She could not remember a happier one.

An old man with light eyes strode toward the table.

"Ho, *aluf!*" called Karl Haller. He released Aisha's
hand, almost surprised to find himself holding it.

"What's wrong with him?" Aisha asked. For all the
kumiss she had drunk, she was instantly sober, instantly
alert.

"Dammit, I'm not on call," muttered Haller. "All
we need . . ."

The newcomer's face was sweaty. His hands shook

visibly, not with age, but with anger. Seeing him, Karl Haller rose so fast he almost overset her chair.

"*Oom* Avi," he greeted the newcomer. Whispers informed Aisha that Avi Allon was the oldest healer in the valley, so much respected that he never accompanied warriors or caravans, but worked with the women's doctors, helping to birth the next generation. "What's happened? Has there been an accident?"

"There certainly has been," said the old physician. Aisha rose and tried to give him her chair.

"Thank you. First time in the valley? First child? I haven't seen you before."

He doesn't know me. He thinks I'm someone's wife. I could pass for normal here. I could. I could.

"My niece," Chaya told him firmly. "Aisha."

Now was the time for him to recoil at the outcast. Instead, he shook his head, dismissing the subject. "Hold on, Karl. I said there was an accident."

"I'll have to get my kit unless . . ." But the elder healer's hands were empty.

"No one's hurt. But some pigeater broke into the dispensary. No, no drugs or knives are missing. And you don't know how relieved I am about that."

"We can station guards," Barak suggested. "But what *was* taken?"

The fire began to cool in Avi Allon's eyes. When Barak slid a drink across the table, he picked it up in hands that no longer shook with rage.

"Medical records. All my files have been rifled."

The Judge had to have been standing ten meters away in a crowd that made about as much noise as a tamerlane balked of its dinner. But she heard. Almost at once, she was at her son's side, listening, her eyes flicking across the tables of feasters, trying to pick out who was and who was not there. Naturally, Kemal stood at her side: the watcher at the feast. It was as important for him to ferret out signs of trouble as it was for him to see a show of Bandari strength. Alliances could rise and fall for less.

"Who would be interested in medical records?" Barak asked.

"How should I know?" Allon snapped. "You maybe. Your mother. Your own doctor. Your records were one of the set that's gone missing."

Barak looked at the old healer, puzzled. Then he threw back his head and laughed.

"For what?" he asked. "The arm I broke when I tried to shoot *Kapetein* Mordecai's rifle when I was eight? Every scratch I took in training? Obviously, someone's pouring from a bad barrel of beer! Why don't we get a new one and forget all this?"

"I need those records, ben Heber!" snapped Allon. "There's other things in them than broken arms!"

"*Scheiss!*" hissed Karl Haller. "The old man just lost it."

Maybe it was the kumiss. Aisha blinked at him. Barak still laughed, and even Judge Chaya forced a grin, ghastly though it was.

"Waiting to see if you die in a fit, *Sauron!*" shouted Hans Haller. "Maybe they didn't throw your granma on the scrap heap for nothing!"

"You fucking bastard!" Barak screamed, and leaped for the Edenite's throat. Three men hurled themselves forward to stop the fight.

Judge Chaya stood, as frozen as Aisha herself, watching Karl Haller. They must know what was in those records—another curse? Please Allah it would not bring ruin down upon this last of her kin: Chaya blind, Chaya cast out to wander—hardened as Aisha thought herself to be, she cringed until the screams alerted her once more.

Aisha had heard tribesmen scream in rage. She had heard outraged Bandari before. But she had never imagined the sheer volume of outrage and curses that she heard now.

"I don't give a damn, Haller," the old healer spat. "Confidential be damned. Sealed files be damned. Those are medical records, and we need them. Make up your mind, man. Are you a doctor or a politician?"

"I'm trying to keep the damn Pale from splintering!" the younger man shouted. "I suggest you do the same."

She reached for her belt-knife. They all had belt-knives, even Kemal and his men, who backed toward each other. Their eyes flicked around the infuriated Bandari. Abruptly, Aisha's own blood cooled. Time, as she thought of it, slowed, and her thoughts clicked past like beads on an abacus, adding into a sum she didn't like.

Something about those looks. They meant more than concern that the brawl turn into a riot and from there, deteriorate to a feud in which not even honored guests were safe. They were more than apprehension; call it satisfaction, perhaps? Aisha didn't like the look of them.

A peripheral flick of her own memory, and she recalled how *meid* Sannie had left with cousins.

Cousins? Gimbutas cousins—and she of an Edenite *kumpany?* Gimbutas were swarthy; Gimbutas were tricksy . . . like nomads. Gimbutas from an outlying territory, perhaps cousins who lived outside the Pale altogether.

"SHUT IT DOWN!" shouted Judge Chaya with all the power in her Sauron-bred body.

Aisha smelled blood in the air, the result of some lucky punches. Its hot-copper scent made her adrenaline spike up, to be subsumed in that readiness that was the mark of the Sauron-born.

Kemal and his men froze, hands falling away from their belt knives. Carefully, as if setting up an ambush, they began to back out of the crowd. Aisha followed them with her eyes, aware that the Judge was administering a tongue-lashing such as she hoped *never* to deserve: something about "reasonable concern for future health" turned into a blistering attack on lack of respect for Bandari customs ... "disgrace before important guests" and "indecent breach of mourning for our *kapetein*." The Sauron part of Aisha's memory would "store" that lecture for when she would have time to retrieve it from memory. Maybe in a hundred years.

For now, however, she concentrated on being inconspicuous, on passing unnoticed in a storm of reproaches and accusing glares. Like Kemal, she backed away from the center of the fight. Into the shadows, where she could hide and think and plan. She had never been too good at thinking and planning for more than a day ahead. One thing, though, she knew.

This was not a time to warn Judge Chaya that the Pale was filled with spies. Perhaps, if she could bring proof, none of those stares would touch her. She would have brought honor to the Bandari—and perhaps they could help her restore her own.

Gradually, the shouting subsided—into sullenness on the part of some of the Edenites, mutters broken by Karl Haller's earnest, persuasive voice; and into loud, even drunken self-blame on the part of the Bandari, who began to stage a reconciliation that would have made a wedding festival look staid by comparison.

Her senses alert to catch the *warmth* of the spies that she always sensed but no one but her father (and the Judge or another Sauron) could, her nostrils flaring to catch the scent of the men she suspected, Aisha prowled. Her boots squeaked with newness, so she shed them and walked about the camp that way. She wanted silence for her thoughts and her own concealment.

Could she be certain Kemal had set spies? How could she find out? And, even if she found out, how could she bring proof against them, exile that she was? This was a problem Judge Chaya *might* have been able to handle with all the resources of the Pale behind her.

Cat's Eye jeered down at her. *You had a girl's training and then a refugee's. What do you think* you *can do?*

Not trip over the child who wandered into her path, surely.

"*Meid? Tante,*" the girl corrected herself. Her eyes held an unchildlike curiosity that reminded Aisha of Karl Haller. (She wished she could bring this problem to him. That was the problem when a wild thing was tamed; it looked to the tamer for protection and aid.) "Why aren't you at the feast?"

Aisha put out a hand to tip up the girl's chin. Like all children in the Pale, she was respectful but utterly at ease with adults: in the Pale, all adults were protectors of children, or else painfully dead.

"I had eaten and drunk enough," she answered with the first words that came to mind. "And you? What is your name, little sister?"

"Erika," said the girl. "I followed my sister Shulamit and her friend . . ." Her eyes creased into merriment, and Aisha revised upward her estimate of the child's age. "No, not like that. They said they went on a new hunt. Not for tamerlanes but for men. I heard them say it. For spies."

Aisha stared at the girl. *Allah, do you send a child to aid me?*

"I like you," she confided. "You do not laugh at me for what I said. Shulamit said people would laugh if I told them."

"You are Bandari," Aisha said. "Even young as you are, you would not say . . ."

"They go to find proof now, Shulamit and Karl do. But they make noise when they hunt!" Outrage quivered in the girl's soft voice. "You do not make noise when you walk." She pointed at Aisha's bare feet.

"Why do you tell me?"

"Because you are kin to Barak and the Judge. You know . . ." she glanced around before mouthing the name of the nomad chieftain, not daring even a breath of sound. "I watched you."

Had Aisha been all that much older than this Erika when she had left Tallinn? That seemed as long ago now as the time when Haven turned cold.

Aisha squatted down beside the girl. "What makes you think . . . ?" she whispered.

"Shulamit travels . . . much. She says she never saw the cousins who call themselves Gimbutas before, and when she greeted them, they watched her as if she were a *nafkeh* . . . a whore," she translated. "Our clan would not do so."

She cocked her head at the girl. *Where?* Wide-eyed, Erika pointed. *That way.* Aisha glanced down at her feet and grinned in appreciation: not having Sauron blood, the girl couldn't risk the loss of toes or worse by going barefoot. But she had worn soft slippers, rather than boots. A clever child. Allah send she have a better fate than Aisha.

Silently, they prowled, past yurt, wagon, and home. Lamps, torches, and fires confused the senses Aisha had learned to rely on in her years of wandering the steppes; the nightsounds of a town, sinking to rest after the emotions of a feast, a binge, and a near-riot, blocked her hearing.

"This isn't going to work," she whispered to Erika. "Go find your sister and go home."

"They said it would be someplace private." Her eyes danced with sudden, wholly unmalicious humor. "They know a lot of places to go. That's why they thought they could find the spies."

A boy and a girl, scarcely adult, more intent on each other than on caution; Aisha wanted to groan.

"Do you know of such places?" she asked the girl. Erika promptly raised a hand and began to tick what had to be half the meeting places of the Bandari young folk off on her fingers.

Privacy, Aisha thought. It was scarcer than rubies of the type that glittered on her hand, either in the tribes or among the Bandari. And yet, if reports had been stolen and were to be passed to the men who had stolen them, it must be done in private. Assuming the spies were Kemal's men, she didn't think an exchange could be made in Kemal's yurts—too closely watched. Assuming—which she didn't—that the spies were Gimbutas, she couldn't imagine any privacy at all in that clan; and, again, if they masqueraded as Gimbutas, they wouldn't risk exposure.

The Bandari of Eden ... memories clicked and flashed into place: the bunker, where Ruth had been held; where Judge Chaya had hidden as a child. Honored now, but little used; and far enough away that no one might watch it. It was a wild guess, but it was better than the nothing she had turned up in a long night of wandering.

You know, Aisha told herself, *you could be making all this up, you and a little, left-out meid who wants attention. Can't you see it now?* "Oh, that's our crazy cousin." *Really a great political asset, just when you mean to help.*

She recognized that voice; it was the inner killer you heard when the winds lashed you, you hadn't eaten for days, you had a fever, and all you thought you wanted was to lie down and sleep forever. She had practice in ignoring it, and she hadn't lived this long by distrusting her hunches.

First, get the child away.

"Erika, do you know where Judge Chaya lives? I want you to get her . . . please. And tell her that her niece, Aisha . . . bat Juchi, can you remember that? thinks she's found some answers. You can say you helped; you did. Ask her if she can come to the bunker"—Erika's eyes widened—"as soon as she can. Armed. Then, *you go home,* do you hear me? And if you meet your sister and Big Karl, tell them to go home, too."

"*Ja, tante,*" Erika nodded and padded off so fast that Aisha would have taken hot iron in her hand and sworn that the girl would obey all her instructions. Except, perhaps, the last one.

The Judge was half Sauron. And Barak wouldn't let her go alone. Three half-breeds ought to be enough to take out a nest of spies.

Stealthily, Aisha crept toward the bunker. The approaches and the half-ruined stonework offered some sturdy places for hands and feet: she didn't want to leave a blood trail on the rocks for men or beasts. She took a deep breath of air and waited, utterly motionless, surveying the place with all her senses. From within a cracked wall came the sense of heat. Well enough, but it could be a beast, or beasts. She flared her nostrils. Human scent, unmistakable, but without the spoor of rut that even she could identify. Four people: she counted the invisible sources of heat.

The cyborg she had slain knew by training as well as instinct *how* to use the senses she fumbled even now to control. No point regretting it. Aisha edged closer . . . no, that handhold looked like it would crumble . . . three points anchored . . . lever the leg *over* now, quietly, you fat musky!

The pulse in her temples distracted her so she ignored it, focusing on the heat, the voices up ahead . . . by instinct, she crept up the rocks, picking a vantage-point, a place where she could listen and watch and, if the time came, when the time came, intervene.

"What do they say?" The voice bore the accent of Tallinn, but weighted with heavy sarcasm. "Bring the *hakim* along, you said; one *hakim* can understand the words of another."

Aisha heard whispered curses and a scrabbling through pages. "They're in *bandarit*, even to the letters. Allah wither them!"

"Then we get someone to read them," came a third voice. *Kemal.* "The fool slut who helped us gain them. Fetch her. She can refuse us nothing now."

"I'll go, lord," said a man whose arms were almost as fine as Kemal's own.

Aisha shifted into shadow as one of the nomads slipped from the bunker. She would know his scent again, if anyone would believe her.

Sannie? Somehow, that made sense. She wanted Barak, and she wanted him to be *kapetein*. Seize the records, hide them. If nothing in them hurt Barak, betray Kemal and let them be "found." Or find them yourself and reap the harvest of gratitude that might follow and be wife to the *kapetein*—and healer of the rift between Eden and *Ivrit*, if Sannie cared for that.

But if the medical records held . . . oh, Aisha did not know what . . . taints in the blood, the threat of disease, the nomads had what they could not read and would probably destroy. And the files would hold no dangers for Barak.

It was all dishonor, greater than her own in leaving her father's corpse unburied.

Grimly, Aisha shook her head. If they planned hunts as badly as they planned this, they would have starved to death. The wind blew and she sheltered against the rock as the night passed. How long, dammit, how long would it take for the Judge to come or for Sannie to betray herself? She had wintered on the steppe, and the Pale's weather was gentle in comparison; but she didn't think she could wait that long before she *must* attack.

"Douse that flame! Someone's coming!"

Darkness.

Aisha didn't think that Barak or the Judge would make the noise she heard, a confident crunch/crunch/crunch of boots on rock. Obviously, someone did not fear disclosure. Other bootsteps followed.

A new light flashed into the darkness, deliberately glinting on the long barrel of a pistol. "You've got the medical records? Hand them over."

The accent was burred, harsh, that of an Edenite. Aisha had last heard that voice upbraiding her kinfolk. Hans Haller? Had *he* set the spies?

"I had Sannie watched. Should have known she'd do something stupid. These women ... what we get for letting them think they run things ... even our esteemed Judge."

Incongruously, Kemal laughed. "You'd shoot a guest?"

"I'd say you outwore your welcome when you turned spy. So I'll take these, and you can just leave quietly. Or you can have a fight and be known as the men who turned on their hosts."

How many people had come up here? Aisha wondered. The more who knew of this, the less chance for a decent concealment.

"The new *kapetein* would hardly approve of this. . . ."

Haller gestured at the records. "*Those* prove he's no more fit to be *kapetein* . . ."

"Than who?" a woman's voice pierced the night. "Than you, Hans Haller? Who is *your* candidate? Or had you planned to hold whatever *might* be in those records over Barak's head? Blackmail is as much a crime, you know, as theft. Or spying."

So quietly that Aisha had never heard it, Judge Chaya and her son had come up the rocks and fanned out into position. Two clicks sounded.

"I would like to know," the Judge's voice was assured, even a little humorous, "who is whose catspaw in this. Sannie? A willing tool. She might not even guess who put her up to it. Or did someone . . . one of her own . . . egg her on. *Steal* the records since your attempt to get Karl to disclose their contents failed miserably. Never mind what harm it might do our medical care. Steal them, discredit Kemal for spying, throw me out of office? That's another way to look at it. Or, let's look at it from Kemal's point of view. Cast the Bandari into ferment, maybe into civil war, and then move in, if you can.

"A pretty mess."

"You're a fine one to talk about messes," Haller snarled at the Judge. "Righteous, aren't you? You don't want your son to be *kapetein*? You want it so bad you can taste it. But he's just not qualified, is he? Not of old Piet's line, is he? Because *you're* not. We all know that, just like we know why that woman you brought in wears the ring you used to have. She's bad seed, isn't she? You all are. We never saw you with your husband. How do we know . . ."

The bullet that punched the life out of Hans Haller came from behind Aisha. He looked astonished, then agonized, and then like nothing at all. As Haller's guards whirled, trying to find the source of the shot, the tribesmen jumped. Aisha saw knives glint and then streams of blood, rapidly cooling in the night.

Barak dropped to his feet and walked into the bunker. "Everyone don't move. Haller just went too far. And you heard it. One move, though, and you'll go farther."

Incongruously, Kemal chuckled. "What about you?"

Barak shrugged. To Aisha's senses, his breath and pulse were normal . . . Soldier normal . . . and he wasn't sweating at all. Half-blood that he was, he should have shown more stress than that. "A man's mother—she's sacred, or should be. All right, Kemal. This has all gone too far. Hand over the records."

Kemal prodded at Hans Haller with his toe. "I

never liked him," he said. "This was well done, all but the blood feud it will bring."

"We don't have feuds," said Barak. "We have laws. I'll have to stand trial."

Kemal grinned sardonically. "So you say. Say it again if you live that long. But hear what I say, man of law: If the Pale casts you out for this night's work, I'll make a place for you in the tribe."

Absently, Barak flipped through the crumpled leaves. "Sure. After all, I'm of your blood. Just like Aisha. Come on in, why don't you, cousin? You, too, mother. Let's make it a family party."

Kemal shook his head as if admiring what? Enemy? Ally? Aisha sought for a word and found it in *accomplice*.

Judge Chaya slipped in through a fissure in the wall. "We ought to burn those," she muttered.

Barak laughed, a sound Aisha distrusted. "Kemal, you were right about law, weren't you? God, that I should live to see the day. The Judge urging her son to break the law? Why?"

He bent over the records. "I could understand concern over my . . . our Sauron blood. But I'd have thought it was diluted. You're only half-blood, so I'm a quarter Sauron. Shouldn't make for any trouble. Unless," he froze. "Unless . . ."

Light glinted off the ruby on Aisha's hand and caught Chaya's attention. Abruptly, she seemed to shrink in on herself; for the first time, she looked old. She looked at Aisha, who knew in that moment that both faced the same walking nightmare every day of their lives.

"Blood," Judge Chaya murmured. "So much blood. Always calling for more." She looked down at the bodies lying in the darkness that spread out from beneath them. "The God-bloody Saurons." Her eyes darkened as if she stared into hell. "They took him from me. Took Heber. And I never even saw his body."

"*Ama* . . ." Barak's voice was gentle on the word.

"She's got to let it out," Aisha's voice was so ruthless she could barely recognize it. "All these years, the wound has festered. What did you do, kinswoman? The Saurons stole a life from you, so you . . . stole one back?"

Chaya nodded. "You aren't the only woman who kills Saurons, girl. Left him dead on the plain with a spike through his head. My son's *mine*. He was just the means."

"So I'm not of Piet's line on either side," Barak said. "You didn't want to admit what you'd done. Instead, you discouraged thoughts of me becoming *kapetein*. But what if I had? What would have become of your law if I had?"

"It was all in the blood!" Chaya snarled, then seized control of herself. "The law would have been broken. But no one would have known. Just me. I would have taken the blame on my soul. The Pale would have had a strong leader. *And would that have been so bad?*"

"It can't happen now," Barak said.

Chaya nodded her head and dared to look at her son.

"You don't hate me?"

"I just wish you'd told me earlier. I could have done something to . . . take myself out of the running. Well," he stared down at Hans Haller's body, "at least now I've taken care of that."

"What about us?" asked Kemal.

He and his men knew too much to live now. He stank of fear, and he must know that the three who faced him could smell it; but Aisha was proud of his courage in that moment.

"Dishonored," said the Judge. "Spying. Conspiring with *him*. I wouldn't stoop to kill you. Tell about this night's work, and I'll see no one believes you. Ever. Get out of here. Come back with your warriors and we'll give you a fight. Come back with more spies . . ." She spat.

"Some more are coming," Barak observed, almost as if he counted heads at a feast. "They're not making very good time."

But then, they don't have Sauron blood.

"A tribesman," Aisha said. "Kemal sent him to bring in Sannie." Her lips quivered. "He wanted her to translate the medical records for him. Want me to tell her that her services aren't required?"

Barak shook his head. "She has to see. There has been too much hidden."

"It would not have been dishonor if my plan had worked," Kemal said. Color flushed his high cheekbones. "And my blood is still dishonored." He gestured at Aisha.

"I'm not about to kill myself to cleanse it," she told him.

He shook his head. "Not what I meant, girl. Your father, not you. We cast him out. You *chose* to go with him, a loyal daughter, worthy of honor. It's not your fault."

She shed years in that moment, years and defenses. Tears rose briefly, then subsided. Karl Haller had said the same thing. Forgiveness. Mercy. Those were . . . what? Miracles? Avenging one's blood, though, was a law.

"But it is my blood," Aisha said softly. "And my father's cries up to heaven for vengeance."

"You go," Kemal gestured to his men. "I'll see this through."

"But, *khan* . . ."

"I said, go! I am no *khan*, who am a dishonored man. Or do I slay you for your disobedience? Tell them, I shall return when I have cleansed my name."

The nomads left quickly, pushing past their comrade with his reluctant companion on the way.

"Come on in, Sannie," said Barak.

The Eden woman's eyes widened with dismay, whether at the sight of Barak or the bodies on the bunker's floor, Aisha couldn't say. But only for a moment. In the next, she controlled herself as well as any half-Sauron woman might.

"What did you hope to gain?" Chaya asked gently. "You couldn't have known what was in those records."

"He . . . *Oom* Hans . . . he wanted to know, thought there might be *something* when Karl wouldn't talk. I thought . . . I thought . . . best to get rid of them. And you would have been *kapetein*, Barak. And the Pale would have been strong. *All* of us, Eden and *Ivrit*, just as Karl's dinned into my ears since before I could ride. *And would that have been so bad?*"

Even Kemal burst out laughing. Sannie flushed with shame.

Chaya shook her head. "For the first time, Sannie, I think I could approve of you as a daughter-in-law. My thoughts exactly. But it's too late now. And the law is the law, no matter how much could we think we might have done by breaking it.

"You can't go firing off pistols—even after a feast— in the Pale and not expect someone to investigate. So I'm here. I'm investigating. What do I see? I see evidence of a fight. We could rearrange things, you know. Give one of *them* my son's pistol, say he stole it, shot at Haller, who tried to get the records back from him. Eden's got a hero; you've got a spy or two you can disavow, Kemal; and we've got a new *kapetein*. We get you installed, son, and then we can start thinking about what to do to the Saurons for *this*—just one more grudge we owe the bastards.

"Anyone game?"

"That *smells* gamey," Barak observed. "We can't live a lie like that."

Kemal grimaced, and Sannie looked sick: conspirators confronted with the results of their inept schemes. *How like Mother she looks, when Badri saw the truth crash down upon her and no idea of where to hide or how to live with the shame.*

She was a proud woman, that Judge. And she had raised a fine son, done much good for the Pale. Was she to be dishonored now?

"What other choices have we?" whispered the Judge, no Judge now but a woman who feared the ruin of her world.

Aisha stepped forward. "My choice," she said. "Exile. I left the tribe when I learned that the poison in my blood disgraced it."

She reached forward and seized Chaya's hand. It was, most surprisingly, cold. She slipped the ruby from her own finger and placed it back upon the older woman's hand. "Your husband gave you this. You gave it to me when I left Tallinn. Take it back now, and don't feel you dishonored the vows you made. Heber has a fine son to his name."

"No one need know," she hissed. "Not that. We can tell the truth. The truth is that this is a scandal. It discredits us all."

"Can't have a discredited man as *kapetein*, can you?" Barak asked. "The election will have to go elsewhere. Maybe to Old Barak. He'll kill me if he gets stuck with the job."

"Anyone who wants it *deserves* to get it," Chaya said. "You would have been a good *kapetein*. I'm sorry."

"I'm not. So, cousin, you aren't finished yet, are you? Are you suggesting we all exile ourselves till the trouble dies down?"

"Until we avenge the disgrace the Saurons have set upon us. The bloody Saurons, who have made us break our laws and most sacred oaths. I see no reason why Barak ben Heber cannot *be* Barak ben Heber," she went on rapidly. "You never saw your husband's body. Maybe he wasn't dead when . . ."

Chaya's laugh sounded like a file on iron. "Sister, you reason like a true *Ivrit!*"

"He cannot be *kapetein*, then. Fine. That is the law. But there are laws above the laws. And one of them is the law of blood. My father's blood lies upon the gates of Nûrnen, and no one has avenged it. I swore to, but my kinsfolk brought me here instead. I hoped"—*oh how I did hope*, Aisha realized with a pang as she thought of Karl Haller's weathered face and kind, *djinni*-shrewd eyes—"for a refuge and for aid. Now I do not ask for help. I *demand* it!"

"You're in no position to demand anything," Kemal observed.

"Am I not? I am the only one not touched by what has gone on tonight. And I offer you a way of wiping out the stain on your honor. Ride with me to Nûrnen to save my father's bones from their disgrace! Or, in the name of Allah, the merciful, the compassionate, and the livingkind, I go alone and fight Saurons till I die!"

Barak's growl of assent was not the only one Aisha heard.

"I saw your mother, lady, in happier times," Kemal told her. "Whether or not you succeed in this madness, you honor her. I ride with you."

"And I," said his companion. At Kemal's glare, "Your father would cut off my ears, not to mention anything else, if I came back without you. And it will be a good raid, a fine story."

Chaya stared down at her ring. "I do not think I could bear to hear myself called 'Your Honor' one more time. I'll come. And Juchi was my brother."

"I wouldn't miss it," Barak bared his teeth. "Sannie-girl?" He held out his hand, and Sannie took it and carried it to her cheek.

"I'll make it up to you," she promised. "I will. A pledge between Eden and *Ivrit*—we'll have it yet."

Aisha glanced out. The sky was lightening. Below

the bunker, the heat-shapes that meant a crowd lay waiting. No doubt, they planned an attack, just as they had so many years ago.

"I'll lead," said Chaya. "And I'll explain. Once the new *kapetein* is named—and a new Judge—we can ride."

"And when we're through?" asked Sannie. "Do we come back?"

Kemal raised a brow at her. "Do you truly expect to live to return home? We wipe out the offense to our blood in blood," he said.

"We *try*," said Aisha, who always had.

She slipped out of her jacket. "Give me your saber," she ordered. Sticking its blade through the soft, pale leather, she handed her improvised flag to Chaya. "Just in case."

It was bad law, Chaya said after her resignation, and worse precedent, but the investigation of the shooting at Ruth's Bunker probably set a record in terms of speed and efficiency. It wasn't that anyone *lied* precisely. . . .

Aisha had the sense that the Pale would be *very* glad to see the backs of everyone involved. And the fewer questions asked about their destination, the better. A few were asked, by the new *kapetein*, by the Hallers, especially Karl—but they were not addressed to her.

Aisha found she was not sorry to be leaving. Always, if she had made the Pale her home, she would have had the sense that she was betraying her blood for the life it had denied her. The decision left her feeling light, as if she had recovered from another fever, but relieved.

At the very last, only a few people turned out to see them off. One of them was young *meid* Erika, who ran up to Aisha and held out her fist. In it was a gold chain, with a medallion enameled in blue: the Eye that wards off evil.

"It's old!" the girl said. "To keep off the Lidless Eye!"

Aisha leaned down and kissed her. "Keep it for yourself. And may Allah grant you a happier fate than mine."

The new *kapetein*, as Chaya predicted, had indeed turned out to be Old Barak, and a very angry Old Barak at that. So angry that he refused to say farewell to his old friend Chaya and his namesake.

The former Judge was undisturbed. "He'll shout and rant for a day or two, then cool down. He knows where we're going. I wouldn't be surprised if he sent riders after us. Or be sorry, either.

"I just regret . . ." her voice trailed off.

You haven't *had much of a life, have you, Aisha?* Chaya had promised her a life, a place, even a home and husband of her own. Instead, she had joined Aisha in exile and a quest for vengeance.

Aisha shrugged, wordless. At least, when her sister and aunt's life fell apart, she had a new purpose she could turn to. It was more than their mother had. They would not die for nothing, if it came to that.

She ordered herself not to glance around. Karl Haller must be sick of the thought of her, much less the sight. And he had his clan, stunned by the death of their leader, to comfort. If anyone would listen to him.

A word Aisha had heard in the Pale crept into her thoughts. *Dayenu.* It would have been enough to slay the Sauron. It would have been enough to die cleanly on the steppe thereafter, to find kinsfolk, honor, even, and aid for this private *jihad* of hers. And it was enough to find that *jihad* shared.

Not much of a life? It was hers. And it was enough.

They rode in silence up from the valley, without banners or acclaim. That too was enough.

At the border of the Pale, a silent rider waited for them. His leathers were worn and comfortable, his armor somewhat less so, as if he seldom wore it. But he carried his weapons easily, and the fat roll behind his saddle was marked with the twisted serpents of his art.

"And what do you think *you're* doing?" Aisha shouted. She was abruptly, gloriously furious. And she was afraid.

"The way you're acting, I wouldn't let the lot of you cross the street alone," Karl Haller retorted. "Someone's got to look after you. And you're not the only ones who've made the Pale too hot to hold you."

Aisha glared at him. "That's all, then."

His *djinni's* glance always had seen too much. "For now."

Haller's musky fell in with the pace of the other six. No one spoke, though irrepressible Barak gestured thumbs up.

Now we are seven, Aisha thought.

That, too, was more than enough.

From *Report on Sector Seven*, Citadel Intelligence, Archives, Threat Analysis Division, Ethic Substudies, by Analyst Fifth Rank Grishnak, 2920; ammend:

. . . unfortunately, logistical difficulties constrain operations from Angband Base against the cattle territory known as *the Pale*, inhabited by the *haBandari*.

The haBandari are a post-Sauron-contact ethnic group. Linguistic and genetic analysis indicate very mixed background, now stabilized as a neorace; see references, *Ashkenazim, Leituas, Harmony/ Americ*. Significant deviations from human-norm clines are traceable to admixtures of *Frystaat* ancestry; extreme selective pressures among the human-norm settlers of that planet produced genetic modifications comparable in a few respects to those introduced on Homeworld by the eugenics programs of the Sauron Unified State before the wars with the Empire (see *genetic analysis, attached*). The haBandari population is in excess of 200,000; the Pale also contains some 150,000 of the Americ-descended religio-political subgroup known as *Edenites*, who are associated with the haBandari in a dominance/symbiosis linkage. The haBandari speak a language of their own, *Bandarit*; computer analysis indicates this arose as a creolized contact-pidgin between *Americ* and *New*

Hebrew, with substantial contributions from *Afrikaans* and *Lithuanian* (see *linquistic analysis, attached*).

As indicated by the population density, the haBandari practice a mixed economy, with sedentary livestock ranching on their unusually productive steppe and mixed irrigation farming in the *Eden Valley,* a large and relatively fertile lowland with air pressure sufficient for low-risk pregnancy among human norms. Yields are compatible with extensive investment and empirical understanding of plant/animal genetics. Research indicates highly developed handicrafts and intermediate-technology extractive-manufacturing industries, including paper, flintlock firearms, gunpowder, glass, small quantities of high-carbon steel; the above goods are exported in some quantity, mainly in exchange for raw materials. Government is an elective monarchy with oligarchic and democratic features and highly effective military forces, by cattle standards.

My analysis indicates the extreme desirability of bringing the haBandari under our hegemony and levying genetic and economic tribute from this rich source of goods and desirable genes. Further Intelligence operations are imperative.

* * *

From: *Annual Field Intelligence Reports,* Angband Base, relayed to Citadel Intelligence Division, Archives, Threat Analysis Division, Ethic Substudies, 2920; ammend:

. . . *item 17:* Analyst Fourth Rank Grishnak, seven periods without reports while on detached duty with *haBandari Project,* presumed lost while infiltrating enemy territory. *item 18:* maintenance on . . .

SHAME AND HONOR

S.M. Stirling

Prologue

Base First Rank Urthak nodded as he entered the Quilland Base computer room. "That will be all," he said. The Technical Rank specialists nodded in return and left with swift silence.

Urthak sat before the Threat Analysis computer and laid his palm on the screen. It identified him and unlocked; he gave one last glance around the dimly lit room with its blue-glowing screens, using his IR-sensitive eyes. Paranoia, perhaps, but . . .

"THREATS TO QUILLAND BASE—RANK ORDER," he typed. There was a second of waiting, as the computer called on the computational power of the Base mainframe, as much optical-chip circuitry as anyone had on Haven these days.

1. THE CITADEL
2. THE NEWLY ASSIGNED PERSONNEL FROM THE CITADEL
3. THE HABANDARI
4. STEPPE NOMADS, CLANS SUBJECT TO YESUGEI KHAN
5. COSSAKI, *STANITSA* OF BERGENOV

7. OTHERS TOO LOW A PROBABILITY TO BE CALCULATED

Urthak smiled thinly. That was the good thing about computers; they had only those loyalties that you programmed into them. Unlike Soldiers, whatever the cattle thought. Sauron Soldiers could have irritatingly complicated allegiances; for example, they could obstinately insist that the Quilland Base CO should follow every minor directive that came in from the Citadel, whether it reflected accurate understanding of local conditions or not. They might construe his programming of the Citadel as a threat possibility to be treason.

This reflects a refusal to acknowledge reality, he thought. *To acknowledge the passing of three centuries.* Quilland Base had been founded thirty years after the arrival of the Saurons on Haven, in the first flush of victory, when they had believed this world of refuge lay open to them like the legs of a well-trained breeder. When it seemed that the Sauron Unified State would rise again almost immediately, beyond the reach or knowledge of the Imperials who had defeated the first Sauron attempt at supreme power and destroyed Homeworld.

Only natural that they should think in those terms, he thought. The founders had been of the first generation; from lost Homeworld, or raised by those who were. The *Dol Guldur* had brought fifty thousand pedigree Sauron ova, and the Soldiers of that day had supersonic transports, energy weapons, every sort of communications device. But the weapons wore out, and then the machine-tools to build replacements, and the alloys. The breeding program slowed as well, once the ova and the gene-splicing equipment was gone. Saurons produced three male births for every female, and many Sauron-Sauron crossings were not viable; a simple matter on Homeworld, where the eugenics laboratories could handle problems like that. On Haven, it meant centuries of relentless inbreeding and culling; only now were they producing numbers of Soldiers equal to the ancestral stock.

Better, actually, Urthak mused. Less given to dying in convulsions or suffering strokes from blood that clotted too fast.

And only now were they able to begin reestablishing a true unified command; Quilland Base had been an independent satrapy in fact for two centuries. Down south, Angband Base had held on on its own for a hundred and fifty years, until the cattle took it. Unity was needed, but too many at the Citadel thought in terms of the old Sauron Unified State; coldly rational, centralized, bureaucratic. Urthak snorted. On a world where horses and muskeylopes and marching men were the fastest transport? Where the remaining radios were precious relics, used only in an emergency? A network of baronies, owing loose allegiance to the Citadel and united by faith, faith in the mission of the Race—now *that* was possible.

And that Base First Rank Urthak should be the founder of the most powerful baronial line, that is also possible, the Sauron thought. His fingers moved again on the keyboard:

"THREATS TO CO, QUILLAND BASE—RANK ORDER." This time there was no pause before the glowing letters formed:

1. THE CITADEL
2. DIVISION LEADER RANK DEATHMASTER BOYLE
3. THE NEWLY ASSIGNED PERSONNEL FROM THE CITADEL
4. THE HABANDARI
5. STEPPE NOMADS, CLANS SUBJECT TO YESUGEI KHAN
6. COSSAKI, *STANITSA* OF BERGENOV

7. OTHERS TOO LOW A PROBABILITY TO BE CALCULATED

Urthak blanked the screen and for a moment sat thinking before he pressed the buzzer for a runner. He waited impassively until the servant entered and bowed. "Fetch me Division Leader Rank Deathmaster Boyle," he said.

Boyle had been back from the Tayok expedition for a day, long enough to rest and debrief. The minutes that stretched until his second-in-command arrived were neither tense nor boring; they reminded him of his youth, of campaigning against rebel Dinneh bands up in the Tierra del Muerte country. Most of the time had been spent like this, waiting behind a rock. . . .

"First Rank," the Deathmaster said, saluting with impeccable correctness. He was a tall man, nearly two meters, lean as a tamerlane in close-fitting field gray, with the skull insignia *Totenkopf* on his collar tabs. Pale eyes under heavy ridges, long boney face, lank straw-colored hair against olive-white skin; more in the traditional Sauron mold than Urthak, whose squat build and slanted black eyes favored his tribute-maiden mother.

"I've assimilated your report on the proposed Tayok Base," Urthak said. "I note the subsistence difficulties."

Boyle nodded. "The valley the Bergenov *stanitsa* controlled is fertile, and low enough to support successful childbirth," he said. Low by Haven standards, of course: on long-lost Terra it would be considered equivalent to Bogota or Addis Abbaba. Valleys like that were rare outside the inaccessible coastlines and the great lowland of Shangri-La, which could only be reached from the far eastern pass dominated by the Sauron Citadel. Rare and more precious than any gold, and bitterly contested. "Better organization will increase the crop yields, but the steppe population must be reduced."

Urthak leaned forward and steepled his fingers, conscious that even Soldier senses would detect nothing but eagerness. The new Base must hold at least a battalion of Soldiers, a thousand fighting men with their women and children, servants and laborers. No easy burden on a world as harsh as this, and a Soldier consumed many times as much in the way of calories as an unmodified man. The enhanced abilities did not come free; the fast-burning Sauron metabolism had to be stoked, and frequently. For that matter, their dependents usually had a better standard of living than most cattle.

"Yes. The grazing lands of the Cossaki north of the valley must be emptied. They can be leased to other nomads, those the Base takes as tributaries."

That was the usual arrangement, allowing favored steppe tribes to pass into a Base's lowlands for winter grazing and to bear their children, in return for tribute of food and stock and women. Such tribes grew stronger and took the grazing of their enemies; they hated the Saurons, but knew their dependence.

"Exterminating them would be costly," Urthak continued. Boyle nodded expressionlessly; the casualty ratios and estimated expenditures were in his report. "I have decided that we should drive them instead. Using them as a tool to weaken other enemies before they die."

The Deathmaster raised one eyebrow and rubbed his chin. "Difficult; our expedition has already weakened them, and the tribes to the west would resist."

For a moment Urthak's smile made his face more of a skull than the other Sauron's collar-tabs. "We will step up our tribute expeditions among the tribes to the west, especially around Ashkabad," he said. "And perhaps give some direct help to the Cossaki, if they see reason."

No more was necessary to another Soldier of Boyle's rank. "The Yesugei clans have grown uncomfortably strong in the last generation," he said. "Driving the Bergenov Cossaki against their subject tribes would weaken them considerably."

"Chain reaction, to the south," Urthak said, and Boyle's smile matched his. The steppes were prone to billiard-ball migrations; one horde displaced another, that one fell on its neighbors, and in the end war could sweep across half a continent. The great northern steppe across Haven's main landmass was shaped like a giant L laid on its side with the short arm pointing south. Quilland Base was at the joining, and down at the end of the short arm were the haBandari of the Pale; they had been a problem since the Soldiers first came to Haven, three centuries before. Sweeping a nomad migration onto their frontiers would weaken them severely.

"I will be field commander?" Boyle asked, with a trace of shark-eagerness in his voice. He had campaigned against the haBandari in the past.

"I would not think of anyone else," Urthak said sincerely. *What was that Terran legend?* he mused. *Uriah the Hittite?* A Deathmaster commanded from the front, a risky position. "We can make use of the new personnel from the Citadel, give them the blooding they need." He unfolded a map. "Here are the preliminary dispositions. . . ."

Six Terran months later

Byers' Sun and Cat's Eye were both up, throwing light blue and red and banded orange down the huge jagged shapes of the valley, confusing the eye with overlapping shadow. The air was thin and almost hot, here on the slopes of the northern Afritsberg; Assault Leader Gorthaur blinked eyes dry with lack of sleep and scanned down the rocky length that led out onto the steppe. The mountains behind him were high enough that their snowpeaks were as much carbon dioxide as water. It would be very cold here after First Cycle sundown; too high for the air to hold heat, even in late summer. Cold, and no fuel even if they dared a fire. . . .

Dared. We, Saurons, do not dare to light a fire, because of cattle.

It had been three centuries since the Saurons came to Haven. A backwater planet, the only remarkable thing about it the fact that it was the moon of a brown-dwarf gas giant. A CoDominium deportation colony for Earth's criminals and troublesome ethnic minorities in the 21st century, and rarely visited later, even in the heyday of the Empire of Man. Abandoned long before the final battles of the Secession Wars. Perfect for the last shipload of Sauron Soldiers, fleeing the destruction of Homeworld; a place to regroup while the Empire's remnants ripped their own flesh like a brain-shot landgator. A place to remake the Sauron dream, a master-race of genetically superior warriors.

Assault Leader Gorthaur felt his teeth grind together a little. *What would First Rank Diettinger think of us now?* Memory had almost deified the man—the Soldier—who had led the Saurons to their new home, but Gorthaur doubted he had intended them to spend centuries skirmishing with cattle. The crippled *Dol Guldur* had destroyed all high-energy technology on Haven, what little there had been of it, all according to Diettinger's calculations. The loss of the ship had been quite unplanned. . . . The Saurons still had superior technology: bolt-action rifles and Gatling guns. Around the Citadel, at the entry to the Sauron-dominated Shangri-La Valley, it was easy to believe the rebirth of the Race was proceeding smoothly. Here in the far west . . .

We are not engineers, Gorthaur admitted to himself. *But we have the superior genes.*

He forced his attention back to the matter at hand; fifty hours without sleep was making his mind ramble. Meanwhile, the warm rock made it difficult to see body-heat against the background, and the cattle might be trying to set position for an ambush.

"Assault Leader," one of the five Soldiers left of his group whispered behind him. "Do you think we have lost them?"

"Silence. Keep your eyes on the heights, Baugril, these cattle climb too well for my taste."

The Soldier turned obediently and looked back at the rocky heights that overlapped the little depression in which they had paused. Gorthaur could feel a slowness in the movement, an insolence. These Quilland Base Soldiers disliked him, he knew. Disliked him because he was from the draft of reinforcements from the Citadel, the base of Sauron power thousands of kilometers to the east, sent to bolster Quilland Base.

And to get rid of us, he admitted; the breeding program was going all too well, at home. Dislike he could have handled; it was like the odd accent and eccentric customs these western Soldiers had developed, a minor annoyance. It was the lack of *respect* that he could not tolerate. They thought him a . . . tenderfoot, that was the phrase. Unfamiliar with local conditions.

They are too *familiar with the local conditions*, he concluded grimly, focusing on the slopes below. Too respectful of these haBandari; granted that they were capable cattle, but genes were genes.

Was that movement? His ears cocked forward, enhanced senses straining. Muffled hoofbeats? Not many horses, either that or they were far away, the echoes made it difficult to say. Horses. They had lost their own, in the mad scramble up the heights three nights ago. This time his teeth ground audibly. It had been a successful patrol, until a week ago. Taking twenty Soldiers out of Quilland Base to show the flag, to collect tribute, to break opposition. Thirty fertile breeders collected, over a hundred nomad cattle dead in clashes, and only two Soldiers lost ... then the haBandari had struck in overwhelming force.

"Anything?" he asked.

"No, Assault Group Leader," Baugril said, lowering his rifle and rising slightly as he completed his scan of the rear slope. "Not even a haBandari could—"

Crack. A puff of white smoke from the cliff above, from between a notch of rocks. The Soldier pitched backward as the heavy soft-lead slug tore off the top of his head. The retaliation was blinding-swift even by Sauron standards, and a dark-clothed figure toppled forward, somersaulting through the air as the stone around the notch disintegrated under the firepower of five magazine rifles.

"Cease-fire!"

The enemy weapon bounced down to lie smashed at his feet. A flintlock. He picked it up. Beautifully made, although handcrafted rather than lathed. A breechloader, with an ingenious lever mechanism and a brass ring to seal against the combustion gasses. Not as good as the brass-cartridge magazine weapons the Citadel made ... but much better than anything else the cattle of Haven could produce. *The Citadel must receive better reports on these haBandari,* he mused.

Hoofbeats below jerked his attention back to the present. "Their timing's a little off," he said. "Orkhun, Shog, you take them out. Don't kill the horses unless you have to. Everyone else reload, fix bayonets, to the front; they may try and storm." *I hope so,* he thought. The little rocky bowl was an excellent defensive position.

There were two riders coming up the valley on big shaggy horses, and he grudgingly acknowledged their skill to gallop over ground like this; the horses were shod, too, from the sound. "Fire at 800 meters," he said; that was standard procedure.

"Damn," Orkhun muttered a moment later.

The two riders had vanished into dead ground nine hundred meters out, a gully, and the Soldier's shot had been a moment too late. The hoofbeats continued. Gorthaur squinted to read the terrain; it was not easy, with the conflicting shadows.

"They'll have to come into the clear after that sandstone boulder," he said.

Shog made a sound that might almost have been a snort. "I know . . . Assault Group Leader," he said. The rifles leveled, and the other Soldiers remained alert for haBandari using the diversion to advance on foot. The hoofbeats came louder, and—

"Damn you, why didn't you fire?"

"*Sir*, you said not to shoot the horses, and they went past the gap hanging off the opposite sides of their mounts!"

Gorthaur bit back a retort; the war manuals said an officer should never argue with his men. He was uneasily conscious of the fact that they averaged a decade older than him, and collectively had nearly a T-century of field experience. He glanced aside at Baugril's body, with the brains leaking out of the huge exit hole at the back of his head. His first independent command could scarcely be called a success, either.

"They'll have to come up over that ridge, there." It was a hundred meters ahead, sheltered, but the rocks were only knee high, not enough to give cover even for a prone man. "You can shoot the horses, this time." They were edible, at least.

"Now!"

Two shots rang out, and the horses fell as if poleaxed. Riderless, and the two haBandari were down behind thousand-pound meat barricades. At least they couldn't fire without exposing themselves—

A flat bass *snap* from behind one of the dead horses, and a flash of hands; something flew glittering into the

air, hung, twisted, and plunged down to take Thokuz
in the calf. A blue-fletched arrow.

That's a hundred meters! a voice in the back of
Gorthaur's mind screamed. Aloud: "Supressive fire, all
of you." The five rifles began banging, steady, aimed
fire at any hint of movement, or trying for a ricochet
off the nearby rocks. A pebble landed by Gorthaur's
foot, as he worked the bolt of his rifle. He turned just
in time to see the nine haBandari warriors, as they
leaped from above. Seeming to hang suspended,
shields and gleaming swords and dark mottled leather
clothes.

Gorthaur was never quite clear on what had happened next. Some things he remembered sharply.
Orkhun shooting one of the enemy and swinging his
rifle in a blurring-swift arc that would have broken
another in half; the haBandari had leapt *over* it, come
down and sliced halfway through the Soldier's neck.
Gorthaur's own bayonet had punched through that
one's leather breastplate, and then he had been back-
pedalling, the rifle spinning in his hands as two saber-
wielders came at him, sparks and clangor. Neither was
anywhere near as fast or strong as he, of course . . .
but for cattle they were very good indeed, and there
were two of them, with longer weapons, helmets,
shields, and body armor. Fifteen seconds, and his rifle
butt cracked the neck of one. Sixteen, and a desperate
twist avoided the lunge of the other; they were breast
to breast, and Gorthaur swept him up in an arm-hold-
ing bear hug. *Crack* and *crack*, the helmeted head
smashed into his face, while his arms tightened, crushing armor and ribs and spine. Then a stunning impact
and he was overbalanced, fell, with the dead weight
of a strong man coming down on his right forearm
when it landed just wrong against unyielding granite.
The wet sickening sound of bone popping.

Silence. He made the pain recede, came to his feet.

Death, the heavy salt blood and voided bowel scent of it; the tamerlanes and sobor would be sniffing and gathering already. Half a dozen minor wounds, cuts and abrasions; and the major one, his right arm useless until it healed, unlikely to heal unless set and tended. Bodies, four Saurons and . . . eleven cattle, the two behind the horses had charged into the melee.

Movement. A body moved, the form beneath rose. *Amazing,* he thought. One of the cattle. Gorthaur snuffled, spat blood. The broken nose had already clotted; he focused on the haBandari, the first he had seen at close quarters except to fight, as he moved forward carefully. He . . . no, *she* was on her feet, too.

Stocky and broad, that was his first impression. Broad shoulders, broad hips, heavy bones. Her torso was covered in armor of overlapping plates of lacquered bullhide, with armguards of the same material. A sledgehammer drawn on the armor, over a six-pointed star. Leather pants, high boots with horn splints on them, hide gauntlets; a course, blue-linen shirt under the breastplate. Her helmet had been torn away, and he saw a square, blade-nosed face, olive skinned, narrow blue eyes, a braid of black hair down her back. Blood from a graze on her cheek. A long red-wet saber in one hand, a shield in the other. White teeth showed as she bared her lips and twitched the blade back and forth, *wheet, wheeet.*

Ah. She was favoring one knee.

"No further, Sauron." A heavy accent to her Americ, liquid and guttural.

"I can probably draw my pistol faster left-handed than you can attack me with that saber," Gorthaur pointed out. Meanwhile, he made sure, looking with eyes that saw into the IR frequencies; yes, the bodies were all cooling fast. All dead.

Unexpectedly, she laughed; more of a sour chuckle, but still . . . *What a woman to sire Soldier sons upon!* the Assault Group Leader thought in sincere admiration. *Only a dozen cattle to kill four Soldiers, and this one survived. Alone and confronted with an armed Sauron, she laughed. What genes!*

"Why do you laugh?"

"To hear two corpses threaten each other," she said.

"Corpses?"

"Your arm is broken. I have a wrenched knee. We are each a thousand klicks from home, no horses, scavengers coming, and the nomads around here scratch their heads to decide if they hate Saurons more than haBandari."

"Ah." Not stupid, either. Gorthaur looked about at his dead men, up at the woman. *Nobody has ever brought a haBandari breeder into a Base*, he thought, with part of his consciousness. The rest was pure readiness.

The woman waited, almost as tiger-relaxed; then he saw her pupils dilate slightly, sign of interest or concentration in a human-norm. Saurons had that reflex under conscious control, of course. She spoke a sentence in her own language; Gorthaur shook his head impatiently, never having been commanded to learn that bastard offspring of Americ and Afrikaans, Hebrew and Balt. If he had, he might have hesitated longer.

"You owe me a blood debt, Sauron. More than you can pay with your life," the haBandari muttered to herself. Then, in Americ: "A bargain, Sauron."

"What do you propose?"

"A truce until we reach Ashkabad." That was a trading town, down on the plains. Tributary to Quilland Base, but not governed by it. "There are merchants of my people there."

"Agreed," he said decisively. There were overtones of double meaning in her voice, but that was only to be expected. "I am Assault Leader Gorthaur, Quilland Base."

The woman's expression turned feral. "First give me the Soldier's Oath," she said.

His eyes narrowed. "What do you know of the Soldier's Oath?" he said.

"Enough. We have schools, in the Pale. Swear, or we fight now."

If she knows that much, she probably knows the wording, he thought. He spoke, and saw her narrow-focused attention to the terms. "Now you," he finished.

"By Yeweh and all the p'rknz, by the anima of the ancestors and the spirits of Piet and Ruth, and by the honor of *Kompany* Gimbutas, I swear truce until one hour after we reach the borders of the town of Ashkabad, and before this I will help and assist you in all matters of journey and fight, taking nothing of yours without consent. May I be shunned if I break this oath, I, *meid Shulamit bat Miriam fan Gumbutas, ben haBandari*," she said. At his frown: "Meid means I'm unmarried. My name is Shulamit, my mother was Miriam, my *kompany*—clan—is Gumbutas; I'm a haBandari." She wiped the saber carefully and looked around. "Let's get to work."

They made camp ten kilometers down the valley; Shulamit had bound her knee tightly, and kept walking until it began to swell past safety. Gorthaur admired that, and the practical way she had sorted through the gear, according to what they could expect to carry; her superstition in covering the haBandari dead with rocks he tolerated, even if it cost a little time. There was no need to take the horsemeat, she seemed repulsed by the idea as well. *What does "tryf" mean?* he wondered, then dismissed the thought.

The fire was small and carefully banked to be invisible from a distance when sheltered by a blanket; just enough to heat water for eggbush tea. *Water will be a problem,* he decided. Not so much for him, he could go a week or more without, but for the woman. He called up a map with eiditic memory while the two of them coordinated the work of making camp; with three each of sound hands and legs it was more difficult than doing alone. They sat and gnawed dried meat and hardtack in silence for a long time, after the sketchy work of setting up was done. Gorthaur was at a loss for words; what did one say to a woman who was neither Base-born nor a tribute maiden? In the end, he found it was easier to suppress the pain of his splinted arm than the memory of the men he had led to their deaths; tactics seemed a safe subject.

"How did you find us?" he asked.

Shulamit looked up from the pistol she had been turning in her hands; he remembered lessons in reading cattle body language, but so much of it was culture-specific, and he knew little of her tribe. *Tension and controlled fear,* he decided. *And something . . .*

"Chance," she said. "A dozen of us had hired on as caravan guards, and the merchants didn't need us past Ashkabad. Riding back, we heard from the *hotnotts,* the nomads, that you *Soldati* were out raiding. It was too good a chance to miss, we gathered a couple of hundred of nomad warriors and jumped you."

Gorthaur frowned. "Why?" he said. The nomads wanted revenge, and their women back. What was the haBandari's motivation? They lived far south. Angbad Base was there, in the Tallinn Valley just northwest of the Pale, but that had fallen a generation ago and had never been reestablished.

"You're *Soldati*, Saurons," she said with a shrug. "Don't you know the saying, *'haBandari will crawl a thousand clicks across burning stone to do a Sauron an injury'?* That feud's older than the hills." She looked up at him under heavy black brows. "Then we couldn't cut our way out through the nomads, they were between us and home and turned on us, we were too few to control them once the ambush was over. We decided we might as well get a few more Saurons before we died. You're lucky it was a scratch party.

Just youngsters, and none of them kin or clan-brothers or sworn *chavre* of mine, so I'm not bloodbound to kill you in particular.

"Besides," she continued with a grin, "we won."

Gorthaur shrugged in his turn; it was true. He watched as she arranged her bedroll and began stripping off the equipment. The breastplate was held by latches, he noticed. . . . Everything piled neatly, just-so. *Good habits she has.* His nostrils flared slightly as she removed the last of her clothing and began undoing the pressure bandage around her knee; he could smell that she was in the middle of her cycle, ovulating. *Curse this arm,* he thought dismally; he was in no shape to subdue her. *Besides, I did promise.* Now that she was naked he could see the strength in arms and thighs, too. . . .

"Well?" she said, working the injured leg, and then lying back on her elbows, looking at him expectantly. "If you think I'm crawling over there and getting on top with this knee, you're crazy, Sauron."

"Fahise!" The shriek echoed from the buildings. *Whore.*

Erika bat Miriam turned in the saddle to look behind her, craning to see past the other haBandari to the crowded Ashkabad street.

No harlots that I can see, she thought in puzzlement. There were a few in Strang, the main settlement of the Pale, although none in her hometown of Ilona'-sstaad. *It would be hard to tell, here.* Ashkabad was well outside the Pale, its population mostly Tadjik-muslim. Townswomen wore the head-to-toe black tent of the chador, and the female nomads in for the trade fair used the shorter face-covering *yashmak*.

"Fahise Yahud!" the man screeched again, pointing: *Jew whore!* He was an elderly Ashkabadian in a long black robe and a turban as snowy-white as his beard, blue eyes wide with anger.

He means me, Erika thought. *How odd.*

Karl bar Yigal cursed softly beside her, and something in the words and tone made her mouth go papery with fear; she had been married less than a T-year, but that was long enough to know that her husband did not swear often or without cause. The street was emptying, she saw a woman sweep up her child and dodge through a plank door that banged shut behind her. But there was a knot of men around the white-bearded mullah, dressed like him but younger; others were drifting closer as he launched into a sermon in Tadjik, town laborers in rags and nomads in leather and sheepskins. Some were bending to pick up rocks or lumps of horse dung, and there were more on the flat roofs of the mud-brick houses to either side. No firearms that she could see, but of course everyone carried a knife, and many of the nomads wore their *shamshir*-sabers always. . . .

Riot, Erika thought. *Pogrom.* She reached down and unlatched the cover of the bowcase in front of her left knee, acutely conscious of the compound bow within, of the saber slung across her back, and of the double-barreled flintlock pistol on her hip that had been a wedding gift from her half-sister Shulamit. She had been trained to fight, all haBandari were, but . . .

There was a rattle and click behind her, from the others of their party. She glanced over a shoulder. Only a few were wearing their armor, but some were reaching for the bucket-shaped helmets at their saddlebows. Sannie bat Brigid gave her a wolfish grin as she lifted her lance out of the scabbard and let the butt rest on the toe of her boot. Several others had readied their bows; one plucked at the string, a flat snapping throb that cut through crowd-murmur. Tom Jerrison growled and heeled his horse forward to Karl's left side. Bodyguard and companion, he served Karl as he had Karl's father, who had taken him in when the elders of his church congregation back in the Eden Valley cast him out. Erika had never liked him, a slouching troll-shaggy unspeaking presence at Karl's side, but now there was something comforting in his gaunt gray massiveness and the sledgehammer that seemed feather-light in one scarred fist.

Karl cursed again, and pulled off his shapeless bag-hat. The bright yellow coil of his hair fell down loose to his waist; even then, she felt a thrill at his beauty.

"Honored Imam," he said, in a tone that cut across the mullah's tirade: he used the Turkic *lingua franca* of the steppes. "What complaint have you against us, who come as peaceful traders?"

"You bring Allah's wrath upon us, riding with your shameless harlots through the streets of a decent town!" The mullah shifted back into Turkic, finding insult unsatisfying when the recipient did not understand the language. His finger jabbed out at Erika; she blinked bewilderment back at him. "You Jew dogs carry Shaitan's ill-luck as a cur does fleas!"

I'm wearing *a shirt*, she thought resentfully; that was manners, among strangers, even on a hot day. Shirt and trousers and boots and hat; what did he expect, a tent? Anger replaced puzzlement as the meaning of *yahudi kopekleri* sank in, and she let her hand drop to the pistol; she was not *Ivrit* herself, but an insult to any of the Three Faiths was an insult to all the People.

Sannie bat Brigid walked her mount level with Karl's and dropped the point of her weapon; a Bandari lance was twice the wielder's height, and that put the leaf-shaped steel head within a meter of the muslim priest's throat.

"Give me the word, *aluf*," she said in guttural Bandarit. "I'll put it right through that lice-ridden beard and out the back of his empty head."

"Shut up!" Karl snarled, and struck up the shaft hard enough to nearly tear it from her hand. The blood of Frystaat ran strong in him, and that showed in strength and speed as well as blond hair, green eyes, and mahogany-dark skin. Forcing his smile back, he continued talking to the townsman.

"Does it not say in the first of the Medina *surahs*, 'Indeed, there shall be no coercion in matters of religion'? You have your customs of dress and behavior, and we have ours." His smile grew slightly wider; he did not need to move the rifle that lay across his saddlebow.

A ripple of hesitation went through the crowd; one invariable custom that the folk of the Pale followed was tenfold revenge for unprovoked attack. The mullah had blinked in startlement as the lancehead flashed up from before his face, and again as the haBandari leader quoted the Koran; now he looked around, plainly calculating. His students would stand by him, but they were not fighting men; neither were the town roughs. The Turki nomads in for the fair were at least nominal Muslims and always game for a fight ... but there were a dozen haBandari, well-armed, some of them armored, mounted on the tall warhorses of the Pale. Another voice shouted from the milling pack around him:

"You take the grain from our mouths, the cloth from our children's backs!"

Karl shrugged, eyes searching for the face behind the mullah. "We pay well for what we buy. If you think your merchants sell too much, talk to them. Or your *khan*."

There was another stir through the brown-and-gray mass of the crowd. Ashkabad lay on the southern slope of a range of hills that ran out from the Iron Limper mountains, in the neck of steppe where they swung west away from the east-tending Afritsberg. *Quanats* and springs made a string of villages possible, and this was a natural meeting-place for trade, the products of the Pale and the southern valleys and ranges for the goods of the great Northern Steppes. That also made it a natural target for raiders and conquerors; Quilland Base levied tribute for the Saurons, and two generations before the Yek Mongol clans had swept down from the northwest to conquer and hold. The crowd glanced upslope, toward the stone-walled citadel that dominated the mud-brick buildings of the town. The *khan* was Buddhist, and had excellent relations with the Pale ... and his men-at-arms would welcome a chance to teach the townsfolk a lesson.

There was a clatter as stones were dropped. Erika sensed Karl's leashed patience as the crowd dispersed; his eyes stayed locked on the mullah's until the little clump in black robes was again an island in the busy traffic of the street. The haBandari spurred past them at a fast walk; Sannie let her mount's shoulder brush one of the students and sent him reeling, answering his raised fist with a mocking grin and upright finger.

"Rein back, bat Brigid," Karl said tightly.

"They're only ragheads, *aluf*," she said protestingly.

"This is their territory. Keep that in mind!" To Erika: "This is worse than usual; I'm glad to be back, father's not well and he needs me to see to things." A wave to indicate the locals. "They've got some reason for complaint, actually."

She raised her canteen and drank, passed it to her husband. "Why?" she said, gazing about in fascination once more. They were moving upslope, into a district where whitewash covered the mud-brick outer walls of the houses. Here went a litter, bearing a stout merchant in curly-toed slippers and sequined vest; there a coffle of slaves, yoked neck-and-neck; a bush-bearded Christian priest stood outside an onion-domed church like none she had ever seen, fingering the silver cross on his breast; a yellow-robed lama passed him with a wave, and more and more.... The air was thick with dust from the overgrazed plains around the town, rank with the smells of spices and dung fires and human excrement.

"It's been dry, these past few years," Karl said. "I should have remembered."

Tom Jerrison surprised her with a grunted comment: "Dry in the Pale, too. The *hottnots* don't know how to care for the land."

Karl shrugged. "Still, they're short. Yes, we pay for what we buy: with luxury goods, weapons, craftwork. The grain and wool and meat the *khan* and his merchants sell us comes out of rent and taxes. The Saurons take their tribute good weather or bad, the *khan* takes his, the farmers and herders get what's left. Why should he care, as long as enough live? He's a Mongol and so are his troops, *they* aren't going to starve."

"That's your friend Toktai?" Erika asked. "I thought you said he was a good sort, for a *gayam*?"

"His father's *khan*, he's the *noyon*, prince and heir," Karl said, neck-reining his horse around a blind beggar. "Toktai's a nice fellow to hunt gazelle with, good fighter—we went after those Quechua bandits together, did I tell you?—and he'd give his shirt to a friend; we're *anada*, blood brothers. Otherwise, anyone outside his own clans are *suru*, sheep to be fleeced." Karl chuckled. "At that, he's a miracle of humanity compared to his mother, *khatun* Hoelun. You'll be meeting her, and—"

"*Sssst!*" Assault Leader Gorthaur hissed.

Shulamit dropped flat behind the boulder. Waiting, she strained her ears. It was minutes before she heard the hoofbeats and bleating, the laughter and men's voices echoing up the slope, bouncing from the crags of the narrow rock-cleft they had followed down to the edge of the plains.

Impressive, she thought, fighting to keep that from her face. Then: *kaak, they're between us and the water.* Her mouth was dry and more than dry, despite the smooth pebble she had been sucking on. The well down below was the only one in three days' foot-travel, four in the state her leg was in. She and the Sauron had carried as many canteens as they could, and they had not been enough; the last of it had been drunken three days ago. Steppe air was dry as well as thin; it sucked the water out through your skin and mouth and lungs. And it was near Truenight, sun almost down and Cat's Eye a sliver near the horizon; little light, and that orange-brown from the banded planet. Conflicting shadows moved across the reddish, tumbled stone.

Cold tonight, she thought, assessing herself. She had lived hard most of her life, always the wild one. Ill content in the valley, happiest out on the Western Steppes with her family's herds, or even better outside the Pale altogether. But there were limits. Desiccation did more than swell your tongue and make the eyes burn, drive a spike of pain between the eyes. Enough of it could kill.

The Sauron—*Gorthaur,* she thought: all things considered it would be silly not to think of him as an individual—looked nearly as fresh as he had in the fight four T-days ago. *He doesn't even pee when the water's short,* she mused resentfully. The long-dead Breedmasters who designed the Soldiers had known their business.

Slowly, she raised her head to a crack in the boulder. The well was four hundred meters downslope, where a last line of boulders marked the edge of the Afritsberg foothills and the beginning of the rolling steppe; four hundred clicks to Ashkabad, over in the outliers of the Iron Limper range. The well was a circle of mortared stone, with a low dun-green egg-bush tree beside it. A wooden lid as well, priceless, but even the worst outlaw would think three times before damaging a water source. The haBandari pulled a small spyglass from her belt and focused it. Images sprang close, tiny circular close-ups: the worn bone of a saber-hilt, a man's broken nose, the deep pink crater of a horse's nostril.

Raiding party, she decided. A dozen men, all on horses though they had muskylopes along; a couple of pack-camels, too, the two-humped breed common on the high Northern Steppes, and half a hundred sheep. Some of the warriors were wounded, crude bandages on limbs or torsos; tallish bandy-legged men, their heads shaven except for scalplocks, but with long mustaches, a few beards. Some were blonds, and they seemed to favor brightly colored baggy pantaloons, brimless caps with tassels, Astrakhan-wool vests; they were armed to the teeth, the leader positively dripping with weapons. Saber, knives thrust through his sash, two long-barreled pistols and a musket with an odd curled butt as well . . . that was the only firearm; the others had the usual horn-backed plainsman's bows. They pitched camp quickly, hobbling their beasts, laying out blanket-rolls and kindling a small fire of dried dung.

Shulamit ducked her head behind the boulder, then started slightly to find Gorthaur beside her. He had crawled over, one handed, on fingertips and toes. She knew better than to offer the spyglass; a Sauron's eyes were binoculars in themselves. His long slab-and-angle face was impassive as always; the only time she had seen any discernible expression on it was during orgasm, and not always then. The odd-looking gray eyes seemed to glitter slightly, as the hawk-style central focus shifted.

"Cossaki," he whispered. Shulamit made an inquiring sound.

"Related to the Russki," he continued. "Steppe dwellers, though." That was unusual; most of that breed were valley farmers or townsmen, like the Americ. "East of Quillard, a month's journey."

The haBandari raised her eyebrows; that was a third of the way to the Citadel. There was always a flow of raid and counterraid on the plains, and it had been growing worse most of her life, quarrels over grazing and water, but things must be getting very bad.

"We will wait for them to leave, then lie up by the well for a T-day or two," Gorthaur decided.

Shulamit gave him a hard glare, then shrugged: It was the best thing to do. Then a scream brought her head around, a long, shrill sound.

She raised her head again, and the scene below sprang into jiggling focus in the optic of her spyglass. The raiders had brought out more of their loot, two women who had been tied over the back of a dromedary. She could see the beweaponed leader laughing with head thrown back as they struggled with his men. More screams as they were stripped and thrown on their backs, men holding them by arms and legs. More laughter from the leader as he knelt and began to unfasten his pantaloons. Almost of itself, her hands brought up the Sauron rifle.

"No." Shulamit raised her head, looked over at Gorthaur. "No need to take the risk," he said. "We can stand another cold camp, and they will leave in the morning."

Shulamit sighed and shrugged, leaning her cheek back on the stock of the rifle. It was a well-made weapon, sighted out to a thousand meters; blade foresight, adjustable notch backsight, much like the rifles her own people made. *Of course*, she thought, *this is a magazine weapon. Ten rounds. Flatter trajectory, too*. She brought them together, resting the aimpoint between the Cossaki's shoulderblades, then moved it down his spine.

"Gorthaur," she husked, raspy from a dry throat. *Bastard didn't even look to see if I agreed with him.* He had turned his back on her, scanning out toward the western plains with his Sauron vision. She heard a faint interrogatory sound. "Blow it out your ear, Gorthaur," she continued, and squeezed the trigger.

"Thank the p'rknz," Erika said, as the Pale compound came into sight.

"Good to see the rag again, nu?" Karl replied, waving. The flag of the People was flying above the gate; a six-pointed white star on a field of dark blue, flanked by flaming swords, overlain by a leaping antelope. The wall behind was whitewashed adobe brick, lance-high and thick; the gate was laminated steeltree wood, strapped with black iron, wide enough for four horsemen to ride through abreast and left half-open.

"Yes. But . . ." she hesitated. "I'm a little anxious, too, darling. All those friends and relations I've never met, and, and, well—they know Shulamit, not me."

Karl cocked an eyebrow at her. "Afraid they'll resent you for beating her out?" he said dryly. "I'm not the prize ram at a Piet's Day archery contest, you know." Erika felt herself flush. "Don't worry, they'll all love you." A grin. "Shulamit was too like me, anyway, and everyone knew it; we'd have quarreled all the time."

Erika smiled shyly and gave his hand a squeeze; it was still a miracle to her. It had seemed only natural that the dashing young merchant-prince would love the eldest of the daughters of Miriam. The darling, adventurous, adored Shulamit, leader in every scrape and trouble, who had left the quiet of Ilona'sstaad for stockdrives and hunts, gone prospecting for shimmerstones in the thin air of the Afritsburg, gone roving outside the Pale itself. Their quarrels had been a bewilderment; that he should turn to *her*, the mousy, bookish second sister, glory beyond words. *And Shulamit never said a hard word to me, nothing maztov when I told her*, she thought. But she had gotten drunk at the wedding, and ridden quietly off on the second day of the feast. *I . . . hope she's here. It's been a whole year now; we should be close again.*

The guards at the entrance to the compound had

caught sight of the haBandari party; one of them blew a sharp note on an oxhorn.

"Shalom!" Karl shouted it out to the gate guard as they cut through the crowd waiting for entrance.

The guard officer grinned delightedly and returned the greeting; a haBandari in horsehair-crested helmet, with a rifle slung over his shoulder. His men were from the Pale but not of the People; Edenites, descendants of the Church of New Harmony farmers who had held the Eden Valley before the coming of the haBandari, three centuries ago. Big dour-looking men in breastplates and bar-visored helms, leaning on their long pikes or the helves of two-handed axes; some had crossbows slung over their backs, others war-hammers. Mostly of Americ descent, taller and fairer than their haBandari fellow-citizens.

Funny, Erika thought: *Back home, you think of Edenites as surly and stupid and foreign, but out here they look as homelike as clan-brothers.* Strange, but then, you traveled to see new things.

"Shalom, chaver: Mordekhai bar Jacob fan Allon, at your service," the officer replied formally. Then to his troops: "Eddie, Hagen, David, clear the gate; Righteous, go tell Yigal his son's here." The three lowered their pikes and used the poles to sweep clear a path through protesting locals while the fourth pelted off.

"Karl bar Yigal fan Reenan," her husband replied, equally mannered. They dismounted. ". . . bar Jacob . . . Not Dvora bat Margaret's brother? We were in that Quipchak trouble together. She used to have this post, last year?"

"The same, and she's told me enough about you!" the man said, advancing to shake their hands. "She's off east with the Citadel caravan, these last six months; I was up northwest, San Ynez town hired some of us to clear out a band of Lafranche bandits on the road to the sea. . . ." He took Erika's hands, winked. "Worse luck, I missed the wedding, and didn't get to kiss the bride—from the letters, half the Pale attended. My third cousin's aunt Sarah bat Janet fan Zvi was there."

"*Ja,* I remember her *baklava,*" Erika said, taking the hint and giving him a quick peck on the lips, a little embarrassed by his frank regard. *Everyone thinks I'm pretty because Karl married me,* she thought. *Actually I'm plain.* Short and slight, more oval-faced than was common among haBandari, with the usual dark eyes and hair. *Shulamit's much more striking.* "Sarah's married to my great-uncle Paul, that makes *us* relatives."

Karl laughed and bowed introduction. "My wife, *fraw* Erika bat Miriam fan Gimbut—ah, fan Reenan, now. No, only about a quarter of the population came; the rum ran out before we could pack more in." He waved a hand behind him. "These *chaveri* are with us, the House of the Tree caravan?"

The soldier's brows rose. "You're expected," he said. "The wagons came through yesterday. The party's been preparing ever since."

Crack. The Sauron rifle hammered back into Shulamit's shoulder; not as heavy a blow as a haBandari flintlock would have made, and there was no puff of smoke.

Gorthaur gave a shout of rage and startlement, but his first round snapped out before she could finish working the bolt, and she had practiced diligently. The man she had been aiming at pitched forward, thrashing and screaming in the shocked high-pitched tone of surprise and agony. There was an instant of stunned immobility in the camp below, less than a heartbeat, and then they exploded into movement. Another Cossaki took two steps and pitched forward flat on his face, still; that would be the Soldier's bullet. Shulamit barred her teeth as her own next round kicked up dust at the heels of another; worked the bolt again, smelling the harsh cordite stink and the scent of hot brass as the cartridge went *ting* off a rock at her right. *Lead* the running man, *squeeze* the trigger—*crack* and the raider spun, then fell and crawled with one hand clamped to a spouting thigh. Ten seconds, and there was nothing visible but the dead and wounded.

Five, she counted. Plus at least one more who would be out of an active fight. Three of those were Gorthaur's kills, and all of them were motionless; all through the head or torso. Astonishing shooting, considering the lack of warning, and the fact that the Soldier was using a rifle one-handed. *It isn't the weaponry, it's the genes,* she thought resentfully. It was a good thing for the Pale, for all of Haven, that the Saurons were few. But they were increasing. . . . She turned the rifle's bolt up and pulled it all the way back, leaving it there while she thumbed two five-round stripper clips into the magazine and then slapped it forward and down to chamber a round.

Gorthaur had been doing likewise. "You insubordinate *bitch*," he swore, agitated enough to drop into his native tongue. That was close enough to the Edenite dialect of Americ for Shulamit to follow; like him, she replied without taking her eyes from the camp below.

"Who died and made you a god, Gorthaur?" She spared her left hand for an obscene gesture. "They're not going to stay down there. Let's see if you fight as well as you fuck, Sauron: I'm not in any shape to flank them."

Gorthaur gave an inarticulate growl and then laid his rifle down. "Hold them," he said, drawing his pistol.

The haBandari crawled on hands and knees to a different cleft in the rock and eased her eyes up. Four hundred meters was just beyond extreme range with a heavy horn-backed bow. . . . Not a very steep slope, but littered with rockfall from the cliff behind them.

The path down from the cliffs had been difficult enough for the two of them, the Sauron with his broken arm and her with a bad knee; out of the question to retreat with enemies at their backs.

There. Two figures dashing from one piece of cover to the next; she snapped off a shot that sent them diving behind a ridge of rock. *There*. Another pair, and this time she heard a yell; the bullet must have struck, or a rock-spall. *I like these Sauron guns*, she thought delightedly. Much more firepower than a haBandari rifle, enough to keep the attackers from swarming over her in a single rush. As good as a compound bow, and more range and stopping power. . . . Out of the corner of her eye she saw a flicker, and Gorthaur was gone, over the boulder and down into the scree. *Ignore him*.

A moment of waiting. The Cossaki would be thinking; balancing the risk of further advance against the risk to their animals and plunder. If they had raided, they were probably pursued; and to be left without mounts on the steppe was virtually a sentence of death. *They'll probably want to wait for Truedark and close in*, she thought. *Or they could push a little closer and try to drop shafts on me*. She would have to fire occasionally to keep them back, and they could use arching shots to search out her position behind the rocks.

"But *I* know something *you* don't know," she called out in Bandarit, which would do them little good.

Then there was a shot from down near the base of the hill; a Quilland Base-made pistol shot, a scream, another shot, silence.

Half a dozen men on the slope below began calling out to each other; Shulamit recognized some of the words, they spoke Russki in the Tallinn Valley northwest of the Pale, and she had visited there. The haBandari noted the positions for future reference. A final call for silence; then a flicker of movement moving upslope, field-gray uniform against gray-brown rock.

"Should I shoot him?" Shulamit asked herself. *No, I did promise, and he hasn't broken the terms yet. Besides, I'm not certain.* She pulled her lips back from her teeth; Gorthaur was going to give her a prize to take back to the Pale, will he nor nil he.

This time the raiders were looking downslope as well as up; the Sauron's next victim had time to shout three words before his voice ended in a brief shriek of agony. The others exploded from their positions, racing upward in dodging zigzagging runs. The hunters were hunted now; this position of hers was their only hope against the killer at their backs.

Shulamit rose to her knees and flung the rifle to her shoulder. *Crack.* One, chest shot. *Don't get fancy, through the center of mass.* The voice in her head sounded like her father. *Crack.* Another down. *Crack. Crack. Crack.* One more hit, good showing against moving targets in this bad light. Three moving enemy came over the ridge as she threw down the rifle and drew her pistols.

The haBandari was springing back and to her feet as they rushed her, faces demon-dark in the gloaming, eyes and teeth white. Three meters away, seven, nine. Two with swords, shouts and glinting steel. The furthest had a bow, arrow nocked, drawing. Nine meters, and at that range it would go through her curiass as if the bullhide and drillbit gut were linen. This time the voice in her head was old Kristiaan, the Gimbutas clan Drillmaster, explaining melee tactics.

A sword can't hurt you until it gets within arm's reach. Until then, it might as well be on Terra. Get the distance-weapon first. Her right hand came up with the massive Bandari horse-pistol, double-barreled. She jerked at the triggers, instinct-aiming, time slowed like wading through spring mud. Last light breaking off the three edges of the arrowhead as the stranger drew to the angle of his jaw, and *click* the hammers went forward and *scrit-ting* the flints struck the steel of the frizzens and the priming powder flared, then the half-heartbeat wait and *whump*. Twin lances of dull-red fire, massive hammering impact on her wrist, the twin loads of double buckshot spreading out into a cloud that pulped the bowman's face off the bone.

The first man was using a *yataghan,* meter-long and inward-curved for slashing. A big man, ape-long arms and driving speed behind the cut that arched toward her neck. Her right hand was too numb to do more than drop the haBandari pistol, but the left brought the Sauron revolver up, fired. Another flash of light, brighter and sharper than the black-powder weapon. The bullet took the swordsman off-center, spinning him around so that she could see the fist-sized exit hole of the hollowpoint round; this time she did not need to drop the weapon, the Soldier-strength charge had left her hand strengthless from the wrist down. The last Cossaki had shouldered his dying comrade out of the way and attacked, cutting down in a backhand blow.

Kristiaan's voice again: *A cutting sword can only damage in the half-meter between its point and the blade's center. Once you're inside that, all it does is tie up your enemy's hand.*

Go *in*. Step-falling forward, when every nerve ordered her to dodge. Left hand up, forearm against the man's wrist, right hand stripping the knife out of the sheath sewn on her thigh. Better to cut, a knife stab rarely killed quickly, but there was no time. *Ah*. His shield hand had slapped down on her knife wrist, and the tough leather of his sheepskin jacket turned the light pressure of the edge she could muster from this position. Not a big man, but wirey-tough as any Haven plainsman must be; young, downy blond stubble on his cheeks. Mouth gaping across snag teeth, distorted with rage and effort. They were close; close enough for her to see him sweat, smell the stale *wadiki* and bad teeth odors on his breath.

Shulamit saw the Cossaki's eyes open, and then go wide; as he realized he was fighting a woman, and then as he felt the strength in her arms. For a moment they strained almost chest-to-chest, feet stamping and grinding in the loose gravel and broken rock. A whisper from her mother's fund spoke across the back of her mind: *Don't wrestle with men.* A stab of pain from her injured knee seconded it. Some of the haBandari's ancestors had been from Frystaat, a heavy-G world that made Haven seem gentle by comparison. A full-blooded woman of that race could probably have picked the raider up and snapped his spine.

But I'm not a Frystaater, she thought, her own snarl matching the Cossaki's. She threw her mind into her arms, let the man feel her attention riveted to the losing struggle.

He smiled in triumph, began to twist against her knife to turn it on her, press down with the sword to bring the hilt within hammering-range of her head. Then her body made three precise movements; snapping her forehead into his face, straightening the crooked arm that blocked his saber, driving her knee up toward his groin. Shulamit's eyes starred with tears of pain, but she felt his nose smash flat, heard his roar. The released pressure on his sword arm made it slide down, the hilt of his saber thudding into her curlass just below the arm; he twisted desperately and took most of the force of her knee blow on his thigh, most of the rest on the hard leather jock that guarded his testicles. There was still enough pain to distract him, focus attention while she clamped his wrist in her armpit and whipped her arm around under his to lever his elbow locked and straight.

They swayed. Shulamit's leg twisted around, got a heel behind the Cossaki's knee, *pulled.* They went over, and the weight of their bodies was thrown against his arm, near three hundred pounds forcing the joint to move in ways unsuited to the construction and manner and purpose of elbows. There was a sound like dry oilstalks breaking, and the man shrieked the way a rabbit did when the stobor's jaws closed on it. They landed heavily, her on top, and the strength went out of his grip, her knife was gone but she doubled her fist and smashed it into his throat again and again, wet salt on her lips and again and again—

"He's dead!"

The Sauron's voice shouted in her ear, and his hand gripped hers like a thing of resilient steel. Shulamit stopped, looked at the joined hands. They were both dark to the elbow with something wet that glistened.

Blood, she thought, and tried to speak. Nothing came out of her mouth but a dry "hnhh-*huh*," over and over as she dragged the thin steppe air into lungs that felt burning tight. She used the Sauron's grip to haul herself erect, then wrenched free and hobbled down the slope. Gorthaur was speaking; the words buzzed past her ears until he shrugged and fell behind. Shots rang out as he made sure of the enemy wounded, an essential after-battle chore.

There was a folding leather bucket resting on the coming beside the well. Shulamit limped grimly up to it, knelt, and thrust her head into the water.

"Ahhh."

There were few moments of pure pleasure in life, but surely this was one. She raised her face to the sky, feeling the cold liquid sinking into thirsty skin. A mouthful soothed tongue and lips; she let a little trickle down her throat. Typical steppe-well water, cold, mineral-bitter, and sour, utterly delicious. The haBandari swished the rest around her mouth and spat it out, drank again in slow careful sips. Her fingers found the catches of her armor; she let it slip free, propped harness and weapons safely against the well copping and stood to pour the bucket over her head. Cold rucked her skin to gooseflesh as the air sucked the moisture, but the coarse blue linen of her shirt was dry by the time she had pulled another bucket from the well.

"Picking this fight was stupid as well as disobedient," Gorthaur said coldly. This time she had seen him coming, out of the corner of one eye.

Shulamit began to speak, husked, spat, drank again, and continued: "We won, Sauron. Besides, I don't recall promising to obey you, just to help you get to Ashkabad. Don't get above yourself because *I* invited you to bounce the bedroll, superman." She held out the bucket. "Now we have horses and gear."

Gorthaur accepted it, raising the thirty-pound weight one-handed to his lips, as easily as he might a wine glass. He drank long and deep; no need for *him* to fear overburdening his digestive tract. A Soldier ate like a landgator and drank like a camel, for much the same reason—to store fuel.

"True," he said. "But the risk to the genetic—" he began, then turned away, shrugging.

Shulamit laughed as she buckled on her weapons belt. "To *Ashkabad*, Gorthaur, that's what I promised. If you think you can drag me out of town to your Quilland Base stud farm, think again." The Sauron did not bother to turn toward her, or even to shrug again as he went to round up the hobbled ponies.

The haBandari walked past him to the first man she had shot, the Cossaki leader. He had bled out beside the captive woman from the wound that half tore off one arm, but not before he buried a knife beneath her ribs; her eyes stared sightless at the bright steady stars of the high steppe. Shulamit bent to close them, then hooked the man's body off with the toe of her boot before spitting in his face. The haBandari kept no slaves, and despised those who did; and anyone who committed rape within the Pale would be lucky to live long enough to be formally tried and stoned to death. Being staked out by the victim's friends and kinsfolk with a cage of hungry drillbits strapped over the crotch was far more likely.

Gayam, she thought contemptuously, using the Bandarit term for someone not of the People. *Savages.*

A sound brought her head up with a snap, her hand to the hilt of her saber. It was the other captive; she had lain huddled while the fight went on. Now she was up and trying to sidle backwards; the fact that her pants were down about her ankles made it difficult, and the dagger clenched awkwardly in her tightly bound hands. The howling laughter of a stobor pack echoed from the darkness behind her. The prisoner's head whipped around in the direction of the sound, then back at the haBandari. Shulamit smiled and held her open hands up in the peace sign.

"Jo Bandarit ha'taal davva?" the haBandari asked. The other started at the words, swallowed, seemed to focus and realize she was facing another woman. She shook her head, replied in an unknown throaty language.

Well, not likely she would speak the taal, Shulamit decided. Certainly she was of no race or tribe the haBandari had ever seen. The coiled black hair was common enough, but her face was flatter than any Shulamit knew, the nose a snub button, the eyes not just slanted but almost slits above broad high cheekbones and green at that; her skin was a peculiar ruddy brown. She looked like a Turkmen as much as anything, but not very.

"Turku bilr misniz?" Shulamit said.

"Turku bilmiyorum," the girl replied in that language, and shook her head. *I don't speak it.*

At least I know she means no *by that,* Shulamit thought, and tried again:

"Ya spikka da Americ? S'ablan Spanjol? Yeweh dammit, *daver Ivrit?"* More negatives. *"Russki?"*

A tentative nod, and a fractional relaxation. Shulamit sighed in vexation; it *would* be a language she had so little of. *What am I going to do with her?* One of the woman's eyes was nearly swollen shut with a bruise; there were more bruises on her thighs, along with streaks of dried blood, and scratches on her breasts. About sixteen, Shulamit judged. Well fed up until the last few days, not hard-worked; the ripped-open jacket that hung from her shoulders was quietly rich, fine wool dyed scarlet and green and embroidered along the hems with dragons and elk. Some merchant's or tribal chief's daughter, then. *Give her a horse and let her go?* Equivalent to a sentence of death, but not her business. The haBandari were not a cruel people, except by necessity in war, but Haven had little place for altruism outside the bonds of clan and kin.

The foreign woman tottered backward and brought up her knife again; Shulamit heard footsteps behind her, and hoofbeats. Gorthaur finished staking out the lead-line near the well and tied the horses to it before coming to her side.

"Who is she?" he asked.

Shulamit made the haBandari gesture of bafflement, a shrug with palms turned up. "I should know? Speaks a little Russki."

The girl stared at the Sauron, mouth dropping open a little as she recognized him for what he was. There were few indeed on Haven who had not heard the tales, at least, and none who could mistake the flame-encircled Lidless Eye he wore on the pocket of his field jacket. Then her expression firmed; she reversed the knife with a quick motion and drove it toward her own heart. The Soldier hardly seemed to move; he *blurred,* and the would-be suicide found her bound hands held. She wrenched at them, with as much effect as if they had been set in concrete, and kicked at the Assault Group Leader's legs with similar results.

"Bind her," Gorthaur said. "It would be a pity to waste a healthy breeder with good reflexes, now that we have transport."

Shulamit drew her Sauron revolver as she stepped up to the struggling pair—*no, she's the only one struggling*—and checked that the cylinder had turned to a fresh cartridge. A deep breath, for calmness; a long, slow exhale, and she worked her fingers on the pistol's grip. A little too big for her hands.

"You will not need that," Gorthaur said, frowning.

"Nu?" Shulamit replied. And wheeled, pointing the weapon at the man's head. He froze for a crucial instant, torn between releasing the woman's hands and countering the sudden threat: then the muzzle of the pistol was seated firmly in his ear. She grinned mirthlessly. The best reflexes in the world were valueless when the mind hesitated, and she was not so slow, either.

"P'rknz of the Oak, and people say we haBandari are arrogant!" Shulamit said in wonder. "No, don't try it, Gorthaur. Jarring my wrists would set it off before you could move the muzzle." *Probably* true. "Just hold still for a second."

She pressed harder; the ear twitched, disturbingly mobile; the tales said there was something beastlike about Saurons, and the haBandari was coming to believe it. Her left hand snaked around to take the knife-hilt from the stranger girl, then sawed open the twist of rawhide that bound her. *Rawhide*, she thought with disgust. And buried in the swollen flesh; hadn't it occurred to the raiders that the girl's hands would mortify, or freeze as soon as night came? The stranger stepped back, pulling the cord free with only a grimace and a grunt at what must be the brutal shock of pain, rubbing at her wrists and flexing the stiff fingers. A moment, and she was pulling up her clothes and staring from the haBandari to the Sauron and back.

Shulamit extended the knife on her palm, hilt first. *"Chaver,"* she said: *friend,* in her own language. She repeated it in Americ and Russki: "Migo. T'varsh."

The blade was snatched out of her hand, and the girl wheeled to face the Sauron. She knew how to hold a knife, too; hilt down, point up.

Much good it would do us, Shulamit thought, as she stepped back. The Sauron turned to face her with the smooth economy of a cliff lion, face blank except for the flare of nostrils. His eyes glinted for a moment in the red light of the fire, catching the color of the flames like a cat's.

"Once and for all, Gorthaur," Shulamit said softly. "Don't push. You can kill me; you can't threaten me, or order me. Understand?" He stared at her for three long seconds, nodded slightly, and turned on his heel.

"Had enough of exotic foreign places?" Karl asked teasingly as they dismounted and handed their reins to the grooms.

"For a while," Erika said with relief, looking around. The haBandari quarter covered several hectares, the largest settlement of the People outside the Pale.

Home, she thought. In two senses of the word; this was an enclave of the Pale by treaty, under haBandari law. And where she would make their home, while Karl oversaw the House of the Tree's caravans to the north. To be sure, she would have her tasks as well; accounting, women's work among haBandari.

There was a broad, cleared strip within the wall about the compound, paved with slabs of sandstone. Much of it was covered with orderly piles of goods. Pyramids of threshed barley and ryticale and oats, stacks of rough cloth or baled wool or hides, the sort of bulk produce the Pale imported, safe enough outside in the dry season. Among them were caravan wagons, huge vehicles of laminated bloodwood and steel, with man-high wheels covered in tyres of woven drill-bit gut; she recognized some of them, had ridden by their sides the long weeks up from Kidmi Fort on the northern border of the Pale. One corner of the outer-wall held a brick reservoir and the high frame of a creaking windmill that ran the pumps to fill it, another homely sight she had not seen among the outlanders.

They passed the inner wall of the compound, one barely head-high.

"It's like an Eden Valley town," Erika exclaimed, as they walked down the cobbled streets.

"A little," Karl said. "You'll learn the differences." The laneways were not crowded, but he had to stop often to return greetings. The news of their arrival washed out like a bow-wave before them, gathering well-wishers. "More like a herder's camp, in some ways. Less than a thousand of us all told, so we stick together."

"Well, it *smells* better than Ashkabad," she replied, watching with pride as he answered the greetings. She could see that Karl's family was more than well-to-do; it was popular, and you could not buy liking among haBandari. *My family, now.*

They had passed through the area of warehouses, into streets of houses and shops and workshops. Erika could see what her husband meant; many of the people she saw were *gayam*, laborers or customers come to buy. But the smells were homelike, spices and cloth, horses and soap, and there were familiar sights in plenty; the bright geometric patterns on the white-washed walls, a street-cleaner sweeping rubbish into a handcart, a water-seller with his cups and leather sack, a school where boys and girls sat cross-legged over slateboards. A goldsmith in her leather apron arguing with a client, the whicker of pedal-driven looms, loud arm-waving bargaining over a pile of ten-thousand-knot carpets like scattered jewels with their patterns of flowers and warriors, sages and stars and hunting

scenes. She found her eyes drawn to the colors of the rugs, to piles of bright spices in a confectioner's shop, to the pots of herbs and flowers that hung below most windows; it was natural, after so long on the steppe. The high plains of Haven were dull-green in the spring, reddish brown most of the year, white-flecked gray in winter. Your eyes starved for something besides the eternal sameness of it, and now she could sympathize with the color-hunger of the haBandari herders who flocked into the valley towns for the festivals.

There was a crowd of a hundred or more around them when they spilled out into the courtyard before Karl's father's house; that was a substantial stone building, two stories under a slate roof with windows of real Eisenstaad glass. Questions flew thick and fast, especially about the wedding; someone had produced a fiddle, and someone else a flute, with the sound of a snaka drum bringing up the rear. Hands thrust a cup of hot honey-wine into her hands, and a garland of sweet-smelling dried flowers over her head. They passed a synagogue, with the rabbi standing on the steps smiling, prayer shawl over his shoulders; a Christian church of the sort haBandari used, low and plain but the windows gorgeous with stained glass; a shrine to the ancestors with statues of Piet and Ruth beside the door—the Three Faiths, together as always. Voices rang in her ears:

"Mastov, Karl!"

"Hey, man, good to see you again, *kerel!*"

Erika found herself laughing with them; laughing as the circles formed and began dancing around them, counter-rotating. Karl groaned theatrically and tried to push his way through.

"Have heart, *chaveri,* we're just in from a—"

"Half-day's ride, you need to dance out the kinks!"

Somebody reached up and drew Karl's saber from over his shoulder, tossed it to his wife. She caught the heavy weapon easily and drew her own lighter blade, poised with the swords crossed above her head. He gave a grinning shrug of resignation and raised his own hands, snapping his fingers in rhythm to the "la-*la*-la-*yey*-ha-*hey*" chant-song. Erika spun, swinging the swords in figure-eights; Karl danced with her, bending and weaving and swaying. It was one of those dances that started slowly, to show your control. Then it went *fast*, for speed: fun, and a test, to show these hard-bitten frontier-folk that the young scholar from Illona'sstaad was no sheltered flower. She finished with a blurring propellor-whirl and tossed the sabers into the air.

"*My* turn," Karl whispered with a wicked smile. They were back to back for a second, turning to follow the circle of leaping, singing figures about them. They faced each other, Erika pulling out the long white handkerchief she would wave as she danced around the edged steel.

Then the music died away. Erika looked up; it was *Oom*—no, she corrected herself, *Father-in-law*—Yigal, and Karl's mother Hagar bat Katherine. And two *gayam*. Who must be important guests; an older woman in robes of Citadel-made silk, embroidered with dragons and lightning bolts, and a man in lamelar armor of steel splint mail and a high spired helmet. The woman was unveiled, and she was of the same race as the man, flat-faced and high-cheeked, eyes narrow slits; as hard-eyed as the warrior.

The two haBandari sheathed their weapons and made polite bows.

"Prince Toktai son of Yuechi, *khatun* Hoelun," Yigal began. "My son Karl you know; this is his wife, Erika bat Miriam—"

"No," Shulamit said.
The girl—*Borte*, she said her name was—looked up. The three of them had dragged the enemy corpses

away from the fire; that much fresh meat in the hungry season toward the end of summer would attract predators. Stobor for certain, possibly enough to be dangerous once they went into a feeding frenzy. Tamerlanes possibly, and a pair of the big cliff lions was nothing to trifle with, even three armed humans. A landgator would be worst of all, some of the pseudosaurians here along the foothills grew up to five meters in length, and they were damnably hard to kill. There was little smell; the temperature was falling rapidly now that Byers' Sun was down, already near freezing.

"No," Shulamit said again, as Borte looked down and continued to push the Cossaki leader's breeches open with the butt-end of a salvaged lance.

There was a knife in her other hand, and the same fixed stare in her eyes that she had worn since the haBandari woman faced down the Sauron. She had gone off a little into the rocks to wash, dressed warmly if more drably in clothes salvaged from the raider's packs; Shulamit had allowed it, and Gorthaur did not seem to be in a mood to argue. Dragging the bodies had made her shake with effort—not physical, just with the strain of forcing herself to touch the men who had abducted her. Now she obviously had a little posthumous revenge in mind. . . .

Shulamit stepped close enough to grip the other's knife wrist. "*Nyet*," she repeated firmly, clamping the wrist steadily against the increasingly frantic jerks of the girl.

"Why? Why . . . no?" Borte said at last.

"Because . . ." Shulamit struggled with the unfamiliar language; she had the sort of minimal command of Russki that you needed as part of a warband or caravan guard. *How much?* or *Give me kvass* or *Where is the water?* or *Go away or I'll boot your balls.* She doubted that this Borte had ever killed anyone. How to translate what the drillmasters said?

"You remember," she said, pointing to the bodies and then tapping her head.

You remembered fighting, stress and pain fixed it in your memory. It had been . . . what, four years ago, at Agarsfield up near Fort Kidmi, when that fan Allon *mediko* had pulled an arrowhead out of her thigh with the pincers, and she could still remember the stitching on his glove like it was yesterday. You had to remember the details, not seeing the ones you fought as human beings, not the look in their eyes when they knew they were going to die. People you had to kill weren't people, they were targets, tactical problems. You could remember tactical problems without puking; targets didn't come back in the night, when you were eating, when you were playing with kids or making love with your man.

Targets didn't shove their dead faces into yours with their bloody genitals hanging out their mouths.

"You do this, remember when not want. Remember too much," Shulamit said desperately. "Not good. Not help forget." The wrist under her hand went limp, and Borte's face suddenly crumpled; she dropped the weapon and pressed her face into the collar of Shulamit's sheepskin coat and clung. Shaking at first, then sobbing more and more loudly; Shulamit put an awkward arm around her shoulders, patting her back and making soothing noises.

Hell, she thought dismally: *I always hated being cried on, even by Erika or Sannie.* Not that her half-sisters had cried often, though Yeweh and all the p'rknz this poor bitch had reason . . . Shulamit had been more given to red-faced tantrums and howling fits than tears—

Borte pulled herself upright and shot a glance that was half gratitude and half suspicion in Shulamit's direction. The haBandari handed her a kerchief, almost clean.

"I go horses," she said, and waved to the camp. "You sort gear, *da*?"

The mounts were something of a surprise. Twenty-one, to begin with, that meant none of the raiders had been riding muskylopes; the awkward, shaggy native quadrupeds were slower but more enduring than horses and needed less feed and water than even a camel, but you could not fight effectively from their backs. From the degree of jostling and bickering the horses were doing even on a widely spaced picket line most of them were strangers to each other, looted, probably. She ran a stockbreeder's eye over them; most were ordinary steppe ponies, stiff-maned and hammer-headed little beasts about twelve hands high. Six were of another breed, a hand or two higher and longer in the leg, not much by the standards of the Pale but better than nothing.

On a hunch, she went over to the baggage camels and examined the leather-and-wicker hampers. "Fodder," she said, holding up a handful; cracked ryticaly grains mixed with pellets of dried alfalfa. Quite a bit of it, enough to keep horses going without stopping to let them graze for the hours needed on thin steppe forage. For that matter the mounts looked in pretty good condition, harder-ridden than she liked and far too roughly harnessed for a haBandari's liking, some with saddle-galls, but well-fed.

Gorthaur walked up, casually slapping the nose of a camel who looked at him sidelong and visibly considered spitting. Borte shied around him and took the bucket to the other end of the picket line, beginning the process of watering the horses.

"This is unusual?" he said. Soldiers used pack and riding animals, but less than most. A Sauron could run as fast as a horse, for much longer, and on much less in the way of supplies; it simplified their logistics.

"Quite," she replied. "But useful." To Borte: "Feed all horse from this. Half bucket. Understand?"

"Da."

"Quite unusual," she continued to the Sauron. "For a normal raid . . . but then, it isn't usual for raiders to go so far from their normal stamping grounds; *hotnots* usually steal from their neighbors. They're better armed, too . . . more what I'd expect for scouts out from a big warband. But then why are they bothering to pick up livestock?"

Gorthaur shrugged, wordless; plainly he felt speculation was useless. The three set about making ready; in hostile country you had to be prepared to run the minute you awoke, that went without saying among Havenites. Shulamit selected the best of the horses for her own, counting on the Sauron being less familiar with the points of bloodstock, picked a saddle and tack and laid them out; she would ride with a half-dozen remounts on a leading rope, switching every couple of hours. The camels could keep pace; Bactrians were slower than horses in a gallop, but had more endurance. And the free horses could carry loads; it had grated on her to leave so much valuable gear with her dead comrades four T-days ago. Silver and jewelry went into her saddlebags, and she made a bundle of the weapons. Good steel, some of them; the leader's muskets and pistols were crude stuff by haBandari standards, but would fetch a good price in Ashkabad. Or . . .

She stepped over to where Borte was stoking the fire, feeding the thin flames with scraps of dried twig and fat from the sheep carcass beside her; it was always difficult to keep flame alive on the high steppe, the oxygen content of the air was too thin. Another thousand meters up, and even Haven-born such as they would faint and die.

"Here," she said, offering the weapons belt. It held the Cossaki chieftain's two long-barreled pistols, with bullet pouch and powder horn. More practical than a knife if worse came to worst; Shulamit flattered herself that she *might* be able to take a weaponless Sauron who had broken an arm, provided she had a saber and armor and plenty of warning. Borke might just get off a shot that hit, through sheer *p'rknz*-joke luck, if it came to it. "You know how use?"

About what I expected, Erika thought, looking around her in-laws' dining hall. Very much like their house in Strang, where the three-week wedding celebrations had been held. The families that controlled the House of the Tree were traditional to a fault; none of the newfangled chair-style backrests for them. They sat on cushions, around low tables, in a room floored with rugs and hung with tapestries to keep out what drafts the thick stone allowed. A yellow and scarlet *chagal*-tile stove sat in one corner, taking off the chill. The heads of the household and their honored guests ate here, at the table nearest the stove; their retainers and servants of the People elsewhere in the room.

Today the food was feast-style, with luxuries like risen wheat-bred and hot Nomad'sheart juice sweetened with beet-sugar. The centerpiece was whole roast lamb on a bed of steamed groats, stuffed with eggs and sausage and seasoned with paprika and garlic; there were sliced muskylope steaks marinated in herbs and grilled with ear-mushrooms, fried liver with onions, hard-boiled eggs with dill, salads of summer greens dressed in oil, deep-fried potato slices with dried tomato paste, pickled baby onions ... Prince Toktai belched politely as the meat courses were removed and followed by cheese, dried fruit, and the elaborate sweet pastries that the haBandari were famous for. Servants poured eggbush tea and nearcoffee, set out decanters and glasses of clownfruit brandy and wadiki.

"My thanks," the Mongol said, as he sipped. He looked admiringly at the hangings, the colored and wheel-cut glass of the table service, the inlaid brass of the tables. "My friend Karl said he would return my hospitality, and he has done so tenfold."

He bowed from the waist to Erika. "It grieved me that I could not attend his wedding, noble lady, after he and I had hunted and fought together. Affairs of state; I was called to the court of my liegelord the Gur-Khan Yesugei, son of Yesugei, overlord of the Yek and the Merkit, the earth lies at his feet." The latter was in a perfunctory sing-song. Erika recalled what Karl had told her; Ashkabad and the tribes surrounding had been allowed to keep their lands by the Mongol conquerors, two generations ago, subject to tribute and levies in time of war; the fortress of Ashkabad-town was held by a kinsman as vassal *khan*, with a garrison of Yek warriors.

The *noyon* continued: "But it was fortunate for me; my mother"—a nod to Hoelun, who had spoken perhaps half a dozen words during the meal—"arranged for my own betrothal to the maiden Borke, daughter of the *gur-khan*'s younger brother Hulagu." Obviously a dynastic union, but Toktai seemed pleased enough. "We expect her at any time, her caravan left the Black Tents two weeks ago." Those were Haven weeks, each of three 87-hour days; nearly a T-month. "You and your lady and your honored sire would please me greatly if you attended. So say I and my father, the Khan Yuechi, whom the *Wantegri* bless."

Karl's father Yigal bowed in turn, equally courtly. "May the favor of Yeweh lie on him," he said.

Erika looked up sharply; there was a slight breathiness to his voice. *Too gaunt,* she thought with worry; the older man's square boney face seemed to have fallen in on the strong slab shapes in the year since he had danced at her wedding. Her eyes met her mother-in-law's with shared concern; Yigal was darker than his son, but otherwise much like him. The heritage of Frystaat showed in the massiveness of their bones, and would internally as well. That folk had not used genetic engineering to adapt to their planet as the Saurons had, but eight tenths of the original immigrants had died within a generation. Their descendants seldom lived past fifty; the supercharged hearts and lungs needed to stand the killing gravity burned themselves out.

"His friendship and yours honors my House," Yigal continued. "Indeed, the whole Pale values the regard of the House of Yesugei, son of Yesugei, the earth lies at his feet." Which was quite true, since Ashkabad was crucial to all the northern trade. "Our *kapetein*—" the Mongol would hear that as *"khan"*; in fact, the ruler of the haBandari was elected, although always from the descendants of Piet van Reenan "—entrusted my son with these tokens of our regard."

The packages came forward. Silk robes for the *khatun*, embroidered in metallic thread of platinum and gold, with tiny chips of ruby and shimmerstone for the eyes of the dragons and landgators and firebirds that sprawled across it; a mirror of real silvered glass in a frame of worked bronze, completed the set. For her son, weapons; his hands were eager as he took the belt that bore them. The outer surface was black beefleather, tooled and stamped with silver designs of running tamerlanes and cliff lions, the whole lined with tough drillbit gut. He drew the saber; the hilt was searay ivory, and the basket guard brass inlaid with nacre. The meter length of blade was severely plain by contrast, except for the patterns in the steel itself, wave-shapes where layers of soft iron and hard steel had been bent, heated, and hammered together, again and again.

"Ahhh," Toktai said. "Look, the edge is as hard as glass, sharp enough to cut a drifting thread, but the rear of the blade is as flexible and tough as a crowbar! How do you do it?" He seemed a little taken aback when Erika answered:

"Layer forging and surface-hardening," she said,

reaching over to flick a nail against the edge; it rang. "A strip of wootz steel welded onto the edge; you cover the sword with fireclay, thick at the back and leaving the edge clear. Then pack it in a stone box full of powdered charcoal and keep it at red heat for several days." She grinned impishly. "Plus tempering, grinding, all the things a van Gimbutas smith could tell you."

Toktai nodded thanks. "Your lady Erika has . . . considerable knowledge," he said.

"A scholar," Karl answered with pride. To his father: "That's why we didn't come in with the caravan. Erika wanted to see the old ruins, the ones Aldigiras bar Voldemaris found during the Aydin War." That had been twenty years ago, in the turmoil that followed the fall of Angband Base and the last Sauron raid on the Eden Valley.

The two Mongols both made signs against evil. "Imperial things?" Hoelun asked. "Ill-luck to meddle with them. Atoms."

"Ahh—" Erika paused to marshal a diplomatic answer. "We have a way of finding those which are dangerous." Paper soaked in salts of silver, but rarely needed these days; it had been a *long* three centuries since the Sauron nuclear bombardment. "Not Imperial by origin, I think. Older, right back to the CoDominium." The young haBandari woman shivered slightly, remembering the shock of finding the ancient sigil of Earth's last state, the Americ eagle combined with the Russki hammer and sickle. Ceramic as fresh and unfaded as the day it was made nine hundred years ago, amid the crumbled sand-drifted concrete.

"Abandoned for a while, then used for many different things during the Imperial period." There had been a covered borehole, useless now but precious in those far-off days when electric pumps were available. She reached into a pocket of her second-best trousers and pulled out a plastic-coated alloy buckle, with double lightning-flash 7's superimposed on the Phoenix blazon of the Empire of Man.

"This is what interested me, I thought there might be something like this from hints bar Voldemaris left in his reports. The Seventy-Seventh must have had a unit there, just before the end."

Everyone knew what she meant; despite the centuries since their withdrawal during the Secession Wars the name of the Land Gators, the 77th Imperial Marine Division, still lived on in Haven legend. Ruth bat Boaz's famous *Lament* had its narrator calling their spirits home, when the Saurons came and found Haven defenseless. Erika remembered reciting it to herself as she stood among the tumbled stones; there had been another relic, a faded holograph of a young woman with a child, lost in a hasty evacuation. *Was she left behind?* Erika had wondered. *Did he remember her, dying on some planet far away? Did she remember him, when the* Dol Guldur *came?*

"Your pardon, lady," Toktai said, "but what exactly was it you were a scholar of?"

"Oh, the usual things," Erika said. All haBandari children learned letters and numbers, and the traditions of the People. Illona'sstaad was a center for learning, as well. "Accounting. And, ah, military history, mainly."

"Well, I'd not say anything against the luck of those who can make gifts as royal as these," Toktai said politely, resheathing the sword with visible reluctance. "They say you haBandari are tight-fisted and hard bargainers, but now I can testify that you know how to give like chieftains."

Hoelun muttered something in the barking syllables of her native tongue, then continued in common Turkic: "Wealth must come to those fortunate enough to pay no tribute to the Saurons," she said, ignoring her son's frown.

Karl showed his teeth in a smile. "They've tried

taking it, often enough," he said evenly. Then to Tok-tai: "But it was a stroke of inspiration by the Founder"—so the haBandari called Piet van Reenan, even those who did not make sacrifice to his shrine or believe his spirit abided to guard the People—"to sieze the Eden Valley as the heart of the Pale. Nothing south of us but wilderness and the sea beyond that, and it's as far from Quilland Base as you can get."

The Mongol prince nodded unhappily. His people held good grazing by the tens of thousands of square kilometers, but little lowland. There was the northern seacoast, but that was hideously difficult to reach across the Tierra del Muerte, barriered with deadly marsh, frozen almost all the year. To the west the only pass to the coastlands was held by the city-state of San Ynez; high enough to kill some with altitude sickness in summer, frozen in winter, altogether too risky to send pregnant women along. Which left Quilland Base's territory as the only practical alternative.

"It's a shame to us, even though the tribute we pay for passage is lighter than most," he said. "Worse shame that we let their tax collectors go freely among our tributaries here, whey-faced Turks though they are, but it was their price for not interfering when we took Ashkabad from the Kalmuks. I'd hoped we could arrange to use the Eden Valley, or Tallinn."

Yigal spread his hands. "We already take in many, *noyon*," he said. "It's not a matter of gold, but of grain." The land would feed just so many unproductive expectant mothers, after the women from the higher parts of the Pale were accommodated.

Toktai sighed. "And so we must tolerate the arrogance of the Lidless Eye," he said with some bitterness. "Even now a patrol is out taking women and stock from the clans hereabouts, and killing any who resist. The Buddha curse them to miserable rebirth!"

"Amen," the haBandari echoed; many of the People believed that souls returned. Then Yigal stiffened:

"Karl . . . Shulamit was going to meet you south of here."

Erika's eyes tracked to her father-in-law. "When?" she said.

"They left four days ago. Her and a dozen others, guards and mercenaries, *wildechaveri,* young hot-bloods who'd been hanging about after their caravans disbanded."

Karl's mouth had gone tight. "They could have missed us when we turned west to the ruins," he said bleakly. Erika answered with his own thought:

"Shulamit? She could track a ghost over a glacier!" Their eyes met. *Shulamit,* their shared thought ran. *Who hates Saurons even more than most.* Twenty years before the Soldiers had raided the Eden Valley, part of a probing expedition after the fall of Angband Base. Shulamit's father had fallen defending the Bashan Pass; at her Bat Mizvah his daughter had sworn to kill a Sauron for every year her father had missed of his threescore and ten. *Shulamit, who's been wilder than ever since Karl bar Yigal ended their stormy love affair by proposing to her younger sister.*

Karl opened his mouth to speak, closed it at the shouting outside the door. It burst open, and a figure staggered through to fall prone at Toktai's feet. Tom Jerrison followed, scowling, his sledgehammer ready in his hand.

"*Da hijputa wunna alto,*" he said in Americ: *The bastard wouldn't stop.*

Erika caught her breath. The man was of Toktai's race, still dressed in leather armor and plainsman's wool. A cut from brow to upper lip had left one eye a cratered ruin that oozed; the wound itself was bone-deep, and it wept pus. A stab under the lower ribs on one side had left a sheet of dried blood down that leg, and more ran in a sluggish trickle as he lay. Pink foam was on his lips as he struggled to grunt out his message; he ignored it, as he ignored the quick skilled hands of Karl's mother; Hagar bat Katherine had been born to the fan Allon clan, and trained as a mediko.

"Lucie, get my kit," she snapped, using a sharp clean carving knife to slice through the straps of the curiass and the cloth beneath. "Bandages, mould-powder, a saline drip, hot water, *quickly*."

Toktai listened to the wounded man, answered, touched his forehead with a curious gentleness. Erika forced herself not to flinch at the expression on the flat, hard face.

"My bride," he said. "Borte, the *gur-khan's* brother's daughter. The caravan was ambushed. Most slaughtered, she and her attendant carried off."

"Saurons?" Karl said. Yigal had called several of his retainers, speaking quickly and softly.

"No. It might as well be," Toktai said. "Cossaki dogs, of the Bergenov *stanitsa*. We beat them in my father's time, and my grandfather's. The Saurons have taken their valley of Belogrod, and now they are driving them west. Into our lands!" He nodded bitterly. "Now we know why they have sent their tribute-takers through the tribes; to weaken them for the Cossaki, so that their defeat may weaken *us*. Psin"—his foot indicated the wounded man, unconscious as his host's wife worked to save him—"says they saw a Sauron patrol pass one Haven-day before the attack; the Cossaki came in the Soldier's footsteps." He stood, faced Karl. "Is this your fight, my *anada*?"

Karl's hand gripped his. "My kinswoman Shulamit is out there, too," he said, in a voice equally flat. "And if she were not, an oath is an oath. Three hours, by the east gate?"

Toktai nodded silently and stalked from the room. Karl was already calling to faces in the banquet crowd:

"Shimon, Itzak, Kosti, Jadwiga," he barked. "Everybody who'll come except the gate guard; you vet them, no shopkeepers or clerks, full kit, three remounts each and see they won't founder. Father, we can draw on the settlement stores?" Like any haBandari town, the Ashkabad enclave had its armory and communal store-houses that any of the People could use at need. "Kosti, take half the rifles and a hundred rounds each. Let's *move*, people!"

Erika waited in the silence that filled the room as they left, swallowing. *Shulamit*, she thought. *Oh, sister . . . if you're dead, how can you forgive me? The* anima *of the ancestors will cast my soul out of the People. . . .*

She looked down at her mother-in-law. "Will he live?" she said, as the older woman sat back on her heels and wiped her blood-smeared hands.

"Perhaps," Hagar sighed. "He's got a collapsed lung, that's not good up here." This was the high steppe, where even the barrel-chested products of a thousand years of natural selection were at risk. "We'll see."

Hoelun snorted as she came to her feet. Erika started slightly; she had not even been conscious of the Mongol woman's presence.

"We may all see our men brought back dead," she said heavily. "They are born to such things . . ." More softly: "Borte was a merry child, who grew into a girl worthy of her blood; she and Toktai would have made a good match. Now her hopes are dust even if she lives, and I may see no grandchildren." She turned her head to look at Erika, greenish slit eyes meeting hazel. "I will light joss sticks to the boddhavistas," she said. "What will you do, young scholar?"

The haBandari looked at her in puzzlement. "Ride with my man," she said, raising her brows. "What else?"

"Danke," Shulamit said, taking the bowl and a round of stale flatbread from Borte's hands.

The smell was intoxicating, the first hot food in more days than she cared to count. Stew, slices of mutton boiled in water thickened with powdered dried milk, bits of liver and kidney and heart from the sheep they had slaughtered . . . but there was business first. Gorthaur had placed her bedroll beside his. Shulamit kicked it over to the other side of the fire in its circle of rock, sinking down with the rolled leather and duck-down between her buttocks and the cold rock. *Damned if I'm going to screw with an audience,* she thought. Coldly: *Let's see, they say five times to take . . . probably more than enough.*

"Shul-mit," the girl said.

"Mmurph?" Shulamit replied, through a mouthful of stew. The rich fat was intoxicating, after weeks on biltong. The sticks of dried meat would keep you going, but they were lean; the body craved calories, burned them fast when you had to move and fight in steppe weather. *Thank Yeweh it isn't winter,* she thought, watching her breath steam in the night air. The hairs on the inside of her nostrils were crinkling anyway. Cat's Eye was a crescent a handspan over the northern horizon, the darkened three-quarters a dull, red glow next to the banded brightness of the visible slice. Two of the other moons were up, whetted sickles. . . .

"You Sauron's woman?" Borte continued, busying herself with a pan. The fire burned acridly, dung and mineral-heavy native Haven scrub and the fat-wrapped bones of the sheep, but the stones piled around it would keep the glow from showing far.

"No." Shulamit grinned at her back. *I'm an unwillingly unmarried meid who plans ahead,* she thought to herself. Aloud: "I *my* woman. Maybe Gorthaur think different."

Borte turned her head over her shoulder, and surprised the other woman with a slight smile. "I remember," she said; she passed the haBandari a cup of eggbush tea and served herself a bowl of the stew. "How you, him, ride together?"

"Long story," Shulamit said.

"Long night," Borte said, bringing over the pan. It held rags, heated in a little of the precious cooking oil they had found with the raiders. Shulamit rolled up her pantleg over the injured knee and sighed with relief as the hot cloth settled over it. The swelling had gone down, and the pain was less. *Better,* she thought, supressing a nagging worry. Knee injuries were tricky, and it might never be as good as it had been . . . "Long night, long story," Borte prompted again.

The haBandari laughed. *"Da,"* she said, searching for the words. *Why can't everyone speak Bandarit, or at least Americ?* she thought. "Shto—"

Gorthaur returned while she was telling the tale; he stopped and glanced at his bedding where it lay across the fire from the others'. Shulamit gave him a cool smile, without interrupting the flow of words. *Take it in hand and walk to the Citadel with it, Sauron,* she thought; from what she knew of Sauron custom, frustration of this sort was *not* something Gorthaur would be used to. Far too early for him to force a confrontation, and meanwhile her knee was healing faster than his arm, the greater degree of injury making up for the superior Sauron metabolism. *Bit of a relief.* Bedding him had been . . . odd. It was the first time she had done it without affection and with an ulterior motive, for one thing. *For another, he's got all the finesse of a forgemill triphammer. And the staying power: I'm sore.*

Gorthaur helped himself to the food, stoking himself with methodical calm and taking long pulls at a flash of wadiki between mouthfulls; alcohol affected his breed much less than human norms, and there was a good deal of food energy in it. *But a little of drowning sorrows, too,* Shulamit thought maliciously, as she came to the end of her story. Borte was staring rapt.

"I"—she pointed to herself—"Yek Mongol. You?"

"HaBandari," Shulamit replied. *This one must be from a long way away.* A haBandari was distinctive enough, and a haBandari *woman* doubly so. "Go Ashkabad? Take Borte there, your people?"

The Mongol girl's face went dull, expression draining out of it; she turned away, rolling herself into the blankets.

What did I say? Shulamit thought, and then dismissed it; it was surprising how well the other had born up, actually, better than many of the People would have in the same circumstances. She unbuckled her boots, put her weapons by her saddle and slid into her own bag; Pale-made, with a quilted lining and quick-release latches.

"There?" she said to Gorthaur, pointing to where one of the moons would be in six hours: they had divided the watches six and four, in practical recognition of the Sauron's lesser need for sleep.

"Yes," he said shortly, picking up a loose-woven wolfcloak of tamerlane fur and stalking away to a vantage point.

The haBandari lay back, feeling her teeth show in an unpleasant grin as he stalked away, unconsciously tracking his boots on the loose rock. It was difficult, he was extremely quiet for a man of the weight she remembered. She gathered the upper flap of her bag around her head, breathing through the fringe of cliff lion underfur, that had the unique property of shedding moisture. Sleep came quickly; rest was life, you could not afford to waste it. But it was light, a doze that left her half-conscious of outside noise; after an hour or so she blinked back to wakefulness.

What is that? A low whimpering and rustling behind her, three meters away. *Oh.* Borte was stirring in her sleep, in the grip of nightmare.

"Yewehdammit. Some p'rknz is playing a joke on me." *It followed me home, ma: do I have to keep it?* she asked herself rhetorically. To the People there was no particular obligation to aid a stranger, but she could scarcely withdraw help once given. *I'll hand her over*

*to whoever her kin are in town and that'll be the end
of it,* Shulamit thought. Which left the little matter of
getting there, it was four hundred kilometers of hostile
territory. In theory a haBandari ought to be able to
cross the steppe hereabouts, the Pale had a treaty with
the rulers of Ashkabad for safe-transit. Practice was
another matter entirely.

Sighing, she wormed her way over to the Mongol
like a caterpillar in a sleeping-bag cocoon and tapped
her on the shoulder. Borte came half awake with a
start.

"It's all right," Shulamit said muzzily. "Go back to
sleep."

The cold had turned bitter when Gorthaur awoke
her, scuffing his foot through the scree an arm's length
away. Reflex brought her up with the pistol in her
hand, and frost crackled off the fur of the bag's flap.
Her first thought was resentment that he had awak-
ened her before the time. That died as she saw the
wary crouch of his stance: she slid silently out of the
bag and refastened her boots. The fire had died to
cold ash, and the breeze blew whisps of it about her,
a sad bitter smell. The wind was down from the
heights, cold air falling toward the relative warmth of
the steppe trough.

"I hope this is important," she whispered, following
the Sauron to a rock-ridge. He pointed toward the
western plain, that fell away from the foothills in a
rolling plateau slashed with erosion gulleys. Shulamit
closed her eyes as she pulled on her gloves, working
stiffened fingers in the lambswool lining, then used
them to shield her nightsight from the light of Cat's
Eye while she scanned; it was just a little too dim to
be able to tell a white thread from a black. *Nothing,*
she thought, peering out from beneath. *Absolutely
nothing.* Of course, low-light night like this was worse

for long-distance sight than the rare occasions of total dark.

"Well?" she said.

"Campfires, and large bodies of men and animals," he said; his tone was as flat as ever, but she thought the crisp-vowelled Sauron accent was heavier. "I can see their heat."

Shulamit winced, and drew her spyglass. "Point me," she said. After a minute: "I think I can see one or two. I'll take your word for the rest . . . what patterns?"

"Nothing regular," Gorthaur said. "Larger fires, then smaller scattered around, with the animal sources further out still. Several dozen in all. Six to twelve kilometers from here, and directly on our route."

The haBandari grunted. Not Saurons, then; they lit fires the way they did everything else, by the numbers and in straight lines. An army of the People was unlikely in the extreme, but even if there had been a haBandari force it would be grouped by squads and clan regiments. . . . Locals, then or—

"More of those Cossaki?" she asked.

"Impossible to say," the Sauron said thoughtfully. "There have been operations in their sector—" he shut his mouth with a snap. "They have just made camp; if we leave within an hour, we will have the best chance of evading their pickets."

"North or south?" she asked. Neither of them knew the ground in detail. *South puts us closer to the Pale if we can't make Ashkabad. North is closer to Quilland Base.*

Gorthaur stared out into the night. "Logically, either might be better. Therefore there is only one sensible method of deciding." He smiled and drew a silver coin from one of the patch-pockets that half covered his field uniform; Citadel-minted, the only stamped currency on Haven. One side bore the dagger shape of the *Dol Guldur*, the other an ancient motto of the Saurons in the Old Americ tongue: *KILL 'EM ALL AND LET GOD SORT 'EM OUT.* "Print or Pirate?" he said.

"I didn't quite believe you, when you said your people could keep up with mine," Toktai son of Yuechi said, watching the two columns pass below the hillcrest. "Those tall horses of yours look fine, but I'd have sworn they couldn't keep up with our ponies."

There were a hundred and fifty haBandari, as many of his household retainers. Twenty hours out from Ashkabad there was little difference in appearance, although the Mongols had started the journey more colorfully dressed; now both were the reddish-brown color of steppe dust. The warriors of the Pale were equipped alike, corselets and thigh-guards of overlapping bullhide plates on a backing of woven drillbit gut, bucket-shaped helmets; his men wore what they could afford, from a few with steel armor like his to a majority in lacquered leather. The haBandari weapons were similar to his; bow, saber, and knife, and a third carried lances as well. And a dozen bore rifles: the prince supressed a moment of envy at that. His own pistols were the sole powder weapons among his band, more ornament than weapon. Well, the hornbow was the *khan* of weapons on the steppe, and the Mongol were second to none with *that*.

"Oh, they can't," Karl said, keeping his binoculars to his eyes and scanning westward; the party from Ashkabad was keeping to the edge of a string of volcanic hills, to reduce the plume of betraying dust. Of course, the gravel and sharp-edged rock was harder on the unshod nomad horses, but it was worth it. "Not for more than a week or so. War's more confined, down here in the southern steppe." A week's hard ride from the Afritsberg to the Iron Limpers, and five from Quilland Base to the scrub-forests at the southern border of the Pale.

"Dust," he continued, and passed the glasses to his ally.

"*Tcha*," Toktai muttered, focusing them. "I wish your *kapetein* would sell us more of these ... ahhh. Enough for five hundred men, in loose formation."

"Or ten scouts dragging brush, or a herd of cattle," Karl said, naming two of the classic tricks of open-country warfare. "We could put out a scout-screen? We need to know how many, their leaders—we need prisoners and reports."

Toktai looked down at the passing warriors, thudding clatter of hoofs, creak of leather, rattle of iron; the light of the quarter-Cat's Eye painted the edges of the lanceheads with blood.

"Yes. And that also warn *them*," he said, beating one fist on his thigh. "Curse those turki dogs for fools and cowards!" His rage at the Turkmen tributaries of his folk seemed almost as great as what he felt for the invaders. "We've already come across two camps of them burned out by the Cossaki, yet they flee us as if we were the enemy!"

Karl shrugged. "I see the hand of Quilland Base in this," he said. "Those tribute parties probably passed the word to some of the clan chiefs; and the Cossaki are heading straight south like an arrow, killing everything in their path. The local tribes figure if they get out of the way they won't suffer: and they're more afraid of the Saurons than of you, my friend.

"Erika," he turned to his wife, where she sat with compass and mapboard. She looked up at him, and a cold knot turned tighter in his gut at the calm confidence in her hazel eyes. *Spirit of Piet, I wish I could send her out,* he thought. "Courier back to Ashkabad, and priority to Fort Kidmi; minimum two thousand sabers heading south. This is going to be the biggest fracas since the Aydin War." She pulled out a scrap of brown rag-paper and began to write.

"In the meantime, our kinswomen are behind that,"

Toktai said, jerking his chin toward the eastern horizon. "To rescue, or avenge."

"Yes, there is that." Karl bar Yigal grinned, teeth white against the dirt-caked brown of his skin. Erika looked up from her note taking and stared at the expression wide-eyed; it was not a pleasant one, or something she had seen on her husband's face before. "So if we can't scout them, we'd better hit before they realize we're coming." Cut through the screen of outriders any force on the steppe drew about itself, cleave like a lancehead to the core of the enemy host, slash their way out again.

Whup.

"Shit!" Shulamit yelled, as the arrow split the air a meter from her ear. "Back, you cowfucker!" More yells from the pursuers, a high *yip-yip-yip* like animals in pain.

She twisted in the saddle; the long swooping rhythm of the gallop made that easy, wind cuffing at her face, huge muscles bunching and straightening beneath her knees. The bow came up in her hands and she locked a thumb over the shaft and drew. A Pale-made bow, the unique *bare* first crafted by the legendary weaponsmith Kosti Gimbutas, at the beginning of the People. With a rigid centerpiece, cut from the heart of the clownfruit tree; a molded pistol grip, with a cutout rest for the arrow, and a sighting ring above it; thick laminated arms, with the string running over offset bronze wheels at the tip of either stave.

Knock to the string, shaft to the ear, and loose, she thought, as the crosshairs fell on the Cossaki's chest: there was the familiar rattle and hum, the *snap* of the string and the blurring trajectory, almost too swift and flat to see. Three hundred meters behind her the foremost Cossaki checked, threw himself flat along his mount's neck as the arrow wasp-whined through the space he had occupied a second earlier; the other seven behind him came on, howling like stobor. Rabid stobor they were, but she had taught them respect for the haBandari bow; there had been ten of them, to begin with. It had taken that many for them to realize she outranged them by a third. Grudging respect: *But they can ride and shoot, curse them.*

She clamped her knees tighter, leaned forward again with the horse's mane whipping into her eyes, that made less of a target—*though it means if they do hit me it's in the rump*—if they hit the horse, she was dead, that was all—

"Come on, *myn lekke,* my sweet," she crooned to the animal; its head was plunging, pumping up and down to the *brrrt-brrrt-brrrt* of its hooves on the sandy dirt. Lather streaked its flanks and spattered musky across her face, but she could feel the spirit of a beast that would run until the heart burst in its chest. "*Greut ferd, g'rion ferd,* great horse, hero horse, you shall graze in clover and bear foals to the finest stallions in the Pale, *run* you bitch, *run.*"

The slope was coming up towards her, half a thousand meters high of sand and tumbled rock and bush; the Cossaki would be expecting to pin her against it or shoot her down as she climbed. And the mouth of the gully, wide enough for three riders abreast, shadow and the green-gray-red banded volcanic rock. Shulamit pressed inward with her toes, and the horse slowed fractionally as they plunged into the gloom; even with a mount as fine as this, you did not take rough ground *that* fast. A dogleg, right, left, cliffs like walls on either side where long-ago floods had carved the rock. Echoes, pounding hooves back redoubled and—

Yes. The file-on-rock shrieks of the Cossaki, loud enough to make her mare start and roll its eyes, almost crashing them into a boulder.

"Yeweh Mog'n haBandari!" she muttered in wonder, as hands and knees and weight made their dance of control with the horse. "*Yeweh Shield of the People!* Gorthaur was right, they followed me right in!"

Rock blurred by on either side, reaching for her with fingers of thorny *qosbush*. This was going to be tricky, the accursed *gayam* weren't slowing down at *all*, only the twists of the gulley were keeping them off her back, and—

Light slapped at her eyes as the walls fell away; the opening was egg-shaped, a hundred meters broad and twice as long. "*Heeeeeeeyaaaiiii!*" she screamed, hauling the reins back. The horse screamed as well, high and shrill, neck arching, haunches sinking almost into a squat, almost going over but not quite, rearing and pig-jumping forward as it shed momentum. She brought it up and around again, wheeling in place, dropping just in time to let her snatch another shaft from the quiver before her right knee.

The first Cossaki came into the ampitheatre at a flat gallop that stretched his horse out along the ground, secure in the saddle as a centaur or an ancient Terran Commanche. There was nothing wrong with his reflexes either; he was drawing on her even as her arrow punched *crack* through the horn scales sewn to his long leather coat, through breastbone and spine with a wet crunch to flip him over his horse's tail; the beast bucked and ran, circling the cliff and bugling its panic. Gorthaur had been waiting in the shadow by the narrow slit in the rock, with his saber cocked back over one shoulder. He was not an expert rider, nor trained to the sword. He did not need to be; the steel was a shining arc in his hand, and the next Cossaki tumbled to the gravel cut almost in half.

Then the others were out, bursting past the ambushcade, turning their mounts and drawing steel. Shulamit had just enough time to drop the bow into its case, snatch her buckler and draw before two of them came at her. Two to one was bad odds; she clapped heels to her mount and passed them on their left, ducking under a cut and slashing a blindside backswing behind her. The saber jarred in her hand as the armor over the man's shoulder blades turned it.

"*HaBandar!*" she shouted as she reined about. The two foemen had done likewise; in a frozen moment she could hear a clash and scream from the group about Gorthaur, but there was no time to worry about that. If only they could use their pistols ... no, that was death, the echoes carried too far in these badlands.

Two men, one in a leather breastplate and spiked steel helm, the other in sheepskin cap and jacket. Sharp-curved swords, plainsmen's *shamshirs,* small bucklers like hers with central handgrips. Her armor was better, something of an advantage. She would need it.

"*HaBandar!*" The horses bounded forward off their haunches; she headed for the slight gap between her opponents. There was a brutal jarring as her tall mare slammed its shoulder into that of one man's mount. That threw his cut off; Shulamit caught the stroke, his partner on her own sword, held it for a crucial moment while her left hand chopped the iron rim of her shield into the nose of the first man's horse. It reared, bucked, twisted, out of control for crucial moments.

Kill him, kill him, kill him now, she thought, as the shamshir scraped along her saber with a long *shungggg* of steel on steel. They wheeled and cut, hard jarring in her wrist and arm as blade beat on shield, on blade, on shield. *Shit, he's too good,* she thought, pushing despair back below the surface of the combat-mind. Man and horse both, he seemed to have never heard of the point but he was *fast,* she'd have to work his blade out of line. . . .

A flicker from the corner of her eye, the other Cossaki getting his horse in hand, but she *couldn't* spare the attention, his friend was beating on her guard like a smith on an anvil—*once* and she brought the buckler around and up in a circle, protection without covering her eyes. The scimitar snicked off the curved leather with a hard bang, deflected, reversed, came at her again in a smooth backhand cut. She pulled the hilt of her sword back, saw his eyes widen—*thought I'd lock hilts and you could disarm me, didn't you, gayam*—and *two* she ducked and felt the edge ring off her helmet, stars and lights before her eyes, sick pain in her neck, but the point of her sword flicked forward. Sharp point, on a blade built to thrust as often as cut; punching through the leather coat, into muscle and gut that felt soft and heavy against her wrist.

Swordfighting was close work, no elegant affair of arrows where tiny doll figures fell off model horses while you rode away. Close enough to hear your opponent pant, close enough to smell his sweat. Shulamit set her teeth and withdrew as she had been taught, with a wrenching twist; making herself see the man's face as a thing of shapes and colors, not human, not a mouth flaring out in pain, not eyes that knew their own death. Her blade shed an arc of red drops as she wheeled to guard against the other. The other who should have killed her already, Gorthaur was still fighting . . .

He was on the ground; beside a horse that dragged itself along on its forelegs, hamstrung. The man was dragging himself, too, crawling doggedly as Borte hacked at him, holding a saber in a two-handed grip like a farmer threshing grain. The Mongol girl was spattered from knees to face with the products of her earnest, clumsy butchery; Shulamit could hear it, whacking sounds as the sword turned on his hard-leather backplate, chunking as the notched edge met flesh. One wild flail crossed the back of his neck, and he stopped, spasmed, died.

Borte dropped the sword, looked up at Shulamit. "I

cut the horse," she said calmly. "It threw him, he landed on his face. Then I cut him."

"You saved my life," Shulamit said, feeling the same glassy detachment.

"You avenged my honor, even though blood cannot wipe out my shame," Borte replied formally. Then she knelt and began retching bile.

The haBandari blinked bewilderment, even as she turned to confirm what peripheral vision had told her, that all the Sauron's opponents were down. *Shame?* she thought. *Doing pretty dam' well, for a gayam.* Especially a gayam woman, untrained to arms. Was she ashamed because she lacked a warrior's skills? Some non-Bandari thought like that; the People held that war was waste, not glory, and trained to it because they must. There were some fire-eating youngsters who thought differently, of course; she wiped at the sticky drops on her face and wished that she could have some of them here.

"Are you injured?" Gorthaur called to her sharply. That brought her back to herself; she took a deep breath and forced alertness. *Actual detectable concern in his voice,* she thought sardonically. *Why, Gorthaur, I didn't know you cared.* Her horse cantered over to the ampitheatre's only exit, then shied at something that twitched.

"No," she said, looking down. The sight caught her attention; hand-to-hand combat with edged weapons was always gruesome, but this . . . Once she had worked for a summer in a wind-powered sawmill, on the southern border of the Pale; there had been an accident, one of the workers thrown into the path of the circular saw. This was like that, only repeated four times. She looked up to meet Gorthaur's eyes; they were more alive than she had seen them, darting about, and she could see a flush on his cheeks. *Maybe I was being overoptimistic,* she thought, remembering her estimate that she could take the Soldier, wounded and unarmed. *He* let *me live. Probably because I'm a woman: the more fool him.*

"I—" he glanced at the sword in his hand, began to wipe it. "We do not do much of this sort of combat," he said. "At close quarters, like this. Against doctrine," he continued, almost caressing the steel. There were a few superficial cuts on his face and arms, clotting even as she watched.

"Your doctrine sucks wet muskylope farts," Shulamit answered sincerely. "Your ancestors should have used more bombs, wiped out everyone who knew how to make gunpowder weapons. Hand to hand, there'd be no stopping you."

"There were considerations—" Gorthaur stopped, and his voice returned to the neutral tone. "This was . . . exhilarating, nonetheless," he said. "Come."

Shulamit nodded; they had punched a hole in the enemy's screen, thanks to a reckless bloodlust that Gorthaur had described and she had scarcely been able to believe. Now they had to get through it before it closed.

"Borte!" she shouted. "Poed bruk, ans trek!" *Damn, I'm forgetting.* "Get our stuff, we've got to *move.*"

Exhilarating, she mused, as the Mongol led out their remounts. HaBandari records went back to the coming of the *Dol Guldur,* if scantily; the Founder had written that the Empire of Man destroyed itself to crush the Saurons and scorch their homeworld. *Now I see why.*

"Remember to lead him," Erika told herself, snuggling her cheek into the cold wood of the rifle stock. "Breathe in. And out. Don't think, this isn't the time or place." The tremor died out of her hands.

The haBandari main body was nearly a thousand meters to her front, dipping in and out of sight as they galloped in a compact body before three times their number of pursuers. *A mob,* she thought. *I can't*

*believe they're going to fall for the same trick again.
With another trick inside it, this time.* For that matter,
it was taking these Cossaki a long time to grasp that
their bows simply did not have the range of the
haBandari *bare*; there was a long train of bodies across
the steppe, almost all enemy. *Every one of them a
human being.* "He who saves the life of one, it is as if
he has saved the whole human race—"

"Stop that!" she scolded herself sharply. "If a man
come up against thee, to slay thee, slay him first."
That was also the Law. Hooves made a thunder that
vibrated the earth beneath her belly; the scent of
horse and dirt and gun-oil was like a hunting trip, a
drill, homelike. "Just a firing exercise," she told herself. "The clan regiment's out, and you're showing
what you're made of."

The snipers of the Pale were lying in a staggered
row, sighting across the saddles of horses trained to
lie flat. Erika was in the center of that line, waiting as
the chase drew nearer. Waiting, eight hundred meters,
seven hundred, the horses turning from points to dolls
to reality, looming out of the cloud of dust—

Five hundred meters, she was sure of it. That was
what the rifle's sights were set for; she had always
guessed right in the school range-estimation games,
almost as often right as Shulamit; when was Itzhak
going to—

Crack. A dozen more; Erika's finger stroked across
the trigger. The flintlock kicked back into her shoulder; was that a man down, a horse tumbling, her
doing, a life snuffed out? Impossible to tell; her hands
moved, jerked at the lever that formed the trig-
gerguard of the rifle. The mechanism clicked; a wedge
swung down, and the iron and brass tube that sealed
the breech popped up. Erika's hand was already going
back to the bandalier at her side for another of the
paper cartridges as she blew sharply on the breech to
make sure there were no sparks left.

Bite the cartridge open, taste of sulphur and wax. Thumb over the end, use your hand to push the L-shaped pan cover and frizzen up. The first pinch of powder into the pan, the rest into the loading tube. Let the stubby cone of the bullet drop into your palm, thumb it into the barrel, jerk the lever forward. Visual check, to make sure the tube had slid forward into the breech, the wedge up behind to lock it. Pull the hammer back to full cock, *click*. Another target, not a man, a target, that was what Shulamit had told her, impatient when she asked what fighting was *really* like. And stroke the trigger, squeezing gently . . .

Six times a minute in skilled hands, and the dozen rifles beat out a metronomic rhythm. The Cossaki band wavered, its pursuit of the haBandari turned to slaughter. *If they run—* Erika thought, as her hands moved through the drill. But they did not; instead they turned to the line of white puffs that marked the rifles and charged. There were still better than two hundred of them, only five hundred meters away. Half that, and they would be in arrow-range, dropping shafts on the marksmen hidden behind their mounts. There was not enough firepower in the haBandari firing line to stop them, not even with the mounted warband wheeling to race along behind their former pursuers. Not against men as brave as these; and these *gayam* were brave as *g'rioni*, heroes, you had to admit that. Erika saw Itzahk turn to wave behind, down the low slope at their backs.

A jingling sounded, a clatter building to a thunder as the Mongols came up the rise that had concealed them. They threaded through the line of haBandari, building speed; the Cossaki band did not slow, it rippled with metal that blinked honed sharpness as the warriors cased their bows and drew steel. The warriors of the Pale did likewise, couching lance and laying sabers point-forward as they charged in wedge formation, a boulder-solid mass riding boot to boot. Erika expected a crash when the lines met, but instead there was only a sudden swelling of sound, scrap metal falling on stone, screaming, horses and warriors down in a mist of dust that rose saddle-high and glinted with movement.

She sprang to her own feet, straddled her horse. "Up, Flower," she called; the animal rose in a surge, and she slid the rifle home in its scabbard as her feet found the stirrups.

"Wait up," Izthak called sharply, as she drew her saber. Her arm remembered the feel of the edge on meat; the clan drillmasters had students practice on animal carcasses occasionally, to get the sensation. It had been mildly disgusting at the time. Now it set her teeth on edge.

"Wait up, you wildechaver," the older man said again, as the snipers formed up in line. "Orders." They were not to risk the firearms without need.

But Karl's down there! she cried within.

"How many rounds?" he said.

"Twenty-seven," she replied automatically. The others spoke in turn; she was second-highest. *That's the price of eleven hundred sheep we've fired off today,* some far-off irrelevant bookkeeper's part of her mind recorded: Haven had many volcanoes but little sulfur. Ammunition was *expensive,* that was one of the many reasons firearms were rare.

Itzhak's eyes saw more than hers in the melee. "They're breaking," he said with satisfaction. First a scattering fleeing in all directions, like spattered droplets, then the whole of them, half as many as there had been a half hour before. "Right, let's move."

Gorthaur reined in; his horse made a small sound of pain at the heavy tug on the reins. His head turned to the northwest, motionless for a moment. Then he dismounted briefly, pressing an ear to the ground.

"There is a battle going on there," he said as he

rose and swung back into the saddle; he did it swiftly, but without grace.

"Nu?" Shulamit's mount halted to the swing of her balance; she narrowed her eyes and peered. "Dust, yes, but we've been seeing that all day."

"Battle," the Sauron said firmly. "I heard multiple firearms, and the hoofbeats indicate a sizable mounted force in rapid motion. Not my people, black-powder weapons."

"Mmmm." Shulamit blinked. She was exhausted, with a sick tiredness that owed more than a little to the blow she had taken five hours before; you paid for things like that. *Think, cow,* she told herself. "Well, that accounts for our getting through clear, once we took out those scouts, they pulled everything to meet whoever-it-is." She reached for her canteen, then forced her hand away. There was not much left, and they had had to leave the camels. "South?" They should be nearly through the badlands in any case.

Gorthaur nodded wordlessly and turned his horse's head to the left.

"Not going to win any prizes for small talk," Shulamit muttered, following.

"I was wrong," Karl said, looking about. The Mongol troopers were walking their mounts delicately among the enemy fallen, spearing the wounded. Work the haBandari were glad to leave to their allies, essential though it was.

Erika ignored the red-brown stickiness that coated her husband's arm to the elbow and ran liquid on his sword; they leaned together in the saddle for a brief one-armed embrace.

"I was wrong," he said again, weariness in his voice. "This isn't a warband on a raid, it isn't even an army. It's a fucking folk-migration, that's what it is, and my temper got us right into the vanguard of it." His shield-hand touched her on the cheek with a moment's gentleness. "I'm sorry, Erika."

"I'm right where I want to be, Karl," she said quietly. "With you."

They both looked up as Toktai reined in beside them with a spurt of gravel; there was a carnivore satisfaction on his face.

"We gave them an expensive lesson," he said.

"Not one we can deal out again," Karl replied, straightening. He pulled a cloth from his belt, looked at it, and threw it away, rummaging for a clean one in his saddlebags; even in an emergency, you did not sheath a blade with blood on it. "We're running short of arrows, and most of my riflemen are down to a dozen rounds. Also there'll be more of them, next time." He looked down at the clump of enemy dead, at the scattering that trailed off across the rolling steppe. "They're excellent individual fighters, but not very well ordered."

Toktai snorted. "Ordered? Stobor fighting over a dead horse have more discipline. One *touman* of my *gur-khan*'s troops could slaughter the lot of them." He looked admiringly at the stolid clump of haBandari, caring for their wounded and seeing to their weapons. "If they come against your people twenty thousand sabers strong, you will turn them into our advance, Karl my brother."

"Yes, we will," Erika said sharply. "And still there will be orphans, maimed, homes burned, and lives wrecked, even for those who live."

The Mongol looked at her with kindly tolerance; Erika felt her temper flare for the first time that day, and was glad when he turned back to her husband without answering.

"We're nearly to the canyon country," Toktai continued. "We've punched right through, just as you said. In there, not ten times their number could find us, and I think they won't stop."

"I don't think they *can* stop, not if they have the Saurons at their back," Karl said. His gaze swung consideringly to their north. "We've seen fighting men, mostly, only a few wagon trains." Widely spread out, as any large movement must be, to give the draught animals grass and water. "The last two bands hit us too close together for my taste. They've got all the tactical cohesion of a tavern brawl, but *somebody* is directing them, and not badly. We'd better get moving; it all depends if whoever-it-is can get enough riders in front of us fast enough."

Toktai nodded. "Those we came to rescue . . ." he shrugged. "They were caught like travellers in an avalanche; now we must rescue ourselves." Grimly: "But vengeance we have had, and will."

"Vengeance tastes better as dessert than as appetizer," Karl quoted: another saying of the Founder. "Let's move."

"Down!" Gorthaur barked. Then: "No matter. They have identified us."

The Sauron was a little ahead of her on the slope, taking point while Shulamit rode beside Borte and the remount string; she spurred up beside him, peering ahead.

"You certain?" she asked. The riders were a clump nearly three kilometers off, too far to make out details.

The Soldier spared her a glance: "I said so," he continued dryly. "They have altered direction toward us." The three fugitives had been heading south and east, the party of Cossaki directly north. "Evidently they have a telescope of some sort."

"Yeweh dammit," Shulamit said, feeling weight pressing down her shoulders. They *should* have been all right, the Cossaki should have assumed they were a part of this warband-army-host whatever. "I'm too old for this shit." *If—when—I get home, I'm going to endow a synagogue and buy a whole* flock *of sheep to sacrifice to the anima of the Founders. I must have done* something *horrendous to deserve this. You hear me, Yeweh? Piet? Ruth?*

Gorthaur blinked at her; a hundred hours at close quarters had shown her that was his equivalent of a puzzled frown. "I thought you were only twenty-one T-years," he said.

"That's twenty-one T-years too many for this," she said. "Which way do we run? Northeast?"

This time Gorthaur did scowl. "Yes. Bad, but better than backtracking." It would mean heading toward the action he had heard, but there were advantages to that; battle bred confusion. "Shulamit . . ."

She looked up at his tone. "Shulamit, I have been . . . impressed with your abilities. Yours are obviously superior genes; it is . . . irresponsible that they should be wasted. When we have eluded pursuit, come with me to Quilland Base; you will have considerable status as my woman. You will be free of danger and labor, then; you deserve a civilized environment, and all you need do is bear Soldiers."

The haBandari stared at him, feeling her jaw drop slightly. She closed it with a snap. *I thought jaws dropping in astonishment was a cliche,* she told herself.

"Nu, Gorthaur," she replied. "Why don't you give up being a Sauron and come to the Pale? I'll get you a job in a coalmine, nice safe work."

They stared at each other for a moment in mutual bafflement, and then the Soldier shrugged the rifle off his back. "There is a horsetail banner with that party of Cossaki," he said in a matter-of-fact tone. "I can bring down a few of their commanders before they disperse; that will keep them from pressing us too closely, we may be able to lose them in favorable terrain." He dismounted and trotted forward to find a prone firing position.

Borte came up beside her. "What did Sauron say?" she asked as the first shot rang out.

"I think he just . . . proposed marriage," Shulamit answered. They looked at each other, and the haBandari saw the Mongol suddenly break into a grin.

"Not . . . how say, not right time?" Borte said. Shulamit snorted.

"You should have been born haBandari," she said. "Now, let's *go*."

"Yeweh's eternal curse," Karl said, lowering the binoculars. He turned to look behind them, and to either side.

"What is it?" Erika rasped. This time she allowed herself a swallow of the brackish, bitter-tasting water in her canteen; it was glorious.

"More Cossaki. Ahead of us. Between us and the badlands."

Itzhak bar David was near enough to hear. And for Erika to hear the phrase he murmured to himself, in a language far older than Bandarit: *"Hear, O Israel, the Lord our God, the Lord is One."*

"Oh." Erika found herself making the same circuit of the horizon as her husband, past the exhaustion-slumped warriors sitting horses as droop-necked as themselves. There were converging dust plumes from east and southeast and northeast; and now directly ahead, from the west that had offered the false promise of safety. *Dust,* she thought bitterly, spitting to clear her throat and blowing her nose into the wadded linen of her handkerchief.

"How many, my brother?" Toktai's voice was almost as hoarse as hers.

"Two hundred." Less than the force they had left, but enough to hold them for the pursuers. Karl raised the field glasses again. "We underestimated whoever commands . . . wait." His fingers moved on the beveled wood of the focusing screw. "Wait a minute, there's somebody between them and us." A pause. "Three riders, going flat out. Coming our way, they'll get here first." He shook his head. "Piet was right: luck *does* matter more than skill, at seventh and last. They're being chased, whoever they are, and leading those Cossaki right into us."

Toktai growled something in barking Mongolian and spat on his hands before he drew his sword; their quivers were all empty, now. "Cut our way through them, eh?" he said. Karl forced a tired grin and fisted him on the shoulder.

"As you say." After the prince had wheeled off to take position before his countrymen, the haBandari spoke once more to his wife.

"At my side, love."

"Always." She took stance to his right and half a length behind, locking her toe underneath his stirrup iron. Tom Jerrison was on the other side, crusted sledge over his shoulder.

With a hard snap, Karl called to Itzhak: "Sound charge, bar David!"

The ram's horn gave its dunting wail.

"HABANDAR!" roared out from a hundred throats.

"No!" Shulamit said and shifted again, putting herself between Gorthaur and the haBandari guns. *"I gave my word!"*

"We didn't," one of the riflemen said grimly, pressing a leg to his mount's flank. The horse skittered sideways and the flintlock leveled.

"Put that up, Adigirdis, or you answer to me," Karl bar Yigal said flatly. To his sister-in-law: "There had better be a good explanation for this, bat Miriam."

"There is; my honor on it." Shulamit was conscious of how utterly still Gorthaur stood at her back, his one good hand gripping his horse's reins. *That is a brave man,* she admitted to herself: it took more than battle-courage to be so calm crippled among enemies. "Shalom, little sister," she added, with a wry smile. "Sorry to include you in my bad luck."

"Shalom, sister." Even then, Shulamit felt a warmth that unknotted some of the tension beneath her breastbone at the well-remembered smile. "So, this is adventure?"

Shulamit looked around. It was wheels within wheels. The last of the Cossaki who had been after her were grouped around their standard, a double-headed eagle mounted on a shaft festooned with horsetails; no more than a dozen of them, when they agreed to a truce. Six-score of her people and the Mongol allies. And beyond *them* top of a little knoll encircled by enough enraged Cossaki to roll over them all, but not before the last of those around the standard died.

She thought for a moment, then uncorked her canteen and rinsed out her mouth, spat, drank deep. "No, this would be an adventure if it were happening to somebody else, far away and long ago, daughter of Miriam," she said. "As it's us, here and now, it's simply some very bad shit."

That startled a giggle out of Erika; that faded as the young Cossaki who had accepted the truce returned to confront her husband and Toktai.

"We have rested," he said, in fluent Turki. "What point in waiting further? You will kill me, as your Sauron killed my father the Hetman"—he crossed himself—"who is with Bog and the Saints where I will join him while you heathen dogs will burn in hell. And the Sir Brothers of the Bergenov Stanitsa will kill you all in turn."

"He's not my Sauron," Karl said, crushing his cap in one hand. Shulamit heard him add in Bandarit: *Yeweh give me strength*. "We didn't ask you to come into our lands, boy!"

"We had no choice!" Shulamit could see where tears had cut streaks through the dust on the young man's cheeks, down into a cropped beard the color of

ripe barley: grief, she judged, and rage. Certainly not
fear; the light gray eyes were steady.

"The Saurons drove us out, Satan drag them down
to hell. There was nowhere else for us to go!" He
turned the pale glare on Toktai. "Should we charge
rifles and Gatlings with sabers? Will you Tartars welcome us as brothers and share your grazing?" He
looked at Karl and the dusty, bloody figures behind
him. "The Saurons told us that there were only Jew
merchants south of here, that we could take new
homes. They lied, as they always lie."

Shulamit had seen Erika stiffen. "Nowhere else to
go," the younger of the bat Miriam sisters murmured
to herself. Then she called out to Karl in Bandarit:
"The Xanadu road! *The Xanadu road!*"

The haBandari commander turned to gape at her
for a second, then grinned incredulously and blew her
a fisted kiss. "Daughter of Miriam, my love, Ruth's
spirit spoke in your ear," he said: there were few
higher compliments, among the People. Ruth bat Boaz
had been their first Judge, as Piet van Reenan had
been first *kapetein*: her name was still a synonym for
wisdom, twelve generations later.

"Wait." He spread his hands, closed his eyes for a
moment to marshal words. "Ivan Bogdanevitch, do
you know what lies *south* of the Pale?"

The Cossaki's eyes narrowed in suspicion. "Haven
forest, down the escarpment." Which meant wir-
eweed, snapper worms, a dozen types of deadliness,
as any Haven-born knew. Even logging the outskirts
of such was dangerous work. "Better clean death in
battle, even for our women and children."

Karl hesitated. "Now I risk more than my life," he
said. "I risk a secret of my people . . . one that will
be known everywhere, soon, but . . . We know what
is beyond the forest, because the haBandari have built
a road through it. A clear road good enough to take
wagons, with clean water and resting places. Beyond

the forest and the hills, a strip of land lower than the Eden Valley, more air-rich, as fertile as any on this world—which we plan to take for ourselves, I will not lie. Marshland beyond that, which we will reclaim in due time. But east of that, a thin line of passable country, to the mouth of the Xanadu River, where it enters the swamps."

Shulamit heard Gorthaur grunt with surprise; heard a similar sound come from her own throat. Certain mysteries made sense, now: taxes that the clan chiefs had been suspiciously eager to grant the *kapetein*, restrictions on travel imposed to prevent "accidents" along the forest fringe . . . *Xanadu*, she thought. That was the river that drained the Shangri-La Valley, Haven's greatest lowland, half a continent of the richest land on the planet and the center of most of its civilization. She could see the Cossaki fighting down hope.

"The Saurons . . ." he began.

". . . rule the *eastern* third of the Shangri-La Valley no more. Man, it's four thousand kilometers from the mouth of the Xanadu to the Citadel! Yes, you'd have to fight to take territory there, but only against the dwellers. They're no friends of ours; we'd be glad to have a friendly power there. A long journey, yes, difficult, with a war at the end—but would you rather break yourselves on the frontiers of the Pale, while the *gur-khan*'s armies come up behind you, hammer to the anvil?"

Toktai was looking at his friend with something approaching awe. Then he smiled unpleasantly and added: "Cossaki, while you wait, your people need not starve. Plunder these Turkmen swine hereabout, feast on their herds and ravish their women, empty the steppe: I give you leave, I Toktai son of Yuechi, heir to the vassal khanate of Ashkabad. Since they prefer to follow the commands of Saurons, let them ask Quilland Base for protection . . . afterwards, I will call for clans of the Yek and Merkit to come take their places. We can use the extra grazing, and I will have warriors I can trust."

Ivan Bogdanevitch nodded thoughtfully. "You, Karl bar Yigal . . . have you authority to make such an offer?"

"No," Karl said promptly. "I'm a relative of our *kapetein* with something of a name, and son and heir to an influential family. But I'll speak with all my power, and I do say that the *kapetein* and council will probably agree. It costs us little, and gains us much. Not least, it injures the Lidless Eye." He shrugged. "If I *did* have authority to offer it, could you accept for your people?"

"That has the sound of an honest man's words," Ivan said. "I speak likewise: no. The Sir Brothers are free men, not slaves: we must elect a Hetman. But we acted as Sauron catspaws from need, not choice. They would have hailed me lord of the *seich* in any case; doubly so, now that I can show them a better hope."

He frowned. "This is only a beginning. There must be exchange of hostages, councils called among your folk and mine. . . ." Ivan looked at Toktai, weighed a thought. "To prove my good faith, this. The Saurons told us that there was revolt planned among your subjects in Ashkabad town, to bring it under Quilland Base directly; to encourage us, they thought. We knew better than to think a Tadjik muslim rabble could threaten the folk of the black tents, but said nothing. This word is my gift to you."

"My thanks," Toktai said, fist tight on the hilt of his saber. "A culling of flocks will be made." Turning to Karl. "My brother—"

Assault Leader Gorthaur allowed himself one inward sigh, looking aside at Shulamit; the taste of her mouth came back to him, that first time. *At least I*

will not die without handing on my genes, he thought;
the scent was fairly definite, even this early.

Then he became all Sauron, a tactical computer that
happened to be colloid compounds rather than silicon.
Yes, a very high probability of success, he decided.
Nothing in his vulnerable quadrant but Borte, a negligible factor. Only one enemy between him and his
target. His slow, inconspicuous shift had put living
shields between him and the haBandari firearms: the
probability that they could redirect their attention to
him, shift, aim and fire before he killed Bogdanevitch
was vanishingly small. And once the Cossaki leader
was dead, the war among the cattle Quilland Base had
planned would continue on schedule. *It would have
been more efficient to give me an adequate briefing*,
he thought severely, as he took a deep breath and
repeated a mnemonic formula.

All humans possess the capacity for berserkergang,
the phenomenon the Malays had called *amok*: hysteri-
cal strength, immunity to pain and shock. Soldiers had
nearly that in their normal state, and *their* berserkergang was a controlled and rational thing. Gorthaur
felt his perceptions alter to a diamond clarity that was
the most beautiful instant he had ever experienced:
suddenly the very dust-motes in the air froze as if in
amber, and light flared to the edge of pain. *This is
what it is to be a cyborg*, he thought. A step that fell
like thunder, and he had ripped Shulamit's knife from
its sheath. She fell sideways, moving with glacial slowness, would still be falling when his work was done.
Another, and his fist drove into the neck of the big
Edenite with the sledgehammer, even as he turned,
eyes going wide and the ponderous weapon beginning
a swing that would never be completed. Six more
steps, and the three young leaders were only starting
to react, expression and motion like freeze-frame
blinks to the charging Soldier.

Crack. So heightened were his senses that he heard

the snap of the pistol trigger behind him before the ball struck. Enough time to begin a dodge, a motion that threw his spine directly into its path. *Borte*. Not a negligible factor after all, she must have been considering it even before he moved. *I made a mistake*. No pain, only a crackle of bone. Sensation vanished from the waist down; even then his arm was coming forward, converting his slash to a throw. *Crack*. The second ball took him high in one shoulder, just enough to put the blade into a trajectory that clipped the Cossaki's ear rather than slamming into his throat. Defeat tasted of copper and iron, as his body flexed and drove into the ground. It bounced, bone cracking: more slow *crack* sounds, as other weapons fired. Some struck, chest, arm, shoulder, lung. He could feel his blindly efficient mind shutting down the injured arteries.

Perception returned to something like normal for a moment, to show him Shulamit's face. He called on will, tried to force words that came as lip movements and a wheeze of pink froth:

"Still . . . you . . . bear . . . Soldier . . . to . . . me."
Yet she heard.

"No, Sauron," she answered. "You never understood. I will bear a haBandari who can *beat* the Soldiers."

Blackness, soft arms lifting him against softness.
Mother.

"Wait, wait, wait!" Shulamit said, taking another nip at the flask of clownfruit brandy. *Have to give this up for a while,* she realized. *Bad for the baby.* The sweet liqueur sang in her blood, warmed the stomach. "Two hours isn't enough to get it all straight, two *years* won't, it's *over*, I want to *sleep*." She grinned at the brother-in-law who had been her lover once. "Thought you'd get a quiet life by standing me up, eh? You should be so lucky."

"Oy, *Shulamit,* really!" Erika said.

Karl laughed and reached for the bottle. The motion froze at the sound that came from Toktai. The three haBandari exchanged glances, then turned back to the Mongols. Borte was standing before her affianced, head down. She spoke another sentence and Toktai shouted again, clapping his hand to his sword and turning towards the fire where the Cossaki sat, a hundred meters away.

"No, my lord, no!" Borte threw herself on Toktai, holding down his arm until the haBandari were about him: the Mongol troopers were just starting up from their own fires, running to the call of their prince. Borte continued in Russki:

"No, they did not know who I was, they are dead; Shulamit killed the ones who did the thing, you will only spread my shame for all to know! Think of our people, my lord!"

Toktai halted, with an effort that brought a sheen of sweat to his flat brown face; the firelight and Cat's Eye together turned it to a film of blood. Only the eyes were alive as he waved his followers back to their seats with a savage chop of one palm and made a stiff bow to Shulamit.

"I am in your debt, warrior woman," he said stiffly, his voice thick, shaking.

The haBandari released him; Borte fell to her knees before his boots, covering her face with her hands. Shulamit waited a moment, until it seemed that Toktai would leave without speaking.

"Noyon," she said sharply. "Would you tell me what is going on here, please? Is there some problem, your betrothed has told you?" She spoke Turkic, but Borte took the meaning.

"I cannot lie to the Noyon Toktai," she said tonelessly, not looking up. "I must tell him that the Cossaki defile me, I have no honor to give him."

"*What?*" Shulamit said. Erika was gaping, and she

realized that her own expression was a twin to it. *Did I drink that much? Am I missing something?*

"I am not a virgin," Borte whispered.

Shulamit found herself speechless. Strict *Ivrit* among the People attached importance to that, Edenites considerably more; for that matter, most haBandari considered it evidence of bad character if a girl took too many lovers before she married, and all were strict about faithfulness after vows. But this . . .

"You—" She looked up at Toktai, holding onto her temper with both hands. "She was *raped*, you idiot *gaya*—ah, Prince. What choice do you think she had?"

Borte spoke again, in the same toneless voice. "It does not matter. A *noyon* cannot marry a woman who has been shamed; no decent man could. There is no place for me anywhere."

"Do you mean to tell me," Shulamit continued— Karl tensed at the flat reasonableness of her tone— "that this girl—woman—who saved *my* life and *your* life and stopped a *war* is not *good* enough for you because some *shlyml* bandit assaulted her?"

Toktai's mouth twisted in tragic grief. "Yes," he said. "It is the custom."

"Oh, *you* are sorry, it's the *custom*, well, that *explains* it," Shulamit said. Mentally, she felt herself relax both hands. "Excuse me, did you say you were in my debt?"

"Yes," Toktai nodded. "Vengeance is my duty, but you have fulfilled it."

Shulamit smiled sweetly and leaned forward. "*Well, fuck you very much, too!*" she hissed, and swept her shin upwards between his legs with blurring speed.

There was a dull *clank* as the shinguard of her boot connected with the steel cup under Toktai's trousers and arming-doublet. "Gurk," he said, and staggered backward clutching at his groin. Shouts rose from around the Mongol fires, and the sound of blades being drawn.

The *noyon* was a warrior; gray faced and running with sweat, he managed to stand erect and signal his troopers back. He even mustered a smile.

"I . . . am . . . still . . . indebted," he husked, and walked away with slow straggle-legged dignity.

"Shulamit!" Karl said angrily. "Don't be an idiot, you don't understand their customs—"

She wheeled and shot a finger in his face. "You understand them all too well, Karl bar Yigal: start remembering *ours*, why don't you? About obligations? Who stopped the Sauron? Men!"

Erika wrenched her hand out of his and fell in beside her sister, crossing her arms over her chest. "Now, that's a good idea, husband; because until you *do* remember it, you're sleeping alone!"

Shulamit reached down and pulled Borte to her feet. "Borte," she said firmly. "Borte!" The Mongol girl blinked back to awareness from the place where she had gone. Shulamit drew her knife and made a small, precise cut at the base of her own thumb. "Give me your hand." She repeated it with Borte, and pressed the tiny wounds together. "Now you're my sister, understand? Blood-sister, clan sister—there are formalities later, but forget about that. You're Erika's sister, too, and even this useless lump of blond litvak stupidity's sister." She calmed. "You have a place with us."

Erika put an arm around the younger girl's shoulders. "Come on, sister. We'll take you to the mediko." A warm smile. "And if you want, when we get back to the Pale, we'll even see a *babshka* about finding you a husband. Although," she continued austerely, glancing at Karl, "there are times when a woman without a man—"

"—is like a horse without a synagogue," Shulamit finished. "Let's go."

"*Oive*," Karl muttered after a moment, into a silence that echoed. "And she took the flask, too."

"I've got another," Itzhak bar David said, coming up beside him. He coughed discretely. "Couldn't help but overhear. Anyway," he continued, as the young leader drank deeply. "It could be worse, *chaver*. We could have lost."

Karl laughed, then sobered. He looked down: the dead Sauron lay staring up at Cat's Eye, and for a moment the light caught his eyes, turning them into silver-red circles, glowing.

"We still could," he said. It was time to sleep, and the work of the day awaited. "We still could."